THE WATCH GODS

THE WATCH GODS
Barbara Wood

NEW ENGLISH LIBRARY

For Barbara Young

First published in Great Britain in 1981
by New English Library

First NEL Paperback Edition May 1982

NEL Books are published by
New English Library,
Barnard's Inn, Holborn,
London EC1N 2JR,
a division of Hodder and Stoughton Ltd.

Printed and bound in Great Britain by
©ollins, Glasgow.

0 450 05382 2

EGYPT – THE PRESENT

He PAUSED in the dark passageway to wipe the sweat out of his eyes and thought: So this is what it's like to die . . .

He had crawled a long way, using his one good arm, half-dragging, half-slithering down the shaft that was a hundred feet long, and he knew, without the benefit of a flashlight, that he was near the ante-chamber; the air smelled rancid.

He was lying on his stomach, sweat dripping from his forehead, a screaming pain in his right shoulder where the arm had been slashed. It dangled now, the bone having been severed neatly through, and caught occasionally on the rough-hewn walls of the narrow shaft. He was the last one left of the expedition; the other six, all dead. He was the last member alive and he knew he had little time left. He was going to die a long and agonising death, but he didn't care. All that mattered now, before the demons laid hands on him, was to get to the coffins. Then it would finally be over.

Knowing that time was rapidly running out, he clenched his teeth, hoisted himself up on his good arm and dragged himself the last few feet.

Suddenly the floor ended and he felt himself falling in the blackness. The cold stone floor of the ante-chamber rose up and slammed against him, knocking the breath out of him. He lay on his side for a moment, stunned, his mouth stretched in mute agony.

I'll just stay like this, he thought, and die. It would be so goddamned easy . . .

But he knew he couldn't, not yet, not until he did what he had to do with the coffins. Then he could reward himself with the luxury of the final sleep.

A pain in his thigh caused him to gasp and roll over. He felt beneath it and drew out a long metal object. A flashlight. Dropped earlier by someone running in blind panic.

He pushed the switch and an amber light filled the small room. He saw that he was not alone.

'Ah,' he whispered, struggling to sit up, 'here you are.'

Seven eery figures, their faces turned in profile, stared dispassionately down at the intruder, each fixing one cold eye upon him.

'You bastards,' he whispered, breathing laboriously. His throat rattled. 'You haven't won yet. Not while I have breath left in me. I'm not . . . beaten yet . . .'

They did not reply, the Seven, for they were but figures painted on the wall:

Amon the Hidden One, gold and naked and muscular.

Am-mut the Devourer, a beast with the hind legs of a hippo, the front legs of a lion, and the head of a crocodile.

Apep, Belonging To The Cobra, a man with a snake rising up between his shoulders where his head should have been.

Akhekh the Winged One, an antelope with wings and the head of a grotesque bird.

The Upreared One, a wild boar with human arms and standing on its hind legs.

She-Who-Binds-The-Dead-In-Chains, a slender shapely woman with scorpion's head.

And finally, Set the Slayer of Osiris, the most formidable of all ancient Egyptian demons, a primeval beast of terror with flaming red hair and gleaming red eyes . . .

The man felt his throat constrict in anger; a groan escaped. Letting the flashlight drop and his head fall back, he cried, '*You will not win!*'

Visions flashed in his head, burning his brain with memories he tried to fight; the images of six inhuman and unspeakable deaths. Each one, each member of the expedition, one by one felled by an invisible and unearthly power; each one the brutalised victim of one of the Seven who guarded the tomb. One by one, all dead, all gone, leaving him alone – the last to fight.

The man started to sob. 'I'll fight you . . . I'll get to those coffins and I'll win . . .'

The chamber started to swim; he knew he was dying. Shock had stopped the haemorrhage from his shoulder, soon it would stop *him*.

He fell back, banging his head on the stone floor. Darkness ebbed and flowed about him; he hovered for a moment in a twilight realm, then all came into sharp focus again. He heard his voice saying, 'You sons of bitches. Did you have to kill *her*? Did you have to do *that*?'

Then he remembered the coffins. The reason for his having come here in the first place – not now, but three weeks before. The sealed coffins which held the answers to all the mysteries. Three calamitous and hellish weeks; but before that, four months. Four months and so many events since it had all begun, all leading to this incredible moment.

To find out who slept here, who lay buried here, and why their secret had been so carefully, so *painfully* guarded . . .

ONE

'SEXUAL ATTITUDES of the ancient Egyptians were such that they have no parallel in today's society. While the Wisdom Literature instructs in the ways of righteousness and honesty, to the point at times of sounding proto-Christian, and while the Book of the Dead lists the sins for which a man might be denied the right to Heaven, the question of sexual rectitude was never an issue. That is not to say, however, that they condoned promiscuity, for we know that adultery was condemned and punished; however, this did not spring out of morality, as it does in our Puritan-rooted society, but out of necessity for keeping public order. In other words, Mark Davison, you are talking, as usual, through your ass.'

Lifting his thumb off the 'record' button, Mark gazed for a moment out of the window. Before him, to the misty horizon, stretched a furious and abyssal sea. Below, beneath the floor of his bedroom which stood on stilts, the surf thundered against rocks and every so often the wood-frame house shuddered. Mark lifted the microphone to his mouth again and said softly, 'Erase that last paragraph. It stinks.'

Giving the ocean one final scowl, Mark Davison picked up his empty glass and went to the bar, where he poured himself a shot of bourbon with one cube of ice. The living room was growing dark and gloomy but he made no move to turn on a light.

This afternoon his life had taken a hundred-and-eighty degree turn: Grimm's phone call. That sonofabitch. Apt name, Grimm.

'Sorry, Mark,' like a computer voice, 'they voted you down. I'm really sorry. But I want to assure you that . . .'

Mark hadn't heard the rest. Something about you can still keep your teaching post and maybe next year if there's a seat vacant blah blah blah. All he could fix upon now was the final crunching verdict that had marked the end of twelve months of rising hopes. This morning, getting up to a dazzlingly sharp blue February sky, Dr Mark Davison, thirty-six year old Egyptologist, had felt sure he was going to get the vote. And just the night before – only last night for Chrissake – Grimm had sat here on this very sofa and said, 'I tell you, Mark, you've got it. There isn't a single vote you don't have.'

And then *slam*, the impersonal phone call and the bottom drops out of Mark Davison's life.

He tossed down the last of his drink and, keeping his eyes on the rolling dark ocean, poured a refill.

Mark thought of the half-dictated magazine article; then he thought of the years ahead and of the hundreds of articles that would fill them. He conjured up the books he would write, and the lectures he would give – to women's clubs, night classes, weekend seminars. Projects to fill the time, to bring in the money and make Mark Davison feel like he was doing something with his profession.

Because one thing was certain, he wasn't professing. That associate professorship at UCLA should have been his. He had worked hard for it. Teaching on a lower rung for six years, publishing his last book for the university rather than for himself, giving them all the credit; politicking, campaigning, ingratiating himself with the academic cliques. Working, *praying* toward getting that associate professorship.

And then Grimm says: 'Sorry, Mark . . . '

This time he left out the ice and drank the bourbon down in one swallow.

The trouble with Egyptology today was: it was a dead end.

Mark left his glass on the bar and wandered over to the sofa. Flicking on a small lamp that stood on the end table, he considered lighting a fire. It was getting cold and damp in the house. He went over to the fireplace and paused, looking at the three faces that stared down at him from the mantelpiece. On the right and left, Nefertiti and Akhnaton; not originals but damn good replicas. Mark concentrated on the third face before him, the one in the mirror with the tired eyes; the bearded one that probably looked a little older than the face really was.

He had been told he was handsome, but he didn't think so. Cynicism had etched two deep lines in his cheeks and the dark beard hid the creases which ran from the edge of each nostril down to the corners of his mouth. His eyes were okay, a little jaded perhaps, but the forehead looked like that of an older man. The black hair was prematurely grey at the temples, but Mark wasn't sure if there was such a thing as maturely grey. Anyway, what mattered was the fact that he was thirty-six, and looking older and rapidly running down the road toward anonymity.

Grimm, of course, didn't agree. 'You're a successful man, Mark. You're what these days they call a "popular scientist". You know, like Carl Sagan. Someone who brings science into the home for the average person. The public loves your books on Egypt.'

The public was also fickle, and unless he could turn out a book every few years, he would soon be a popular nobody. And in Egyptology, if there was no digging going on and no new discoveries being made, which there weren't, then it was pretty difficult to keep coming up with something new and fresh to write about.

Mark bent his head and rested it on his folded arms. He glared into the charred fireplace, at the layer of ash and few stumps of blackened driftwood, and felt that he had come to the end of his line.

The knocking at the door was so reserved that, at first, Mark didn't hear it. When it finally registered, he glanced at his watch, which said five-thirty, and then at the front

10

door. When the knock sounded a third time, he went to answer it.

On the threshold, against the backdrop of cars speeding by on the Pacific Coast Highway, stood a man whom Mark had never seen before.

In his late fifties, tall and distinguished, with silvery implacable hair and meticulous moustache, the stranger was dressed in a conservative three-piece suit and carrying a black attaché case. He inclined himself a little and said in a soft, nasal voice, 'Dr Davison? Dr Mark Davison?'

Mark eyed him warily. 'Yes . . .'

'I have something here that will be of interest to you.'

Mark glanced down at the attaché case and said, as he started to close the door, 'I already have a cemetery plot, thanks.'

'Excuse me, Dr Davison, it was Professor Grimm who told me I would find you in.'

'He's not supposed to give out my address.'

'He did not, I assure you. Dr Davison, please, a storm is gathering. May I come in?'

'No.'

'Dr Davison, my name is Halstead. Sanford Halstead.' The man paused as if expecting some sign of recognition, then said, 'I assure you that I have here something of the utmost interest to you –'

'I'm not in the mood for visitors, Mr Sanford.'

'Halstead,' said the stranger quickly. 'Yes, I can appreciate your not wanting to see anyone right now, Dr Davison. I understand how you must feel about losing the professorship.'

Mark frowned and took a closer look at the man's face, illuminated by the frail light of the naked bulb over Mark's front door. There was an acuity about the eyes of the stranger he had not at first seen, and a self-assurance about the thin mouth. The man stood uncommonly erect, like a mannequin, yet he also gave the impression of utter ease and confidence. 'How did you know about that?'

'Professor Grimm warned me that you would not be

taking visitors and explained why. But I assure you, D
Davison, that once you see what I have to show you –'

'All right.' Suddenly having a pretty good idea why the
man was here, Mark stood back and held the door open.

The stranger followed him into the living room and took
a seat on the sofa. Noticing that raindrops had started to
spatter the floor-to-ceiling windows, Mark took a seat
opposite his visitor.

The attaché case remained in Sanford Halstead's lap as
he spoke. 'I have come to you, Dr Davison, because I am
in need of expert advice. Your reputation is not small,
even among the public, and you came highly recom-
mended to me by two of your colleagues on the east
coast.'

While the stranger spoke, his voice cultured and measured, Mark picked up his pipe and started to fill it.
Everything about his visitor, he noticed, was phenomenal-
ly immaculate, down to the manicured fingernails.

'Your credentials are impressive, Dr Davison. Fulbright
Lecturer in 1967. You have personally directed four
excavations in the Nile Valley and assist-directed two
others. You were the lead technical adviser on the Dendur
Temple Project, and you have taught archaeology at
UCLA for the past six years. I have read all of your books
and magazine articles.'

Mark tamped his tobacco, touched a flame to it and
puffed the Borkum Riff into brilliance. As purple smoke
swirled before him, the refined voice of his visitor continued.

'The reason I am here, Dr Davison, is that I require
your advice on a matter that is of the utmost concern to
me.'

Mark's eyes flickered again to the attaché case. He
knew what was coming. It was a story he had heard a
hundred times before. Archaeologists were always being
approached by people who were sure they had gotten
their hands on an object of astronomical pricelessness. A
bronze statue, a clay tablet, even a papyrus. But most of

the time they were either forgeries or in deplorable condition or too commonplace to bother with, such as a scarab. Eyeing the attaché case Mr Sanford Halstead cradled with great care, Mark tried to guess what it might contain.

'I will come directly to the point, Dr Davison. What I wish to do is go to Egypt.'

Mark puffed thoughtfully on his pipe and watched the rain fall harder against the windows. 'There's a travel agency on Sunset, Mr Halstead.'

'I think you know what I mean, Dr Davison. What I have in my possession is an item which I believe will impel you, as it has done me, to go at once to Egypt.'

'Isn't that for me to decide?'

'Most assuredly.'

'That is, if I even want to bother. Which I'm not sure I do. You see, Mr Halstead, I'm a busy man. I don't have time –'

'I understand, Dr Davison,' the stranger rejoined smoothly. His mouth, which appeared unused to smiling, seemed to curve up slightly at the corners. 'You are currently involved in writing an article on ancient Egyptian sexual standards for a popular women's magazine.'

Mark's eyebrows shot up.

'And you are also roughly drafting out your next book, which will deal with the question of who was the real Pharaoh of the Exodus. I believe you hold to the rather unpopular Akhnaton theory, as did Sigmund Freud.'

Mark took the pipe out of his mouth and leaned forward. 'How did –'

'I know a lot of things about you, Dr Davison. It might surprise you just how much I know. For example, your dissatisfaction with the state of Egyptology today. You believe your science is in a crisis. There is not enough interest to keep it alive these days; money that might otherwise go into excavations is being put toward stopping seal killers and protesting against the building of nuclear power plants.'

13

Mark gazed at the man, stunned.

'I am only repeating your own words, Dr Davison, and I assure you that I agree with you entirely. What I am, Dr Davison, is a man willing to finance a dig, something you had been thinking would never come your way again. Not since the building of the High Dam at Aswan has there been any significant digging in the Nile Valley. As we both know, Dr Davison, there is no interest in ancient Egypt today. Nowadays one cannot find a financial backer such as were numerous decades ago, like Carnarvon and Davies. Today's Egyptologist must be content with the classroom or with the analysis of objects unearthed long ago and trying to come up with new theories for them.'

Mark tried to fight down his rising anger. 'You seem to know a lot about me. You even quote my opinions accurately, although I can't imagine how you heard some of those things since I only voiced them to close friends. Whatever,' Mark rose abruptly. 'I'm no longer interested in what it is you have to show me.'

Sanford Halstead remained unperturbed. 'Please, Dr Davison, hear me out. This is for your benefit as well as mine. I am placing before you the opportunity to get out into the field again, which I know is something you desperately wish to do.'

'Well, Mr Halstead, there's one thing about me that you don't know, and that is I don't like people to tell me what I'm thinking. Or how I'm going to feel about something. So I suggest you take your precious artefact and get out of here.'

The stranger rose and seemed to fill the room. 'Dr Davison,' he said coolly, 'you cannot afford to turn me down. I am offering you the one thing in life you most desperately want. The field.'

'Please leave, Mr Halstead.'

'Very well.' But instead of turning and leaving, the oblique Sanford Halstead did a strange thing. He paused to gaze out at the slaty, turbulent ocean, and then very methodically set his attaché case on the driftwood coffee table, opened it and lifted out a square, paper-wrapped bundle. Leaving this on the table, he straightened, stared directly at Mark Davison, said, 'I will return tomorrow evening at six,' and then left.

The man's gestures had been so unexpected and mesmerising that Mark had simply stood and watched him go, barely glimpsing, as the front door opened, the rain-glistened Rolls-Royce that idled in front of his house.

A long moment after the door closed behind the enigmatic Mr Halstead, Mark strode over to the bar and poured himself a bourbon.

Before him raged a furious storm. Water pelted the floor-to-ceiling windows in a rage which matched the passion charging Mark's soul. Whoever Halstead was, he hated him. Hated him for knowing so well the frustration that was eating away at his mind.

What was really troubling him on this stormy evening was Nancy, his fiancée. That damned associate professorship had meant more to her than it had to him; it was what *she* had wanted, so they could get married and have kids and settle down like normal people. Right now, his teaching salary wasn't enough to support her and a family; every month the rent on this rickety Malibu shack went up a notch. Nancy, the first woman to whom he had ever uttered the words: 'I love you', the first woman for whom he had ever committed sacrifices. When they had first met seven years earlier he had been a practicing field archaeologist, but she had expressed dissatisfaction with his frequent absences, and so, out of love and need for her, Mark had tried to fit himself into the academic niche, teaching, writing, lecturing, so that he and Nancy could spend more time together. Upon receiving the professorship they were going to get married and start a permanent life together. And he had been so certain of the appointment they had even set a wedding date.

Only, now, he didn't have the professorship and he didn't know how to break it to Nancy.

He muttered, 'Piss,' and refilled his glass.

The dismal living room, cluttered with real and replicated antiquities, stacked haphazardly with books and dust, was becoming a cage. Halstead was right: Mark needed the field. What he yearned for was the challenge and physical exertion of the dig: the sun-drenched days of sifting through sand for clues to ancient mysteries and sweating amid the ruins of a people he so greatly admired, seeking to understand them.

He settled his gaze at last upon the paper-wrapped bundle left by Halstead.

The sound of the pickaxe striking stone, the feel of a spade sinking into dirt, the cries of the Arab workers whenever something was found . . .

He stared fixedly at the package.

Who the hell was Halstead anyway? A crackpot who thought he had in his possession a priceless artefact that would send any archaeologist running off to Egypt with shovel in hand.

Depositing his empty glass on the bar, Mark approached the coffee table with a mixture of curiosity and indifference. The bourbon had softened him, made him a little more receptive.

Deciding to give Halstead's gewgaw a quick look over, Mark sat down on the edge of the couch and slowly unwrapped the brown paper.

To his great amazement, what emerged before him was a large, leather-bound antique book.

TWO

He awoke shortly after sunrise, squinting and turning his head away from the ray of dawn that broke through the rain clouds. Hearing his own groan, he blinked and looked around the living room. Realising he had fallen asleep in the easy chair after finishing reading Neville Ramsgate's Journal, Mark Davison rubbed his neck and came shakily to his feet.

'I'll be damned,' he muttered, looking down at the heavy, leather-bound book that lay at his feet. 'I'll be goddamned . . .'

Mark groped his way through the gloom to the bathroom, stripped down and got under a hot shower. Scrubbing his hair and beard, he saw the events of the previous evening fall slowly back into place: Grimm's crushing phone call; his feeble attempt to continue the magazine article; the unexpected visit of Sanford Halstead; the Journal.

A few minutes later, vigorously toweling off and trying to pump some life back into his body, Mark reflected on the remarkable story he had read during the night.

Dressed and feeling a little better, but with a vague pounding in his head and the gnawing ache of hunger in his stomach, Mark Davison went straight to his bedroom phone. He dialed Ron Farmer's number, let it ring twenty times and then hung up. He turned to the picture windows and saw that, some time during the night, the rain had stopped.

Making a quick decision, Mark spun about, strode into

the living room and reached for his windbreaker which hung on a hook near the front door. Outside, his battered Volvo, with the license plate 'DIGGER', stood exposed to the elements. Warming up the motor, Mark thought again about the incredible story he had read through the night.

The memoirs of a pioneer Egyptologist who lived in the nineteenth century, Neville Ramsgate's Journal was the personal account of one man's exploration of the ancient city of Akhet-Aton in Egypt. Mark had heard of Neville Ramsgate and had read of the old professor's expeditions along the Nile. It was known that in 1881 Ramsgate had headed an excavation somewhere in the region of Tell el-Amarna and that he had been looking for the fabled tomb of King Akhnaton. However, nothing was known about what became of Neville Ramsgate or his expedition. All anyone knew today was that the Victorian explorer had, one hundred years before, set up a dig somewhere around Tell el-Amarna, had worked there for a while, and then had mysteriously disappeared, never to be heard from again.

That was what Mark and every other archaeologist in the world knew of Neville Ramsgate. Until this morning. Until a stranger named Sanford Halstead presented himself on Dr Mark Davison's doorstep holding a journal written by the curious Neville Ramsgate himself.

After the Volvo had been given sufficient time to warm up, Mark watched for a break in the heavy morning traffic along the Pacific Coast Highway and pulled out, heading south.

Half an hour later he arrived at Marina del Rey.

Driving slowly along the line of parked cars on Channel B, which were few this early in the morning, Mark spotted Ron Farmer's old Skylark, with its bumper sticker that read: ARCHAEOLOGISTS DIG OLDER WOMEN, and pulled in next to it. Killing the engine, he waited for a moment and gathered his thoughts.

Ron Farmer was never difficult to find. He existed in

only one of three places: the darkroom in his house, the UCLA library, or on his boat. Since Mark had gotten no answer at Ron's house, and since the library was not yet open, he knew where his best friend would be at this hour.

The gate was open and Mark was able to get down to the slips without having to climb the fence. Ron was moored at the very end, so Mark had to pass between two rows of gently bobbing, creaking boats, all of which glistened in the grey light of morning. Coming to the last slip, Mark saw his friend squatting on the starboard pontoon of his boat, a twenty-six foot Cross trimaran named *King Tut*.

'Hello!' called Mark.

Ron glanced up, gave a little wave, then returned to glaring angrily down into the hatch of the starboard hull.

Mark jumped on board, grabbed a shroud to steady himself, and said, 'Got problems?'

Ron didn't look up. 'Rainwater in the bilge, dammit.'

Mark forced a smile and rubbed his hands impatiently.

Ron Farmer, thirty-five years old and looking much younger, was dressed in patched blue jeans and a stained navy-blue sweatshirt that had BRUINS emblazoned on it in peeling gold. His long blond hair fell forward over his shoulders, obscuring the look of displeasure on his face.

Mark glanced down into the cockpit and saw on the torn vinyl cushion his friend's familiar accoutrements, Ron Farmer's trademarks: a jug of Gallo chianti, a Stanislaw Lem novel, and his OM-2. Mark knew the routine; Ron would sail out past the channel, heave to, luff the sails, and sit out on the swells until the wine was gone. Sometimes he disappeared for days, deciding at the last minute to sail up to the Channel Islands or over to Catalina. And then Mark wouldn't see him for a week. He was damn glad he had caught his friend in time.

'Ron?' Mark shivered a little in the biting ocean air.

The younger man finally gave a shrug, let the hatch cover drop and stood up. Although the same height as Mark, Ron's lankiness and lean, angular frame made him seem taller than his friend. He also appeared to be more than just one year younger; with his smooth face, cornflower blue eyes and platinum hair that reached his shoulder-blades, Dr Ronald Farmer looked like a seventeen-year-old surfer.

'What's up?' he asked. 'I never see you down here at this hour. God, you look awful!'

'I feel awful, Ron, I've been up all night. I want you to come home with me. I have something to show you.'

'Now? I've got work to do. Gotta pump this water out of the bilge before it rots the hull.'

Mark ran his hands through his hair and looked around the *King Tut*. For all the work Ron was constantly doing on his boat, it always appeared to be in a state of dereliction. But then, Ron never cared about looks. *King Tut* could do thirteen knots at a close reach.

'Ron, have you ever heard of Neville Ramsgate?'

The younger man dropped down into the cockpit and started rummaging around. 'Yeah,' he called back. 'One of the first Egyptologists. Before Petrie, I think. Did a lot of measuring of the Pyramids.'

'He excavated Tell el-Amarna, too.'

'So I read.' Ron thrust his hands into the storage compartments that were built into the pontoons and muttered, 'Shit.'

'What's wrong?'

'Can't find the pump.'

'Ron, can you do this later?'

Ron Farmer finally straightened up. 'What's this all about?'

Mark wanted to blurt it out, share the incredible excitement that was gripping his stomach. But he held himself back. 'There's something I want you to see, back at my house.'

Ron pushed wisps of blond hair out of his face. 'An artefact?'

'Come home with me.'

'Can't it wait?'

Mark solemnly shook his head.

'Well . . .' Ron squinted up at the sky and released a sigh. 'Looks like it's going to rain again anyway.'

They went in Mark's Volvo. Along the way, Mark recounted the brief, puzzling visit of Sanford Halstead, trying to remember everything the man had said. He touched upon, but did not disclose, the nature of Halstead's package, and ended with: 'I was afraid Grimm's news had put me in a vulnerable mood, like where I'd grab at anything that came along. This Halstead, wanting me to go to Egypt and dig, it sounds too good. So I thought I'd better let you assess the situation and tell me what you think.'

As they climbed out of the Volvo, feeling the first drizzle of rain hit their faces, Ron said, 'You've got to give me coffee first. I've been up most of the night, too.'

Mark fumbled for his house key. 'Working on your Akhnaton paper?'

'Developing that roll of dolphin pictures I shot off Catalina. Got one good shot out of thirty-six.'

The chill dampness of the house made Ron wrap his long arms around himself. 'How can you stand it like this?'

'Light a fire if you want,' called Mark as he went into the cluttered kitchen.

Five minutes later, with the rain starting to pelt down the two Egyptologists were seated before a roaring fire and sipping hot coffee. Mark wordlessly handed the antique book to Ron.

'This looks old!'

'A hundred years, to be exact. Read the front page.'

Ron slowly scanned the swirling Spenderian hand. 'Neville Ramsgate, how about that . . .'

'This is what Sanford Halstead brought me last night. I read the entire thing, but you don't need to. The first part is a lot of purple prose about Cairo and Ramsgate's trip up

21

the Nile by steamer. Turn to June, it's about halfway, and start reading around the twentieth.'

Ron lifted his ice-blue eyes and said, 'Does it say what he found at Tell el-Amarna?'

Mark avoided his gaze and, looking into the fire, said quietly, 'Just read it . . .'

THREE

'WELL?'

Ron Farmer looked up, his face puzzled. 'He didn't finish it. The last entry ends abruptly in the middle of a sentence.'

'What do you think of Ramsgate's story?'

Ron closed the Journal and laid it gently on the coffee table. Then he stood up, stretched and walked to the sliding glass door. Watching the grey ocean rise in swells to catch the heavy rain, he said quietly, 'I'd say Neville Ramsgate found Akhnaton's tomb.'

Behind him, still leaning against the fireplace mantel, Mark was fighting to contain himself. Ron's words had made a reality of the wild hope he had harbored since reading the Journal. 'One hundred years ago,' he said softly, forcing calmness into his voice, 'Neville Ramsgate headed a seven-member expedition up the Nile to Tell el-Amarna where he set up camp and expected to excavate the ruins on the plain. Then, by a stroke of luck, evidence of an unexplored tomb fell into his lap. He shifted his attention to searching for that tomb – which he suspected belonged to Pharaoh Akhnaton – and by following a sequence of clues, found it. However . . .' Mark's voice dropped, 'the Journal ends on the eve of opening the tomb door . . .'

Ron stared at the torrent of water washing down the other side of the glass; his eyes went from crisp blue to slate, the color of the ocean, and his face took on a pale aspect. Turning, Ron leaned against the cold glass and folded his arms. 'I'd say it's a pretty safe guess that the tomb is still there and unopened. In the last Journal entry, Ramsgate said they had cleared away the final step and could see the entire door . . .'

'Which still had the priests' seals on it.'

'Something must have happened to Ramsgate before he could open it because, number one: he didn't finish the Journal, and number two: I have never heard of the tomb he describes. It seems likely that he died before it was opened and that, for some reason, no one ever came along after him to open the tomb.'

'The secret must have died with him, Ron,' said Mark, scowling down at the heavy book. 'Everything we just read happened a hundred years ago. Egyptology was so primitive then you could hardly call it a science. Neville Ramsgate stumbled upon the tomb by accident, died before he could open it, and the secret of its whereabouts, its existence even, died with him.' Mark pushed away from the mantel and slumped down on the sofa. 'That tomb is still out there somewhere, untouched.'

Ron gazed thoughtfully at Mark for a moment, then said, 'Do you think it could be found again?'

'Jesus, Ron,' he whispered. 'The tomb of Akhnaton. The most famous, most notorious of Egyptian Pharaohs. His tomb would be a more sensational discovery than Tutankhamon's. And for the man who finds it . . .'

'Limitless fame and fortune. He would be a hero, more famous than Howard Carter. If . . .' Ron unfolded his arms and crossed the living room in four easy strides. He dropped down on the sofa next to Mark. '*If* it can be found again.'

Mark regarded his friend with anxious eyes. 'Ramsgate found it, didn't he?'

'Sure, but according to the Journal, most of it was luck. That old woman giving him the first stone fragment.'

'But Ron,' said Mark quickly, 'all we have to do is reconstruct Ramsgate's actions.'

'I don't know, Mark, there are so many blank spaces.

24

Ramsgate wasn't writing this Journal for someone a hundred years later. It was a personal memoir. *He* knew what he was talking about, therefore there was no need to fill in details. Like where the tomb is precisely.'

'But still, he gives enough evidence. Like, we know it's at Tell el-Amarna.'

'And that's about all we know. Hell, Mark, you're talking about twenty-four square miles of sand and canyons and ravines! The clues he does give us are only half-clues. And *those* he only stumbled upon. Listen to this.' Ron picked up the Journal and carefully leafed through the brittle pages. 'Here.' He spread it open on his lap and read quietly:

'July 1, 1881: Shortly after sunset an old woman entered our camp leading a donkey. She told Mohammed that she had been foraging through the ruins for *sebbakh* (ancient mud-brick which the locals use as fertiliser for their crops) when she came upon something she was certain "the strangers from the north" would be interested in. Mohammed was about to drive her off when I intervened, recalling that many of the precious artefacts now housed in the new British Museum had fallen into European hands in just such a manner, and I said I should gladly inspect her offering.

Imagine my surprise when those gnarled old hands drew from the sack upon the donkey's back the perfectly preserved topstone of a stela such as are found carved into the cliffs in this area. But, alas, it was not the complete stone, and I deduced from the line of fracture that the stela had been broken into three parts. Holding my interest to a minimum lest the old *sebbakha* demanded an outrageous price, I enquired where she had found the stone.

Mohammed translated for me, as I am not accustomed to the dialect of this region. The fragment had been lodged in the sand on the plain, not far from the mouth of the great wadi.

I asked the old woman where the other fragments were, for I suspected her of the old Arab trick of breaking up one artefact and selling it as three for a higher profit, and was further surprised when she claimed not to know.

Our dialogue here deteriorated, for the *sebbakha* seemed to grow afraid and made to lead her donkey away. I instructed Mohammed to offer her one Egyptian pound (which surely was a fortune to her!) for this fragment and two pounds if she would help us locate the other two, but she refused, saying she wanted no money at all!

Sir Robert and I suspected a trick, for there exists no greedier race than the Arabs, but Mohammed explained that the villagers were *glad* to be rid of the stone, for, ever since a freak rain had washed it down from the wadi months before, bad luck had befallen them.

As they talked, with Mohammed trying to stay the old creature and to learn from her more information, I took a careful look at what I held in my hands, and as it came to me that this fragment was part of a funerary stela – that is, a stone marking the entrance to a tomb – and as it appeared to indicate the burial place of Royalty, I grew excited.

Did this come from the so-called Royal Tomb? I asked through Mohammed. Had this stone originally stood before the tomb that is four miles up into the wadi?

She shook her head wildly, saying something about a Forbidden Area.

I tried to press her, but there was no holding the old woman. I raised my offer of money but she again refused, chattering excitedly in her garbled tongue. After she had gone, Mohammed translated this last for me, and what the old woman had uttered before she hurried fearfully away was this: that the stone had marked a Forbidden Spot which her people had for centuries known to avoid, but now lightning and rain had broken the marker which had stood under the Dog and scattered the fragments. Now the devils were set free.

Those were her exact words, Mohammed said.'

Ron looked up at Mark. 'Clue number one. The stela marking the entrance of the tomb had stood underneath a Dog, but lightning had broken it into three pieces and a flash-flood had washed one of the pieces down on to the plain. Now, Ramsgate set out to try to find the tomb by using this fragment and looking for the Dog, whatever that was –'

'And found it.'

'Yes, but again, only by accident! Not because of that stone fragment. He goes on for pages about his search for that Dog, and when he finds it he doesn't say where it is, merely, "I've found the Dog at last." '

'I imagine it's an outcropping of rock that resembles a dog.'

Ron shrugged. 'Now for clue number two.' As he turned the yellowed pages, a streak of lightning tore through the rolling clouds, followed a second later by a deafening crack of thunder.

'Storm's right on top of us,' murmured Mark, looking up at the ceiling.

'Here,' said Ron softly.

'*July 3, 1881:* There is something queer about the stela. I made a close scrutiny of its carvings last night and have come to the astonishing discovery that this stela is not at all like any in known existence. It neither resembles the usual commemorative slab depicting a king engaged in battle, nor the sort of funerary stelae upon which the deceased is shown worshipping Osiris and Anubis. Indeed, there is portrayed not a single human being on the crown of the stone, but instead seven rather curious and intriguing figures which I assume to be gods. One name alone is distinguishable, and it is the cartouche of an unknown Pharaoh named Tut-ankh-ammon. I have never heard of him, nor has Sir Robert.

It appears to be a marker of some sort, and yet the hieroglyphs which run in horizontal columns and which read from right to left seem to be extolling a warning . . .'

Ron turned the page and another explosion of thunder shook the wood-frame house.

'*July 4, 1881:* I have translated the stone. It is, as I suspected, a funerary marker and it designates the location of a tomb belonging to someone referred to as He-Who-Has-No-Name. Unfortunately, here the stela breaks off and I cannot decipher the identity of He-Who-Has-No-Name.'

'That would be Akhnaton,' said Mark, gazing out at the violent ocean. 'After the collapse of his reign, the priests of Amon made it a crime to speak his name.'

More pages turned beneath Ron's slender hands. 'Then his foreman Mohammed found the second stela fragment on 10 July, but Ramsgate doesn't say where. Now, Mark, listen to this.' Ron's voice grew muted, he read breathlessly.

'*July 12, 1881:* A compulsion has gripped all of us to find the Dog and to find the third fragment. In translating the second section, I detected the barest beginning of a passage which I am certain gives the whereabouts of the tomb.'

Ron looked up, the Journal still open on his lap. 'In all of these pages, Mark, Ramsgate goes on and on about the excavation – the trenches, the circular pits, the test holes, even life in the camp, which was pretty strenuous in those days. But nowhere, Mark, does he say *where* he is excavating.'

'Read ahead, Ron. Read that passage about the riddle.'

'Ah yes, the riddle. Clue number three.' He flipped ahead, then slammed his palm flat on the page. 'The crucial passage.'

'*July 16, 1881:* Shortly after sunrise, when the teams were already at work in the wadi, the third fragment was found. It is not a loose stone but a base of firm rock growing in the sand. The stela was carved from living rock. The base is therefore permanent, immovable. While in more deplorable condition than its mates, this fragment's inscription is nonetheless readable, and I have been hard at work all day to translate the last of the hieroglyphics. While poor Amanda sleeps restlessly beneath her covers, moaning with those nightmares, I puzzle now over the words I have brought to light.

The warning continues, bidding the traveller in countless repetitions to stay away, until the last column, which reads: "When Amon-Ra travelleth downstream, the Criminal lieth beneath; to be provided with the Eye of Isis."

Sir Robert and I have worked all evening trying to unravel the riddle. There can be no doubt that this last line refers to the location of the tomb, and yet I find no mention of a "dog". How does this passage relate to what the old *sebbakha* told us?'

'Damn him,' muttered Mark, striding to the bar. 'He gives us enough to drive us to distraction!' As Mark poured himself a shot of bourbon, glowering at the unrelenting ocean, Ron continued to re-read the Journal.

After a few minutes of silence, broken occasionally by a thunder-clap, Ron said in a hushed voice, 'This is the part that intrigues me the most. The inscription Ramsgate found on the door of the tomb . . .'

Mark wasn't listening. As he stared at the churning grey water and felt his house shudder with each surge, he was caught up in the turmoil of his own indecision.

Halstead had asked him to go to Egypt. And only one thing was stopping him from jumping at it: a promise.

Mark thought again about Nancy, pictured her lovely face, heard her soft comforting laughter. He had met her seven years earlier at the Los Angeles Museum of Art when he had given a lecture on Queen Nefertiti. Their relationship had started out casually, growing in intensity with each of Mark's returns from Egypt, until his last return made them both realise that they were in love and did not want to be separated again. But Nancy hated traveling and longed for permanency, and somewhere along the line, during their long and loving nights together in his bed, Mark had come to agree with her.

He had promised her his digging days were over, that he would settle down and give her permanency. And until yesterday, up to Grimm's phone call, Mark had stuck by his promise. But then, Halstead had appeared and offered him the one golden opportunity of an Egyptologist's lifetime. Only a fool, no matter how much in love with Nancy, would pass it up.

Behind him, Ron's voice seemed to come from far away. 'The seven demons and the seven curses on the door of the tomb, Mark, I've never heard of anything like it, not in all my years of studying Egypt. Jesus, listen to this:

Behold the Guardians of the Heretic, for they watch in eternal vigilance. Such is the vengeance of the Terrible Ones:
One will make of thee a pillar of fire and consume thee.
One will make thee to eat thy own excrement.
One will wrench the hair from thy head, pulling the scalp off thy skull.
One will come and dismember thee.
One will come as a hundred scorpions.
One will command the insects of the air to devour thee.
One will cause an awesome bleeding to drain thy body unto death.'

Ron sat back and gently closed the Journal. 'That can't be right. Ramsgate must have mistranslated. The Egyptians never put anything like that on their tombs . . .'

Ron's voice receded as Mark continued to wrestle with his thoughts. He knew he had no right to break his promise to Nancy; but he also had to be true to himself.

Mark gripped his glass so tightly that his fingers were bloodless white. He trembled in indecision.

Egyptology had meant everything to him, for as far back as he could remember.

Mark Davison was a first generation Bakersfield Okie. His father, a thick-necked slab of a man, had dragged his family from the Dust Bowl to the San Joaquin Valley, following the crops and hammering into his four sons a narrow respect for the Virgin Mary.

Mark had not known rebellion as a youth, only a deepseated mixture of awe and hatred for his father. Stooping in the fields of Salinas beneath the hot sun with his father and three brothers, grubbing in the dirt for artichokes, Mark had started to sense, even at the age of five, that he was destined for something better. He didn't know when the love of ancient things first budded within him, but he had never known a day when there wasn't dirt under his fingernails. It had been difficult at first for young Mark, as his father was contemptuous of education and the family never stayed in one place long enough for him to finish an entire year of school. But time went by and George Davison started to succumb to decades of drinking and disillusionment, and as the older brothers took off one by one, leaving Mark alone with a drunken father and a shadow of a mother, he was consumed by a blind need to make something of himself.

He worked in gas stations and went to school at night. He applied for and received a scholarship to go to the University of Chicago. A professor with flair and a sales pitch had ignited Mark with an obsessive interest in Egypt; Mark had had to work hard and sacrifice for his dream, holding down two jobs and spending every free moment studying and working on the thesis that was going to give him his PhD at the age of twenty-five. He had known nothing of a social life, had martyred himself for the science of Egyptology, emerging into the scientific world completely alone and protected by a tough shell of self-sufficiency. And, above all, fiercely dedicated to Egyptology. All those years of study and sacrifice, for this moment . . .

Impulsively, Mark spun around and said, 'Ron, I'm going.'

'What about Nancy?'

Mark's fingers worked nervously around his glass. It could mean losing her, he knew that. 'I don't know. I can only hope she'll understand. Ron, that tomb is out there and it's *mine*.'

Ron leaned back against the sofa cushions and scrutinised his friend. He hadn't seen Mark so determined, so full of ambition since the Dendur Temple Project five years before. And, knowing what his friend was feeling right now – the excitement, the prospect of a sensational find – imbued Ron with some of that electricity.

They gazed at one another across the gloom, each thinking of the divergent paths that had brought them to this momentous hour.

Mark and Ron were products of the post-war 'baby boom'. Both of them, all through their growing years, had had to sit in crowded classrooms and be part of massive graduating classes. In college they had flooded the campuses; after receiving their degrees they had tried to fight for a place in the already glutted job market. There had been nowhere for them to go with their brand new degrees. With no digs going on and no finds to analyse, their options consisted of teaching or working in museums – and for every position open, there were ten qualified Egyptologists. Many had had to turn elsewhere for work; one mutual friend had gone to a Los Angeles trade school to learn auto mechanics. He was now making more money than Ron or Mark.

Mark, however, had been fairly lucky. He had managed to get in on the few digs the Aswan Dam had generated, had written a few popular books and, as a consequence, had been offered a teaching post at UCLA. Ron, on the other hand had had to go out of his field to survive. To pay the rent on his canal shack in Venice, California, Ron wrote gothic romances under three different female pen-names. His royalties kept him in camera and darkroom equipment; he maintained contact with his profession by turning out scholarly works which regularly received accolades from the archaeological community. Three of his papers, written for the *Journal of Near Eastern Studies* – 'Male Homosexuality in Egypt', 'The Fallacy of Female Dominance in Egypt', and 'Bes: the Phallic God' – had been included in a new textbook which was being used by anthropology students all over the country.

Mummies were his speciality. Ever since his doctoral thesis, 'The Use of Roentgenography In Determining Filial Relationships of New Kingdom Pharaohs', Ron had managed, through his writing, to build a modest reputation in this area. The previous year, he had been invited by Wesleyan University in Connecticut to assist a team of medical doctors in unwrapping and analysing a Twentieth Dynasty mummy that had been donated to their natural history museum.

Mark and Ron had met fighting. The occasion had been a seminar in Boston, eight years back, where the two had been invited to speak. Mark's talk had been a case for the co-regency theory of Akhnaton and Amenhotep III; Ron's had been the rebuttal. Making each other's acquaintance for the first time at an introductory brunch, they had begun their debate over Eggs Benedict, carried it into the amphitheater, continued it over cocktails and dinner, and then into the night until the bar closed. The next morning they had gravitated together, to the exclusion of the rest of the attending members, and had immersed themselves in each other's opposing views for the rest of the week.

Their differences had been their bond. In their own ways, each was a better Egyptologist than the other, and each had come grudgingly to acknowledge this. Mark had a feeling for the earth, knew where and where not to look, and could dig up an artefact without disturbing one grain of sand. But Ron's mind worked in the abstract, he saw the story behind the artefact; he could take one hieroglyph, one strip of linen, and one lock of hair and decipher the drama behind them. Ron hated the dirt and Mark was only second best with analysis. But together, as a team, they totaled more than the sum of both of them.

'Ron,' said Mark softly, 'I want you to go with me.'

His friend smiled and slowly shook his head. 'Why?'

'For one thing, we'll be needing a photographer. For another, if we do find a mummy, you're the expert to examine it.'

'I agree, Mark, however,' Ron stood and stretched his lanky frame. 'I've got a deadline on my Akhnaton paper . . .'

'That's cow puckey and you know it. Here's a chance for you to handle the body of the very man you're writing about, an opportunity to see for yourself if Akhnaton was asexual or not, a chance goddamit,' Mark slapped his knee, 'to write a book that will knock the socks off the *New York Times* Best Seller List, and all you can think about is a deadline for some pissy magazine that has a circulation of two hundred.'

'Hey, don't get mad. I just don't want to go, that's all.'

'What are you afraid of, Ron?'

'I'm not afraid of anything. Just because you have a secret desire to live like Wayne Newton doesn't mean I do.'

'You live in a shanty in Venice and wear clothes Goodwill throws out and you write romances and sail in a bucket that only floats on a prayer, when you know goddamn well you could be at the top of your field!'

'It's different for you, I'm happy the way I am.'

'Are you? Look at you, Ron, twisting around old facts to make them fit your latest far-out theory. You don't really believe Akhnaton was asexual –'

'Hey, I really do –'

'Sure you do. A year ago it never occurred to you, even

34

though you'd seen photographs of that statue a hundred times. But your boat needs its hulls scraped and that's expensive, so all of a sudden you realise there's been nothing written about a statue of a king that shows him naked without any genitals! You're prostituting your profession, Ron.'

Ron remained silent, staring into the cold black pit of the fireplace.

Mark said, 'Ron, if we find that tomb and there's a mummy in it, I want you there to be the first to inspect it.' He walked over to him and dropped a heavy hand on Ron's shoulder. 'And I need a photographer. The best person for that on a dig is someone who's an Egyptologist. Now's the chance to put all that expensive equipment of yours to good purpose.'

'I have no field experience, Mark. It's one thing having a darkroom in your closet, another having it in a tent.'

'You could use one of the tombs.'

'Sacrilege.'

'Come with me, Ron. You'll earn enough money to scrap the *King Tut* and buy yourself a boat that'll win you the Trans Pac.'

Ron thought a moment, then said, 'Do you think you can find it?'

'I don't know. Amarna's a pretty big area and it's been rather thoroughly explored. And the Journal doesn't give us much to go on.'

'Where would you look?'

'I guess I'd first try to find out where Ramsgate's campsite was, and then do a little detective work to see if I can locate those stela fragments. They must still be there, somewhere under the sand. Then I'd look for that Dog, whatever it is, to solve the riddle. Ramsgate says all the clues are there, it's only a matter of working them out.'

'That riddle, Mark, it doesn't make sense. For one thing, Amon-Ra doesn't travel downstream. The sun goes from east to west, not south to north, even in Egypt. And

35

I've never heard of an Eye of Isis, or that any of her manifestations was as a dog. I suspect Ramsgate mistranslated.'

'Even so, Ron, he found the tomb.'

'Yes, he did . . .'

'And he never got inside it. It's still there.' Mark turned away and went back to the bar. He saw that the storm was abating. 'What do you suppose got into his workers, making them desert at the end like that? And those two bizarre deaths . . .'

Ron shrugged. 'It's my guess the locals wanted to get rid of the gringos so they could have the treasure to themselves. It happens all over Egypt, even today, look at the trouble in Qurna. I would imagine the honchos of the villages either paid Ramsgate's *fellaheen* to run off or they scared them off. Those two deaths sound like a couple of nasty murders to me.'

'But I wonder why, if the villagers went to that much trouble to get rid of the foreigners, they never ended up opening the tomb. Anyway,' Mark dropped an ice cube in his glass, 'there's been a running feud between El Till and Hag Qandil for years; I hope we don't get caught in the crossfire.'

Ron walked away from the fireplace and stood spread-legged before the window, watching the rolling ocean. 'What do you know about this Halstead character?'

'Nothing. He wasn't here ten minutes.'

'Has he got money?'

'I think so.'

'How do you know he's legit?'

'I don't.'

'Where'd he get this book?'

Mark shrugged.

'It's probably a wild goose chase,' said Ron.

'Probably.'

'And besides,' Ron rubbed his arms, suddenly aware of the chill in the room, 'it's been a hundred years. There's been a lot of vandalism at Tell el-Amarna. A lot of theft.

The tomb could have been pillaged and we don't know it.'

'Ron, I want you here tonight when Halstead returns.'

'Got any wine?'

'Only a magnum. But I can run to the liquor store for you.'

Ron smiled at his friend. Then a new thought straightened his face. 'Does Nancy know you didn't get the professorship?'

Mark scowled at the drink in his hand then drank it down in one long burning gulp. 'I'm going to have to find a way to break this to her.'

'Take her to Egypt with you.'

'No. She hates traveling and hates the desert even more. It's not going to be pleasant, whatever . . .'

'One thing bothers me, though,' said Ron, thrusting his hands into the pockets of his jeans.

'What's that?'

'What happened to Ramsgate? Why was he never heard from again, or any member of his expedition?'

'I don't know.'

'And why did he end his Journal in the middle of a sentence?'

FOUR

'THAT'S HIM.'

Ron jumped to his feet and looked at his watch. 'Punctual. Smack on six.'

They had been relaxing after an early dinner of fried chicken which they had ordered by phone.

Mark wished he weren't so anxious, it made his palms moist, and no matter how frequently he wiped them down his pants, they remained clammy.

He opened the door in time to see the Rolls-Royce slowly pull away from the house, a shadowy figure behind the wheel. Before him stood Sanford Halstead, appearing exactly as he had the night before, except this time he had nothing in his hands. In the background, the ceaseless traffic of the Pacific Coast Highway sped along the glistening pavement.

'Right on time,' said Mark, holding the door open.

Sanford Halstead nodded politely and stepped inside. As the door closed behind him, he caught sight of Ron Farmer standing by the fire and said in a smooth, nasal voice, 'Dr Farmer, I see you were able to join us.'

Mark and Ron exchanged glances, and both noticed, as the tall, grave visitor came in, that the ambience of warmth and coziness in the living room suddenly seemed to chill a little.

'Would you care for a drink, Mr Halstead?'

'No, thank you, Dr Davison. I do not take alcohol. Nor do I smoke.'

'Well then, have a seat and we can get down to business.'

When the three were settled, with the glow of the fire illuminating their profiles, Halstead said, 'I presume you read the Journal?'

'Yes, we both did.'

'And what do you think?'

'I won't make any promises, but there's a good chance the tomb exists.'

'And that it has remained unopened?'

'Mr Halstead, when a tomb is discovered, it is either reported to the authorities or it is kept secret for the illegal sale of its contents. In the first case, the legal reporting will appear in official journals and will generally become known to the scientific community very quickly. In the second case, even the most secretive of discoveries is heard about through the circulation of illegal antiquities on the black market. Especially in items that are related to burial; funerary objects get immediate attention because that means a new and unreported tomb. Over the past few years, there hasn't been much in the way of anything new. A few statues, maybe, jewelry and scarabs. Before that, nothing that would seem to have come from an Eighteenth Dynasty tomb.'

'But the tomb might have been empty to begin with.'

'I doubt that. Ramsgate says the priestly seals hadn't been disturbed. That means that whoever was buried there still had all his possessions, because that's how the Egyptians were buried, with all their possessions.'

'What are our chances of finding the tomb?'

'That depends on a lot of things. First we have to go to Amarna and scout the area. Look for Ramsgate's camp, which will not be easy to find. See if the stela fragments are still there somewhere. Remember, we don't know what became of the Ramsgate expedition. I'll have to get more information from Cairo before I can estimate our chances of finding anything.'

'How will you go about looking for the tomb?'

Mark leaned forward, elbows on knees, and clasped his

hands together. 'The Journal gives us three clues: the scattered fragments of the stone stela which marked the tomb's entrance; the Dog; and the riddle on the stela base.'

'Were you able to make sense of the riddle, Dr Davison?'

Mark picked up the Journal and opened it out on the coffee table to the entry dated July 16, 1881. He read aloud: ' "When Amon-Ra travelleth downstream, the Criminal lieth beneath; to be provided with the Eye of Isis." ' He closed the book and leaned back. 'According to Ramsgate, the tomb is indeed where the riddle says it is. *And*, beneath the Dog, whatever that is.'

'But there is no mention of a dog in the riddle.'

Mark spread out his hands. 'We supposedly have all the facts we need right here. However, they are obviously not enough, since Dr Farmer and I cannot make sense of the riddle. You see, Mr Halstead, Amon-Ra is the sun, and downstream means north. The riddle is saying that when the sun travels north —'

'Then there's a mistake there.'

'You would think so, except Ramsgate doesn't mention that in the Journal. When he does finally find the Dog – by accident – he says it corroborates the riddle perfectly.'

Sanford Halstead considered this, then asked, 'Dr Davison, do you think it is the tomb of Akhnaton?'

'Ramsgate found no names on the door of the tomb, but the stela referred to the Criminal. That was the name given to Akhnaton by the priests of Amon after he died. You see, the Egyptians believed very strongly in the power of a man's name. If you used a man's name, you gave him strength and power. By robbing him of his name, you robbed him of his identity and therefore his potency. That is why all mummies and all graves had to have names inscribed on them, or else the spirit of the dead person didn't know its identity, and without an identity it could not have any afterlife. Because Akhnaton had tried to do away with all the many ancient gods and force his people to worship only one god, the Aton, the priests of Amon took their revenge by making his name illegal after his death, thereby robbing his spirit of its identity. Yes, Mr Halstead, I believe Ramsgate found the tomb of Akhnaton.'

'Why wasn't he buried in the so-called Royal Tomb that was excavated in one of the canyons in 1936?'

Reaching for his pipe, Mark replied, 'Because no one was buried in any of the tombs at Amarna, Mr Halstead.' He filled the bowl, tamped the tobacco, then said, 'When Akhnaton died, the city was abandoned. Relatives who had people buried in the tombs removed them and had them re-interred at Thebes. Akhet-Aton, as Akhnaton's city was called, was declared accursed ground by the Amon priests, so no one wanted to leave their dead there. Even Akhnaton's mother and eldest daughter were removed from their tombs at Amarna and reburied at Thebes. His father, two brothers, sister and other daughters were also buried at Thebes. One of his brothers, I'm sure you know, was Tutankhamon.'

'Then why was Akhnaton not buried at Thebes with the rest of his family?'

'I would imagine the Amon priests didn't want him desecrating their holy ground. Remember, Mr Halstead, Akhnaton was a heretic. By the time he came to the throne, around 1350 BC, when his name was Amenhotep the Fourth, Egypt had flourished for two thousand years, and in all that time they had worshipped hundreds of gods. When young Amenhotep came to the throne and changed his name to Akhnaton, he decided to do away with polytheism, the worship of many gods, and forced his people to worship one benevolent deity, the Aton. The priests of the other gods went into hiding during Akhnaton's reign, because he closed their temples, and plotted their secret revenge. So, when he died suddenly in his sacred city at Tell el-Amarna, the priests came out in the open, declared his god false and made it illegal to utter Akhnaton's name. He was called The Criminal of Akhet-

Aton. Therefore, the priests wouldn't have wanted his body buried in their holy ground in the Valley of the Kings, for then his spirit would have been nearby to haunt them. I imagine they wanted to leave him where he was, in his own accursed ground.'

Sanford Halstead pursed his lips. 'Dr Davison, if the priests of Amon hated and feared Akhnaton so much, why didn't they just destroy his body? I understand in Egyptian theology that without the body the soul cannot exist. Why did they go to the trouble of burying him?'

'Because, Mr Halstead, they were highly religious men, and according to Egyptian religion the Pharaoh was a god, even if he was Akhnaton and much hated. He was a god and they would not risk the wrath of the other gods by harming his body. It's my guess they both feared and hated him, so they buried him on his own ground to keep his spirit far away from themselves, but nonetheless buried him to placate him.'

'Then why construct a whole new tomb? Why not use the one already in existence, the one called the Royal Tomb?'

Mark cast a quick glance at Ron and frowned. 'That, Mr Halstead, is something I'm afraid I cannot figure out. It is just one more of the many mysteries that surround the calamitous end of the Eighteenth Dynasty, and I suppose when we find the tomb we'll find the answer.'

Sanford Halstead nodded slowly, his silvery hair catching the firelight. 'Dr Davison, can we get the concession?'

'If there's no other archaeological work going on there at the moment, yes.'

'Can you arrange everything?'

'How much freedom do I have?'

'I want you to do everything, Dr Davison. Hire whom you wish, buy what you need. Now tell me, when can we go?'

'The season for digging is usually from October to April. I'll find out when Ramadan is taking place this year; the Moslems use the lunar calendar so their months aren't fixed like ours.'

'Ramadan?'

'The holy month of fasting. They don't eat or swallow a thing from dawn till sunset, not even their own saliva. Believe me, it's impossible to get any work done at that time. October is the best, so that gives us seven or eight months to get ready.'

'Dr Davison, I wish to go as soon as possible.'

Mark shook his head. 'You wouldn't want to go before October, believe me.'

'Dr Davison, just tell me how quickly you can arrange everything.'

'Conservatively, it would take three months, maybe four.'

'Excellent, then that is when we'll go.'

Mark laid his pipe down in the ashtray and leaned forward in earnest. 'Mr Halstead, no one digs in Egypt in June or July! The heat is unbearable!'

'*As soon as possible, Dr Davison.*'

As Mark tethered his impatience and glared at Sanford Halstead, Ron Farmer quietly spoke up, 'Tell me, Mr Halstead, has anyone besides the three of us seen the Journal?'

'Only my wife.'

'Where did you get it?' asked Mark.

'I purchased it at an estate auction some months back. I am a collector of antiques and antiquities, Dr Davison. The woman whose estate contained the Journal was an old Beverly Hills dowager who died at the age of ninety-six without an heir. The Journal was part of the estate, which sold for several million dollars. I purchased her art collection and a mélange of Victorian memorabilia that I did not sort through until long after it had been delivered. After an enquiry to her attorney, I learned that the Journal had been in the old woman's possession for decades.'

'Do you know how she came to have it?'

'I do not. All I know about the Journal is what I read in

it, and *that* I did not get around to doing until some time after it was delivered, for I am a very busy man.'

'But the minute you read it,' said Mark, carefully studying his visitor's austere features, 'you recognised it for what it was.'

'Quite the contrary, Dr Davison. After finishing the Journal I had only the barest notion of what I had purchased. I was merely interested in the value of the book itself, not in what was written upon the pages. I contacted an old friend in Boston, an Assyriologist, and described the Journal to him. He believed it had great value and suggested I speak to someone whose specialty was Egypt. So I contacted an Egyptologist in New York City, a Dr Hawksbill. Do you know him?'

Mark smiled crookedly and picked up his pipe. 'Yes, he's the one who's been spreading those crackpot theories that the Egyptians were ancient astronauts from another galaxy.'

'Nonetheless, he is an Egyptologist.'

'At one end of the spectrum.'

'Without disclosing the contents of the Journal, I explained the nature of the book to Dr Hawksbill and he became most excited. Neville Ramsgate, I learned, was quite a ground-breaker in your science – and I intend no pun – so that a Journal written by him would have immense value. Not to mention the tomb he wrote about.'

'So you then decided to go after the tomb yourself.'

'Will you accept the job, Dr Davison?'

Mark rose from the couch and walked over to the picture windows which overlooked his sundeck. A new storm was churning over the ocean; bloated black clouds slowly rolled toward the coast in a fury that matched the violence of the water below it. Mark knew it was only a matter of minutes before Malibu would be hit.

'You knew before you came here tonight that I'd take the job.'

'Then we must begin preparations at once.'

'If you want to dig in June,' said Mark after a few puffs

on his pipe, 'I'll have to get started tomorrow. There are people to get in touch with. I have to find out if my usual foreman, Abdul, is free. I'll have to contact the Department of Antiquities in Cairo. There's equipment to be bought, supplies, tents –'

'I leave all that entirely up to you, Dr Davison.'

'You do understand, I assume, that anything we find has to remain in Egypt?'

'My interest is not in the treasure, Dr Davison, but in learning once and for all the true nature of the mysterious Akhnaton.'

Surprised, Mark turned around.

The ghost of a smile touched Halstead's thin mouth. 'That surprises you, Dr Davison?'

'Let's just say I suspected other motives.'

'Dr Davison, I am an immensely wealthy man, I have no need of a few ancient treasures, especially illegal ones. My sole concern is with discovery and enlightenment. I am interested only in uncovering the truth of the legendary Pharaoh who has sparked more controversies than any other king in history.'

Mark settled his gaze on a replicated limestone carving which hung on the wall near the kitchen, a profile of Pharaoh Akhnaton worshipping his revolutionary god, Aton. He stared at the strange body of the king, the feminine breasts and large thighs, the sagging belly, the long prognathous face, the inescapable *ugliness* of the man. Who or *what* was he, this enigmatic being who had eluded scholars for centuries? Some people, Sigmund Freud for one, thought he was the man who first introduced monotheism to the Hebrews. Others believed he was simply the victim of a bizarre disease; a deranged king. Ron Farmer believed he was asexual, neither male nor female. Mark Davison thought Akhnaton had simply been an ugly dreamer, whom no one had understood.

'I have read a little about Pharaoh Akhnaton,' said Sanford Halstead, 'and I have learned that no one knows what happened to the heretic king. He reigned for seventeen tumultous years and then, most mysteriously, vanished. Akhnaton followed his father Amenhotep the Third to the throne, moved the court away from Thebes and built his own city, Akhet-Aton, on a spot of barren ground many miles down the Nile to worship his new god in peace. But upon his death, his beautiful city was abandoned, the people went back to the old ways, and the name of Akhnaton was accursed. But what became of his famous wife Nefertiti? Who was she, where did *she* come from? And Tutankhamon, his brother, why was he murdered after a few short years on the throne? It is my hope, Dr Davison, that the tomb Neville Ramsgate is leading us to will have the answers.'

Mark pushed away from the glass, went over to the bar and poured himself a bourbon.

Halstead rose smoothly, cat-like. 'You will please keep me informed of your progress. My secretary will contact you every Monday morning at precisely nine o'clock, at which time you will report how you are doing and what money you need. The cheque will be mailed to you every Monday by three.'

When Halstead turned to go, Mark said, 'Wait a minute, we haven't discussed salary or anything.'

'My secretary will have contracts mailed to you and a breakdown of the terms of payment. All will be to your liking, I assure you.'

'But can't I get a hold of you when I need to?'

'There will be no need for you to contact me, Dr Davison. The next time we meet will be at the airport, departing for Egypt.'

Mark followed him to the door, noticing that for a man nearly sixty years old, Sanford Halstead was in remarkable physical shape. 'I'll let you know when we're leaving as soon as I can.'

Halstead turned at the door and said, as if he had been waiting for the right moment, 'There is one more thing, Dr Davison, my wife will be accompanying me.'

Mark opened the door and saw, through the driving

rain, the sleek black Rolls; the passenger door stood open and next to it, holding a black umbrella over his head, the shadowy chauffeur. 'Just as long as she understands it won't be a picnic.'

'I assure you, Dr Davison, my wife is quite up to it. Good evening, gentlemen.'

After the door had closed and he heard the Rolls pull away from the curb, Mark felt Ron's presence at his side. Then he heard his friend say softly, 'Looks like I'm going to *have* to go with you. I don't trust that man, Mark.'

And Mark Davison, his eyes still on the closed door, murmured, 'Neither do I, my friend, neither do I.'

EGYPT – FOUR MONTHS LATER

FIVE

MARK WAS glad of the long, uninterrupted train ride; it gave him a chance to organise his thoughts to come to terms with his charged emotions. There was so much to think about.

He sat with his shoulder against the window, watching but not seeing the endless fields of sugarcane speed past. It was early morning and the Nile dwellers were active: donkeys trotted along dirt paths beneath mounds of cane; naked children and starved dogs ran down to the tracks to hail the passing train; black-clad women balancing water jugs on their heads paused to stare. The populated area had been passed an hour before; once the dwindling suburbs of Cairo fell behind, the ancient, changeless scene of the Nile Valley came into view.

But Mark Davison was not appreciating it. Sitting in a first-class coach with his five silent companions, he sucked meditatively on his cold pipe and tried to approach each of the issues plaguing him objectively.

The problem with Nancy, the major cause of his three sleepless nights at the Nile Hilton in Cairo, could not be handled without emotion. As much as he would like to put it out of his mind and concentrate on the thousand details of the expedition, Mark could not help going over and over their last night together.

When he had told Nancy that he had been voted out of the professorship, she had been kind and understanding. There would be better opportunities, she had said, and if not, at least he was contracted to write another book for his publisher and she would help and support him with it. When she had steered the conversation toward the subject of marriage, Mark had told her about the dig.

Mark had known she had a temper; he had been at the eye of that Irish-Latin storm more than once. So when he had dropped the news on her and had braced himself for battle, he had been stunned to see her stare at him for a long, shocked moment, then deflate, melt down and finally gaze up at him with sad resignation. Then she had said, 'I suppose I've known all along it would be like this. It was childish of me to think I could keep you here or expect you to hold to your promise.'

When he had started to protest, she had said in a killingly gentle tone: 'I'm more in love with you now than I ever have been. Enough to let you go. I don't mean just to Egypt, but out of my life. You need to dig, Mark, and I need a home and babies. No, I won't go with you, and no, I won't marry you this afternoon. That wouldn't change anything. Do what you have to do, Mark, and if I'm still here when you come back . . .'

She hadn't finished her sentence, and what he dwelled upon mostly now, as the train clacked along irrigation canals, was that last night in her arms, making love and loving, clinging to her while she sobbed quietly into his neck. She hadn't come to the airport to see him off, and when he had tried calling her apartment from the first-class lounge, he had gotten a recording that the phone had been disconnected.

The rustling of papers brought Mark back to the present. He tore his eyes away from the window and looked at Ron who, sitting opposite him so that he rode backwards, was bent over his notebook and scribbling avidly. Ron had put his three days in Cairo to productive use, having gone to the Egyptian Museum and made the acquaintance of the curator. He had been able to visit the private, non-public mummy vault and had taken two rolls of pictures of the ancient kings and queens, after which he had spent another roll of film on the much speculated-about Akhnaton statue.

Ron Farmer's specialty was ancient anatomy and it was upon various statues and carvings of Akhnaton that he was basing his new theory: that the king had had no sex organs. Ron had taken further pictures of certain disputed bas-relief inscriptions in the museum which supported his thesis, in that they indicated that the famous six daughters of Akhnaton might not in fact have been his daughters but his sisters.

With such a controversial thesis consuming him, Ron paid no attention to the fact that they were entering Middle Egypt and nearing their destination.

Mark looked around at the others in the first-class car.

Sanford Halstead sat with his head back and his eyes closed, barely moving, barely breathing; so serene and composed he appeared dead. Next to him, flipping through a fashion magazine so that the jade bracelets upon her thin wrists jangled, was Halstead's astonishing wife, Alexis.

Mark had been surprised when he had met Alexis Halstead three days earlier at Los Angeles International Airport; he had been waiting in the first-class lounge and had wondered who the stunning beauty was who walked in with Sanford Halstead. About thirty years younger than her husband, Alexis Halstead was tall and tanned with an athletic body, wild unharnessed red hair and moss green eyes that had all the warmth of a glacial lake. Halstead had introduced her curtly, almost perfunctorily, and had then separated himself and his wife from the two Egyptologists. Alexis had barely glanced at Mark, nodding sparingly, and had not acknowledged Ron at all.

Mark had stared after her as she swept away to sit on the other side of the first-class lounge: on first seeing her, he had thought her strangely familiar. And now, watching her chiseled profile, like a bust carved of brown marble, that elusive familiarity returned.

He pulled his eyes away from her and looked across the aisle at Hazim al-Sheikhly, the young agent from the

Ministry of Antiquities who had been attached to the expedition.

They had met two days before, in Cairo, when Mark had gone to the ministry to see if they had anything in the archives on the Ramsgate party. While the ministry had sadly little on the ill-fated Ramsgate expedition, and what few new facts Mark learned had only created more mysteries, he had learned two astonishing things.

The first surprise had come in the form of a government order, signed by the Pasha in 1881, stating that because the Ramsgate expedition had succumbed to smallpox, the area was to be quarantined and the campsite burned. While this had cleared up the mystery of what had happened to the Ramsgate party, what disturbed Mark was the perplexing discrepancy in dates: the Pasha's order was dated 5 August, 1881, while the last entry written in Ramsgate's Journal was dated August the first.

How did an entire expedition, with no signs or symptoms on 1 August (for Ramsgate made no mention of illness) contract smallpox and die of it four days later – all of them, with no survivors?

The second surprise had come from Mark's scrutiny of the seven yellow, faded death certificates, filled out in Arabic and signed by a Dr Fouad. Neville Ramsgate, his wife Amanda, their foreman Mohammed and three other men were all listed as having died of smallpox. On Sir Robert's certificate, however, the cause of death was listed as cholera.

To add further perplexity, there was no mention in the pitiful file of what had been done with the bodies.

Turning away from the handsome young agent, Mark finally looked at the last member of the expedition, recalling the conversation he had had with his foreman upon arriving at Cairo International Airport three days before.

Abdul Rageb had met the disembarking foursome outside of customs. A tall, austere Arab of aristocratic bearing and indeterminate age, Mark's old friend had been dressed, as usual, in an immaculate white *galabeyah* which exaggerated his leanness and heightened the darkness of his skin. Abdul Rageb had embraced Mark with a characteristic mixture of warmth and reserve, speaking softly in clipped English; he had greeted the visitors as if he were the king of this country, bowing slightly with each introduction, his hands clasped and hidden in the generous sleeves of his robe. He addressed Mark as *effendi*, a Turkish expression belonging to days gone by which led Mark to believe Abdul was much older than he appeared.

They had covered the final details in the Mercedes on the way to the Nile Hilton.

'Are we ready to go up the Nile, Abdul?'

'All is in order, *effendi*, we shall depart in three days, *inshallah*.'

'Everything arrived safely?'

'Yes, *effendi*. The crates arrived undamaged and are now at Rameses Station. Tomorrow I will accompany them up the Nile and set up the camp so that all will be ready for your arrival. I have also reserved an entire first-class car for you on the train, so that you and your companions will not be disturbed.'

'Excellent.' Mark had felt his excitement mount as they left the desert and entered the suburbs of Cairo, passing crowded slums and ill-cared for government buildings. A camel cart had created a pile-up at one intersection, causing a cacophony of car horns. It had felt good to be back in Egypt. 'Now tell me the situation at Amarna. Is there hostility?'

Abdul's expression grew veiled. 'There is nothing that cannot be worked out, *effendi*. I have met with the *'umda* of each village and we have established the pay scale. Ten piastres per day for each man, working on a rotating system with teams so that the crops will not go unattended.'

'But there *is* a problem.'

'No problem, *effendi*. There has been unrest in the villages since you were here last. Many young men have left the farms for the oil camps and phosphate mines on the Red Sea. In this new age, no man is content to till the soil like a slave.'

Mark studied the man's sharp profile. There was something unsettling about Abdul's manner. 'Abdul, is there something wrong?'

'No, *effendi*.'

'All right, then how about accommodations at Amarna?'

'We will have tents. You will not wish to live in the houses of the villages.'

'How about the water situation?'

'I have arranged everything, *effendi*. There will be a cistern and a pump and a man assigned to the task of seeing that it is always filled. When we arrive at Amarna, we will first meet with the *'umda* of El Till, for he is the most powerful. Later, we will visit the others.

'Electricity, bathrooms, cooking facilities?'

'All is well, *effendi*, as it was before.'

Mark looked at the Arab out of the corner of his eye. 'Are you sure they don't mind us being there?'

'The people are excited with the prospect, for you bring them diversion and money. It has been many years since we have worked in the ruins of Amarna.'

Mark raised his eyebrows. 'We? Do you mean you once worked at Amarna?

Abdul continued to avoid his companion's eyes. 'Many years ago, *effendi*, I was an overseer when the British were there. I helped excavate the Northern Palace.'

'I never knew that! You must have been awfully young at the time. Well, you'll be a bigger help to me than I had anticipated.'

The traffic thickened, grew maniacal; horns honked, brakes screeched, sooty buses hunkered by with Arabs spilling out of the windows and hanging on to the sides. 'I want you to set up the camp at the foot of the eastern cliffs, on the south lip of the Royal Wadi. Dr Farmer will be the photographer, so he'll require a tent for his darkroom. As I recall, Abdul, you're familiar with that set-up.'

'Yes, *effendi*.'

'You've seen to the special food for Mr Halstead?'

'All that was in your letters has been done, *effendi*.'

'Great!' As the limousine nosed its way through the press of traffic in Tahrir Square, with the Hilton complex looming on the right and the murky Nile beyond, Mark had excitedly rubbed his hands together. He was lucky to have Abdul Rageb as foreman again. 'One last thing. What about a doctor? I told you in my letters that I want a doctor on the team because we're going to be halfway between nowhere and nowhere, and my patron is a very important man.'

'There was some problem with that, *effendi*, for doctors who are willing to sit in the desert are difficult to find. Even at the generous pay you offered. It will be summer, a time when no sane man works in the sun. And physicians are becoming scarce in Egypt. After medical school, they go to Europe or America where the money is better.'

'Abdul, I won't go up the Nile without some –'

'But I have taken care of it, *effendi*. There is a medical student whom I know well, of good character, and who is willing to join us for the months when school is not in session.'

'Is that the best you could do?'

'This student is in the last year of medical school and already works in a clinic in Cairo.'

'All right, I'll trust your judgement, Abdul. If you think he's what we need, hire him on.'

'The student is not a man, *effendi*, she is a woman. Does this change your mind?'

Mark had had to think about that one, wondering what Halstead might say. Abdul had hastened to add: 'The young lady is familiar with archaeological expeditions and has a great interest in Egypt's ancient past. Her medical knowledge is expert; she is highly spoken of.'

'Okay.' The shiny Mercedes had pulled up the Hilton

drive and a uniformed doorman hurried to open the doors. 'She can come. She'll probably be company for Mrs Halstead.'

Sitting now in the train car and staring at Yasmina Shukri, medical student, Mark thought: How wrong I was on *that*!

The train finally slowed and a faded sign came into view which read MELLAWI in English and Arabic. While his companions slowly rose and stretched, Mark shot up and swung on to the platform while the brakes were still hissing.

Abdul emerged from the shadow of the rickety ticket office. '*Ah-laan, effendi*. All is ready. The camp is set up and the electrical generators have been started. All is as you ordered, *inshallah*.'

The incredible July heat pressed down on the newcomers as, one by one, they descended from the train. A stranger came to stand by Abdul, a man who kept his eyes proudly above the heads of the visitors and whose back was as rigid as if held in place by a ramrod. A hawk-faced man with copper skin pulled taut over hollow cheeks, he was a giant wearing a blue *galabeyah* and turban with a rifle slung over one of his massive shoulders. He reminded Mark of the mummy of Seti I. Abdul introduced him as the chief *ghaffir* responsible for protecting the expedition.

Mark looked the man over, noticing the cloud of trachoma over one eye. 'You've done well, Abdul. *Shokran*. Are the cars here?'

'This way, *effendi*.'

He led the group away from the platform to a dirt track paralleling a brackish canal where the flies were so thick their drone was deafening. At the swampy edge of the water, two men squatted in the dust playing trick-track. Parked on the 'road' were three old Chevrolets, black and dented, on top of which the company's luggage was being lashed. Mark divided everyone up, then climbed into the last car with Ron and Hazim and the *ghaffir*, who hung his rifle out of the window to make more room.

The journey over the bumpy dirt road was jarring as the three cars rattled along canals, through cotton fields and under canopies of date palms. The noon sun flashed through the overhead fronds as the low-slung automobiles bounced in and out of the holes and sped past crowds of children waving and shouting in the storm of dust left behind. By the time they reached the river, not a word had been spoken by anyone. The drivers opened the doors and everyone fell out, coughing and knocking off the dust.

Mark gave a quick look around at his party as he wiped dust out of his eyes. Alexis Halstead, cool and unperturbed, walked away from the car with her hands on her slender hips. Sanford Halstead, dressed in beige slacks and white polo shirt, eyed the approaching feluccas warily. Abdul, aided by the *ghaffir* and his two assistants, helped the drivers unload the luggage and set it on the wooden landing stage. Hazim al-Sheikhly sauntered over to where Yasmina Shukri stood drawing her long black hair into a scarf and struck up a quiet conversation with her.

Ron, with his camera swinging from one shoulder, came up to Mark and muttered, 'Sure is hot!'

Mark kept his eyes on the two boats weaving a path across the river toward him. 'This is only the beginning, my friend.'

The Nile spread out before them like a brown field, its surface rippled by the wakes of the feluccas and a northerly breeze that swept down through the valley. The expedition members took refuge in what shade they could find.

'Mark, what about Hazim? Do you trust him?'

'He's okay, I know his type. Young and green and eager to be of consequence. His government is trying to make up for the lack of foreign excavations in the Nile Valley by training their own people, only it isn't working because no one wants to dig. They all want a badge and a desk. Hazim won't be any trouble. Fresh out of college and full of idealism, corruption hasn't got to him. Yet.'

'When are you going to tell him about the Journal?'

'Tonight.'

Ron fanned a fly away from his face. 'Halstead looks like he's holding up pretty well.'

The fifty-nine-year-old man was leaning against a date palm, pressing his hands together in an isometric exercise. 'He's well preserved, I'll say that for him,' said Mark with a little laugh.

'His wife's quite a looker. Married him for his money, I'll bet. I wonder how long she'll be able to go without maid service.'

Mark watched Alexis as she went to stand at the edge of the water. Her thick hair caught the sunlight in fiery reflections. Dressed, like her husband, as if she were at a polo match, Alexis seemed to be able to keep cool and dust-free. Mark suspected her femininity was deceptive; Alexis Halstead had a fine toned musculature, she appeared ineluctably self-sufficient. Watching her, Mark suddenly felt very grimy.

'I don't think the other one likes us.'

'Which other one?'

Ron inclined his head toward Yasmina Shukri, who was laughing privately with Hazim. 'She didn't exactly throw roses in our path.'

Dressed in khaki slacks and blouse with her hair bound up in a bandana, Yasmina Shukri looked like many young Egyptian women Mark had seen in the last few years: emancipated, educated, breaking away from the old ways. She looked militant, standing on one hip with her arms folded and her head cocked to one side while Hazim spoke to her quietly in Arabic. A rifle on her back would not have been out of place.

Mark thought again about their first meeting that morning at Rameses station. The hostility in her eyes, when he had been introduced to her, had startled him. Although her voice had demurely said, 'I am pleased to meet you, Dr Davison,' her dark, lustrous eyes had said: I hate you but I tolerate you because, for now, my country needs you.

'I'm trusting Abdul's judgement. He says she's sailing through medical school with honors and already has three offers of good positions when she graduates. Besides, she was all we could get.'

Ron shrugged, muttered something about snapping a few pictures, and trudged away.

Mark could not help comparing the only two women in the expedition. They were about ten years apart: he estimated Alexis was thirty-two or three, Yasmina twenty-two or three. Alexis Halstead was cold and dazzling like a sapphire; Yasmina, warm and dark like polished ebony. They were both attractive, but in different ways. They were both quiet, but also in different ways. The disdain in Alexis Halstead's green eyes was due to arrogance and conceit; the resentment in Yasmina's smoldering eyes was a hatred of foreigners. Both women, Mark suspected, for their different reasons, would have to be handled carefully.

He turned away and strolled down to the bank where the water rippled the clay and stood gazing toward the clusters of palms that sprouted on the opposite bank. And beyond, the sandy plain of the ruins of Akhet-Aton.

As he stood with the toes of his boots teasing the water, Mark squinted at the stretch of yellow-brown desolation that reached from the edge of cultivation behind El Till to the foot of the distant cliffs three miles back. He thought again of the frustratingly scant details Ramsgate had left as to the whereabouts of his campsite, wondering if he had come to the correct conclusion that they should set up just below the mouth of the Royal Wadi. Ramsgate could have been anywhere in that twenty-four square mile area. And furthermore, where were they to start searching for the base of that stela? Also, what was the Dog and where could it be? For, according to Ramsgate, the tomb was located directly beneath it.

Mark closed his eyes and, feeling the warm breeze

against his face, tried to conjure up a vision of the blinding white temples and palaces that had once stood on that desolate plain, tried to picture Pharaoh Akhnaton and Queen Nefertiti riding through the streets in their glittering electrum-plated chariot, tried to hear the cheers of a thousand people hailing their Living God. Akhet-Aton, the 'Horizon of Aton', the most romantic and mysterious of ancient cities, was today nothing more than piles of rubble where the ancient buildings had stood.

Something had happened there three thousand years ago, something violent and unexplainable, something which had caused the priests of Amon to declare that patch of wasteland accursed and to seal in an unknown tomb the body of the heretic king . . .

'*Effendi*?'

Mark spun around.

'Pardon, you did not hear me.'

Mark, finally hearing the background shouts and seeing, at the landing stage, a commotion of waving arms and angry faces, said, 'What's happening, Abdul?'

'*Effendi*, there is trouble.'

SIX

THE TROUBLE had been between the two felucca owners, both of whom had claimed the right to transport the party across the river. Mark had solved the fight to everyone's satisfaction by dividing the group between the two boats and paying each boatman five pounds. Abdul took his two assistants, the *ghaffir* and all the luggage aboard one felucca, with Mark keeping the Americans, Yasmina and Hazim together in the other.

It took half an hour for the feluccas to tack across the wide river; everyone sat in silent thought as the ancient river craft creaked on their way. They crouched in the dirty hulls littered with cigarette butts and chewed ends of sugarcane, listening to the Nile lap against the boards.

At the landing on the opposite bank, a crowd had gathered.

The villagers, who had left their plows for the special occasion, watched silently as the strangers stepped on to the clay bank. Abdul's crisp orders were the only sounds to be heard as he supervised the loading of the luggage on to donkeys. As Alexis Halstead, the last to disembark, was being assisted by her husband, a rifle shot suddenly tore the intense noon air. It was joined by a series of reports from the surrounding cliffs, all firing and echoing and filling the valley with temporary thunder. When it died, Abdul came up to Mark and said, 'You have been officially welcomed, *effendi*.'

The crowd of peasants parted before the strangers, their faces broad with curiosity, and when Mark held up a hand

and called out, '*Ah-laan*!', he was answered with an energetic shout of, '*Ah-laan wah sahlaan*!' Then the villagers closed behind and followed.

Abdul led the party along a track that bisected two newly plowed fields: flat tracts of land interrupted by a network of irrigation ditches and an occasional clump of date palms. The winter crop of wheat had been harvested, the ground was being prepared now for the summer bean crop. As the party passed a young *fellaha* squatting in the dirt and kneading maize dough on to round wooden platters set out in the sun, she smiled shyly and lifted her veil up to her mouth. Nearby, the wheels of the village *saqiya* creaked while an ox, his bony mass walking in an eternal circle, turned the shaft. Women gathering water stopped to stare at the passing strangers, hastily covering their faces with their black veils.

The village was a huddled mass of earth on the border between lush cultivation and arid desert. Its ugly mud-brick houses, compacted tightly together and roofed with bundles of brushwood, were camoflaged a little by surrounding palms, acacias and sycamores. The visitors, now treading a dusty path, passed the village *birka*, a greenish stagnant pond which was used as a drinking trough for the animals, a swimming pool for the children, and which provided water for bricks and household washing. Its foul stench caused the foreigners to wrinkle their noses and turn away.

Next to the *birka* was the communal threshing and winnowing floor, a flat patch of ground covered with dust and cow dung, trodden level. A heavy wooden sled fitted with axles for breaking the straw was being guided over the fresh stalks by a *fellah* sitting on the box and steering his buffalo over them. Other men, leaning on their four-pronged winnowing forks, casually eyed the passing group.

Everywhere, the flies and smells were overpowering. Mark glanced once over his shoulder and saw that Alexis Halstead was holding a scented handkerchief to her nose.

The man they were being taken to see was the supreme government of the village. While each province in Egypt was governed by a constable known as the *ma'mur* who had an armed police force at his command, it was ultimately the *'umda*, an elder of the village chosen from among the *fellaheen*, who was the true government. He was a revered man whose prestige was attested to by the fact he usually had the only telephone. The *'umda* of El Till, the largest village at Tell el-Amarna, was a man of unaccountably advanced years, whose house was the only one in the village covered with whitewash.

The visitors were led down a dusty 'street' so narrow they had to walk in single file. At ease now and chattering among themselves, the crowd following on behind ogled Alexis Halstead's flaming red hair and remarked upon the quality of her henna. Smells pervaded from narrow doorways; the pungency of burning buffalo dung predominated. Mark and his companions waged a continuous battle with flies, and by the time they entered a small, sun-filled plaza in front of the *'umda's* white dwelling, they were sweaty and anxious to get on to the camp.

The ritual had to be observed; etiquette could not be breeched.

Lengths of cloth had been spread on the ground for the visitors to sit on, as the *fellah* had little use for the chair, and palm fronds which served as fans and fly swatters were shyly offered by barefooted children. Mark patiently took his seat, sitting cross-legged on the cloth, with his companions doing likewise, and smiled around at the crowd, trying to sense any hint of hostility. There appeared to be none.

He was all too familiar with the ever present problem of feuds between villages along the Nile. Disputes over watering rights, farm boundaries, a daughter's honor could lead to bloody rivalries that ended in death. Five years before, when Mark had been excavating in the Delta, a goat from a nearby village had strayed on to the threshing *qurn* of a neighboring village. The offended *fellah* had stormed up to the owner of the goat and rained insults at him. Hearing the argument, friends and relatives had come running, many of them still holding their harvesting tools; a man was accidentally shoved, he pushed back. A melée ensued and the *ma'mur* had had to send his police in to break it up. Later, during the night when all was quiet again, someone had stolen into the first village and slashed the goat's throat. The next day, the buffalo of the trespassed farmer was poisoned. Two days of bloody battle followed, with both villages rallying to the defense of family and tribal honor. Two men were killed, three critically injured, and the *ma'mur's* police had had to be stationed in the two villages until the bad feelings were forgotten. Which had taken a year.

Mark looked at the peasants clustering about the visitors, at the dark skinned, sturdily built *fellaheen* of El Till. The men wore long dirty *galabeyahs*, were barefooted and grinned with gaps in their teeth. The women, many pregnant and holding infants on their hips with other children hanging on to their skirts, wore faded print dresses that fell to their ankles, colorful plastic bangles on their wrists, and long black veils on their heads which they could draw up in a hurry to hide their faces from strangers. The majority of the women had reddish henna-rinsed hair, palms and cheeks dyed red with henna, and eyes rimmed with thick layers of black *kohl*.

Mark took care not to stare too long at any one woman, for a father or husband or brother could take it as an insult and vent irrational *fellaheen* wrath on both Mark and the woman.

He studied the men. As a race, Mark knew the *fellaheen* were of a pure, isolated stock, protected for centuries by the desert and cliffs that run parallel with the Nile. The broad skulls and faces, narrow foreheads, prominent cheekbones, thick noses and heavy jaws had withstood fifty centuries of foreign invasion; they had not intermarried with the Greeks, Romans, Arabs, French or Turks. These people not only worked and lived the same way their ancestors had done thousands of years before, keeping the ancient traditions despite the infiltration of Islam and Christianity, they also had the same physical appearance. Virtually direct descendants of the Nile Valley peasants of ancient times, the *fellaheen* of El Till were from the same genetic pool that had tilled the land and raised the food for Pharaoh's court. These were Akhnaton's people: unchanged and unchanging.

A stir rippled through the crowd and an old man with the longest, whitest beard Mark had ever seen emerged from the house. Wearing a white *galabeyah* and sandals, he walked with the assistance of a wooden staff. On his head the *'umda* wore a white knitted cap which signified that he had made the pilgrimage to Mecca. Mark saw how the crowd fell silent and turned their eyes to the old man as he came, like a Biblical patriarch, into the sunlight, paused a moment, then stiffly took a seat in the wicker chair that stood by the door. The *'umda* was king here.

'*Ah-laan wah sahlaan*,' he said in an ancient, rasping voice.

Mark returned the greeting, adding: '*Sab-bah in-noor*.'

The old man smiled benevolently and lifted a gnarled hand. At once a young woman appeared from inside the house, her face veiled and wearing brass circlets on her wrists and ankles; she carried a brass tray bearing glasses of tea.

When the tray was presented humbly before Mark, he took his tea, which was served in a Woolworth lunch-counter glass, and knew before tasting it that it would be outrageously sweet: a layer of sugar had settled at the bottom of his glass. Mark took a sip, smacked his lips and said in Arabic, 'The tea is delicious. It is the best I have ever had.'

The *'umda* grinned, exposing dark brown teeth against his white beard and moustache, and said, 'Allah forgive me that I must serve my most honored guest a tea that is not fit for donkeys, but it is all I have.'

Mark, who knew this was from the *'umda's* special

64

reserve and that his wife had spent all morning meticulously brewing it, said, 'I am not worthy to drink it.'

A woman came out of the house and stood behind the
old man. She was small and withered, her red hair white at
the roots, her face crinkled leather, but her hands were
dyed orange and her wrists jangled with bracelets of gold –
she was the most respected and envied woman in El Till.

The *'umda* said, 'I present my wife, Ahmed's mother.'

Mark nodded politely at the old *fellaha* without paying
her excessive attention. It was *fellaheen* custom to refer to
a woman not by her own name but by the name of her
oldest son.

The *'umda* proceeded to welcome, by name, each of the
men in Mark's party, ignoring the women, and ended
with, 'May Allah smile upon your work and bring you
many successes.'

This was the signal for business to begin. Abdul opened
up by explaining to the *'umda* that Mark would need two
teams of ten men apiece, to be changed every two weeks
or as the farming demanded. The *'umda*, whom Abdul
addressed as *haj*, meaning pilgrim, listened graciously.
Then he turned to Mark and said in his Middle Egypt
drawl, 'It serves us all that you have come, Dr Davison.
Our people need the work, you need our help, and we all
revere that which is *qadim*. Too long has it been since
there has been work among the ruins.'

Mark nodded and tried, without gagging, to drain his
unbearably sweet tea. *Qadim* meant anything ancient, and
fellaheen the length of the Nile, in their superstition and
awe of their ancestral past, venerated anything that was
centuries old. They believed there was strong magic in
objects from their distant past.

Sanford Halstead now spoke up, leaning toward Mark
and murmuring, 'Would you kindly translate all this for
us?'

'It's just a formality, Mr Halstead. Abdul took care of
everything weeks ago, everything's arranged. All we're
doing is acting out a little play that custom demands.'

'It's a waste of time.'

'I agree, but we have to do it, otherwise we'll offend the old man and then we'll have ourselves a pack of trouble. He may not look like much, but the *'umda* is supreme lord of the land here and the people do what he says.'

Sanford Halstead straightened up and scowled into his tea. He had not touched it.

'And I suggest you drink that.'

'I'd rather not.'

'It'll offend him, and nobody takes offense more seriously than these people. Refusing an Egyptian's hospitality is as bad as spitting in his face. Please drink it.'

As Sanford Halstead forced the tepid tea between his lips, keeping his face stony, Mark said to the old man, 'My friend would like to know if he could have another glassful.'

The old man grinned and snapped an order to his daughter, who eagerly ducked into the house.

Business continued. 'There will be no problem supplying you with willing workers, Dr Davison. Indeed, everyone wishes to work for the Americans. I have had to make serious decisions these past few weeks; it is not easy choosing who may join you and who must stay with the fields.'

Mark knew this was the crucial part. The rivalry between El Till and the village of Hag Qandil to the south was famous; both *'umdas* would have to be mollified. Mark trusted that Abdul had hired equal numbers of men from each village.

'As to the matter of payment, Dr Davison, ten piastres a day per man is satisfactory. This will buy sugar and a new plow. Each man has his reasons for wishing to work for you. Sami has a son who wants to marry, but he has no money for the bride-price. Mohammed owes money to the moneylender at fifty per cent interest. Rahmi has twin sons who need to be circumcised. We all need extra money, Dr Davison, for you see that we are as poor as the needle, which clothes others but itself remains unclad.'

Mark waited impatiently, knowing what was coming. Therefore he was not surprised when the 'umda said, 'But alas it would seem ten piastres is no longer enough.'

'What will make the job worth your while, *hagg*?' Mark pronounced the title *haj* in Middle Egyptian dialect.

'We wish you to add to the ten piastres a measure of tea to each man.'

Mark looked at Abdul who turned slightly and said in metered English, 'I anticipated this, *effendi*. Among the crates I brought with me two days ago is a shipment of the blackest, purest tea to be found in Egypt. Two *ghaffirs* have been guarding it day and night since it arrived.'

Mark nodded, he had seen this before. The *fellaheen* madness for tea. Denied alcohol because of their Moslem religion, Nile peasants had long since turned to other forms of stimulation, and as hashish was expensive and interfered with work in the fields, tea had become the number one addictive among the millions of peasants. Mark knew that no *fellah* went into the field without his pot of strong, thickly sweetened tea. It was his 'high', his physical entertainment, his one luxury and therefore necessity in life. By the gallons they gulped it, rich black tea spiked with a pound of sugar.

'Very well, *hagg*, you will have your tea.'

'And sugar, Dr Davison.'

'And sugar.'

'I understand,' continued the 'umda, 'that you will also be hiring men from Hag Qandil. I must warn you that they are untrustworthy scoundrels. We have no fight with them at the moment, but I put a board across my door at night.'

'What do you suggest, *hagg*?'

'What I will try to do is act as mediator between you and the men of Hag Qandil. Perhaps if I humble myself . . .' He spread out his bamboo-shoot hands and hoisted his bony shoulders. 'I can speak to them on your behalf.'

Halstead hissed angrily, 'What's going on!'

'It's the old insurance game. You pay us, we don't break your legs.' Mark addressed the 'umda again: 'What can I do to help, *hagg*?'

'I am an old man, Dr Davison. Alas, my days are numbered. How many sunrises I will live to see, only Allah knows. It would be a comfort in my old age and poverty to have some small trifling luxury. Something that would be of no consequence to a great and wealthy man like yourself.' His grin widened. 'I want Coca-Cola.'

Mark shot an impatient glance at Abdul who quickly said in English, 'It arrived with the tea, *effendi*. A crate of it.'

'Does the *'umda* of Hag Qandil know about it?'

'No, *effendi*.'

'Don't let him. All we need is a fucking feudal war over our Coke.' He forced a smile at the *'umda* and said, 'We have a bargain.'

The old patriarch relaxed visibly and sat back in his chair, a contented smile crunching his leathery face into a million creases.

Sanford Halstead, catching sight of a woman picking lice out of a little boy's hair, said to Mark, 'How much longer!'

'Not long. Smile at the old man and gulp down the tea. If you belch loudly, he'll be your friend for life.'

'You can't be serious!'

'When in Rome, Mr Halstead.'

'I can't take much more of this stench, Davison, and I don't think this is very fitting for my wife.'

'Your wife, Mr Halstead, is so inconsequential right now that the *'umda* would think more highly of your donkey, if you had one. A few more minutes, then we'll strike off for camp. I want to ask him a question or two about Ramsgate.'

As he downed the last of his chokingly sweet tea, Mark caught sight of a man at the edge of the crowd who did not seem to belong. Short, fat and oily, he was glaringly out of place among the villagers, especially with his white shirt, which was buttoned right up to his thick neck, and his dark trousers. The face was chubby, the hair long and wavy and shining with grease. The shirt was soiled around the collar and cuffs, and decorated down the front with food stains. The man was leaning against a urine-stained wall picking his ear. His air of casual disinterest alerted Mark.

Mark knew who he was. He was the village Greek, the one merchant, the jobber, the clothier, the wheeler-dealer, the loan shark. There was one in every village from the Delta to the Sudan: a long time ago, the Greeks had come to the Nile Valley and had seen profit in exploiting the peasants who had nowhere to turn for their material goods. The job was handed down from father to son; they rarely intermarried, importing a bride from Greece; lived at the edge of the village; took no part in the social life, and exacted a comfortable living from the gullible *fellaheen*.

Mark etched the man's porcine face on his brain and then returned to the *'umda*. He said, 'I need some information, *hagg*.'

'And I have the answers, *inshallah*.'

'A hundred years ago an Englishman came here to dig in the ruins. He was before Petrie, *hagg*. He died of an illness and the area of his camp and worksite was quarantined. Do you know this place of restriction?'

For the first time since he had come out of the house, the *'umda's* sharp little eyes clouded over. 'That was a long time ago, Dr Davison, and there is no longer an area of restriction. Nor in my memory has there been such a place, and I am over eighty years old.'

'This was in the time of the last Turkish Pasha, before the British took over the government. A paper was issued forbidding anyone to enter a certain area. I believe it was in the hills.'

'My grandfather was *'umda* of this village then, Dr Davison. He told me when I was a boy of the first foreigners who came here to dig. They called themselves scientists, but they were no more than treasure hunters. They uncovered the ruins of our ancestors and took away the beautiful things they found. They shared nothing with us.'

Nothing, thought Mark, except the English pounds they paid you for helping them dig. 'Do you remember one called Ramsgate?'

A barely perceptible pause came before the answer. 'No.'

'Do you remember anything about the restricted area?'

'I do not know why you are asking me these things. If they happened a hundred years ago, what can they matter?'

'They matter, *hagg*. Do you know where the restricted area was? Or is your memory failing you in your old age?'

The bright little eyes flared. 'Age has not dimmed my memory, Dr Davison! Yes, I remember that my grandfather told me of a British explorer who died in the ruins with his wife and friends. They were diseased, he said. And then the government forbade our people to enter the area.'

'Where was it, *hagg*?'

'I do not know. My grandfather never told me. When I was old enough to visit the ancient places on my own, the restriction was no longer enforced, for a new government was in the land, new laws and new police. The old rules were forgotten.'

'When was that?'

The *'umda* looked away. 'When I was young.'

Mark studied the floral pattern of the cloth he sat on and ran a hand over his sweaty neck. 'Is the name Ramsgate familiar?'

'No.'

'Then there are no forbidden places nearby?'

'None.'

'And you will let your grandchildren play where they wish?'

'Yes.'

'You have been most helpful, *hagg*, and I am grateful. One of my men will bring three bottles of Coca-Cola to your house tonight.'

An instantaneous change came over the old man as his

face brightened and beamed like a sunrise. 'Dr Davison, you humble me with your generosity!'

At this point, sensing a pause in the men's conversation, for to interrupt them would mean a beating, the *'umda's* wife leaned close to him and murmured something in his ear. The *'umda's* white bushy eyebrows arched in pleasure. He said, 'Ahmed's mother has requested that you attend a celebration we will be holding tonight.'

'What sort of celebration, *hagg*?'

'It is the circumcision of Hamdi's daughter.'

Halstead tapped Mark on the shoulder. 'What's this about?'

When Mark translated, Alexis Halstead, sitting behind her husband, said, 'Daughter!'

Mark had to twist around a little to look at her. 'Both boy babies and girl babies are circumcised here.'

'But what can they do to girls?'

'They have the clitoris removed.'

Her pencil-thin eyebrows shot up, and Mark turned back. 'You do us great honor, *hagg*, but we have traveled a great distance and are anxious to be at our camp. Tell Ahmed's mother that we are overwhelmed at her generosity and it pains us to have to refuse.'

The *'umda* nodded graciously.

When the requisite well-wishes and good-healths were exchanged, everyone rose and stretched. Yasmina Shukri, who had sat through the visit unmoving like a statue, did a curious thing. She went to the *'umda*, fell to her knees before him and touched her chest, lips and forehead with the fingers of her right hand. As she rose again to her feet, Mark stared at her in mild amazement, all the more so because the *'umda* acknowledged her homage with a patronly smile and did not seem at all surprised.

The *'umda* finally rose and the peasant crowd started to disperse. Mark rubbed his lower back and made a sweep of the little plaza. He looked for the Greek, but the man was gone.

SEVEN

As THE three Land-Rovers raced across the plain away from the setting sun, caroming in and out of gulleys and raising a maelstrom of grit and debris, the expedition members gazed at the ancient city they passed through.

They saw a plain of such utter bleakness and desolation that the soul cried out for some shred, some clue, some tiny memento from the magnificent past. Each one, American and Egyptian, looked out at the mounds of rubble that were all that remained of Akhnaton's city, trying to reconstruct a mental picture of white palaces and tree-lined avenues out of the crumbled walls and dunes of sand. But it could not be done; nothing remained.

Ahead, the sheer wall of limestone cliffs loomed larger and larger as, gradually, the Nile and cultivation fell behind. The cliffs were primeval backdrops of bare, stratified rock like a miniature Grand Canyon; a prehistoric landscape stripped to its geologic layers. When the cluster of tents came into view, Mark wiped the sweat off his forehead and thought: We're going back in time.

The vehicles finally came to a halt and everyone waited for the dust to settle. Through the cloud they could see that they had driven past the Royal Wadi – which was a dried up river-bed; in the south-western United States it would be called an arroyo – and had swung around a stony promontory which jutted out from its south lip. On one side of the promontory could be seen, in the late afternoon sun, a patchwork of waist-high walls that resembled a maze through which a giant rat might run. This was the ruin of what Egyptologists called the Workmen's Village – the little town where ancient tomb workers and their families had lived separately from the main city – and one could see evidence of new habitation in some of the 'rooms'; Abdul's hired crew had chosen to set up their own temporary camp in the ruins to save a daily trek from the villages a few miles away.

On the other side of the promontory, seven large white tents had been erected in a vague circle. They crouched at the foot of the rise of cliff wall, protected from the wind and assured of shade for the first half of the day. Generators hummed beneath a lean-to, and electrical wires led from them to all of the tents. A hundred feet downwind from the camp were two shower stalls and two latrines.

As the hottest part of the day was now upon them, the expedition members lethargically climbed down from the Land-Rovers, knocking dust off their clothes and eyeing the camp skeptically. Ron, the most energetic, immediately fell to taking pictures, running around and snapping everyone in candid poses to capture the mood of setting up camp.

Abdul began barking crisp orders at two *fellaheen* who had hurried over from the Workmen's Village, where their bedrolls and campfire could be seen in the ruins, and Mark slowly walked around, appraising and approving of the set-up.

The rest were directed to their tents. Four were to be private quarters: the Halsteads in one tent, Ron and Mark in another, Hazim and Abdul in the third, and Yasmina Shukri with her medical supplies alone in the last. A fifth tent served as Ron's darkroom, the sixth had been fitted out as a work area, containing excavating, laboratory and surveying equipment, with the seventh and largest tent set up as a mess tent where communal meals would be eaten.

Mark watched Sanford and Alexis Halstead as they were led to their tent, three *fellaheen* struggling behind with the luggage. Halstead had been specific in his requirements for their accommodation, and Mark silently

73

prayed Abdul had been able to comply.

When they disappeared inside, Mark started to turn away. As he did so, an insect flew across his face, buzzing. He took a swipe at it, looking up to get a better aim. He stopped short. Bringing up a hand to shade his eyes, he squinted up at the top of the cliff which towered several hundred feet above the camp. There, silhouetted against the blue sky, stood a silent figure staring down at the activity.

Mark gazed up for a moment, trying to focus on the person who stood on the plateau, then dropped his hand and looked around for Abdul.

He knew that an ancient road existed still on the tableland above the plain, a road that Pharaoh Akhnaton's soldiers had built, and that the local *ghaffirs* now occasionally used in their policing rounds. But this man had not looked like a *ghaffir*. For one thing, he didn't have a rifle; for another, he was without a mule or camel. Nor was Mark even certain it was a man.

Abdul was snapping orders to one of his assistants, the gist of which was to see that the shower reservoirs contained enough water for the bathing of six people. The assistant was waving his arms and pointing and explaining something Mark could not quite hear.

When he looked up at the plateau again, the dark figure was gone.

Mark watched Yasmina Shukri jump down from the Land-Rover and pause to push a few stray hairs from her face. She leaned against the fender and trailed her unreadable expression over the camp. He had not given the young woman any more thought since climbing into the felucca, and only now wondered vaguely why she had volunteered for this unglamorous post. No communication had passed between them since their introduction upon boarding the train, and it appeared she was going to make little effort to ingratiate herself with the group.

Mark watched her as she pushed away from the vehicle and followed one of Abdul's assistants to one of the smaller tents. Then he turned his attention elsewhere.

Yasmina murmured, *'shokran,'* to the *fellah* and waited until he had left the tent before she made a move. Then she turned around, unfurled the roll of mesh over the doorway and zipped it shut. Yasmina knew the problems they would be having with insects.

She inspected the tent from where she stood; the foreman had done a good job. The cot appeared comfortable, a wad of mosquito netting was suspended overhead in a ball. A brightly colored carpet was spread on the floor. There was a chair and a small writing table, plus the special bench and shelves she would need for her medical supplies. Against one wall stood the crate containing her equipment and drugs.

She moved languidly about the tent, trying to gather up her straying thoughts and put them in order. There was so much to think about; she was so full of emotions that needed to be analysed. Yasmina sat on the edge of the cot and wearily untied the scarf from her hair. As the thick waves tumbled over her shoulders and down her back, the young Egyptian woman released a shaky sigh.

This was the first thing, she decided at once, that she would work on: the loneliness. It was a daily battle to which Yasmina Shukri was accustomed: the loneliness that had followed her through years of school and college, in and out of friendships, and which awaited her, she knew, when she received her medical degree and became a practicing physican.

She was not sure why she had joined this expedition, except the money was good, and the foreman, Mr Rageb, had assured her the Americans would be easy to work for.

Yasmina, slouching on the cot with her hands lying lifelessly in her lap, gave a moment's thought to the foreigners, dismissing the Halsteads as people not worthy of her time, and considered the Egyptologists. The blond one seemed nice enough, though not at all professional, but the other one, the leader of the expedition, he was the one she did not trust. Yasmina Shukri had seen enough of Mark Davison's type in her life to know what his motives were and what to expect of him. He would be like the others, the exploiters she had long ago come to despise; so she would maintain her distance and use him to her own ends.

Yasmina felt something brush her cheek. She absently flagged it away with her hand.

Mr Rageb had not told her what the Egyptologists were looking for, and Yasmina was not sure she cared. All that mattered was the salary, which had promised to be good. Plus, the generous patron Mr Halstead had agreed to give her total freedom in purchasing medical supplies. How different from a government infirmary!

Something touched her cheek again. She brushed it away.

Yasmina finally settled her thoughts upon Hazim al-Sheikhly. Although he was possibly a little too solicitous to the Americans – but then, that was his job – Hazim was a young man Yasmina could very easily like. He was handsome and energetic, and seemed, in his approach to her, secure enough within himself not to be threatened by her. So much of Yasmina's loneliness stemmed from the archaic traditions of Islam which dictated that a woman must be inferior to a man. Even her fellow medical students were uncomfortable with her and shied away from more intimate relationships: soon she would be a doctor, and the prospects of finding a husband in this Moslem country who would allow her a career and status of her own were practically nil. Hazim al-Sheikhly was the first man in a long time who seemed . . .

It brushed by again, this time snatching Yasmina out of her thoughts. Bringing her hand up to her cheek, she looked around the tent which was, at the moment, due to the slanting afternoon sun spilling through the mesh

76

doorway, well lighted. She searched for the pesky insect and, not finding it, felt around her face for a possible stray hair.

Yasmina hoped the expedition would last the summer, although Mr Rageb had not been able to promise that. If they lasted the summer she would have enough money to . . .

This time it felt like a tiny slap, like a moth batting a window pane; Yasmina got up and went over to the utility stand which held a pitcher and basin, soap and towels, and above which, fixed to an aluminum strut, hung a mirror. She bent close to examine her face where the pest had hit it and saw on her cheek, just barely surfacing, a tiny red welt.

Yasmina immediately checked the two windows for holes – both were covered with netting – then opened her box of supplies and drew out a packet of fly paper and a spray can of insect repellent.

This was probably going to be the extent of her services for the summer: treating insect bites.

Hazim al-Sheikhly carefully and meticulously unpacked his case and set his toiletries in an orderly row on his night stand. He moved in a disciplined, punctillious way, not wanting his excitement to create sloppiness. Hazim prided himself in his neatness; he hoped the man he was to share this tent with was equally fastidious. Hazim suspected so. Abdul Rageb, by appearance and manner, was conscientious and also enjoyed no small reputation for skill and efficiency. Hazim had been impressed, upon receiving this assignment, to learn he would be working with the much admired and respected Abdul Rageb.

The whole expedition was nearly more than the eager Hazim could bear. It was a choice plum that not a few of his colleagues wanted to get. But having an uncle high up in the ministry had helped. This could be a lucky break for Hazim al-Sheikhly, only two years out of college and doing nothing behind a desk. If the Americans came up with a good find – although Allah alone knew what could possibly be left in this depleted desert – it could mean a promotion and a title for Hazim.

He brought his head up and turned around. 'Yes?' he said.

But the tent was empty. Before him, yellow dust-filled rays poured through the open doorway.

He shook his head and returned to unpacking. Hazim could have sworn that, for the moment, someone had been in the tent with him.

He had taken enough shots of what he considered the 'preliminary chaos' and was now anxious to check out his own facilities, so Ron headed for the tent that was to be used as his darkroom.

Despite the late afternoon Nile breeze and reflecting whiteness of the Dacron walls, the interior was stifling and oven-like. Ron paused inside the doorway to let his eyes adjust, then looked around.

It was incredible. Abdul had done exactly as he had specified, right down to dividing the tent into a 'wet' side and a 'dry' side. Directly in front of him, against the back wall, stood the wooden workbench under which the crates he had personally packed and shipped off back in Los Angeles had been neatly stacked. Over this bench were strung three electrical outlets containing bulbs. Falling to one knee, Ron did a hasty mental check of the cartons and searched each one for a number, satisfying himself that all had arrived.

He immediately set about opening them and, going in order of priority, found the heavy crate marked #101 and which was labeled in red bold letters: FRAGILE! HANDLE WITH EXTREME CARE! He pried the top slats loose with his pocket knife, filling the warm tent with sounds of splintering, and was soon scooping out handfuls of styrofoam packing. This was the crucial box.

Ron relaxed and broke into a grin. Reaching in, he withdrew one of the gallon bottles of Gallo chianti and patted it lovingly.

Alexis Halstead stood with arms akimbo as she surveyed their quarters. The two cots, draped with satin sheets and goosedown comforters, were set as far apart as possible with two ivory-inlaid mahogany night tables between them. Dividing these was a linen curtain, suspended from a rod which Abdul had had bolted to the tent poles. The curtain, now pulled back and secured to the wall, would later serve as a room divider to create two smaller chambers in the tent.

Ignoring her husband, who was going through a suitcase filled with jogging wear and Adidas shoes, Alexis noted the little comforts and luxuries Abdul Rageb had added to their tent.

Glazed ceramic pitchers and bowls stood on separate toilet tables, each with a stack of starched hand towels, a dish of soap, and several lush Turkish bath towels. Over each bed hung an ornate brass lamp operated by a switch near each night table. On the walls were photographs of flowers and Nile sunsets. On each night stand, a little electric fan. On the floor, oriental carpets.

When the *fellah* deposited the last of their suitcases by her bed, Alexis turned around and pulled down the tent flap, plunging the interior into semi-darknes, with the tepid afternoon light filtering through the window netting. She flicked on the light over the bed, wordlessly unfastened the curtain from the wall, and drew it down the length of the beds.

As she was standing over her suitcase in the pattern of light created by the brass lamp, she heard her husband's voice on the other side of the curtain: 'I beg your pardon, Alexis?'

'What?'

'What did you say, Alexis?'

'I didn't say anything.'

He appeared around the edge of the curtain, his shoulders and chest bare. 'You said something. I didn't catch it.'

'Sanford, I haven't uttered a word since sitting in that god-awful village! If you're going to jog, get going. The sun is setting.'

He ducked behind the curtain. 'I could have sworn . . .'

With a paper cup filled to the brim, Ron returned the bottle to its crate and slid the crate back under the developing table. He knew he was going to have to be sparing with his wine; no telling where he was going to get more.

He opened the second most important carton, the one containing his battery-operated cassette player and his collection of Doug Robertson tapes. Choosing his favorite, he slipped the tape into the player, pushed a button, and the stifling air gave way to the delicate strings of classical guitar.

As he started to rise, Ron felt something scurry across his shin. He took a swat at it and then quickly searched the floor. Whatever it was, it had been too quick for him.

'What?' Alexis straightened up impatiently. 'Sanford, what did you say?'

The other side of the curtain was annoyingly silent.

'Are you playing games with me?' she snapped irritably.

When no answer came, Alexis pulled back the curtain.

Her husband was not there.

The developing tanks here, stop-bath there, enlarger over there, safelights strung here, and so on. Ron hummed along with Doug Robertson and took another sip of wine.

'Shit!' he hissed as the thing scampered across his feet again. This was the third time.

Mark felt the setting sun pound his back as he stood and watched Sanford Halstead, sweating and puffing but in enviably good shape, jog around the perimeter of the camp.

Ron got down on his hands and knees and poked his flashlight beam into every crevice and behind every box. Whatever it was, it had felt pretty big. Big enough to find without much trouble.

But he never found it.

Mark gave a last look around the camp. From the darkroom tent came the faint strains of Vivaldi; Mark knew his friend was already at work and would not come out until he had finished developing. Through the gauzy doorways of three of the residential tents Mark could see the hazy outlines of his people settling down. Yasmina Shukri, faintly visible, was creating a miniature infirmary of her tent. Hazim al-Sheikhly was at his little writing table already starting a report to his superiors. And Alexis Halstead, a misty, shapely shadow seen through the tent wall, appeared to be doing nothing at all.

Mark decided to check out the mess tent.

His other senses registered it before his eyes could, since the interior was dark and smoky; he smelled the cooking aromas and heard the crackle and sizzle of frying meat. After a few seconds, his eyes adjusted, and what he saw startled him.

She was the oldest woman Mark Davison had ever seen.

The *fellaha* did not at first look up from her work, but remained intent over her pots and pans. Dressed entirely in black, the old woman was so bent and gnarled and darkly complexioned that she reminded Mark of a piece of driftwood. In the next instant, however, when she raised her head and fixed an astonishingly sharp eye on him, he found himself thinking of the *sebbakha* in Ramsgate's Journal.

'What's your name?' he asked, wondering why he suddenly felt uncomfortable beneath her stare.

The withered *fellaha* held him for another moment – her parchment face, with the forehead and eyebrows covered by her black veil, frozen in an unreadable expression – then she returned to her cooking.

He repeated the question, this time in Arabic. She did not reply.

Then the light from the doorway was obliterated for an instant, and Abdul was standing at his side. 'Who is she?' asked Mark.

'Her name is Samira, *effendi*.'

'Is she deaf?'

'No, *effendi*.'

Mark studied the curvature of the dehydrated body, the knotted hands emerging from voluminous black sleeves, the gold ring in the right nostril. She looked like a shrunken nun.

'Where did you get her?' asked Mark.

'Her home is at Hag Qandil, but she services all villages here.'

'Services?'

Adbul hesitated slightly. 'She is *shaykha*, *effendi*.'

Mark nodded in understanding. Every village in the Nile Valley had one, or her male counterpart: the men were called *shaykh*, meaning magic man or sorcerer. The *shaykha* was the one who had been taught the old magic, handed down from mother to daughter; she was the one who knew the ancient spells, the formulas for warding off the Evil Eye, for helping women to conceive, to cast evil spells on enemies and benevolent spells on one's crops. The *shaykha* knew how to secure the help of the *jinns*, how to make love potions, or how to insure the birth of a male child. The *shaykha* practised the most incompre-

hensible form of mumbo-jumbo, and the more compli-
cated, the more esoteric her magic, the more potent it
was.

'Why did you hire her?'

'It is not easy, *effendi*, to find a woman in this region
who can cook for Americans. She understands your
delicate stomachs and sensitive tastes. I sought her out
personally because her reputation is good. And because
many years ago she worked for the British Egyptologists
when they were clearing away the palaces.'

Mark cast a sideways glance at his reserved foreman,
wondering fleetingly if Abdul still harbored some of his
childhood superstitions, then said, 'I don't care what I eat,
just so long as she understands that Mr Halstead must
have special food.'

'Yes, *effendi*.'

He stepped out into the sunset and inhaled lungfuls of
warm desert air. Ahead of him, a thin ribbon on the
horizon, was the river – green and slow and very old.
Mark could see the distant groves of date palms growing
dark against the globe of the setting sun. He closed his
eyes for an instant.

'Okay, everybody!' rang a voice over the silent camp.

Mark opened his eyes and saw Ron plodding through
the sand toward him. Behind came Hazim al-Sheikhly,
Yasmina Shukri and Sanford Halstead. Ron's camera
swung across his chest as he walked. 'Time for one last
picture!' He was carrying a tripod.

Mark laughed softly and stepped away from the mess
tent.

'Group together now! Where's Mrs Halstead? I want
one good shot of all of us on our first afternoon here. And
the light's perfect right now. Yeah, right there is good!'
Ron waved his arms like a movie director. 'Closer! That's
it! Where's Mrs Halstead?'

She pushed aside the tent flap and emerged into the
daylight like a desert queen. Mark couldn't help staring
for an instant. Alexis paused before stepping away from

the tent, her copper hair lifting in the breeze. After seven years with five-foot-three Nancy, Mark had forgotten how long a woman's legs could be. Dressed in tennis shorts and blouse, Alexis Halstead was the image of towering sexuality. When she walked toward the group, her body moved with well-oiled grace, each swing of the arm a perfect gesture; even the occasional toss of her head, not jerky or affected but wonderfully alluring, was like the toss of a stallion's great mane.

And once again, just as when he had first met her at Los Angeles International Airport, Mark was struck by a haunting familiarity about her face . . .

'This one's for the *National Geographic*!' said Ron, taking Hazim by the arm and moving him closer to Yasmina. 'Let's try to look like we know what we're doing here. Where's Abdul?'

'Forget it, Ron,' said Mark, completing the line by taking a place next to Sanford Halstead. 'I've never known Abdul to allow his picture to be taken. Hurry up, sun's almost down.'

Ron made the final adjustments on the tripod, looked through the viewer one last time, then set the shutter on the timer and ran around in time to throw his arm over Hazim's shoulder before the camera clicked.

'One more!' he said as everyone started to break away.

'Come on, Ron, we're tired and hungry.'

'It's the last one on the roll, Mark. I can develop it tonight.'

Mark laughed wearily as he opened his mouth to protest, but he didn't get a chance to say anything further for, in that instant, the afternoon silence was suddenly ripped apart by a high, piercing inhuman shriek.

EIGHT

'Is THAT what you think killed him? A heart attack?'

Yasmina Shukri was sitting by herself at the smaller of the two tables in the mess tent, sipping coffee. She nodded slowly, thinking of the man they had found in the ruins of the Workmen's Village. He had died in a squatting position; presumably about to brew tea over his campfire. He had been alone.

'Are heart attacks common among these people?' asked Mark.

She murmured, 'No.' She could not shake off the memory of the poor man's face; he must have died suddenly and in tremendous pain. They had found him with his eyes open and staring, his mouth twisted.

Mark turned away from her and scowled down at his coffee. Hell of a way to start the project. And now, when they should be studying the maps, Abdul was at El Till consoling the dead man's widow.

'What is the schedule for tomorrow, Dr Davison?'

Mark looked up at the man sitting across the table from him and forced himself to be as congenial as possible. 'Abdul and I will scout the plain and the plateau to try to determine where we will begin the search. You will recall that Ramsgate's Journal tells us of a funerary stela marking the entrance of the tomb. It was carved out of living rock – that is, from rock jutting up out of the sand – and that at some time in the past, lightning struck the stela, breaking it into three pieces. And then, about a hundred years ago, a flash-flood washed one of the pieces – the top stone – down this ravine behind us and on to the plain. An old woman, a *sebbakha*, brought it into Ramsgate's camp, telling him that it marked the location of a tomb, which she said was 'under the Dog'. Several days later, Ramsgate found the base of the stela, then that Dog, and from there the tomb. What we are going to look for, Mr Halstead, is that stela base and anything that looks like a dog.'

Sanford Halstead listened politely. He did not care for the heat and closeness of the dining tent; a few flies had found their way in and were droning irritatingly. Smells from the Coleman stoves rose to the ceiling and gathered in a suffocating pall over the heads of the six people who had just finished supper.

While Halstead had eaten a salad of raw vegetables and yogurt, the others had devoured old Samira's meal with enthusiasm: roasted lamb and rice in a savory gravy with locally grown broad beans dressed in butter; very cold mint tea and a delicious millet bread baked that afternoon; and for dessert, sweet *mehalabeyah*, the rice pudding speciality of Egypt.

'Precisely how will the search be handled, Dr Davison?'

'Abdul and I have topographical maps of this region. Tomorrow he and I will scout the whole area and work out a grid system. The plain and plateau will be divided into squares, with one man assigned to each square. I plan to concentrate our initial search in the gulleys that drain from the tableland above us.'

'And the Dog?'

Mark could not pinpoint his annoyance, but he had little patience for this aristocrat who had come to Egypt in cream colored slacks and polo shirt. 'I imagine the Dog will be found purely by accident. Abdul and I will instruct the *fellaheen* to keep their eyes open for anything that might resemble a dog.'

'Are they to be trusted? How can you be sure one of these Arabs won't just take a nap instead of exploring his square?'

Mark looked over at Samira who flapped silently over her vegetables. At one point during the meal he had happened to look up and he had seen that her black veil had ridden up on her forehand, revealing what looked like a tattoo. The old *fellaha* had quickly turned away and pulled the veil back into place.

'We have a reward system, Mr Halstead. Any man who uncovers something of value to us will receive a handsome reward. Believe me, it works.'

'What time will we start?'

'Very early. Sunrise. Before it gets too hot.'

'Dr Davison.'

Mark turned to look at Alexis Halstead, mildly surprised to hear her speak. Her eyes of polished malachite seemed to be boldly appraising him. 'I would like to see the tombs in the cliffs.'

Raising his eyebrows slightly, Mark said, 'Certainly. We can include them in our survey of the plain.'

Mark drew off each itchy sock with a sigh of relief and wiggled his toes in the cool evening air. The cot felt good beneath his buttocks, and he knew he would sleep deeply and soundly until Abdul woke him in the morning. Decanting a little bourbon from his flask into the glass on his night table, Mark felt a sense of satisfaction wash over him. This was definitely where he belonged.

Toasting the photograph of Nancy that stood on the table, and thinking: I promise you wedding bells and babies after this one, he downed the whiskey in one gulp.

The tent flap moved aside and Ron Farmer entered. In one hand he held his paper cup of chianti; in the other, newly developed pictures.

'Got some good ones,' he said, sinking on to his own cot and holding the proofsheet out to Mark. 'Hoo! I feel like I could sleep forever!'

'You're working too hard. It could have waited till tomorrow.'

'Felt like doing it. Lot of work to setting up a darkroom. But I'm going to have to check out the tent for holes tomorrow, had a critter running around the floor.'

Mark looked at the photographs. 'God, do I really look like this?'

'Get a load of Halstead. I'll bet he picks his nose with a Q-tip.'

Mark paused over the last picture, the group shot. Six weary, dusty people giving the shutter their best. Ron's grin was the broadest as he hung on to Hazim; next to him Yasmina Shukri, her lips curved uncertainly. Then Alexis Halstead, supremely bored. And Sanford Halstead, cool despite his jogging. Finally, Mark.

He frowned. 'What's this?'

'What's what?'

He handed the proofsheet to Ron. 'The last shot. That shadow behind me.'

Ron brought the photo close to his eyes. 'You got me. Probably a defect in the film.'

'Well,' said Mark, starting to peel off his shirt. 'I'm going to skip down to the shower, if there's any water left after the Halsteads, and then I'm going to go into a coma.'

Ron winked. 'You got it!'

But Mark amazed himself. He couldn't sleep after all. He had come back from the shower to find Ron asleep in his T-shirt and jeans, flat on his back with his mouth agape. Mark had quietly unwound his friend's mosquito netting, spread it over the cot, and secured it at the corners. Then he had climbed naked into his own cocoon and had laid back waiting for sleep to claim him.

But a wave of great apprehension had suffused his body, filling him with a sense of expectancy, of waiting for something to happen . . .

He lay on top of the blanket staring at the tent top through the film of mosquito netting. Ron breathed softly in the darkness. Then a chill suddenly filled the tent, swept over Mark's bare skin and caused him to shiver. The Shell No-Pest Strips, hanging around the door and windows like wolfbane, swayed slightly.

Mark lay unmoving for a long time, late into the night, until not a single sound remained in the desert, then he finally drifted off, not knowing that an intruder, who left no footprints in the sand, walked through the camp.

Sanford Halstead tossed and turned, unable to get comfortable on the camp cot.

The hour was late, the camp was plunged into primeval darkness; an ancient wind played with the Dacron walls of Halstead's tent, reminding him of the eternal sea of black desert beyond. He tried first this position, then that, rising up on an elbow and pounding the satin pillow with a fist. On the other side of the curtain that separated him from Alexis, his wife lay in deep slumber.

Flopping on to his back and kicking off the satin coverlet, Halstead stretched his arms at his sides and closed his eyes.

He was exhausted, there was no doubt about that, and desperately in want of sleep, and yet it would not come. Perhaps he should try concentrating on something boring, force his mind to entertain the mundane and thus rock itself into a stupor – for Sanford, unlike his wife who was pill-dependent, refused to take a sleeping tablet.

He conjured up his stock portfolio and imagined in his mind the dull nasal voice of his stockbroker, reciting in a monotone figures of price/earnings ratios, short and long sales, margin percentages, dividends . . .

He finally drifted off.

It started subtly, in the distance: the plod of heavy footsteps in the cold sand.

Sanford slept as the footfall drew near, outside his tent, accompanied now by a soft, rhythmic breathing.

The heavy feet circled the tent and paused at the flap. Then the Dacron seemed to lift of its own accord and a silhouette stood against the stars.

Sanford moaned softly in his sleep: he was having a nightmare.

The gigantic, angular figure slid smoothly into the tent and came to rest at Sanford's feet. In his dream, Sanford opened his eyes and gazed for a moment at the mosquito netting coming together in a circus-tent peak above him, then, sensing he was not alone, raised his head in alarm.

Through the gauzy net, the intruder could barely be seen, yet it was enough to show that he was a man, tall and muscular, naked and gleaming, his sinewy arms dangling at his sides. It was the eyes which Sanford saw in his nightmare.

They shone as dazzling white ovals. Disembodied eyes, floating in the air with dilated pupils, staring down at him, staring, staring, like something out of a horror movie, not blinking, imprisoning Halstead in a vice-grip that made him break out in a sweat and his body tremble so violently the cot shook.

The eyes burned down upon him, and when the naked, gleaming chest rose and fell and the pectoral muscles cast off frail starlight, Sanford Halstead saw that the intruder was made of gold. His polished, muscular body shone in the wash of moonglow: yellow, metallic, rich, luxurious. The vision was solid gold with two ivory eyes shining like beacons in the black night.

Halstead made a throaty, guttural sound and tried to move, but could not.

Then the massive right arm of the phantom rose up and a gleaming gold finger pointed straight at him and a hoarse whisper, heard only in Halstead's dream, said: *Na-khempur. Na-khempur . . .*

Halstead tried to speak but could not. Locked into those blazing eyes, he heard over and over again: *Na-khempur, na-khempur, na-khempur . . .*

Until, in exhaustion, he slumped back and fell into a dreamless swoon.

Mark awoke to the sound of someone puffing and padding around the camp. He blinked a few times, then groaned and looked up. Ron was sitting on the edge of his own cot vigorously toweling his wet hair.

'Sun's up!' he said.

'What? Oh damn. Where's Abdul?' Mark clawed his way through the mosquito netting and discovered he had a throbbing headache.

'He was in a few minutes ago. I told him I'd wake you up.'

Mark cradled his head in his hands. 'God, my head . . .'

There came a polite throat clearing on the other side of the tent flap. 'Pardon, *effendi*.'

'Okay, Abdul!' Mark called out, wincing. 'Be with you in a few minutes.' He rose unsteadily from the cot and made his way to the pitcher and basin on his toilet table. 'I can't believe I slept so soundly. Didn't even dream. Damn, I had wanted to be out on the plain by sunrise . . .' Bracing himself over the bowl, Mark emptied the pitcher of cold water over his head. 'Jee-SUS!'

As he straightened up and shook his head, he heard the plodding footsteps come and go again.

'That's Halstead,' said Ron, pulling a Greenpeace T-shirt over his head.

Mark grimaced. 'He's in better shape than I am. And he's old enough to be my father.'

'I'm taking both cameras out today,' said Ron, pulling on his boots. 'I'll have the zoom, too. Tell me what you want taken.'

Mark nodded as he massaged his face with a towel. Then, getting into his bush jeans, he looked up and said, 'What's that?'

'Sounds like an argument.'

The two ran out of the tent, padded over the cool sand and arrived at the mess tent in time to hear a high-pitched torrent of Arabic cursing. Inside, Mark and Ron found Yasmina Shukri, her hands on her hips and her face molded in fury, in a screaming match with the old *fellaha*.

Ignoring the entrance of the two men, old Samira

continued her offensive barrage. Then she picked up an empty pot, swung it high in the air, and clanged it down hard on the table.

'What's going on here?' demanded Mark.

Only Yasmina acknowledged him; the *fellaha* continued to fix a brilliant, fiery glare on her opponent.

'Dr Davison,' said the young woman, visibly trying to control herself, 'she refuses to boil the drinking and cooking water.'

'Oh great.' Mark rubbed his bare arms against the morning chill and addressed the *fellaha* in Arabic. To his annoyance, she ignored him, continuing to hold her poisonous stare on Yasmina.

He repeated himself, a little louder and more slowly, and still the old woman ignored him.

'What is this? Doesn't she understand me?'

'She understands you, *effendi*.'

Mark and Ron swung around. Abdul stood in the doorway. 'The old woman says the Nile water is healthy. If you boil it, you will chase the good spirits out.'

Mark gently massaged his eyes. 'Abdul, the water for drinking and cooking is to be boiled before it's used. See that she does it.' He turned to Yasmina. 'Miss Shukri, would you happen to have something for a headache?'

He followed her out of the tent, stepping into a brilliant dawn that made him wince. With the sun behind the cliffs, the camp was in the shade and the sand beneath his bare feet was still cold, but before him stretched a golden counterpane that rose and fell over the ancient mounds like a yellow sea.

Yasmina stepped into her tent, and Mark followed right behind, unaware that his doing so disquieted her.

She took an unmarked bottle off a shelf over her small work-bench and emptied two white tablets into her palm. Mark made a cursory inspection of this 'infirmary' and was impressed.

A starched white cloth covered the table and on top of it sat tongue depressors; scissors; bottles of different colored liquids; a stethoscope; metal basins containing sterile supplies; and, to his amazement, a small microscope. On the shelves overhead stood bottles of drugs and antibiotics; bandages; sutures; surgical gloves; anesthetics; needles and syringes. Dangling from a hook was a blood pressure cuff.

She poured water from a pitcher into a small cup and gave him the pills.

Mark swallowed them both at once with a gulp of water and handed the cup back, trying to smile. 'Let's hope they chase away the evil spirits!'

But Yasmina only gazed at him with a coolness that matched the morning air. Then Mark suddenly realised that he was shirtless and alone in a tent with an unmarried Moslem woman. Trying to pump warmth into his smile, he mentally kicked himself and quickly left.

It was necessary to visit the *'umdas* of the three southern villages, but, as none were as powerful as the *'umda* of El Till, the three audiences were only brief formalities. The main work of the morning consisted of surveying the plain and plateau that existed within the ancient boundaries and working out an excavation plan. They went in two Land-Rovers, with Abdul's assistants driving. In the first rode Mark, Ron, Abdul and Hazim. In the second, Alexis Halstead and Yasmina Shukri with her shoulder bag of emergency medical supplies, and the hawk-faced *ghaffir* with his rifle. Sanford Halstead remained at the camp; his morning jogging had given him a nosebleed.

They followed first the straight edge of the D-shaped plain, paralleling the Nile, and stopped for a rest two hours later at the northern tip where the cliffs arched around to meet the river.

While Ron squatted in the shade of a date palm to change film, Mark walked a short distance away from the Land-Rovers.

Before him stretched a broken maze of humble brown

walls. This was all that was left of Akhnaton's famous Northern Palace. Mark scanned the plain with his Nikon binoculars, and as he traced the stratification in the limestone cliffs three miles away, he felt someone come to stand next to him, and in the next moment he smelled gardenias.

'May I look?' said Alexis Halstead.

'Not much to see.' He handed her the field glasses without looking at her.

'Will we visit all of them?' she asked, holding the binoculars up to her tinted aviator glasses. She eyed a row of gaping black holes cut into the cliff-face halfway up.

'All of what?'

'The tombs.'

'As time will allow. We have to climb up to them and it's already getting hot.'

She gazed for a long moment through the field glasses, her red hair a nimbus of fire about her head in the desert sun. Mark wondered what she stared at for so long, felt himself grow impatient, and did not notice that Alexis Halstead's breathing had changed.

She brought the Nikons down and turned her hard green eyes on him. 'The tomb of Mahu,' she said breathlessly. 'Will there be time for that?'

He felt himself frown. 'If you like. Why the tomb of Mahu?'

She handed the binoculars back to him. 'For the murals, Dr Davison. I want to see . . . the murals . . .'

As he was unable, at that moment, to take his eyes away from hers, Mark was suddenly, acutely aware of how closely she stood to him, and the fragrance of crushed gardenias filled his head.

He was casting about for a reply when he heard a click behind them. Mark looked over his shoulder and saw Ron waving. 'Great candid shot!' Not too far from Ron, leaning against a wide palm, were Yasmina and Hazim, talking quietly.

'Is this the Northern Palace?' asked Alexis, sweeping a

lazy arm over the mounds and ditches.

'That's what Egyptologists call it.'

She kept her eyes fixed straight ahead; her voice grew distant. 'What do you mean by that?'

Mark stepped away from her, picking his way over the rubble and bits of mudbrick that made up the bare outlines of what had been the palace's foundation. 'No one's really sure what any of these buildings were used for, it's all conjecture.' He squatted by a crumbled wall and ran a hand over the brittle stone. White ants had long ago pushed into the mudbrick and eaten out every trace of straw from it. Then the prickly roots of the *halfa* grass had pierced through. Even the roots of palm trees could be seen forcing their way up through the hard dirt floor of the palace.

'Tell el-Amarna is unique in archaeology, Mrs Halstead, in that it is not really a *tell*. A *tell* is an ancient mound made up of layers, each one representing a different age of settlement on the site. As a town was destroyed for one reason or another – like fire or disease or war – a new one was built upon its ruins. Troy, for example. The different strata reveal the different ages of habitation, with the lowest being the earliest. But Akhet-Aton, Mrs Halstead, was built, lived in, and abandoned all in less than two decades. It was deserted and never returned to.' Mark stood up and dashed his hands against his jeans.

Her voice came from far away; it contained a note of sadness, 'Then there should be more left than there is . . .'

Mark shook his head, gazing down at the dirt that had once been a magnificent marble floor. 'When the people left they took everything with them. Their furniture, doors, even the pillars. And then nature took over; the unprotected mudbrick buildings succumbed to three millenia of wind and freak rains. And then tourists, all through the centuries, stopping here and picking up a souvenir to take home. Finally, the local *fellaheen* carried off the mudbrick for fertiliser. It's a miracle there's anything left here at all.'

Mark walked among the fragmented walls, his boots crunching over the rubble, and Alexis walked with him. 'Why aren't you sure this was a palace? I had thought every structure here had been identified.'

They stopped at a flight of stairs leading up to nowhere. 'It's all hypothetical, Mrs Halstead; a bunch of experts agreeing on what they don't know. Like the structure we call Akhnaton's zoological garden. We only call it that because of the tiny, windowless chambers that are too small for bedrooms and that are painted with frescoes of animals and contain curious stone tubs that might have been mangers. For lack of anything else, we called it a zoo.'

Alexis turned her green eyes, hidden behind the tinted glasses, to him and stared for a long moment. Although he didn't quite know why, Mark felt uncomfortable. 'Do *you* believe this was once a palace, Dr Davison?' she asked softly.

He looked away from her. 'I'm not sure. For one thing, there are no kitchens or servants' quarters. There are bathtubs, but they have no drainage like the ones in the private houses. This so-called palace lacks many of the amenities and necessities of a residence. It's almost as if this immense structure was not meant to be lived in, merely to symbolise a house.'

Mark turned around and watched as the rest of the group milled restlessly around the waiting vehicles. 'So what really did once stand on this spot, Mrs Halstead? A palace, or something else? Something the modern mind cannot conceive of, something peculiar to a race of people who lived here three thousand years ago and whose secrets died with them.'

Alexis listened intently, her eyes not moving from his face.

'Like the so-called Palace at Knossos,' Mark went on, 'which archaeologists are beginning to believe was not a palace at all, but a massive sepulcher inhabited not by the living but by the dead. Three thousand years from now, in 4981 AD, what will archaeologists think of merry-go-rounds and pay toilets?'

'Hey you guys!'

Mark looked around. Ron was motioning them back to the Land-Rovers.

'The statue in the Cairo Museum shows him naked and without genitals. You see him here in a dress that looks like a woman's. He appears to have breasts and wide hips. Yet his title is "king".'

Ron's voice filled the cool stillness of the rock-cut chamber. They were all crowded into the tomb of Huya and staring, once their eyes had adjusted to the gloom, at a great carved relief which took up most of the wall. Before them, illuminated by sunlight spilling through the entrance, Pharaoh Akhnaton leaned back in his chair chewing contentedly on a bone. Behind him sat his wife Nefertiti, sipping wine. The relief was slightly blackened by the torches of countless visitors through the centuries.

'One explanation for the controversial statue in the museum,' Ron went on, 'is that Akhnaton was having himself symbolically depicted as the "father and mother of mankind", which was one of his titles. However, Thutmoses the Third was also called "father and mother of mankind", and he was never shown as anything less than a virile male. That theory collapses further in the face of Akhnaton's revolutionary art. For the first time in history, life was to be depicted as it really was, and Akhnaton insisted even his facial ugliness be maintained in the truth of his new art. There is very little in the way of symbolism in the radical artform of Akhnaton's reign, and since the rest of his body was reproduced exactly as it appeared in reality, one must strongly suspect that Akhnaton did not, in fact, have any sexual organs.'

Six pairs of eyes beheld the towering, malformed Pharaoh. Ron wasn't sure anyone was listening to him, but he didn't care. 'There is evidence that the six so-called daughters of Akhnaton were not his daughters at all but his sisters. Wherever one of the princesses' names appears, it is always followed by the title "king's daughter". The king, however, is never named, although the *mother* is. For example, here.' Ron reached up and tapped a column of hieroglyphics. 'What it says here above Princess Baket-Aton is: "Baket-Aton, King's Daughter, of his loins, by the Chief Wife Tiye". We know that Baket-Aton's father was Amenhotep and that she was Akhnaton's sister. However, his so-called daughters are also referred to as "Princess Such-and-Such, King's daughter, born of the Chief Wife Nefertiti". In all cases, they are known simply as the king's daughters, as if his identity were understood, whereas the mother had to be specified.'

Hazim cleared his throat. 'Then you believe, Dr Farmer, that the unnamed king is in all instances Amenhotep?'

'I believe Akhnaton ruled jointly with his father for a number of years – Amenhotep in Thebes, Akhnaton here. When Amenhotep was the sole Pharaoh, his daughters were referred to as the "king's daughters". However, when the *two* Pharaohs ruled jointly, the daughters born to Nefertiti were still referred to as the "king's daughters", while Nefertiti is named. If, when the mother was different, she was named, it would follow that when the father was different, he would be named. Scenes showing Akhnaton with the six princesses have been touted as wonderful examples of paternal affection. I think they could just as easily be taken as illustrations of *fraternal* love.'

Ron's voice settled on the stale air. 'Another mystery surrounding the shrouded figure of Akhnaton is that his loving wife, Nefertiti, left him near the end of his reign and went to live in a separate palace. No one knows why.'

Alexis's voice fell to a whisper. 'Did she really leave him? I thought they were supposed to have been two of history's most famous lovers.'

'There's no doubt that she left him, because after the twelfth year of his reign, Akhnaton is no longer depicted with Nefertiti but with his brother Smenkhara, who is dressed in Nefertiti's clothes and who was given her royal titles. We know the queen was still alive because there is evidence in one of the palaces that she lived there with little Tutankhamon. On one stela, the two brothers are shown with their arms around one another and appear to be kissing.'

'Is that true?' Alexis's eyes widened. 'Can we see it?'

Ron lifted a hand to his forehead; he was perspiring heavily. 'That stela is in the Berlin Museum.' He tried to focus on Mark who was leaning casually against a wall with his arms folded.

'I disagree with your theory, Dr Farmer,' said Hazim al-Sheikhly. 'Just because the king is not named while the mother is . . .'

Ron shifted his attention to the handsome young Arab and was annoyed that the man spoke too softly to be heard.

'. . . there was only one king at the time, Akhnaton, but he had many wives. It was understood who the king was, but . . .'

Ron frowned. 'Would you speak up please, I can't –'

'. . . the wife would have to be named.'

A drop of sweat fell into Ron's eyes, blurring his vision. The heat in the chamber was increasing. He heard himself say, 'But there were *two* kings at the time, Mr Sheikhly . . .' Ron tried to raise a hand to his forehead but hadn't the strength. 'Co-regency was a common practise in the Eighteenth Dynasty. It's probable that, since the son was impotent, the old Pharaoh . . . would have seen to the duty of providing . . . the throne with offspring . . .' Wiping sweat out of his eye, Ron saw his companions stare blankly at him. In the dim shadow, he realised Mark had suddenly pushed away from the wall.

Ron felt his mouth turn to cotton as he tried to

continue: 'There's another theory that Akhnaton was a homosexual . . .' Ron forced a dry tongue over his lips. Five pale ovals stared back at him. One of them, bearded, was pushing its way in slow motion toward him.

'The stela . . . showing Akhnaton in an intimate pose with his brother has been taken by some Egyptologists . . .' murmured Ron, 'to mean that he was not a totally eunuchoid pathic. Jesus, it's hot in here!'

Hazim opened his mouth but no sound came out.

Ron felt the floor start to tilt. 'I need air –'

Then he heard a loud crack, saw a flash of stars, and found himself tumbling into a spiral.

NINE

'How DO you feel?'

Ron blinked up at Mark and found himself sitting in his cot with a blood pressure cuff around his upper arm. 'What happened?'

'Don't you remember?'

'Did I faint?'

Mark nodded. 'Do you remember any of it?'

Ron brought his hands up to his face and squeezed his eyes tight shut, trying to wring out the memories. 'We were in the tomb. I vaguely remember Abdul and the *ghaffir* carrying me down the mountain.' He brought his hands away and looked around at the late afternoon orange glow that suffused the tent. 'How long was I out?'

'Only about two minutes.'

'But that was hours ago! Have I been asleep?'

'Believe it or not, you've been sitting here for the past four hours, talking your head off –'

'Hello.'

They looked up as Yasmina Shukri poked her head around the tent flap. 'How is the patient?'

Mark got to his feet and stepped away to make room for her. Yasmina was carrying her shoulder bag. She sat on the edge of the cot and wordlessly wrapped cool fingers around Ron's wrist.

'Am I going to live?' he asked when she had counted his pulse.

Yasmina smiled and said softly, 'I will let you know in a moment.' Withdrawing her stethoscope from the bag, she inflated the cuff and checked his pressure. She did this twice before removing the scope and gently unwrapping the cuff. What she had been afraid of – bradycardia, a widening pulse pressure, and a rising systole – were not present. Then she took out a small flashlight and checked Ron's pupils for light reflex. They were equal in size and reactive.

She leaned back from him now, studying his face with her liquid brown eyes. 'How do you feel?'

'All right, I guess, except for this lump on my head.'

'Can you tell me your name?'

'Only if you'll tell me yours.'

'Ron,' said Mark, 'cooperate with the lady.'

'Ron Farmer.'

'Do you know the day?'

'Friday.'

'And the date?'

'10 July, 1981. Are you going to tell me what happened?'

'I want you to tell me that.'

'Mark says I've been sitting here talking all afternoon.'

Yasmina nodded, her smile patient. 'It is common after a head injury and unconsciousness for more than a few seconds. You were awake but incoherent. You were a little amnesic and could not recall having been in the tomb. You do remember that now, do you not?'

'Yeah. And all the soliloquising I was doing. That's what made me faint, all that hot air in the tomb.'

'Can you raise both your arms for me please? Now here,' she held out her hands. 'Squeeze my hands as hard as you can.'

After he did so, causing her to grimace a little, she very delicately lifted the hair off each of his ears and inspected them.

'What're you looking for? My brain?'

'I am checking for cerebrospinal fluid.'

'Christ.'

'But you are all right. Now that your level of consciousness has been restored, I think you are out of danger. Your head sustained a nasty bang.'

'Yeah.' He gingerly felt the back of his skull for the lump. 'I heard it.'

Yasmina replaced her equipment in the shoulder bag and rose to her feet. Mark noticed for the first time how small she was; she barely came up to his shoulders. 'Dr Farmer will be all right. But he must rest. And if there is any change at all, such as disorientation or nausea or runny nose, please call me at once.'

'Runny nose!'

She smiled down at Ron. 'That would be a cerebrospinal fluid leak. There is still a chance you have some edema. But I think it is only a mild concussion.'

'Thank you, Miss Shukri,' said Mark as he held aside the tent flap for her. When she was gone, he turned back to his friend, shaking his head. 'You'll do anything for attention, won't you?'

Ron grinned and tried to rest his head against the Dacron wall, but he flinched, brought his head forward again and said, 'I had a friend once who was in a motorcycle accident. He was only out for a minute, but for five hours afterward he didn't make sense. He talked and talked and we couldn't shut him up. And then all of a sudden his head cleared and he remembered everything. I had thought it was all an act to qualify for disability pay.'

Mark sat on the edge of his cot and eyed his friend. 'Was it the heat, Ron?'

'I don't know what it was, and I know what you're thinking. Don't worry, man, I won't pass out on you again.' He tossed back the blanket and started to swing his legs over the bed.

'Where do you think you're going?'

'We've got work to do, Mark. There's the plateau.'

'Abdul and I are going in a few minutes. I estimate three hours of good sunlight left. But you're not coming along.'

'You'll need pictures!'

103

'No one's coming with us on this one. It's a rough trip and I don't want to waste time.' Mark stood up. 'Ron, you've been ordered to bed rest. I expect to find you still here when I get back or I'll rip your epaulets off.'

The plateau, towering four hundred feet above the plain, was a harsh and unforgiving landscape, especially in the hot, dying light of afternoon. Abdul's assistant had to fight his way up the ancient road leading to the Hatnub Quarries, struggling with the steering wheel over a perilously scarred and splintered terrain. While he concentrated on keeping the Land-Rover from plunging into the sudden hundred-foot gorges that scarred the tableland, Mark and Abdul compared their topographical maps with what they saw, making notations and discussing likely places to start work.

As the afternoon dragged on and the heat intensified, the plateau took on an extraterrestrial aspect: the deeply clefted wadis became awesome black pits; broken hills gleamed with alabaster deposits or masses of crystalline carbonate of lime; peaks and gulleys glittered with striations of translucent spar. There was no vegetation, no animal life on this merciless desert, just veins of purple gorges and sharp jutting peaks that caught the sun in fiery brilliance.

The Land-Rover was able to follow the ancient roads once used by Akhnaton's police; the tracks were marked with cairns of limestone and flint. And from up here one could see the plain of Tell el-Amarna below, the farms and Nile beyond, then the cultivation on the other side of the river, and after that more desert stretching like an evaporated sea to the edge of the world.

When they returned to the camp, with the sun dipping below the horizon and twilight rushing in after it, Mark felt drained.

'What have you learned, Dr Davison?' asked Sanford Halstead, sitting in the dining tent over a bowl of alfalfa and almonds and smelling like Brut cologne. He held a starched white handkerchief to his nose.

Mark was on the bench opposite him, cradling his face in his hands. The old *fellaha* worked quickly to serve him, as the others were already eating, but Mark didn't feel very hungry. His stomach was full of sand. 'Not much,' he said, pouring marbled cream into his coffee. 'But, then again, I wasn't expecting to see anything. We got the grid laid out so we can start the teams working in the morning. I also want to take a look at the Royal Tomb.'

'What is the Royal Tomb?' asked Alexis, picking at her food.

'It was the tomb Akhnaton originally built for himself and his family, but it was never finished and Egyptologists doubt it was ever used. I'm going to give it a look over in the morning, although I don't suppose it will give us any clues as to the whereabouts of Ramsgate's tomb.'

Alexis didn't look up from her roast duck. 'Ramsgate wrote that he cleared away a flight of stairs leading down to the Criminal's tomb. Wouldn't they still be visible?'

Mark shook his head and murmured, *Shokran*, as Samira deposited a plate before him. 'A hundred years in the desert will bury anything and leave no trace behind. It's a constant battle in this country, keeping the sand away.'

'Where will the men start looking?'

'On the plateau, at the mouths of all the wadis, and in some of the likeliest gorges.'

The aroma of duck and spiced rice suddenly made Mark ravenous. While he ate, he looked up once or twice at Yasmina who sat by herself at the other table. 'Has someone taken a plate to Ron?'

When no one replied, Yasmina turned to Mark and said, 'He would not stay in bed, Dr Davison. He is in the darkroom and said he will eat after the photographs are done.'

They looked like concentration camp corpses.

The faces were horrifying, as if they had been cremated. Black hollows gaped where the eyes had decayed and fallen back into the skull. Lipless mouths stretched wide over fearsome teeth, grinning in grim parodies of death. Bony shoulders jutted up from caved-in ribcages; bellies were emaciated caverns dressed in tarry skin. The arms and legs were leafless branches of charred wood; hands were stretched rigid in the surprise of death.

Ron smiled in satisfaction. This was the roll he had taken in the mummy vault at the Cairo Museum, and each picture was a gem. He turned now to the photographs he had taken that morning on the plain.

Ron unclipped the film strip which hung from the wire he had stretched across the width of the tent and laid it down on the work table. Turning off the lights except for the amber safelight which hung four feet above the workbench, he withdrew a sheet of photographic paper from its packet on the shelf over the table and laid it on the composition board. He then placed the negatives, dull side down, on the paper and placed a sheet of glass over them. Flicking on the seven-watt bulb which hung two feet above the glass, Ron mentally counted ten Mississippis, then turned off the light, removed the paper from the board and slid it into the developing fluid. As he rocked the tray, he leaned forward and tried to read the thermometer on the shelf.

This was the best time of the day for developing – evening. The temperature was cooler, although right now it seemed a little too high, and there was less chance of light leak. He had spent an hour searching for holes in the tent, then he had taped up the window with black opaque paper and masking tape. A length of black cloth, which he kept rolled up over the door when not developing, was now stretched down and secured tightly. Outside the tent he had hung a Nile Hilton English-Arabic DO NOT DISTURB sign.

Using his free hand to wipe the sweat off his forehead,

Ron lifted the sheet out of the developer, let it drain for a couple of seconds, then slid it into the stop-bath. He rocked the tray for seven Mississippis, then slid the sheet into the fixer. Two minutes later he turned all the lights back on.

Ron examined the photographs, muttered, 'Piss,' and took a long drink from his cup of wine.

Something was wrong with the pictures. He was going to have to do them all over again.

Mark felt a lot better. Abdul had been right: Samira, for all her doubtful looks, was an excellent cook. Now the air was growing appreciably cooler, the moon was rising, and a kind of serenity settled over the camp.

Ten years ago Mark had not smoked, but a seasoned 'digger' had told him that a pipe would keep insects away. So Mark had taken up the pipe and had discovered a degree of freedom from mosquitoes and flies, which were a problem in the Middle East. Tonight, however, as he wandered away from the dining tent, he was smoking for the pleasure and relaxation of it.

He left the circle of light created by the lanterns strung around the camp and strolled over the rocky ground to an ancient mudbrick wall that jutted two feet up through the sand. Settling down on it, Mark withdrew his tobacco pouch and started to fill his pipe.

A few hundred feet to his right, down a slight incline, only barely visible in the moonlight, were the ancient walls of the Workmen's Village. Three thousand years ago laborers and their families had been crammed into that maze of tiny rooms, living in crowded, airless quarters while they slaved in the tombs of the nobility. Evidence showed that the compound had been a prison-like structure, surrounded by high walls and guardhouses. Evidence also showed that many of those workers had secretly continued to worship the old gods.

The ruins were inhabited again, for the first time in

thirty centuries; Mark could see the glowing fires and hear the voices of the *fellaheen* sail away on the evening air. Abdul was with them now, explaining what they would be looking for tomorrow and how they were to go about doing it.

As his Borkum Riff flared brightly, Mark saw a dark figure move quickly and silently against the backdrop of softly glowing tents. It was Samira, her chores done, hurrying to the segregated quarters she had claimed for herself in one corner of the Workmen's Village. Seeing her flit in and out of the light like a black moth, Mark watched her curiously for a moment.

When, however, the *shaykha* dissolved into the shadows, he once again turned his mind to Nancy: he wondered what she was doing at that moment, ten thousand miles away, why she had had her phone disconnected, if she would wait for him. He hoped thinly that she would rejoice with him in his success, if he had any, and would marry him and resign herself to accepting him for what he was.

Footsteps crunching over the sand brought Mark out of his thoughts. Ron was slogging toward him with a paper cup of wine in one hand and a proofsheet in the other. there was just enough room on the broken wall for him to sit next to Mark.

'How's your head?'

'Okay. I'm going to have to do something about ventilation in that tent.'

'Take a fan from the central work tent, then. What do you have there?'

'I don't know. You tell me.' Ron held out the proofsheet.

Mark flicked his pipe lighter and studied the rows of photographs by its flame. He was silent for some time before saying, 'These shadows, what are they?'

'That's what I can't figure. Look, here at Hag Qandil as you're getting out of the Land-Rover. And here, talking with the *'umda* of El Hawata. And here,' Ron's slender finger touched each photo, 'and here, at the Northern Palace. And here, just as you're entering Huya's tomb. Every single goddamned one of them. Not anybody else. Just you. A shadow at your side in every single shot.'

Mark studied the one of him at the Northern Palace, standing in what was called the Throne Room. He and Alexis were talking, their backs to the camera, their shadows, cast by the morning sun, stretching toward the foreground. But the other shadow, the one that appeared in every shot of Mark, was at his left and appeared, like an optical illusion, not to be lying on the ground but vertical, as if standing next to him.

'There's something wrong with this roll of film. Or with your camera.' He handed back the proofsheet.

'It can't be the film. Look, it's the same size and shape in each picture and it's always the same distance from you no matter where you're standing –'

Mark laid a hand on Ron's arm. 'Listen . . . do we have company?'

Ron stiffened, turned in the direction Mark was looking and saw, in the darkness, a grotesque shape slowly ambling toward them. It was accompanied by a rhythmic, plodding footfall. 'What the hell is that!'

Mark got to his feet.

As the monstrous deformity drew near, the two Americans could hear raspy breathing and an eery grunting. Then the outline slowly coalesced into something recognisable until the camel snorted and a voice called out from above, 'Good evening, gentlemen!'

The camel, led by a boy in a *galabeyah*, rocked down to its knees with a grunt of protest, and its rider slid gracelessly to the ground. 'Good evening,' he said again in careful English.

Mark resumed his position on the broken wall and proceeded to re-light his pipe. There was enough illumination from the camp to clearly identify the stranger. It was the Greek from El Till.

'I am Constantine Domenikos,' said the chunky man,

coming to stand before the two seated Egyptologists. 'How do you do?'

Mark inclined his head. 'I guess you already know our names.'

'Everyone in Amarna speaks of the American scientists Davison and Farmer.' His grin was a greedy one. 'I have come to pay you my respects.'

Ron eyed the man with suspicion, vaguely recalling having seen him the day before in the crowd at El Till. Constantine Domenikos was a porcine man with bulging, heavily lidded eyes.

'Is there somewhere we can talk in privacy, gentlemen?'

'Why?' said Mark.

'Business, Dr Davison. I believe I can be of service to you. I would not refuse an offer of tea.'

'What sort of business, Mr Domenikos?'

The reptillian eyes flickered slightly but the smile remained fixed. 'It would be a great honor for me to be of help to your expedition. But please,' he spread his spatulate hands, 'can we not speak in more . . . em, appropriate quarters?'

'This is as good a place as any. Have a seat, Mr Domenikos.'

The Greek looked around, then squatted on a large boulder across from the Americans.

'My expedition has everything it needs,' said Mark.

'Supplies can run short, Dr Davison.'

'My foreman will see that they don't.'

'He cannot foresee all possible mishaps.'

'Such as?'

The Greek drew in a reedy breath. 'There are rumors, Dr Davison, of war coming to this land. We live in restless times, the brittle truce between Egypt and Israel cannot withstand the weight of so much mistrust. I am a man who lives by anticipating, Dr Davison. I anticipate the future and prepare for it.'

'Could you get to your point, if you have one?'

'For example, Dr Davison, this is what my mind has

seen. The Palestinian Liberationists will stage an attack on the Egyptians, making it appear the Israelis did it. President Sadat will counterattack on Israel, and Israel, outraged, will retaliate with all her forces. Your country, Dr Davison, believing Egypt provoked the war, will come to Israel's defense. Diplomatic relations will be broken, President Carter's peace treaty will be torn up, and this country will find itself engaged in the bloodiest conflict it has known since the days of the Pharaohs.'

Mark knocked his pipe against the mudbrick wall and, withdrawing his tobacco pouch, said, 'That's a little far-fetched, Mr Domenikos, but even if you were right, why come to us about it?'

'If war breaks out, you will need friends in Egypt.'

'We have friends.' Mark flicked his lighter and touched the flame to his tobacco. In the brief light he saw the flat, calculating look in the Greek's eyes.

'On closer ground then, gentlemen,' continued the oily voice. 'Surely you are aware of the unrest between El Till and Hag Qandil. There has been an uneasy peace in this valley for the past few years; it is only a matter of time before conflict erupts. You might be caught in the middle, gentlemen, for they will use you as a pawn, each side demanding your alliance. You will lose workers and then the battling *'umdas* will make demands of you.'

'The *ma'mur's* police know how to handle these people.'

'Certainly, but not . . . em, until after considerable damage has been done.'

'And you, of course, Mr Domenikos, are offering us your help because you are a neutral party. With you on our side, we'll be protected. Right?'

'You impress me, Dr Davison.'

Mark got to his feet and stretched. 'Well, we don't need your protection, Domenikos, or your threats.'

'Please, please, Dr Davison. Be seated, for I have not finished. By all the saints, I did not come here to frighten or threaten you! How I have misrepresented myself!'

Constantine struck his barrel chest. 'Please hear me out, Dr Davison!'

Mark remained standing. 'You've got three minutes.'

'I came to discuss business with you, Dr Davison. This is how I can truly be of service to you. The other –' he waved a pudgy hand, 'that was merely idle talk. True, if there is trouble and you need help, I can help you. But what I have come for tonight, gentlemen, is to let you know that I am available to assist you with . . . em, let us say, *distribution* of your merchandise.'

The cool night air hung between them for a hollow moment, then Mark, sitting back down, said, 'Merchandise?'

Constantine Domenikos leaned forward, nearly sliding off the boulder, and lowered his voice. 'You have excavated in Egypt before, Dr Davison, do not pretend with me. You know what I speak of.'

Mark felt Ron shift uneasily. 'You're right, Domenikos, I've excavated in Egypt before, and I've met your type before, too. I'll tell you flat out. I don't deal that way. And besides, you don't know what I'm looking for. You don't know that there's going to be any *merchandise*.'

The Greek remained unperturbed. 'Dr Davison, my father lived in this valley before I was born, and his father before him. I have heard stories. There are myths and legends. Perhaps I, in my boyhood, had thought them products of the old men's imaginations, but now I suspect otherwise. And there was once, a long time ago, a forbidden area. Perhaps, Dr Davison, I *do* know what you are looking for, and perhaps I *do* know that you stand a good chance of unearthing something of great value.'

Mark tethered his revulsion. 'First of all, Domenikos, what we're searching for is none of your business. Secondly, if we find anything, it sure as hell won't end up on the black market. You've come to the wrong man.'

'Dr Davison, I am only a poor Greek, but I represent *a lot of money*. There are men in Paris and Athens who . . .'

Mark stood abruptly. 'You're a slug, Domenikos. Go

112

back under the rock from which you crawled out.'

The Greek smiled in a chilling way. 'Excuse me, Dr Davison, but I have not come to the wrong man. I know that scientists are deplorably underpaid and that your salary cannot possibly match your ambition. We all have our price, Dr Davison, even you, and I know you will agree with me when you hear the contract I am prepared to offer you.'

Mark looked down at Ron. 'How do you say "fuck off" in Greek?'

Constantine Domenikos rose smoothly, still smiling, still unnervingly smug. He made a motion with his hand and the boy in the *galabeyah* jumped up and seized the camel's rein.

'I feel it only fair to warn you, Dr Davison, that there are those in the valley who are not pleased with your arrival.'

'Like who?'

'The old ones, the ones who remember the horror that stalked this land many years ago. I keep my ears open, Dr Davison; the old ones speak quietly and fearfully among themselves. A hundred years ago seven foreigners died here in calamitous circumstances, attempting to find what you are now searching for. And your group is seven, is it not?'

Mark felt himself stiffen. 'I don't know what you're talking about.'

'I think you do. Myself, I am a businessman, I have no faith in the legends. But the old ones, they are superstitious. They whisper that you are going to set the demons loose again, like before, and it will all end, as before, disastrously.'

'Get out of here, Domenikos.'

'I will not come again, Dr Davison,' said the Greek as he mounted the animal, 'for you will come to me. The time will come when you will have great need of me, I promise you that.'

They watched him lumber away into the night, then

113

Mark turned back to the camp. 'Come on, Ron, let's get some shut-eye. Tomorrow we start the search.'

Hazim was having difficulty writing his report. He knew that before long his superiors would expect word on the expedition's progress, and knew also that such a report would trigger the arrival of more important men than himself. He had seen it happen before. Didn't that happen to his best friend Moustafa on the sun temple project in the Delta?

In frustration, Hazim tapped his pen on the little writing desk and so was unaware of a faint scuttling sound by his bare feet.

Poor Moustafa, sent to the Delta to check on the progress of that British expedition, had discovered to his immense delight that an ancient sun temple had been found, and had looked forward to glory and promotion, only to have it all dashed when his superiors arrived after receiving his report and relegated him to nothing more than field secretary.

Something small and yellow and glistening was slithering toward his bare foot.

Well, that wasn't going to happen to *him*. He was pleased Dr Davison had not disclosed the existence of the Journal to the ministry, for then Dr Fawzi himself would have headed this expedition and Hazim would still be back at his desk in Cairo.

He shifted in the chair, moving his feet; startled, the scorpion froze. When Hazim was settled, it resumed its course toward his feet.

They thought this an unimportant project, a folly really, because what could possibly be left in the sands of Amarna? Well, Hazim al-Sheikhly, although fresh out of college, was no fool. His report was going to be . . .

The scorpion, almost touching his bare foot, raised its tail . . .

. . . be as vague as possible, full of ambiguities. Not yet,

114

not until the tomb was found and he was secure in his position as sole government representative would he . . .

Hazim shifted again. His eye caught the movement by his foot.'*Ya Allah!*' He shot up so fast the chair went flying backwards. The scorpion remained where it was, unmoving, tail poised. Shuddering, the young Arab slowly backed away, staring down at the hideous segmented body.

When he backed into the tent wall, Hazim shook himself out of his shock and quickly searched around for something to kill it with.

Picking up a boot, he advanced cautiously upon the scorpion, which still had not moved.

Hazim felt a fine sweat sprout on his forehead, the hairs on his neck prickled, the night air suddenly felt acutely chill.

He brought the boot down squarely on the scorpion.

Trembling, with heart pounding, Hazim held it there for a few seconds, then gingerly raised the boot off the Dacron floor.

The scorpion was gone.

She studied her husband's recumbent form for several minutes, then, certain he was deeply asleep, silently rose from her cot, pushed the netting aside and stole softly across the tent.

A full-length mirror had been installed next to her vanity table, and as Alexis came to stand before it, she stepped into a pool of moonlight. It fell over her like a silver mantle, turning her tanned body into milky calcite; she was a vision of dazzling whiteness and purity. Alexis gazed in fascination at her naked perfection; her eyes followed the lush red waves that tumbled over her pale shoulders and on to her large, firm breasts. Her narrow waist flared into perfect teardrop hips; her legs were long and shapely and as extraordinarily white as the rest of her body.

Alexis brought a hand to rest on her taut abdomen and felt a steadily increasing pulse beneath the muscle. The skin was curiously feverish and cool at once; Alexis imagined that she glowed.

Then she met her gaze in the mirror and smiled dreamily, for although her eyes were open, Alexis Halstead was asleep.

Mark's eyes suddenly snapped open. He cocked his ears to the silence, wondering what had awakened him. He had been called out of a deep, dreamless sleep and he was abruptly, sharply awake. Lying on his back and staring up at the darkness, he could feel his heart pounding, not in his chest but in his abdomen – a heavy rhythmic pulse that made him sit up. A film of sweat erupted over his body, making the night air seem chill. And an aching throb started to fill his head.

Then he heard it. The soft sweet whisper of a woman crying.

Quietly he rose from the cot, aware of every muscle in his arms and legs. His nerves were bowstring taut; he felt as if his body might snap at any moment. Barefooted, Mark stole to the netted doorway, and, listening to Ron's peaceful breathing, slowly unzipped the netting and stepped out.

The glacial air slapped him like a deluge of ice water. He shivered and rubbed his arms, listening. The weeping, still soft and anguished, was louder.

He crept on silent feet to the other tents, listening first at the Halsteads', then at Yasmina's. Nothing. All was dark and silent.

Mark absently massaged his temples; the headache was increasing. Then he turned his head this way and that, raising his face as if to sniff the breeze. Compelled, he followed the sound.

Beyond the periphery of the camp he saw her, draped gracefully over the boulder the Greek had occupied a few hours before, her face buried in the fold of her arms. Her slender back rose and fell with each sob.

Mark watched in fascination. An aura surrounded the woman; a halo glow that seemed to emanate from her body. She was a willowy incandescence, clothed in a flowing white robe that spilled over her fragile body like milk. She was familiar to him, and yet not. A stranger whom he thought he should know.

Mark stared unmoving. His eyes traced the slimness of her legs, curled modestly under her, the suppleness of her arms, the curve of her back.

Then Mark realised that he could see the boulder beneath her arms and the sand beneath her legs and the limestone cliff behind her.

The woman was transparent.

TEN

MARK STIRRED his cold coffee in a mindless exercise. He was waiting for the aspirins to take effect.

The others in the tent, Yasmina and Hazim, were sitting at the other table finishing their breakfast.

Mark had awakened again with a headache and the vaguest sense of having dreamed. But the dream was lost now – he couldn't even remember what it had been about – and all he was left with was a sick ache inside his skull.

Samira tried to force a plate of scrambled eggs on him but he pushed it away. He noticed, as she turned from him, a leather pouch dangling from her belt and wondered, briefly, if the noxious odor that always seemed to surround her came from that pouch. He knew that *shaykhas* carried all sorts of ground-up magic things with them, he also knew they chewed hallucinogenic plants, but there was something *human* about the smell that made him think it came from the woman herself, so Mark made mental note to have Abdul see to it she took a bath.

The doorway netting lifted and Alexis entered the tent.

'Where's your husband?' asked Mark. 'It's almost time to go.'

'Sanford will not be coming with us. He's indisposed.'

'What's wrong? I heard him jogging at sunrise.'

'He has another nosebleed.'

Yasmina looked up from her tea. 'Shall I take a look at him?'

Alexis did not look at the young woman as she said, 'No need to. He'll be all right.' She took a seat opposite Mark,

118

folding her arms on the table, and gazed at him expectantly. The old *fellaha* shuffled up and placed a glass of tea before Alexis; as she did so, her beady little eyes fell upon Mrs Halstead's face. For an instant, the tiny eyes widened in horror, the leathery lips parted in a silent gasp, then the old woman backed away, stumbled against the next table and blindly made her way back to the stove.

'What is the plan, Dr Davison?' asked Alexis, unaware of the *fellaha's* reaction.

He withdrew a rolled sheet of paper from his hip pocket, spread it out on the table and anchored the corners with salt and pepper shakers. 'This is a topographical map of the area, and these lines,' he traced them with a finger, 'form the grid Abdul and I came up with. The teams will be "surface hunting" today, which means each man will do a survey of the square he has been assigned to. More specific exploration will be done tomorrow, and so on until we find a lead.'

'Will *we* be assigned to squares, Dr Davison?'

'I have one picked out for myself, but the rest of you won't be involved in the actual excavation. Your help will be appreciated here in camp once we make the finds.'

Yasmina and Hazim left their table to stand over the grid map.

'These letters marked in red,' said Alexis, 'what do they mean? And why have you connected them with a red line?'

'They represent the boundary stelae which Pharaoh Akhnaton used to define the area of his holy ground. Some of them were carved into the cliffs and can still be seen today. Others were slabs of stone sunk into the earth and which are now in museums. When Akhnaton moved his court from Thebes and established this ground as the site for his new city, he had his stonemasons place markers around the edges of the city. He then drove out to each one in a chariot and swore on each spot, to his new god Aton, to never again set foot outside this area. Not in this life or in the next.'

'Why are they lettered?'

'The first Egyptologists, at the turn of the century, did that as they found them, labelling them in geographical order. The stelae are lettered discontinuously – you'll notice there's no Stela O or T – in case others might be found in the future and can be lettered in the order of their placement.'

'You haven't continued your grid outside the red border.'

'If the priests of Amon were afraid enough of Akhnaton's avenging spirit to bury him in a special tomb, it is my guess they hoped to placate him by burying him within his own consecrated boundaries. So . . .' Mark rolled the map up again and thrust it into his hip pocket. 'From now on, we must try to think like the priests of Amon. Where would *you* have dug that tomb?'

They followed Mark out of the smoky tent and into the crisp morning sunlight where they were joined by Ron. He was wearing a 'Nuke the Whalers' T-shirt and, around his head, a brakeman's bandana. Mark led them to where the two open-topped Land-Rovers were parked and divided the group between the two. Armed *ghaffirs* were the drivers, just as newly recruited *ghaffirs* with rifles now stood outside the large central work tent where the tea and Coke were stored; all because of Constantine Domenikos.

The drive up the Royal Wadi was a messy one with the *ghaffirs* going at reckless speeds and seeming to aim for trenches and boulders. Alexis Halstead, wearing half-tinted aviator glasses and with red filaments of hair, like jets of fire, escaping her scarf and whipping across her face, sat next to Mark in cool silence. In the back seat, Ron tried to protect his tripod and cameras as he flew into the air with each jolt. Behind them, in the second vehicle, Yasmina and Hazim clung to the dashboard in pale-faced terror.

The wadi, which was broad and flat at its mouth, gradually narrowed to a deep cleft in the plateau, and four miles into it was the entrance to the Royal Tomb. As they neared it, Mark raised his hand, signaling to his own driver and the one behind to stop. He grabbed the windshield bar and hoisted himself up to look around. When the sand had settled, he swung himself down, his boots crunching and splintering the rubble on the floor of the wadi.

The sun seemed more intense in this naked ravine. What breeze had been created by the speed of the four-wheel-drive was suddenly gone, and an incredibly concentrated heat pressed down from the thin strip of blue sky above.

As he descended from the Land-Rover, Hazim al-Sheikhly warily searched the sand before putting his feet down. He had not slept well after his experience the night before – he had had nightmares of giant scorpions and of a slender-limbed woman coming to embrace him, whose head, at the last instant, had turned into the pincers of a scorpion. Too weary and on edge to enter the tomb, Hazim decided to hang back and wait by the Land-Rovers.

The government *ghaffir* who guarded the tomb entrance was squatting in the dirt with a yellowed copy of *El Ahram* opened out and draped over his turban. He made a gesture of greeting, slowly got to his feet and fumbled with the keys on his belt.

As the iron gate swung open, Alexis said, 'Does this help?'

'No. The guards can be bribed.'

They saw evidence immediately upon entering the tomb, for on the walls were inscribed centuries of graffiti and signs of vandalism. The interior was grim and depressing. A sloping passageway and a steep flight of stairs led to the burial pit where the sarcophagus had once stood – the gloom was musty and oppressive. Mark led the laconic group past this 'well' and into a hall whose walls were decorated with badly damaged reliefs of the royal family worshipping the sun god, Aton.

'When this tomb was excavated in 1936,' said Mark, holding his flashlight on the caricatures which loomed before them, 'all it contained were a smashed sarcophagus and a few canopic jars, which are containers for the deceased's internal organs. The canopic jars found in this tomb had never been used, and the sarcophagus was empty. It's a safe assumption to make that no one had ever been buried here.'

Ron stepped away from them and began erecting his tripod.

'Why was it never used?' murmured Alexis, raising a hand to the mural but not touching it.

Mark stared at Alexis's upturned profile and was again struck by the haunting familiarity in her face. The way the shadows in the tomb played upon her unique beauty, emphasising the prominence of her cheekbones, the sensual mouth and straight, classical nose. In the eery light of the tomb, Alexis's face seemed to alter; another aspect, not seen in daylight, now appeared to emerge. 'I don't know,' Mark heard himself say.

'The Ramsgate tomb, will it be like this one?' Her voice had altered as well; it was deeper, huskier.

'I don't know . . .'

She turned slightly, her features shifted. Alexis fixed half-closed eyes upon the grotesque shapes on the wall: Akhnaton and Nefertiti, worshipping their peculiar god. Her voice came out in a curiously coarse whisper. 'Why were these murals purposely effaced?'

Mark tried to moisten his lips with his tongue but found his mouth was unexpectedly dry. 'The priests of Amon didn't want Akhnaton and Nefertiti to have life.'

'What do you mean . . .?'

The scent of crushed gardenias filled his head. Another click, sounding unusually loud in the stone chamber, came from the camera behind them. Mark found himself unwittingly whispering. 'To the ancient Egyptians, any figures painted or engraved on walls, once drawn, had life. Animals could move, bird symbols could fly off the wall.'

'And people?'

Mark felt a tightening in his bowels. It must be latent claustrophobia; he suddenly wanted to get out of the tomb. 'People, too. A human figure, once painted on plaster, had life. They could step down any time and walk the land . . .'

She turned away from him, languidly, smoothly, as if moving in a dream, and blended into the darkness of a doorway. Before her yawned a black abyss with no boundaries or definition. 'What's in here?'

Mark remained rooted before the mural, trying to focus on Alexis's milky body. His eyes played tricks on him: she seemed to glow. 'The burial chambers of Akhnaton's daughters.'

'Were they ever used?'

Another click – the slicing sound of a slow shutter – filled the tomb. 'No.'

Alexis turned and regarded him from the inky depths of the doorway, her face hidden in shadow. 'Where were his daughters buried?'

Mark wanted to run a finger under the collar of his shirt but had no control over his arm. 'No one knows . . .'

'No one knows? All six of them vanished?'

Mark forced his gaze away from her and stared up at the mural. His eyes fixed on the face of Nefertiti, on her profile, her profile . . .

Ron's voice, from very far away, said, 'No doubt their tombs were ransacked thousands of years ago,' *click*, 'and their jewelry was melted down for gold coins,' *click*, 'and their mummies ground up for medicinal powders.'

The profile, Nefertiti's profile, *her* profile . . .

Mark's shirt collar grew tight around his neck; he could not swallow. Something crawled around inside his belly. His legs felt suddenly weak.

'Great pictures!' boomed Ron, folding up his tripod with a thundering *clack*. 'Dramatic compositions, mere humans standing at the feet of the gigantic Living God!'

Mark's mouth hung open as he stared up at the towering queen, trapped for eternity on the limestone wall of the tomb, at her profile, Alexis Halstead's profile . . .

Releasing a brief, muffled cry, Mark stumbled back, spun on his heel and said in a tight voice, 'We're wasting time, let's get the hell out of here!'

The mess tent was uncomfortably warm and smoky, but the only alternative was to eat outside with the flies. Two portable fans, running off one of the gasoline generators, kept the air moving, but there was not enough light and the cooking odors were almost overpowering.

Samira, with her sleeves rolled up to her elbows to reveal brown withered arms, was kneading maize flour into a dough, pausing now and then to add a little water and fenugreek. Several round wooden platters awaited the dough, which would be pounded into flat cakes and then baked in the stone oven built at the rear of the tent. The result would be a tasty golden brown bread of two soft crusts with no crumbs; it was called *pitta* bread, *bettaw* in Middle Egyptian, after the ancient Pharaonic word for bread, *ptaw*.

Mark was not aware that he was staring at Samira as he drank his tea. Once, her black veil rose up and the purple tattoo appeared again on her forehead, but the *fellaha* had been quick to re-cover it without breaking her rhythm.

Ron was the only one who ate. He dashed pepper over his *ful*; next to his plate stood a cup of Gallo chianti.

Sanford Halstead, snacking on a bag of raisins and almonds, said, 'When will Abdul be reporting to you?'

'In about an hour.' Mark forced himself to look away from Samira.

'Do you think they found anything?'

Mark tried to maintain congeniality. Halstead, dressed smartly in a tight sports shirt and white slacks, was so irritatingly youthful and vigorous. Mark wondered what the man's secret was; did Alexis rejuvenate him with her sexual vitality? 'If anything significant had been found, Mr

124

Halstead, Abdul would have reported to me immediately.'

'Tell me, Dr Davison,' said Alexis, opposite him. 'Why was Akhnaton's monotheism so violently opposed?'

Now, against the commonplace backdrop of the mess tent and in better lighting, Alexis Halstead was no longer haunting and sinister. She was a strikingly beautiful woman, nothing more. And yet, Mark had to admit, the resemblance remained, it was definitely there. With her hair pulled back and with an application of ancient Egyptian cosmetics, Alexis Halstead could be a reincarnation of Queen Nefertiti.

'Because it upset the established order of things. The ancient Egyptians believed that the world must never change; that what was yesterday must be so today, and also for tomorrow.'

'Why were they so against change?'

Mark glanced at Sanford and saw that a droplet of blood was starting to appear below one nostril. 'Because the Egyptians lived in a land that was itself changeless. Nature in the Nile Valley is static; the climate is predictable, no cataclysms, no surprises. Their religion and philosophy imitated nature. The world was always the same, therefore the people must remain so. That's why there are really no angry or malevolent gods in the Egyptian pantheon.'

Mark looked at Halstead again. He had discreetly dabbed a napkin to his nose, leaving a crimson spot on the cloth.

'Compare the Egyptian gods,' Mark went on, 'with the gods of Mesopotamia. The Sumerians, Babylonians and Assyrians. People who dwelt in a land of unpredictable seasons, unexpected floods and earthquakes. Their gods mirrored nature; they were dark and mysterious, angry and vengeful, like the Jehovah of the Hebrews. The Egyptians on the other hand, dwelling in a balmy changelessness, in a land that barely knew seasons, never conceived of anything but happy and benevolent gods.'

Mark's eyes strayed again to Halstead. Fresh blood was appearing on his upper lip, trickling down into his silver moustache.

'The one exception was the god Set. He was the slayer of Osiris, the red-haired demon who was the god of darkness, derived no doubt from some primeval beast of terror. And there were a few lesser deities that might resemble devils, but they were more like annoying spirits or poltergeists.'

Halstead, now keeping the stained napkin pressed to his nose, said, 'Where did Akhnaton get his monotheism from, Dr Davison?'

'No one knows. There are a lot of theories but nothing concrete. Some people believe he was Jesus in his first incarnation, but that he failed because he had come before the world was ready for him. You see, Akhnaton referred to himself as the Son of God.'

Halstead brought the napkin away from his nose and delicately concealed it beneath the table. 'I have read the Hymn to the Sun. It's remarkable how like the One Hundred and Fourth Psalm it is. No doubt, discovering his tomb and possibly his body and possessions would be a great boon not only to history but theology as well –'

Halstead froze, a look of astonishment on his face, and in the next instant a gush of blood broke, like a bursting dam, from his nose and spattered on to the table.

'*Jesus*!' screamed Ron, jumping up and scrambling backwards over the bench.

Alexis gave a cry, and before Mark could react, Yasmina was on her feet. She threw an arm around Halstead's shoulders, grabbed the tablecloth by a corner and dragged it up to his face.

Mark felt himself slowly stand up, his mouth hanging open. Sanford Halstead was haemorrhaging on to the floor.

'Ice!' snapped Yasmina, by now cradling Halstead's head against her abdomen. The blood soaked through the cloth as quickly as she pressed it in wads against his nose.

'Get me some ice!'

Mark felt himself move. A small refrigerator stood in a corner under several crates. Opening it, he found blocks of meat and butter, bouquets of vegetables, a six-pack of beer, and in the tiny freezer compartment, one small tray of ice. His hands shook as he knocked the cubes into his napkin. When he returned to the table, both Yasmina and Halstead were drenched in red. She cradled him like a doll; he had passed out.

Snatching the ice pack from Mark, Yasmina flung the bloody tablecloth to one side and, securing Halstead's head in the crook of her arm, pinched his nose tightly with the fingers of one hand and held the pack to his face with the other.

For a moment, time stood still. Somewhere behind Mark, Ron groaned faintly. Hazim gazed in stupefaction, trembling so badly that he leaned against Mark. Alexis was sitting down, stunned.

Mark stared for a moment at Halstead's blood-soaked shirt and pants, then at Yasmina's hands and arms, which looked like they had been dipped in buckets of red paint, then he raised his eyes and looked around the tent.

Samira was no longer there.

The heat rolled down off the cliffs in great heavy waves, and as Mark walked across the camp towards Yasmina's tent, he felt his fresh shirt start to grow damp with perspiration. Pausing at the doorway of her tent, he called out, 'Hello? Miss Shukri?'

Her outline appeared on the other side of the gauzy doorway.

'I was wondering if we could talk. May I come in?'

She drew aside the netting. 'Please come in, Dr Davison.'

He followed Yasmina into the tent and allowed a moment for his eyes to adjust before sitting on one of the two folding chairs. Glancing around, he saw he had interrupted some work at the microscope. 'How's Halstead?'

Taking a seat on the other chair, Yasmina clasped her hands in her lap and said in a soft voice, 'He will be fine. I have given him a sedative so that he sleeps now.'

'What caused it?'

'I believe he is too anxious about finding the tomb, it has affected his blood pressure. Or possibly, his nose is sensitive to the sand. I will have him wear a surgical mask from now on.'

'He lost a lot of blood.'

'No more than a pint. Spread around, it looks like much more than it is. It will only make him tired.'

'God, I thought he was bleeding to death.'

'Would you care for some tea?' she asked after a moment's consideration.

Mark shook his head. He tried not to look around the tent but found himself curious. His gaze halted on a strip of fly paper hanging over her bed. It was speckled with flies, some of them still squirming. He looked away and inclined his head toward the microscope. 'May I ask what that is for?'

'It is for my speciality, Dr Davison. I am studying parasitology. In this region the people are plagued with terrible diseases caused by parasites in the soil, which they might be able to prevent with the proper education. Right now I study ancylostomiasis. It is introduced by a hookworm which lives in the soil and which passes through the bare skin. The *fellaheen* will relieve themselves wherever they are, and the infected ones pass the parasite along in their urine to the soil. Later, the people will walk barefoot through the same soil. The larvae will pass into the blood stream and will consume the red corpuscles. A victim can die at the age of twenty-five and not know how easily he could have prevented it.'

Yasmina, embarrassed by her rush of words, looked down. 'I would like to find a cure for these illnesses and a way to educate the people. But they are ignorant.'

'Is that why you don't get along with the old woman?'

She looked up, her pupils flared. 'She despises me for my modern ways.'

'The tattoo on her forehead, do you know what it is?'

'Samira is a Copt. The tattoo is the year she made a pilgrimage to Jerusalem.'

'A Copt . . .'

'Dr Davison,' a smile now played faintly around Yasmina's mouth. 'I could not help overhear your words to Mr Domenikos. I admire what you said to him.'

'Yes, well –' Mark placed his hands flat on his knees and tried to think of a way to wrap up the conversation. 'You need a fan in here. Maybe that'll keep the flies out.'

Her face darkened a little. 'My difficulty, Dr Davison, is that when I open the tent flap to let one fly out, ten will come in. I seem to be particularly plagued by them, for no one else complains.'

His eyes strayed again to the corkscrew hanging from the tent roof. It was now solid with flies. 'Jesus Christ! How long has that been hanging there?'

'Since this morning.'

Mark frowned. 'They must be after drugs or something.'

'And at night, when the flies sleep, the mosquitoes bother me. The netting seems to be of no help.'

'I'll have Abdul check it out.'

Yasmina smiled a second time and it surprised him. In the soft light and warmth of her tent, Mark felt compelled to return her stare. She had a peculiar way of looking at him: it was like an appraisal, as though he were a man she was both suspicious of and attracted to, fascinated with and yet contemptuous of.

Her eyes were incredible. It was as if a veil covered the lower half of her face; the veil her mother and grandmother had been forced to wear. Generations of women, as far back in history as Mohammed, had had to suffer their cheeks, noses, mouths and chins to be hidden, and as a consequence had developed sensuous eyes and a way of looking at a man that was nearly annihilating.

Mark suspected the look was unconscious, that it was genetically produced, and that Yasmina was unaware of the effect her eyes had on him. But he wasn't sure.

'I guess I'd better get Abdul's report. You'll let me know if Mr Halstead's condition changes, won't you?'

Yasmina rose with him. 'Yes, Dr Davison.'

He walked to the netted doorway and turned around. 'Listen, we're probably going to be here all summer and working closely together. Why don't we get on a first name basis right now?'

Yasmina stood a few feet from him with one hand resting on the work table. A long moment went by before she said softly, 'I will try.'

They had found nothing. Six hours of surface hunting had turned up absolutely nothing, but then again, Mark was not surprised. It was going to be the work of the next few weeks that would produce results; intensive exploration of each grid square and possibly the sinking of a few test holes in hunch areas.

He sat at his small desk, reading Ramsgate's Journal by the fluctuating generator light, studying each sentence, each word, hoping to pick up something he had missed. On 1 July the old *sebbakha* had come into Ramsgate's camp with the top fragment of a stela engraved with seven inexplicable figures, and she had told Ramsgate the tomb was 'under the Dog'. On 16 July he found the base of the stela which, in a riddle, gave the whereabouts of the tomb: *When Amon-Ra travelleth downstream, the Criminal lieth beneath; to be provided with the Eye of Isis.* And then finally, on 19 July: *Where my eyes have alit a hundred times, there the Dog finally registered.*

Now I know how childishly simple is the answer to the riddle . . .

Mark sat back and rubbed his neck. It was no use. Ramsgate just wasn't specific enough about where he excavated, simply: *circular trenches in the sand with Mohammed overseeing the teams.*

Mark closed the book, picked up his pipe and tobacco pouch, and went outside.

He crossed the compound, watching the supper fires of the *fellaheen* illuminate the ruins of the Workmen's Village; faintly, he could hear distant groups of men singing ballads to the accompaniment of primitive wooden instruments.

He sat down on the ancient mudbrick wall and lit his pipe. He thought about Nancy and considered writing her a letter and having it dispatched from El Minya. He wished she had come with him. It would be nice to have her here now, to talk to her, to make love, try once again to explain his *need* to be in the field . . .

Mark suddenly smelled gardenias.

'May I join you?'

Startled, he shifted on the mudbrick wall and looked up. Alexis was silhouetted like a Valkyrie against the stars. She had something in her hands.

'Be my guest.' Mark moved a few inches to make room. 'How's your husband?'

'We had to burn the shirt and pants because the blood wouldn't come out. Share a drink with me?'

Mark glanced down at the bottle and two glasses she held; he could barely make out the label, Glenlivet. 'Be happy to.'

She poured a little into each glass and handed one to Mark, placing the Scotch bottle on the sand between her feet.

They sipped in silence for a moment, Alexis frequently lifting her hair off her shoulders and tossing it back, Mark feeling awkward with her. Alexis Halstead had all the warmth of a mountain lake; to make love to her would be like plunging into glacial waters. Invigorating, but not satisfying.

'Dr Davison, when will we complete our tour of the tombs?'

'I'm afraid there's no time for it. Sightseeing is over. We're here to work and each day we waste is one day closer to Ramadan and to the most intense heat of the summer.'

'How unfortunate.'

They fell silent again, close together and almost touching but not looking at one another.

Alexis said, 'I smell hashish.'

'It's coming from the Workmen's Village. They smoke it every night.'

She released a short, mirthless laugh. 'I cannot conceive of their way of life. How utterly worthless and depressing. Imagine cutting off a girl's clitoris. The women don't even know what they're missing.'

Mark didn't respond; he was trying to think of the word in Arabic. Then it came to him: *barda*. It meant cold, icy.

'Dr Davison.'

'Yes?'

'Look at me.'

He did so.

Alexis opened her mouth to speak but hesitated, her moist red lips slightly parted. A veil seemed to fall over her green eyes; her expression froze like an immobilised movie frame. Then it passed and she said softly, 'Tell me again about Egyptian tombs, Dr Davison.'

Puzzled, he said, 'What do you want to know?'

She raked her gaze away from him and settled it on some distant point, her eyes unfocused. 'They went to such lengths to preserve the bodies in death. And they went to such pains, such ingenious deception to hide them in burial. Why?'

'Because the ancient Egyptians believed they could only have an afterlife if the body was intact. For as long as the body was in perfect condition, the soul would enjoy the hereafter, which they called the Western Land. The art of mummification has never been re-created, never been equalled. To this day we don't fully know the ancient Egyptians' secret for preserving the corpse. And as for hiding the body, Mrs Halstead, that was to protect it against tomb robbers. You see, for the soul to have an afterlife, the person's name had to be written somewhere on the body. This was usually done in the form of golden amulets and bracelets. Naturally, the tomb robbers would steal these and when that happened, the soul ceased to exist.'

She drew in a deep breath, held it for a long moment, then released it as she whispered, 'Is that why . . . is that why . . .'

He waited.

Alexis fell into a vacant stare, not breathing, not blinking.

'Is that why *what*, Mrs Halstead?'

She stirred slightly, then finally looked at him, her alabaster forehead creasing in a frown. 'I beg your pardon?'

Mark regarded her for a moment. 'Do you feel all right?'

'Yes . . . I do. Only . . .'

'Only what?'

She looked down at the glass in her hand and seemed surprised to find it there. 'I'm tired, Dr Davison. I had nightmares last night. I woke up feeling as if I hadn't slept.' She rose uncertainly, picking up the bottle of Glenlivet. 'Excuse me, I'll retire now . . .'

Mark watched Alexis glide over the sand, her tanned arms and legs curiously white in the moon's glow. As he tossed back the last of his Scotch, he heard heavy footsteps crossing the compound. A few seconds later, Ron Farmer was standing before him.

'What's the matter?'

'I'm pissed.'

'Have a seat and tell me about it.'

Ron dumped himself down, his shoulders sloped forward, his eyes settling on the sand. 'What's that you're drinking?'

'Scotch. What's up?'

'Here.' He thrust a strip of film at Mark.

'What's this?'

'Negatives of the shots I took in the Royal Tomb.'

Mark tried to examine the film by moonlight. 'And?'

'Fogged. Fucking-fogged.'

'Maybe you had a light leak.'

'Then why aren't the rest of the shots on that roll fogged? The ones before we went in and the ones I took outside afterward. Perfect. Just the ones in the tomb, the ones of you. *Fogged*.'

'Maybe there wasn't enough light in the tomb –'

'That's four hundred speed film, Mark, in an automatic camera! The OM-2 doesn't make mistakes like that!'

'You got me.' Mark handed back the strip. 'Go get some sleep, Ron, Yasmina said you banged your head again when you fell over the bench.'

'Couldn't help it, the dude bled all over my beans!' Ron stood up. 'Tomorrow we explore your grid square?'

'I saved the choicest for myself. Good night, Ron.'

Mark waited until he heard his friend's footsteps fade away before also rising. He was starting to feel the effects of the day. He was hoping he would sleep better tonight.

Then he turned around.

And saw a spectral woman standing in the shadows, watching him.

ELEVEN

MARK GOT down on one knee, scooped sand away from the object, and studied it before picking it up. Then he looked around for Ron.

His friend was nearby, prodding the sand with a stick and examining the canyon floor with a magnifying glass. Sanford Halstead and Yasmina were sitting in the shade of the cliff, their backs against the rock wall, their legs stretched before them. Sanford Halstead had insisted he accompany Mark this morning, and because there was no dissuading the man, Mark had asked Yasmina to come along. Halstead was all right today, no more mishaps with his nose, but he wore the white cloth surgical mask Yasmina had forced on him.

The area Mark had chosen for himself was six miles up the Royal Wadi where a branch of the gorge widened into a sandy box canyon, walled in on three sides by sheer rock face. He had chosen this site for himself because of a hunch: a nagging intuition that had come to him during the night that the priests of Amon might have dug their new tomb not too far from the old one, yet at the absolute limit of Akhnaton's boundary.

After four hours he found something.

'Ron! Pictures!' he shouted, his voice rebounding off the canyon walls.

His friend was beside him in an instant, standing over him and saying, 'Well, will you look at that . . .'

'I want a photograph *in situ* before I unearth it.' Mark withdrew a foot-long scale pole from his clipboard and placed it alongside the object.

'You think it's significant?' asked Ron, focusing through the lens.

'It looks old.'

'But it could have been left here by anyone. A member of the Peet-Woolley expedition could have come up this far, hunting jackals maybe.'

'I wonder . . .' Mark remained kneeling until Ron had completed his six shots, then he gingerly picked the gun out of the sand.

He had been methodically going over the floor of this little canyon square foot by square foot, digging his boots into the sand, rolling boulders to one side, crouching over a large magnifying glass and kneeling down every so often to sift through the sand with his hands. His fingertips had hit something metallic.

'Know anything about guns?'

'You're asking me? A guy who once blocked the Pacific Coast Highway with twenty-four cars to prevent the Dow Chemical trucks from going through?'

Mark weighed the gun in his hands. 'I wonder if it means anything.'

'What have you got there?' called Halstead.

Mark picked up his clipboard and strode over to where Sanford was sitting. He held out the pistol. 'Know anything about these?'

Halstead's eyes widened. Jumping to his feet, he seized the gun and turned it over in his hands. 'I am an expert in weaponry, Dr Davison. I collect antique guns.'

'Can you tell me what this one is and its age?'

'It's a Beaumont-Adams double-action revolver. They were developed in England in the mid-1800s and were popular because trigger pressure cocked it and fired it at the same time. If I recall correctly, it takes centerfire cartridges.' He tried to open the six-chamber cylinder but could not.

'How old is it?'

'That is hard to tell, Dr Davison, for it has been badly

weather damaged.' He turned it over and over in his hands, examining every part of it, until he came to the butt. The wood was bleached and corroded, but an engraving could barely be made out. 'May I?' He took the magnifying glass and silently studied the letters.

'What is it?'

'Unfortunately I cannot make out the entire name, but looks like this pistol belonged to Sir Robert.'

Mark took the gun and the magnifying glass and gave it the same scrutiny. 'You're right,' he murmured. 'At least, that's what it looks like.' He whipped around. 'Okay Ron, let's get to work!'

The box canyon was trapezoidal, with the widest edge at the far end. It narrowed to two hundred feet at the entrance, which then dwindled to a thin cleft winding back to the main wadi. The Land-Rovers had to go slowly and in single file, then the team of workers was deployed over the floor of the canyon using a new grid: this time each man was assigned to a square one fifth the size of the one he had been exploring earlier. Still, it was a large area – the canyon was the size of two football fields – and it would take days to cover completely.

As Abdul and his two assistants oversaw the *fellaheen*, ensuring that they diligently examined every pebble and rock and that they searched the ground as if looking for a lost gold piece, Mark and Ron stayed by the Land-Rovers, where a temporary headquarters had been set up. With his new map spread out on the hood and held down by rocks, Mark periodically scanned the canyon with his Nikons. Yasmina Shukri, sitting inside one of the vehicles, kept herself alert in the noon heat; she was prepared to treat scorpion stings and snake bites. Hazim al-Sheikhly strolled around jotting down words in his notebook. Alexis had chosen to remain back at camp, complaining of a headache.

It was Sanford Halstead who found the fire pit.

Having insisted upon taking part in the search, he had picked out a plot of ground that was in the shade of the cliff wall, and had been levering rocks aside with a crowbar for half an hour when he found it.

His excited shout brought everyone running. Abdul, ordering the *fellaheen* to take a rest, walked quickly and stiffly over the sand. Yasmina, who thought Halstead had encountered a snake, came running with her medical bag. Mark dropped to his knees when he arrived, and Ron started snapping pictures.

'Spoons and forks,' said Mark excitedly. 'All blackened and burnt but recognisable. I see a pair of glasses, the old wire-rim type. What's that? Looks like a fountain pen. A shred of cloth . . .' Mark spoke rapidly and breathlessly but touched nothing.

Then he looked up at the others and said, 'This is more than a cooking pit, this is where the Pasha's men burnt everything.'

A wind swept down from the plateau, whistling through the canyon, and an awesome silence descended as the six gazed down at the pathetic remains of Ramsgate's group. Then Ron saw something that made him shiver in the noon heat.

'Look there. What's that . . .?'

Everyone turned to where he pointed. 'It looks like a bone,' said Hazim.

'Is it human?' whispered someone else.

But no one replied. The wind picked up speed, battering the group around the charred pit and making their hair and clothes fly. Finally, after a long moment, Mark stood up and said, 'I want this pit excavated.'

It was time to get the main work tent ready, and Mark was glad of something to keep him busy. After he and Ron had sunk holes into the sand and roped off the area to be cleared, the *fellaheen* had rolled aside more boulders and had found more charred bones. All human.

There was no longer any question about what had been done with the bodies of the Ramsgate expedition.

Mark couldn't fathom why it should bother him, and yet it did. His whole life was devoted to the study of the dead; he had exhumed corpses before. But this was different: these were the remains of people very much like himself, men not far removed in time or thought; there was an intimacy to handling their bones that had never cropped up in disrobing three-thousand-year-old mummies.

It was Hazim al-Sheikhly who had cast the initial pall. After unearthing a skull with bits of white hair still matted to it, the young Arab had asked, 'Will you want to give them a Christian burial?' Mark had not known what to reply. He was an atheist and did not believe in an afterlife; the suggestion nonplussed him. So he left the question unanswered. Abdul was, at the moment, seeing to it that the bones were carefully deposited in a crate and that all that remained of the Ramsgate party was removed from the pyre. Later, after the box was sealed and stored away, Mark would consider what to do with them.

By the time Abdul's assistants arrived with the first excavated objects, Mark was ready.

This tent was larger than the rest, for it doubled as a store-room for all supplies other than food. Large equipment – pickaxes, shovels, trowels, spikes and poles – lay in unopened crates beneath the work tables. A small fan whirred in one corner to keep the hot air moving as Mark worked. On the 'dirty' workbench he had set out the cleaning implements: brushes, cloths, whisk brooms, paraffin blocks, washing trays, tweezers and various sized knives. Here the *fellaheen* carefully deposited the results of their sifting: blackened and twisted bits of metal, scraps of burnt cloth and paper, shards of wood and stone. After Mark had cleaned and catalogued each piece, he moved it to the 'clean' table which held his drawing pads, pens and pencils, protractor and rulers, draughtsman's triangles, magnifying glass, microscope and log book. He worked in silent concentration.

Yasmina Shukrı returned to the camp with the next delivery, leaving Ron at the site to take pictures and Hazim to record the work while Halstead looked on. She appeared in the doorway of the work tent and cleared her throat politely.

Mark, sitting on a high stool and brushing soot off an ivory comb, looked up. 'Hi, come on in. How's it going?'

'Mr Rageb is sifting the last of it now.'

'Good. Tomorrow we can start the trenches. How's Halstead holding up? Any more problems with his nose?'

She shrugged uncharacteristically and continued to hestitate in the doorway.

Mark reached under the bench and pulled out another stool. 'I'm afraid you're blocking my best light.'

'Excuse me.' Yasmina stepped inside and pulled the stool toward her. Sitting on it and hooking her feet on a rung, she said, 'Dr Davison, may I discuss something that is troubling me?'

He put down the comb and wiped his hands on his army-green bush jeans. 'Sure. What is it?'

The young woman looked around the tent, searching for the opening words. 'It is the bones, Dr Davison, there is something wrong with them. Terribly wrong.'

'Like that?'

Her eyes avoided him as she spoke, and her voice was subdued. 'As the *fellaheen* drew the bones out of the sand and placed them in the box, I examined them. The bones have sustained wounds, Dr Davison, breaks and gashes. One of them, a skull, had been clearly battered.'

'Those boulders were probably the cause. They were either thrown on top by the Pasha's men or they fell from the plateau above –'

'No, Dr Davison. That had occurred to me, yet I could not match the injuries in the bones with the contours of the stones on top of them. Even so, boulders would not account for the *scattering*. Skulls are lying many feet away from ribs and arms. Dr Davison,' Yasmina raised her eyes to his, 'the bodies were, what is the word, *dismembered* before they were cremated.'

Mark felt his neck hairs prickle. 'That's obviously the work of desert scavengers. Jackals, probably.'

'Dr Davison, when a jackal tears apart a body, he will drag it far away to eat it in peace. If these bodies had been touched by the scavengers of the desert, we would have found the bones scattered all over the canyon floor. It as as if . . .'

'As if what?'

'As if the bodies had been cut up and thrown piece by piece on the fire.'

'That's ridiculous. Why would the Pasha's men do that?'

'Perhaps they found them that way.'

Mark stared at her in mild surprise, and was about to speak when his thoughts were interrupted by a sound.

Yasmina turned her head. 'What is that?'

Mark listened. It was a deep oscillating hum that sounded like a reed instrument in the lower register; a contrabassoon. It played four notes in a dull, rhythmic repetition, sounding curiously far away and yet near at the same time. 'A *fellah*,' said Mark with a frown, 'playing a flute.'

She shook her head. 'Someone is singing, Dr Davison. Listen, there are words.'

Out of curiosity, Mark slid off his stool and went outside the tent, with Yasmina following immediately behind. They walked around the camp in the intense afternoon sun until, coming to the rear of the mess tent, they found old Samira sitting cross-legged in the dirt, hunched like a magpie beside the stone oven, swaying and chanting with her eyes closed.

'What's this?'

'She appears to be in a trance.'

The old woman continued to mumble her melodic incantation, oblivious of the intrusion. Mark squatted down in front of her and saw glistening brown juice trickle from the corner of her mouth.

When a shadow fell over him, Mark squinted up at the towering form of Abdul. 'We have finished the sifting, *effendi*. The men have placed the last of the findings in the work tent.'

Mark stood up and put his hands on his hips. 'I want Samira replaced.'

Abdul's deep-set eyes flickered down to the old woman. 'Has she done something wrong, *effendi*?'

'She's on a trip, Abdul, she's chewing leaves. I don't care what she does on her own time, but when she's working for me I want her head clear. Get someone else.'

As Mark turned to walk away, the old *fellaha's* voice suddenly rose to a wail, and when he looked down at her, Mark found her gazing up at him with fiery black eyes. Samira had stopped swaying and was now speaking loudly, urgently.

'What's she saying? I don't understand her.'

'She is warning you of danger, *effendi*.'

Mark frowned down at the wizened face. He watched the thin lips move rapidly over toothless gums, uttering words alien to him and yet which had a strangely familiar ring. 'She isn't speaking Arabic.'

'No, *effendi*, she speaks the old tongue.'

'Coptic?' Mark turned to Abdul. 'Are you sure? I've never heard that dialect before.'

Samira's voice rasped on. Now she was repeating phrases, and Mark was able to pick out a few words he knew.

The study of the Coptic language had been part of Mark's doctoral thesis on the spoken language of ancient Egypt. No one knew how the language of the Pharaoh sounded because the Egyptians omitted vowels in their writing; hieroglyphs were a form of shorthand. The Copts, a Christian sect that began with Saint Mark two thousand years ago, claimed to have maintained the ancient pharaonic tongue, so that Mark Davison, in attempting to reconstruct the language as it might have sounded, had traced the evolution of Coptic root words back to ancient times and had found many of them in hieroglyphic texts. The problem was, Coptic had undergone some degree of corruption due to foreign influence throughout the millenia, so that Mark's theory on how the ancient tongue might have sounded remained unproven.

He looked down at the old woman. Listening carefully, Mark was able to seize upon key words. And as he did so, he felt a small thrill go through him. 'Where does she come from?'

'Her home is at Hag Qandil, *effendi*.'

'No, I mean originally. Where was she born? Where did she spend her childhood?'

'I do not know, *effendi*.'

Intrigued, Mark knelt again before the *fellaha* and the tiny jet eyes followed him like magnets. 'Old woman,' he said in Coptic, 'I want to ask you something.'

But Samira kept up her canticle.

'She does not understand you, *effendi*.'

'She doesn't hear me, you mean. That must be powerful stuff she's sucking on. From her own secret little cactus garden, I'll bet. Old woman, listen to me.'

'Do not bother with her, *effendi*, I will hire another woman.'

Mark help up a hand. 'Tell me what she's saying. I can only grasp the number seven, over and over again.'

'She says there is danger here. She says there are two forces locked in a battle and you are at the center . . .'

'Go on.'

'It does not make sense, *effendi*.'

'Translate, Abdul.'

'She says there is an evil force here, but there is also one of good and that you must learn which is which and allow the one for good to help you. It is nonsense, *effendi*.'

Mark gazed at the old woman in fascination. 'This is incredible! I can understand about half of what she's saying! And it's in a dialect far older than any I've heard. Listen . . .' He stared at her in earnest, barely breathing. '"One will go up in flame". Is that right, Abdul, is that

143

what she's saying?'

'Yes, *effendi*.'

'"One will go up in flame and one will suffer a . . . a . . ."' He squinted up at Abdul.

'A bleeding, *effendi*.'

'. . . "that will drain him unto death". This is fabulous, Abdul! She's actually speaking a dialect not far removed from the ancient language! I have to get this down!'

Abdul Rageb, his stoic face unreadable, gazed ahead with half-lidded eyes. Yasmina, frowning, looked from Mark to the old woman back to Mark. 'What is she talking about?'

He waved a hand. 'That's not important. She's on a hallucinogenic trip. What's important is that she is speaking a dialect damned close to the lost ancient language, and *I* can almost understand it!'

The crone babbled and Mark listened excitedly.

'Demons,' he said. 'That's the word she's saying over and over again. Setting them free –' He frowned suddenly, his memory triggered. Ramsgate's Journal. The old *fellaha* was quoting from Ramsgate's Journal.

Mark shook his head impatiently. 'Abdul, I want to know where she came from. Her family, her village. It's just possible she grew up in a remote pocket up the Nile where the inhabitants were isolated enough to maintain the ancient dialect. She might be of help to me.'

'You do not wish to replace her?'

'Not yet. I can use her.'

As he massaged his temples, Mark made a mental note to talk to Abdul about the tent's ventilation. Even though all the window flaps were up and three fans were going, the smoke and cooking odors were suffocating. Mark pushed his plate away. While his companions heartily devoured the savory lamb kebab and rice, Mark found himself without appetite. His headache was lingering, the one he had gotten the night before when he had thought he had

144

seen a woman in the shadows, but which had turned out to be only an optical illusion. And Alexis Halstead's over-powering gardenia perfume wasn't helping either.

Mark's eyes followed the movements of Samira as she cleared away the plates and put bowls of *mehalabeyah* on the table. She seemed not to remember the afternoon's incident, nor to be any longer under the influence of the drug. She had gone back to not speaking to anyone.

'Dr Davison,' said Sanford Halstead over his plate of nuts and greens. 'Can we talk about today's find?'

Mark was craving a strong drink and wondered if Alexis would part with some of her Glenlivet. But, looking at her as she ate in silence across from him, Mark thought Mrs Halstead looked a little pale and wondered what it was that had kept her in her tent all day. Strange, she appeared to be getting whiter while her companions were getting steadily sunburnt . . .

'Okay, let's talk. What's on your mind?'

'I scanned the entire canyon today, Dr Davison, and found nothing that even remotely resembles a dog. I went over every inch of skyline and there is no rock formation resembling a dog. I was wondering if Neville Ramsgate possibly heard the *sebbakha* incorrectly. Is there another word in Arabic that might sound like the word for dog?'

Mark thought a moment. This was something he had not considered. 'In Arabic the word for dog is *kalb*. The only other ones that sound like it are *alb*, which means heart, and *kahb*, which means the heel of a foot. Now, Ramsgate said he found the Dog. He didn't say that it turned out to be something else, like a heart-shaped rock, or that he was mistaken about the fact that it was a dog.'

'Nonetheless, I am concerned. I think it's too much to presume that the tomb is in that canyon.'

'I never said it was, Mr Halstead, but it's as good a place as any to start looking. We have found Ramsgate's possessions and most likely Ramsgate himself. He said in his Journal that he moved his camp to be near the tomb. Well, we found his camp, so I don't think we're far from the tomb.'

Ron, licking the last of the rice pudding off his spoon, said. 'There's one thing that still bugs me.'

'What's that?'

'The Journal,' he said. 'If everything was burned by the Pasha's men, including the bodies, how did the Journal get out?'

Mark stepped out into the coppery sunset and breathed deeply. Then he stretched his arms above his head and rose up on his toes as if to take hold of the lavender sky. A few yards away, at the edge of the camp, Abdul and the *ghaffirs* were kneeling on mats and bowing toward the east. Outside his own tent and also on a prayer rug, Hazim al-Sheikhly likewise observed the fourth prayer of the day. From behind, soft and soothing, came the strains of Ron's cassette player in the darkroom tent. Dotted throughout the maze of mudbrick walls in the Workmen's Village, supper fires glowed.

Mark smiled in satisfaction and headed for the work tent. Things were going well, better than he had expected. He felt confident.

Resuming his place on the stool, Mark picked through the last of the objects taken out of the pit. More personal effects: a hand mirror, a cufflink, the heel of a boot. All charred and sooty and barely recognisable. In his meticulousness, Abdul had seen to it that absolutely everything of question had been put into the box so that Mark had to go through a lot of throwaway pieces of rock and charcoal. It was a long and tiresome task, and as he was drawn into characteristic concentration, Mark was unaware that the day had slipped away and that night embraced the valley.

Subliminally, coming through the Dacron walls, the storyteller's voice could be heard in the Workmen's Village.

Accompanying himself on the *rababa,* a single-stringed violin with a penetrating tone, the *sha'ir* captivated his listeners with a song-story about the exploits of the heroic Abu Zayd al-Hilali and his band of brave companions. The *sha'ir's* voice, resonant and melodramatic, floated out over the purple night, carrying colorful phrases about the physical charms of Abu Zayd's wife Aliya over the mudbrick walls and into the silent camp.

Mark was so engrossed in his work that he was unaware of the storyteller's song, nor did he hear the occasional shouts of glee from the *fellaheen* audience when they heard marvels that pleased them. Mark was painstakingly brushing black dust off a large flat rock that Abdul had put into a box. It was a limestone fragment approximately one foot long, eight inches wide and three inches thick. Mark was submitting it to the routine cleaning before giving it a quick look over with the magnifying glass and then tossing it away.

The *sha'ir* enthralled his audience with tales of the courage of 'Antar, and as the seated *fellaheen* shouted, 'Allah! Allah!' Mark picked up the glass and inspected the rock. It was smooth.

The *sha'ir,* having ended his rhyming epic, turned now to lofty praises of Mohammed and Jesus, weaving the virtues of both prophets into a superhuman tapestry. The *fellaheen* in the circle at his feet started to beat their hands together in time with his chant.

Mark turned the stone over. He bent close to the magnifying glass. Then he stood up, bringing the stone up closer to the light.

When the *sha'ir* reached the climax of his praises, the *fellaheen* let out whoops and flung their caps in the air.

Mark Davison stared open-mouthed at the stone fragment in his hand.

TWELVE

'Hoo!' SAID Ron. 'It is getting *hot* out here. How much longer are we going to keep on like this?'

Mark looked up from his work, wiped the sweat off his forehead and quickly scanned the canyon.

In the half hour he had been bent over the photographs, every single scrap of shade had disappeared; the sun stood at its zenith and the canyon was a bleached, colorless oven with blinding white walls and white floor. Abdul's teams, working slowly and relentlessly in the heat, were stretched out in rows, armies of long-robed men who wore turbans and skullcaps and who wielded axes and shovels. First the trenches had been roped off, now they were being dug. Another line of young boys and old men carted away the rubble, bucket-brigade style. Abdul Rageb, tall and slender, shimmering like an obelisk in the noon, walked gracefully among them.

Mark pushed his sunglasses on to the bridge of his nose. 'Soon. Another hour I guess.' He returned to the photographs spread out on the hood of the Land-Rover. They were of the limestone fragments he had discovered the previous night.

He and Ron had sat up half the night cleaning and examining the stones, and both had greeted the dawn with frustration. The two shards were pieces of Ramsgate's first fragment. However, they were nowhere near the condition in which Ramsgate had found them. Early this morning Mark had sifted through the fire pit with his own rocking screen, and had come to the bitter realisation that all that remained of Ramsgate's two magnificent stela fragments were these blackened splinters and a handful of pulverised charcoal.

Nonetheless, what they had was enough to tell Mark and Ron that they were in possession of a most remarkable ancient artefact.

For one thing, Ramsgate had been right that there was 'something queer about the stela.' It was indeed, as he had written, not at all like any known in existence. Through careful and lengthy inspection, Mark and Ron had been able to discern the outlines of seven figures carved into the limestone; thus far only four were identifiable: Amon, patron god of Thebes and known as the Hidden One; Am-mut, a beast comprised of parts of different animals and called the Devourer; Akhekh, an antelope with a bird's head; and finally, most distinctly, Set the devil god.

Amon the Hidden One stood in the center with the other six paying homage to him. There was not a single human among them. The cartouche of Tutankhamon was clearly read, evidence of why the gods were not carved in the revolutionary Amarna style. After the fall of Akhnaton, Tutankhamon had succeeded him, and art had returned to the old ways as if the heretic had never existed. This stela had been commissioned by the priests of Amon after tradition had been restored.

Mark lifted his sunglasses and seated them high on his forehead so he could rub the perspiration out of his eyes. 'We need that stela base, Ron. Without it, we haven't a clue where to look for the tomb.'

Hazim al-Sheikhly climbed down from the Land-Rover where he had been writing notes for his report and joined the two Egyptologists. 'I have decided to delay a little longer contacting my superiors in Cairo, Dr Davison, until we have something more substantial to report.'

Mark nodded, understanding. His attention was diverted by the approach of Yasmina who was making her way across the sand. Behind her, propped up against the cliff wall, several *fellaheen* sat with eyes closed and heads

149

lolling. When she neared, Mark saw that a film of perspiration glowed on her cocoa skin. He also found himself appreciating the sight of her: her petiteness and exotic features. He offered her his best smile.

'The shade has gone, Dr Davison. These men must be returned to the camp. They suffer from heat and sun-stroke.'

He nodded, then turned and shouted to Abdul. Getting his foreman's attention, Mark waved his hands over his head. To Yasmina he said, 'We'll quit for the day.'

Sanford Halstead was not pleased with the establishment of a siesta schedule. It seemed a wretched waste of precious time; even if it was over a hundred degrees in the canyon. Weren't these people used to it?

He looked over at the curtain partitioning off the tent and heard his wife's restless tossing and turning as she slept fitfully. He turned away and went back to staring at the tent roof with his hands clasped over his abdomen; he returned to the problem he had been going over and over in his mind all day. This morning, Halstead had disco-vered blood in his urine. Perhaps it was nothing, perhaps he was being an alarmist; still, if the problem persisted, he would discuss the matter privately with Davison.

The *ghaffir* shifted his weight from his right foot to his left, unshouldered his rifle and slung it on the opposite side. His duty was pure drudgery – guarding the central work tent where the tea and Coke were stored – but it paid well. He was earning seven pounds a week on this job and already had plans for the money.

The sun was at its highest so that not even an inch of shade stood out from the tent wall. All expedition mem-bers were quietly sleeping, as he wished he could, and there was nothing but endless rolling sand to relieve the eye. When the torturous heat and supreme boredom started to eat at him, the hawk-faced *ghaffir* thought about the money again.

A sound from behind caused him to look over his shoulder. The white wall of the tent blinded him. He held his breath and listened.

Something was scuttling, like rats, inside the tent.

He made a quick sweep of the compound. No one was about, nothing stirred; the only sound beneath the vast ocean of cloudless sky was the hum of the distant generators.

And inside the tent: *scrape, scrape, scrape* . . .

He narrowed his eyes at the doorway. There was no way anything could have gotten past him and into the tent through there. A hole somewhere, then.

Unshouldering his rifle and holding it firmly and ready in his right hand, the Arab slowly circumnavigated the tent, running his one good eye over the Dacron and pausing every now and then to listen to the scratching sounds inside. Whatever it was, it was either very big or there were a lot of them.

Coming back to where he had started, the *ghaffir* stretched his mouth in a grin. He had been wanting to shoot off his rifle, even if it was only at a few desert rats.

Scrape, scrape . . .

Cautiously, not wanting to let them escape, he hoisted the flap aside and stepped into the darkness. Sunlight poured in around him, illuminating the crates, high stools and workbenches. He scanned the floor. There was nothing there.

Suddenly, the flap was yanked from his hand and it fell across the doorway, plunging him into night. The *ghaffir* only had time to gasp, for the rifle was then wrenched from his hand and a black shape, darker even than the interior of the tent, a silhouette so awesome and formidable that his legs gave way, rose up before him.

The Arab fell to his knees, his eyes and mouth stretched wide in horror. The phantom loomed over him, oval eyes blazed down at him, two massive arms rose high in the air.

151

The *ghaffir* said, 'Allah . . .' and then spoke no more.

Mark held Nancy's picture up at arm's length. He brought her to life and relived happy memories with her: their first meeting, weekends in Santa Barbara, swimming naked in the midnight surf. He wished she was here with him now, lying on the next cot instead of Ron. They could make love while everyone else slept.

His arm grew tired so he let it fall.

No, it wouldn't be like that at all. Nancy wouldn't make love to him here, she wouldn't relax, she would hate it, complain.

He thought of Yasmina, saw her black swimming eyes, her swarthy skin, the smallness of her, the vulnerability of her. The image of Yasmina Shukri was one Mark found himself entertaining with increasing frequency.

A high, screeching noise brought Mark out of his thoughts. It had sounded like an owl or peregrine falcon. When it came again, Mark realised it was a human cry, and in the next instant both he and Ron were on their feet.

Coming out into the sunlight, where they were momentarily blinded, Mark and Ron felt others run past them; they heard Halstead's excited voice, and again, the piercing, bird-like shriek.

Mark and Ron followed the others and came upon old Samira, her arms spread out like black wings, screaming up to the sky. At her feet lay a body.

'Jesus!' shouted Ron. *'Oh Jesus!'*

Mark stopped short, stunned.

On the sand, directly in front of the work tent that he was supposed to be guarding, lay the twisted naked body of the *ghaffir*. His face, eyes glassy and staring, mouth stretched wide, was covered with a brown paste; it filled his mouth and spilled on to the sand. The same substance was smeared over his hands and buttocks.

For an instant, Mark felt the ground lurch beneath his feet, then he recovered and was aware of everyone, in various stages of undress, standing in electrified silence.

Halstead whipped away, clutching his stomach, and started to vomit.

Hazim al-Sheikhly, shirtless like Ron and Mark, fell against the tent wall and slowly sank to the ground.

Mark looked around for Abdul. The somber Arab had just arrived and was standing apart from the group, his veiled eyes fixed on the *ghaffir's* wretched body.

'Mark!' whispered Ron. 'In Ramsgate's Journal . . .'

'Shut up. Abdul!'

The foreman glided toward him. 'Yes, *effendi?*'

'What happened here?'

'I do not know.'

Mark started to tremble with fury. 'You have no idea who did this?'

The Arab's face remained stony. 'No, *effendi.*'

'Remove the body, Abdul, find out who his family is, and then check the tent to see if anything was stolen.'

'I want to know who did it, goddamnit!' shouted Mark, slamming a fist on the table.

Abdul, irritatingly composed, did not speak.

'It wasn't for the Coke, nothing in the tent was touched! So the man was killed for personal reasons! Someone had a grudge against him! Well, I want it to end right now, is that understood?' Mark glared at his foreman and felt, for the first time in their long relationship, the urge to throttle the man. The others in the tent sat in blank-faced silence. Only old Samira moved, going mechanically about her chores. Discovering the body had so upset her that the group had had a difficult time calming her down; only the appearance of a hypodermic syringe from Yasmina's bag had stilled her. The only one who was not among them now was Sanford Halstead, who had come down with another violent nosebleed.

Abdul's voice came out measured. 'He was not a popular man, *effendi*. There was jealousy. I believe he insulted a man's wife.'

'Look Abdul, I don't want my camp turned into a fucking battleground! Let them carry out their vendettas elsewhere, not around here! Do you understand?'

'Yes, *effendi*.'

Mark slumped down on to the bench and buried his face in his hands. The aroma of steaming lentils on the Coleman stove made him gag. 'Does his family know?' he asked wearily.

'The man had an elderly uncle in Hag Qandil and that is all. I will see that he is told and that his nephew is buried and I will give the old man bereavement payment.'

'Okay, go do it. And, Abdul . . .' Mark looked up at his old friend, '. . . thanks.'

No one moved or spoke for a few minutes after Abdul's departure. Everyone avoided everyone else's eyes, staring at their hands or into their tea. Three hours separated them from the incident – they were dressed and composed – but the horror lingered.

Ron broke the silence by saying, 'What I don't understand is . . . there wasn't a sound. I mean, some of us were awake, and there wasn't a single *sound*.'

'That doesn't mean anything,' said Mark in a dull voice. 'It could have happened somewhere else and then the body was dragged back here.'

'But why?'

Oh Lord, thought Mark, if I only knew!

'Why would anyone do something like that? I mean, it actually looked like he really–'

Mark let out a weighty sigh and looked directly at his friend. 'Let's not dwell on the morbid, Ron. I want the incident forgotten.'

'Mark, killing someone is one thing. But making him eat shit–'

'Ron, please . . .'

'It is almost as if . . .' came the soft voice of Hazim al-Sheikhly, 'as if someone wanted to frighten us.'

Mark, feeling himself start to tremble again, clenched

154

and unclenched his fists. He had to get a hold of himself and calm everyone down too. He said quietly. 'I want the incident forgotten. The man was a victim of his people's own form of justice. Let's hope it ends here because we don't want the *ma'mur's* police interrupting our work with an investigation. As to the . . . *manner* of his death, it wasn't intended to frighten us, it was a warning to his friends, or to anyone who might be thinking of avenging his murder. Now I suggest,' Mark rose with an effort, 'we all rest up for supper.'

Mark had spent the evening in the work tent, once again examining the pathetic remains of Ramsgate's party. At one point Yasmina had joined him, saying she was restless and couldn't sleep. They had sat on the high stools drinking cinnamon tea and talking quietly; she had called him Mark and had seemed more relaxed than ever before.

Now he was tired and plodded wearily back to the tent he shared with Ron. He was surprised to see the light still on.

Inside, he found his friend sitting cross-legged on his cot with Ramsgate's Journal opened out in his lap and a photograph of the stela topstone by his left knee. He did not look up when Mark came in.

'What are you doing?' asked Mark, unbuttoning his shirt.

By Ron's right knee was a spiral notebook; he was scribbling hastily in it. 'Identifying these gods.'

Mark turned away, pulled his shirt out of his belt and peeled it off. Flicking on the bulb over his own cot, he slumped down, picked up the bourbon flask and glass on his night table, and poured himself a shot. 'So what have you found?'

Ron dropped his pen and looked up. 'I remembered that Ramsgate had identified the Seven when he found the tomb door and that he lists them in the Journal. You and I were able to identify four of the gods: Amon the Hidden

One, who stands in the center; Am-mut the Devourer, distinct because of its composite body – the hind legs of a hippo, forelegs of a lion, and a crocodile's head; Akhekh the Winged One, also distinguished by its unique body – an antelope with wings and the head of a bird; and finally that hideous primeval beast Set the Slayer of Osiris. Because of the cremation, the other three are indistinguishable except for bare outlines. So I looked in the Journal, and since Ramsgate corroborates the four we identified, I assume the other three are correct.'

Mark refilled his glass. 'Who are they?'

Ron read aloud from the Journal: '*Apep, Belonging to the Cobra – a man with a snake on his shoulders instead of a head and who carries a scythe; the Upreared One – a wild boar with human arms and standing on its hind legs; and lastly, She-Who-Binds-The-Dead-In-Chains . . .*' Ron looked up. '*. . . a woman with a scorpion's head.*'

Mark pulled down the corners of his mouth and raised his eyebrows. 'Quite an impressive line-up.'

'The likes of which has not been seen in five thousand years of ancient Egyptian history.'

Mark put his glass down and pulled off his boots, grunting with the effort. 'I'd say the priests of Amon were determined not to have that tomb disturbed.'

Ron gazed at his friend for a moment, then started to read from the Journal: '*One will make of thee a pillar of fire and consume thee. One will cause an awesome bleeding to drain thy body unto death. One will–*'

'Come off it, Ron, this isn't a Boris Karloff movie.'

Ron kept on reading: '*One will wrench the hair from thy head, pulling the scalp off thy skull. One will come and dismember thee. One will come as a hundred scorpions. One will command the insects of the air to devour thee. And One . . .*' He raised his eyes to Mark, '*. . . One will make thee to eat thy own excrement . . .*'

A lonely wind rose up from the desert, howling through the camp and causing the tent walls to buckle; Mark and Ron stared at one another for a long time, listening to the fine spray of sand pelt the Dacron. Then Mark waved a hand and started pulling off his socks.

'I have a bad feeling, Mark.'

Avoiding Ron's wide blue eyes, Mark reached again for the flask. His head was starting to throb.

'The Ramsgate expedition, Mark, all cut to pieces, skulls bashed in –'

'Cut it out.'

'What did the Pasha's men find when they entered that canyon, Mark? Not the victims of smallpox, that's for sure. The man who filled out those death certificates was so scared he didn't think straight. In his panic he wrote *cholera* for Sir Robert.'

The glass stopped halfway to Mark's lips. As the pulse in his temples intensified, his eyes glazed over for an instant. He was remembering something.

The strange woman crying on the boulder four nights before. The transparent woman.

'I don't like it here, Mark. This whole place gives me the creeps. And when I'm in the darkroom, with the lights out, I have this strong feeling that I'm not alone . . .'

Mark shot to his feet in annoyance. Snatching up his shirt and pulling it on, he said. 'That business with the *ghaffir* has unbalanced you, my friend. That and too much red wine. There's nothing here that isn't in our imagination.'

Then another memory intruded upon his mind. The image of old Samira crouched behind the mess tent jabbering a distorted form of Coptic, saying the number seven over and over again. 'One will go up in flame and one will suffer a bleeding,' she had chanted.

'Mark?'

His hands paused over the buttons of his shirt. How had Samira known of the seven curses? She had never seen the Journal . . .

'Mark are you all right?'

'Have a bastard of a headache. I'm going out for some air.'

'It's cold tonight, Mark, better take a–'

But his friend was gone.

Striding across the compound to the boundary of frail light and limitless night, Mark was surprised to encounter Alexis Halstead. And he was further stunned to find her clad only in a flimsy, transparent nightgown.

'Mrs Halstead!'

She turned in slow motion. Her red lips parted but no voice came out.

He approached her cautiously. 'Mrs Halstead? Are you all right?'

Although her eyes were on his face, they were unfocused, as though she were looking through him, at something on the other side. In the edge of camplight, the waves of her auburn hair looked like tongues of flame licking her white shoulders. 'I . . . I'm looking for something.'

'It's cold out here, Mrs Halstead. Come back inside.' Beneath the diaphanous pleats of her negligee, her large firm breasts, tipped with erect nipples, could be seen. Mark reached out and gently touched her arm, shocked to find her skin hot and feverish. 'Come with me, Mrs Halstead.'

'No . . . you don't understand. I have to talk to you.' She resisted, but feebly.

'We can talk inside. Please, Mrs Halstead.'

The glacial breath of the desert swirled about his bare feet, stinging his ankles. Mark shivered uncontrollably. 'You must be freezing!'

'It is summer . . .'

Tugging gently on her arm, Mark was finally able to lead her back from the edge of the night and into the compound. Although she walked willingly, slowly at his side, Alexis protested in a thin voice, 'Thou must know . . . How can I tell thee . . . We must talk . . .'

As they passed Yasmina's tent, the flap moved to one

158

side and the young woman, tying the sash of her robe, stepped out. 'What is wrong, Mark?'

'She's sleepwalking.'

Yasmina stepped around in front of Alexis and studied the blank, hypnotic stare. 'She has been having nightmares. I gave her some sleeping pills.'

Mark frowned at Yasmina. There was a fresh white bandage on her neck. 'What's that?'

'An insect sting. It is nothing.'

'Have the bugs gotten worse?'

'We must get Mrs Halstead inside. It is too cold out here for her.'

They guided Alexis between them and had no trouble getting her to bed. She lay down like a child and slowly closed her eyes.

When they turned to leave, after securing Alexis's mosquito netting to the corners of her bed, Mark happened to glance at Sanford, who was so deeply asleep he barely breathed.

On his satin pillow was a large, spreading red stain.

THIRTEEN

THE VALLEY was filled with the mournful *waloul* of the women of Hag Qandil. The high-pitched, unearthly wail which accompanied the *ghaffir's* body to his grave sailed out to the cliffs and down the ravines where it became amplified between the limestone walls.

Mark knew it made his workers nervous, but Abdul had assured him that none but his two assistants, whose silence could be counted on, knew the circumstances of the man's death. The *fellaheen* continued to toil as they had the preceding day gradually deepening the trenches.

Occasionally, Mark took a Land-Rover across the canyon floor to check on progress. He and Ron and Yasmina were the only ones at the site. The Halsteads had remained at the camp (Sanford had a cut that would not stop bleeding and Alexis had taken a sleeping pill to get through the day). Hazim was in his tent writing letters.

At noon they quit for the day, and when they arrived back at the camp, Mark found a dirty little boy waiting for them. About twelve-years-old, he was a dark round-faced child with one cloudy eye and several teeth missing. He scrambled to his feet when he saw the vehicles pull up.

'The *'umda* has sent me,' said the boy in rapid Arabic. 'I am from El Till and I was told to speak to the bearded one. Are you the son of David, sir?'

'I'm Dr Davison, what is it, child?'

'Iksander's mother needs the *shaykha*. It is her time.'

'Why does she need the *shaykha*? Are there no midwives?'

'Allah! Iksander's mother is in trouble! She screams for three days and no baby comes. The midwives cannot help. She needs the *shaykha*.'

Yasmina said, 'Did no one call the doctor from El Minya?'

The boy spat on the sand and dragged a sleeve across his mouth. 'Iksander's father will not let the government doctor look upon his wife's privacy. We must hurry, Dr Davison!'

Mark turned to Yasmina and said in English, 'Can Samira really help?'

'All the old witch will do is chant over her. Both mother and baby will be lost. I have seen it many times.'

Mark scratched his beard. 'What about you? You're a woman. They'll let you touch her. Can you do it?'

'I can try, Dr Davison, but these people will be unhappy. They do not trust doctors.'

He smiled. 'Maybe if you chanted while you delivered the baby . . .'

Yasmina returned the smile. 'I will have to get some things from my tent.'

As she hurried off, the boy looked after her uncertainly, so Mark said, 'Yasmina will help Iksander's mother.'

'Allah! I was sent to bring the *shaykha!* I will get the cane!'

As Mark was about to give the lad a reassuring pat on the head, a dark movement caught the corner of his eye. Turning, he found old Samira glowering at him from the doorway of the mess tent. Her expression was so intense he had to look away.

When Yasmina returned a moment later with her bag, the old *fellaha* screeched like a parrot and raised an arm, pointing a knobbled finger. 'You dress like a man and flaunt your immodesty and turn your back on your blood!' she cried in reedy Arabic. 'But strip you naked and you are still *fellaha!*'

Yasmina froze for an instant and could not move, then she felt Mark gently touch her elbow and heard him say,

161

'Let's go.'

The boy dashed ahead of them and scampered into the Land-Rover. He stood up on the back seat, leaning on the roll bar and surveying the camp like a conquering general. After a few words to Ron, Mark got behind the wheel and they drove off.

People stared at the couple as they followed the boy through the narrow streets, but no one spoke. Yasmina was eyed with suspicion and contempt as she walked at Mark's side in her khaki blouse and slacks, and an occasional insult was growled from a dark doorway.

As they neared the hovel, Mark heard a radio blare out the throaty voice of Om Khalsoum, Egypt's Judy Garland, and guessed they were not far from the *'umda's* white-washed house.

In fact, they were met by the *'umda* himself.

He stood outside the doorless opening of the mudbrick house, leaning on his staff and regarding the visitors with pursed lips. The boy dodged down a side alley and could be heard padding off in the distance.

'Good afternoon, *hagg*,' said Mark, raising his hand and smiling. 'Peace unto you and all of your household.'

'I asked for the *shaykha*.'

Mark was immediately on his guard. 'The *shaykha* works for me and cannot come. I have brought instead—'

'You have come alone, Dr Davison.'

Mark whistled between his teeth and felt Yasmina fall back a step. They heard, from inside the house, a woman softly moaning.

'You need help, *hagg*.'

'We need the *shaykha*.'

'I have brought a doctor.'

The *'umda* spat the same way the boy had, then said, 'You do not own the *shaykha*.'

Mark didn't know which aggravated him more, the stubborn old man or the unbearable heat; but as he was about to let fly his temper, a fourth person rounded the corner to join them.

He was a short, plumpish man wearing black trousers and a white shirt with the sleeves rolled up. He leaned against the dirty wall and eyed the visitors with jaded weariness. He said in English, 'They want their witchcraft.'

'Who are you?'

'I am Dr Rahman from the government health center at Minya.'

Mark noticed the young man was carrying a black bag similar to Yasmina's and appeared extremely tired. 'They sent for you?'

Dr Rahman shook his head. 'I was making one of my routine inspections. I cover thirty villages and come to El Till once a month. I found the woman down by the river, about to give birth, trying to eat mud. They believe it will give them a son, you know. I wanted to bring her back, but when I tried to touch her, the men threatened me with pitchforks. I talked to the midwife. The baby is breech. But the mother would sooner die than let me examine her, so what am I to do?'

'Miss Shukri here is a medical student, I thought she could help.'

Dr Rahman gave her a quick look over, appeared uninterested, then said, 'These *fellah* dogs deserve what they get.'

'Allah!' whispered Yasmina.

Dr Rahman pushed away from the wall and idly brushed off his arm. 'I do not pretend to be a savior. I am no longer idealistic. Whatever the dreams I had when I graduated from medical school all disappeared after one year with the government clinic. I am paid fifty pounds a month and I must see to two thousand peasants, all of whom mistrust and resent me. They are ignorant, and I must fight every time I wish to help them.'

'They have a right to mistrust you,' said Yasmina suddenly, surprising Mark. 'You will not even look at a sick *fellah* until he can pay you five pounds. And if his family cannot come up with the money, you will let him die.'

Dr Rahman shrugged. 'I have never done that, but I cannot blame my colleagues who do. The government overworks us and does not pay us enough. Why should we treat these animals for free when we have worked hard for our education and deserve to be paid like everyone else? The *fellah* will not give away his crop, why should I give away medical treatment?'

'Where is the woman?' asked Mark.

'Her husband will not allow you in. I know Habib, and I will tell you what kind of man he is. Last year he came to my clinic for treatment and I sent him away with some medicine. When I next saw him, he was still afflicted, so I asked him: Did you take the medicine I gave you? And Habib replied: "I could not, doctor, for the spoon is too large to enter the bottle!" '

Mark turned to the *'umda*. 'Let Miss Shukri see the woman. Perhaps she can help.'

'Habib is my nephew,' said the old man. 'His child will be of my family. I must be careful.'

'What do you want, *hagg?* Tea? Coca-Cola?'

Dr Rahman snorted. 'What a backward world this is! Now the doctor must pay the patient!'

But the *'umda* fell strangely silent, his tiny eyes fused into place. He seemed to be considering something. Then he said, 'We are praying to Allah for Iksander's mother.'

At that moment a figure appeared in the doorway, a grey haired *fellah* who was alternatively wringing his hands and wiping tears off his cheeks. He spoke to the *'umda* so rapidly that Mark couldn't catch it, but Yasmina, again surprising him, spoke up. 'I had a dream last night, *hagg,* in which an angel came to me. He told me that I would have a son today and there would be rejoicing in the valley. I put away the dream as nonsense but now I see it was an omen. Let me help Habib's wife, *hagg.*'

Mark waited outside the house for three hours, during which time many of the men of El Till came to sit with him. The aromas of tea and hashish mingled with the casual conversation of the peasants and the frequent screams of the woman inside. Several times, a veiled *fellaha* ran out of the house with an earthenware bowl of bloody fluid, to return a few minutes later with fresh water from the Nile. Crouched against the wall with his arms wrapped around his knees, Mark fervently wished the ordeal would end.

A few minutes before sunset, Yasmina emerged from the house with a slimy, screaming baby in her arms and the men jumped to their feet. She laid the child, which had a blue bead hung around its neck to ward off the Evil Eye, at Habib's feet, then she spread the cloth to show it was a boy. As the men shouted and laughed and clapped one another on the back a *fellaha* came out of the house bearing a little bag containing a few grains of corn and the umbilical cord, which she was going to plant in Habib's field. Inside the house, she had already buried the afterbirth.

Mark was shocked by Yasmina's appearance. Her usual dusty copper complexion had turned to an ashen pallor, and her eyes, usually lustrously black, were dull and flat. The front of her blouse was covered with blood.

'Are you all right?' he asked.

'Yes,' she sighed. 'But we must go now.'

They drove across the plain as the setting sun left darkness in its wake; the waist-high ruins of Akhet-Aton seemed to stretch and slither over the sand as the Land-Rover bounced by. Yasmina leaned against the door with her forehead against the window, her eyes closed.

'You were remarkable,' said Mark after a long silence. 'Did you really have that dream?'

'No.'

Guiding the four-wheel-drive over mounds and around jutting ruins, Mark chanced a look at the young woman

165

next to him. She was introspective, almost sullen. 'Yasmina, what's wrong? You saved the baby!'

'Yes, Mark, but the woman died.'

It was his favorite time of day – twilight. Supper was over, the major work was done, and the worst heat of the afternoon was turning into tropical balminess. Mark could distinguish the *fellaheen* in the Workmen's Village clapping their hands and singing; he heard the classical guitar of Doug Robertson coming from Ron's darkroom; a clatter of dishes and pans told him Samira was finishing up.

As he set his lighter to the Borkum Riff, Mark decided he would try approaching the old *fellaha* tonight on her way out of the camp. Maybe a special deal could be made: a *kadah* of hashish in return for her Coptic verb forms.

He puffed contentedly a few yards from the camp, sitting again on the broken ancient wall, then he realised he was about to have company. First the gardenias, then her voice. 'May I join you?'

Mark looked up and eyed her warily. 'Please do. How's your husband?'

'Sanford is all right now. In fact, he's doing calisthenics.'

Mark tried to think of something else to say. 'Are you enjoying yourself so far, Mrs Halstead?'

The pencil-brows arched. 'I didn't come on this trip for pleasure, Dr Davison. I came to find the tomb.'

'Still, it must be boring for you.'

She sat close to him, almost touching, but Mark could feel no warmth from her body. 'Dr Davison, how do you presume to know what would bore me?'

Frosty eyes and frosty voice. Mark almost shivered. 'I don't, but the majority of people who come along on expeditions and who aren't directly involved in the work generally lose interest after a while. We might be here for a long time, Mrs Halstead.'

'I'm patient.'

Mark recalled the way she had looked the night before, mesmerised, walking about in a flimsy nightgown. He searched for something to say, to fill the growing silence. 'I must say, Mrs Halstead, that certainly is ... *potent* perfume you're wearing.'

'I beg your pardon?'

'Your perfume. Jungle gardenia, isn't it?'

'Dr Davison, I am not wearing perfume. I never do, I don't believe in it. Perfume is artificial and unnatural. I don't even have a bottle in my possession.'

He gaped at her, speechless, then snapped his eyes away. Why she would lie about something so obvious as that pungent scent she doused herself with – well, it was none of his business.

'By the way, Dr Davison, I had a most interesting chat with Mr Domenikos this morning.'

He jerked his head around. 'What!'

'The abominable man came into the camp this morning while you were at the dig. He approached my husband with a deal.'

'For chrissake! How did he get past the *ghaffirs?* Never mind, I know the answer to that. And your husband?'

'Don't underestimate us, Dr Davison. There is nothing in the world Domenikos could offer us that would induce us to deal with him. My husband has no intention of allowing any of our finds into larcenous hands.'

'And you, Mrs Halstead?'

She focused her hard green eyes on him, and as she stared, it seemed to Mark the malachite irises softened a little to moss. He suddenly wished she weren't sitting so close.

Alexis abruptly looked away and, wincing slightly, brought a fingertip to her temple.

'Is something wrong?'

She didn't answer immediately, but bent her head as if concentrating, then her hand fell away and she turned back to Mark. She was smiling warmly. 'It's the sand. I'm not used to it . . .'

As Mark kept his eyes on her face, he wondered if he had imagined the softening in her voice.

'You think the tomb is in the canyon, don't you?'

'Yes, I do . . .' It was not his imagination that Alexis now leaned against him. 'Ramsgate said he moved his camp to be nearer to the tomb, and I'm pretty sure the black pit is the site of Ramsgate's camp.'

'What are the trenches for?'

'I'm expecting either to come upon the stela base, which contains the riddle telling us where the tomb is, or the stairs leading down to the tomb itself. Ramsgate said there were thirteen steps. Mrs Halstead . . .' Mark stood. 'You'll have to excuse me, but I have work to do.'

When she looked up at him, a ripple of confusion swept across her face, then Alexis said, 'It is late, Dr Davison, and my husband and I intend to join you at the dig in the morning.' She drew herself up and stood unsteadily. 'I . . . haven't been sleeping well . . .'

Mark watched her walk across the sand and enter her tent, then he started toward his own tent.

When he reached the edge of the circle of light cast by the lanterns, Mark suddenly knew he was not alone. He stopped where he was and listened. The camp was silent. Ron's darkroom was still and deserted, and at one point during his conversation with Alexis, old Samira had left the mess tent. Twilight had given way to full night; everyone slept.

Mark turned around and saw a woman standing a few yards from him, watching him. He recognised her; he had seen her twice before. This time, however, as he cautiously approached her, the woman did not disappear.

When he was ten feet from her, she slowly lifted her hand and uttered a single word.

Mark tilted his head. 'What?'

She repeated it.

'I don't understand you. Who are you?'

A pause preceded her reply, then, when she answered,

it was in words Mark could not grasp. While she spoke, he saw she wore the same flowing white gown as before – weeping over the boulder and watching him from the shadows – so that he wondered if he was dreaming again. He also noticed, as the woman repeated the same phrase over and over again, that although her lips moved, the sound of her voice came from inside his head. It was a gentle whisper against his brain; a totally foreign language.

'Who are you?' he said again, feeling the throb of a headache start at his temples.

She spoke again, patiently, the same soft sweet whisper inside his mind.

Then Mark noticed that her feet were not touching the ground and that she rose and fell slightly, as if floating on an invisible tide.

'Dr Davison!'

He spun around.

'Davison, there you are!' Sanford Halstead was marching over the cold sand. 'I'm glad you're still up, I need to talk to you. The damndest thing has happened!'

Mark blinked dumbly at the man. Feeling the back of his neck prickle, he knew without turning around that the woman was no longer there.

FOURTEEN

MARK KEPT shifting his weight on the seat in an effort to maintain his attention. Hazim was going on about a dig in the Delta that had produced an unexpected sun temple, and Mark was having difficulty in appearing interested.

It was ten o'clock and the teams were well into the trenches. Five long and straight ditches now scored the canyon floor, while a mound of excavated rubble gradually rose up a narrow gorge. At the head of each trench stood a wooden crate ready to take anything of interest found in the rocking screens – so far the crates were empty.

Ron had his sleeves rolled up and was methodically photographing the trenches. The Halsteads sat on wooden chairs in the shade of the cliff wall sipping cold tea from a Thermos. Yasmina was treating a man for a scorpion sting. Mark was acutely aware of the sun beating down on the roof of the Land-Rover.

'How long do you intend to work in this canyon, Dr Davison?'

Mark frowned slightly at Hazim. 'I beg your pardon?'

'Have you set a deadline yet?'

'Uh . . . no.' Mark was trying to think of what he had read about the effects of too much sun as a cause of hallucinations. That transparent woman again last night . . .

'If you will excuse me, Dr Davison, I will take a look and see what progress has been made.'

Mark felt the vehicle dip a little as the young man swung to the ground. A moment later he saw Yasmina heading

170

back toward the Land-Rovers. When she climbed in next to him, knocking dust off her legs, Mark suddenly found his concentration had returned.

'How is he?'

'The man will be all right. I was able to tie off his arm with a tourniquet in time and give him an injection of antivenin. However, he cannot work for a few days.'

'We've been lucky so far. Not many injuries.'

Yasmina regarded him quizzically, opened her mouth to say something, then, changing her mind, remained silent.

The two sat quietly for some time, watching the teams of workers through the windshield, then Mark turned to her and said, 'What's wrong with your arm?'

Yasmina laid a hand over her bandaged wrist. 'I have another insect bite. It will not heal.'

'They have a peculiar fondness for you.'

'Yes.'

'I know I've already said it, but I was really impressed with you yesterday. They resented you in that village.'

'Dr Davison, they *hated* me.'

'So why did you fight to help them?'

Her shrug was unconvincing.

'Yesterday you called me Mark.'

She said nothing.

Mark studied her for a moment, enjoying her nearness, then said, 'That Dr Rahman wasn't much help.'

'In a way, I cannot blame him. His is a futile and thankless job. Many times, after a *fellah* is cured, he will re-infect himself without knowing it. Even though he is told the mud contains diseases, he will still walk barefoot through it and die at an early age. The government doctors must bang their heads against a wall of ignorance. For every step forward they take, they are pushed back two.'

Mark watched her face as she spoke, thinking how lovely she was, how pleasurable to be with. 'I'm glad you joined us. You're going to make a terrific doctor.'

'Thank you.'

Mark considered something for a moment, then said, 'May I ask you a personal question?'

She paused. 'Yes.'

'Yesterday, what did the old woman mean when she said you were *fellaha?*'

Yasmina toyed with the edges of her bandage, her skin dark against the white gauze. Her voice was soft, almost a whisper. 'Because I *am fellaha.* I was born in a very small village up the Nile and I grew up there. I will not tell you its name, for it is smaller even than El Till. I was my father's only child and he wished I were a son, so he taught me to read and write and work with numbers. The *'umda* of my village saw that I was not as dull as other children and arranged for me to travel each day to a missionary school near Aswan. When my father and the *'umda* heard from the sisters that I was their brightest pupil, my father brought me to the attention of the *mudir* of our province. I was fourteen then, and I was very smart with books, but not so smart with . . . people.'

Yasmina's head was bowed as she spoke; she seemed to have forgotten Mark was there. 'The *mudir* told me about Cairo and its wonderful schools, and he told me that, if I *earned* it, I could go to such a school and become one of the learned people of my village. A *shaykha,* perhaps. Of course, I wanted these things. He made an arrangement with my father. I stayed with the *mudir* for one year.'

Her slender brown fingers picked at the frayed bandage. 'After that time, the obligations were fulfilled and the *mudir* made good his promise. I was sent to Cairo and my education was paid for.'

Yasmina raised her head and gazed boldly at Mark. 'My father is dead now and I have no family. Even the fat old *mudir* is gone, no one is left to remember those days. But I do. I fought for what I have, just as the government doctors must fight for each piastre. But my enemy is a different one. I want to release the *fellaheen* from their bonds.'

When her voice died away, an awkward silence followed in which Mark found himself captivated by her liquid eyes. And then he felt a sudden impulse, a basic urge that he had not experienced since his first days with Nancy seven years before.

Sounds of pickaxes striking rock enabled him to break away. 'Listen,' he said, clearing his throat, 'before anyone comes back, I want to discuss something with you. It's Mr Halstead, he has a problem.'

She listened in silence while Mark related the talk he had had with Halstead the previous night. He ended with: 'He doesn't want to go to Minya to see a doctor and he won't let you examine him.'

'What did he think you could do for him?'

'Talk to you about it. He was hoping you could give him something for it.'

'He needs to be examined. I cannot give him medication without knowing the cause of his problem. Mr Halstead says he has blood in his urine. That is only a symptom. Possibly it is a bladder infection, but you say there is no pain or burning. Possibly then it is a kidney infection or a stone. It could have been brought on by so much running every day. He might need antibiotics, or even surgery. A man of his age can develop any number of urinary problems. If he will not let me examine him then he must see a specialist in Cairo.'

'That's what I told him but he refuses to leave the dig.'

'What will he do?'

'He said if you can't give him something for it, he'll just wait and see if it goes away. If not, or if it gets worse, he wants a doctor flown from Cairo—'

'*Yahoo!*'

Mark and Yasmina looked up and saw Ron waving his red bandana over his head. There was a commotion at the end of the trench farthest from the Land-Rovers, and Mark could see Abdul in the sand on his hands and knees peering over the edge.

The Halsteads were on their feet and running, along with Hazim; the *fellaheen* straightened up from their labor and watched.

By the time Mark and Yasmina crossed the canyon floor, Ron had cleared away the top of a buried limestone fragment. It measured twenty-four inches by three inches and rose about an inch above the floor of the trench. Its top was rough, broken; how far down it went, no one could guess. The stone would not move beneath Mark's hand.

'It's the stela base!' said Ron, reaching for his camera.

Mark stood up and brushed off his hands. 'Ron, you and I will excavate this fragment. Abdul, keep the teams working just as they are.'

'Yes, *effendi*.'

'We'll need brushes and knives, a trowel, spikes for flags, two rocking screens, a line level–' He turned to Yasmina and placed a hand on her arm. 'I want you to take over the field book and do the logging for me, all right? Oh, and Abdul,' Mark spoke so rapidly that he missed the look of sudden displeasure that flashed in the foreman's eyes. 'I'll need a slate board and heavy twine. Rig up a sunshade, we'll be working through the afternoon. And post an armed *ghaffir* on this rock right now!'

'It's no fucking use, man!'

Mark did not look up from his work. Although his back ached beyond endurance and the canvas did little to allay the heat, and although his friend was angrily kicking up dirt with his boots, Mark remained intent upon his labor. In two hours he had cleared six inches of the stone.

'I don't know what it is!' continued Ron, glaring at the proofsheet in his hand. 'Fogged again!'

'Get another camera.'

'Look!' Ron jumped down into the trench next to Mark. 'These were taken just before the stone was found. Every single one perfect. And here, twelve shots later, a

174

wide-angle of the canyon, absolutely perfect. But these twelve, in the middle of the roll, Mark, fogged. Just the pictures of the stone. I can't figure it!'

'Your film must have gotten damaged in shipping.'

'No way. It wouldn't be this clearly defined. One negative sharp and clear, the next one in line totally blank.'

Mark finally rested back on his heels and dragged a sleeve across his forehead. His eyebrows and beard glistened with sweat. 'Ron, you're the photographer. Me, I'm just an artichoke picker, okay? Look here, you haven't seen the progress I've made.'

Ron got down to his knees. On the face of the large flat stone, sticking six inches out of the sand, were horizontal rows of distinctly carved hieroglyphics.

'Jaysus,' he whispered, 'this really is it!'

'No doubt about it. Read here.' Mark tapped the farthest right-hand column with the tip of a paint brush.

'*The Criminal of Akhet-Aton.* God . . .'

'I don't know how far down this thing goes, but we should soon be reading the riddle to the whereabouts of the tomb. Then we can decide for ourselves if Ramsgate made a mistake or not.'

Ron licked his lips. 'I can't believe it . . .' He pushed back and settled down on his buttocks. Now he noticed the others sitting in the shade of Abdul's flapping tarpaulin. Yasmina, cross-legged in the sand, was writing a minute by minute record of the work in progress. Sanford and Alexis Halstead, sitting like royalty on their folding wooden chairs, might have been watching a tennis match – their faces expressionless. Hazim was writing down his own notes, and Abdul Rageb stood serenely next to the armed *ghaffir*. The only sound in the canyon was the hot wind sweeping down from the plateau high overhead. The *fellaheen* had been returned to the Workmen's Village.

'Ron, we'll need pictures. Good, sharp clear ones. If this stela was carved out of living rock we won't be able to move it. The only way we can study the inscription is from

175

photographs.'

Ron's head bobbed up and down. 'Okay, I brought fresh film that was packed in lead-lined bags. I'll try a few experiments with the cameras, too. But clear and distinct, that won't be easy. The characters aren't more than a sixteenth of an inch in relief. Contrast will be nil. Let's see, if I get some sun coming in from this angle . . .'

Mark's back hurt so badly he thought he would never straighten up again, but it was a good pain. He had felt it before, crouching for hours over a buried artefact, so immersed in concentration that he forgot his body. Now, sitting in the mess tent with his feet up and his dinner plate licked clean, Mark savored the aches and pains because of what they stood for.

He estimated that half the stela had been exposed.

'Sorry about the pictures,' said Ron.

Mark waved a hand and picked up his cup of wine. 'Don't sweat it. We'll work on that tomorrow. I only hope the lower-half is as well preserved as what we've uncovered so far. If it is, we should have no difficulty in reading the message.'

'What I can't figure is why a stela that unique and valuable was never removed by later Egyptologists.'

'No mystery, my friend, they never found it. The Pasha's order quarantined that area for several decades. In that time, no one dared enter the canyon, and so the drifting sand buried the stela and Ramsgate's memory faded.'

'And the Journal?'

'Like I said the other night, maybe a *fellah* snuck it out before the soldiers arrived. Who knows? It's not important.'

Ron stared darkly into his wine. He and Mark were alone in the tent, except for Samira who shuffled silently in her cooking corner like an arthritic raven. 'I have a bad feeling about my pictures, Mark.'

'What do you mean?'

'In Ramsgate's Journal, he says Sir Robert was having trouble with his "camera box". When the plate was developed it came out black. Then he used a flash of magnesium powder and took a shot of Ramsgate and his wife. The resulting picture, he says, exhibited a curious flaw. An unexplainable shadow, like a column of smoke, appears next to Amanda. Sound familiar?'

Mark did not answer. He was recalling another passage in the Journal: *My Amanda has taken to sleepwalking. She is plagued by strange nightmares and prattles in an incomprehensible tongue. When she is lucid and seemingly in touch with reality, she claims to have seen the spectre of a woman dressed in glowing white robes walking through the camp...*

'Let's get some sleep,' Mark said abruptly. 'Tomorrow should be D-Day.'

The night had grown cold during their talk; the stars covered the sky like a spray of shattered ice. Mark and Ron shivered as they crossed the compound.

'It's a wonder this country doesn't crack with these rapid temperature changes! Where are you going, Ron?'

'To the darkroom for a while. Got to figure out what's happening to my film.'

'Easy on the wine, my friend,' murmured Mark, watching Ron walk away.

As he was about to step into his tent, Mark felt a cold tendril snake down his back. Reflexively his shoulder-blades contracted, as if someone had dropped an ice cube down his shirt, and he shivered; he held himself rigid, one hand still poised on the tent flap. The pulse in his temples started to throb.

Then he heard it.

The flat thuck of heavy footfall.

It came from beyond the circle of camp light, somewhere in the inky region behind his tent, a dull, rhythmic *plock-plock*. A sickening sound, like the plodding steps of a drugged animal.

177

It made the back of his neck crawl. He wanted to look and yet he dared not; his fingers involuntarily curled around the Dacron, clutching at the tent to keep himself from falling.

Plock-plock. Plock-plock.

A *fellah* in a hash stupor. But no, this sounded much heavier, it had the weight of a horse. The Greek's camel, then. The bastard was coming back to bargain some more.

Mark started to tremble. He felt half-moons of sweat sprout under his armpits. That was no camel; it was no quadruped. Whatever it was that was steadily thumping toward him was upright on two feet –

A wind rushed up, frigid and chilling to the bone, and whistled through his tent. The suspended lanterns swayed, causing shadows to sashay in and out of the compound. Mark felt an awesome fear creep through his bowels. His head throbbed painfully.

Plock-plock. Louder, closer. *Plock-plock.*

He was overcome with dread and anguish, a sudden, inexplicable need to fall to his knees and sob, an emptying of his soul; whatever was coming toward him from the depths of the night was *evil* . . .

And then, all of a sudden, a queer glow. Before him, he saw his silhouette sharply etched on the wall of the tent. The incandescence, illuminating the compound with a preternatural light, was behind him, not coming from the direction of the approaching evil. Then the wind dropped and the night fell abnormally still and quiet.

The *plock-plock* ceased.

Mark turned awkwardly, with great difficulty, as if he were swathed in a layer of cotton. He turned his back on the tent, on the horror at the edge of darkness, and beheld the shimmering vision at the center of the compound.

She appeared exactly as she had the previous three times: milky, luminescent.

She beheld him with sorrowful, oriental eyes; her berry-red lips moved in slow motion. And as Mark stared in stupefaction across the glacial night, he heard once again, or rather *felt,* the soft tickle of her voice against his brain.

'*Entek setemet er anxui-k.*'

Mark became aware that perspiration drenched his shirt; the arctic air turned the sweat to ice.

'*Sexem-a em utu arit er-a tep ta.*'

His breathing slowed; a tremor took hold of his body. Staring transfixed, Mark suddenly had no control over himself, he could no longer do anything of his own will.

The woman's lips moved and his mind heard a dreamlike murmur: '*Un-na! Nima tra tu entek? Nuk ua em ten. Nima enti hena-k?*'

Mark opened his mouth but his tongue was not his to command.

'*Nima tra tu entek?*'

His breath came out slowly, painfully. Mark thought in stunned horror: I almost know! I almost know!

'*Nima tra tu entek?*'

The words are familiar. I can almost—

'*Nima tra tu entek?*'

He trembled violently now and his shirt was soaked through. His eyes were fixed upon the woman's lips. They moved, and he heard: '*Nima tra tu entek?*'

Yes! I almost understand! Almost—

Another voice suddenly filled his head; it crashed through his ears and nearly knocked him off his feet. The woman in white vanished and lights suddenly flooded the compound. Mark brought a hand up to his eyes.

Someone was screaming.

He ran with the others to Yasmina's tent; her cries of terror splintered the night. Mark and Ron ripped up the outer flap, then hurriedly unzipped the inner netting. Inside, the tent was dark, but they heard Yasmina thrashing about and screaming for help.

When he dashed inside, Mark felt something hit his face. It was as if someone had thrown a handful of gravel at him. A deafening buzz filled the air; a thousand pinpricks attacked his bare arms.

Through the darkness Ron fumbled for the light, and when it came on, he cried out. Yasmina's tent was alive with swarms of insects, thick and droning, cramming the air and crawling over every surface, and at the center, in a thin nightdress, flailing her arms and screaming, was Yasmina.

They were all over her skin, in her hair, covering her face like a black mask: mosquitoes, wasps, flies, locusts. Droning, humming, stinging.

Mark seized her around the waist and dragged her out of the tent. Gaping back inside at the solid cloud of insects he saw Ron fight his way out, shouting and waving his arms. Everyone else stood and looked on in dumbfoundment as Mark held the crying young woman in his arms.

He brushed them off her and the insects fell away, dropping on to the sand and then flying off into the night. Mark listened in horror to the din of thousands of insects, then he turned to Abdul and said, 'Get them out of there! Get that tent cleared!'

'Yes, *effendi.*' The tall Arab kept his face expressionless, but his eyes were suddenly charged with hostility.

'Ron, you and I'll sleep in the work tent tonight. Yasmina can have my bed.'

Her sobbing subsided but she continued to cling to him. In her nightgown, Yasmina seemed very small and vulnerable in his arms, like a little girl. Her face was buried against his chest, and as he continued to hold her, Mark could feel the countless welts and bites on her arms and back.

When he finally forced himself to look again into the tent, the insects were gone.

The heat rose up from the sand in waves, distorting the cliffs on the other side; and pools of mercury, disappearing when neared, spotted the canyon floor. Everyone's attention was at the same time fixed and waning; they did not want to leave the dig, but they were weary of waiting.

Mark, after five hours of work, was clearing away the last line of hieroglyphics.

His own concentration was as refracted as his companions'; the horror of Yasmina's attack had stayed with him, while at the same time he could not get the woman in white out of his mind. He had slept on and off most of the night on the floor of the work tent, waking up out of nightmares to Ron's relaxed breathing. Even now, troweling away the last of the dirt to reveal the stone's cryptic message, Mark felt a fearful apprehension, like a premonition, take command of his soul.

Yasmina had insisted upon coming to the site this morning; she sat above him now, writing in the log book with bandaged fingers. Her face, swollen at dawn, was starting to look better; all that remained of last night's catastrophe were a few nicks and bites.

Ron was sitting next to her, his knees drawn up to his chest, his face darkly preoccupied. He was watching a lizard dig in the sand for scorpions, but he was thinking of his futile efforts to produce one single photograph of the stela.

Alexis Halstead sat apart from the others, sitting on the sand with a queer expression on her face: her head was tilted to one side as if she were listening to a whisper in the wind.

Her husband, next to her, was not his usual self this morning: he had had the nightmare again – a towering man made of gold standing at the foot of his cot, disembodied eyes blazing in the night, and a voice that came from everywhere at once: *Na-khempur, na-khempur* . . .

Hazim al-Sheikhly was the only one thoroughly embroiled in Mark's progress. With the clearing of each hieroglyph, he was able to put out of his mind memories of his own recurring nightmare . . . of being seduced by the scorpion-headed woman – and concentrate on the sensational find that was going to give him a big promotion in the ministry.

Mark dropped the trowel, wiped his face and neck with a cloth, then sat back with a groan. 'Well, that's it. The final message. The whereabouts of the tomb . . .'

FIFTEEN

'WHEN AMON-RA traveleth downstream, the Criminal lieth beneath, to be provided with the Eye of Isis.'

'Are you sure?'

Mark threw down his pencil with a scowl. 'Ron and I have gone over it microscopically. That's what it says.'

'You must be wrong.'

'Mr Halstead, my field of expertise is the language of the ancient Egyptians. I can read hieroglyphics as easily as I can English. I know my stuff.'

'But it doesn't make sense!'

'You're telling me!'

Hazim cleared his throat and said quietly, 'Our tempers are shortening, gentlemen. It is not for the good of the expedition that we argue. Perhaps we should set aside the inscription for–'

'We haven't the time,' said Halstead. 'The days are getting hotter and more unbearable. Next month is Ramadan. We have to find that tomb now.'

Mark ran his eyes over the large sheet of paper spread before him; it was as near a perfect replica of the stela as he had been able to draw. Since Ron had had no success in photographing the stela, Mark had resorted to placing a butcher paper over the stone and rubbing it with charcoal. It was a process he had used in the past to study wall reliefs when the contrast was too poor for photography to pick up the finer details. He had then copied the tracing on to a fresh sheet for study, and had come to dinner with the result.

No one was pleased with it.

'Are you sure, Dr Davison, that there is nothing in the rest of the inscription?'

He spread out his hands. 'I read it to you. A warning to keep away, the names of these seven gods, a few hocus-pocus incantations and then, at the bottom, this riddle.'

'You say that Amon-Ra refers to the sun and that downstream means north.'

'Yes, Mr Halstead.'

'Well, there's an error right there. Either it isn't Amon-Ra or it isn't downstream.'

Mark sighed and shook his head. 'It is and it is, Mr Halstead. Believe me, I'm as frustrated as you.'

Ron picked up his cup, drank it down, then refilled it from the wine bottle he had brought to the table. 'What I can't figure is the Eye of Isis. How is the Criminal to be provided with it, and why?'

Mark turned his attention to the lower row of hiero-glyphics, staring at the characters in question. There was, distinctly, the tall triangular symbol which was pro-nounced *sept* and which was the verb *to be provided with*, followed by the seated figure of Isis and the *udjat,* eye.

'And the Dog,' said Halstead. 'It doesn't say anything about a dog?'

'Not by any stretch of the imagination.'

'Dr Davison.' Halstead placed his palms on the table. He was nervous, jittery. 'Neville Ramsgate said he looked up and saw, *where his eyes had alit a hundred times,* the Dog. He then said how childishly simple the answer to the puzzle was. Why can't you figure it out?'

'Why can't you, Mr Halstead?'

'Dammit, Davison, you're the Egyptologist!'

Mark hid his hands beneath the table and clenched his fists as hard as he could. Calmly and evenly he said, 'Abdul has hired two women from Hag Qandil to do our washing. They will be here in the morning. You will want to gather all your dirty laundry together and have it ready for them before we leave for the canyon. If you have any special garments, Mrs Halstead, delicate things perhaps . . . Mrs Halstead?'

Alexis, who had been staring directly at him, blinked and said, 'What?'

After he had repeated himself, Alexis frowned a little and said, 'Oh yes, I have . . . some things . . .'

Mark stood up and rolled the sheet into a tube. As the others slowly got to their feet, he said, 'Until we can decipher this riddle, we'll go back to trench digging. None of you have to come to the site if you don't want–'

'We will be there, Dr Davison.' Sanford Halstead took hold of his wife's elbow and led her to the door of the tent where he paused to murmur something in her ear. But Alexis seemed not to hear, her expression remained distant; she nodded mechanically and stepped out into the sunshine.

When Halstead turned around and came back, limping slightly, Mark was surprised. He was further surprised when Halstead said in a tone so carefully off-handed that it came out grave, 'Davison, I wonder if you can tell me something. I . . . I overheard a word the other day and I was wondering what it means.'

'Let's hear it.'

'*Na-khempur.*'

Mark pursed his lips, thought a moment, then turned to Ron who was getting up to leave. 'You know what *na-khempur* means?'

Ron shook his head.

'Is it . . .' said Halstead hesitantly. 'Is it modern or ancient?'

Mark's eyebrows shot up. 'Well, if you overheard someone say it recently, then it must be modern. But now that you mention it, it does sound like ancient Egyptian.'

'But you don't know what it means.'

'Haven't a clue, sorry.'

'Never mind. It wasn't important.' Halstead turned on his heel and marched out.

Hazim then came up to Mark and said quietly, 'I think it

185

wisest I do not yet contact the ministry. I will wait until the tomb itself is found, you understand.'

Mark nodded wearily.

Instead of leaving, the young man hovered by him for a second and appeared to be mentally debating something. Then Hazim said in a lowered voice, 'Dr Davison, have you or any of the others had problems with scorpions?'

'No, not at all. Have you?'

'Oh, a little. One or two. What can you recommend against them?'

'Well, first examine your tent for holes, then make sure your door is always sealed. It might also be a good idea to stand the feet of your bed in cans of Kerosene. Talk to Abdul about it.'

'Yes, yes. Thank you.' Distracted, Hazim hurried out of the tent. Ron followed behind, wine bottle in hand, muttering something about taking a sledgehammer to his cameras, so that Mark was left alone in the tent with Yasmina and the old *fellaha*.

It was late for Samira to still be here; dinner had long since ended, the cooking fires were out and the dishes put away. Yet she remained, fussing over something unseen in her dark corner.

Mark took a long look at Yasmina. Her hands and arms were still swathed in gauze; her neck and face were spotted with tiny red welts. He recalled how it had felt to hold her in his arms. 'How do you feel?' he asked gently.

'I am all right.'

They had not talked of the insect attack since the night before. Now Yasmina said softly, 'I do not know what happened. I awoke suddenly and the air was full of . . .' Her voice died.

Mark rested a hand on her shoulder. 'It won't happen again. Abdul went over your tent inch by inch. There's no way any bugs can get in.' He paused. Something about his words rang in his ear like a flat note. 'Anyway, the men moved your tent so that it's right next to mine. It was probably originally pitched over something the insects wanted to get at. And I had Abdul set insecticide around the openings. You'll be all right now.'

Her eyes were deep; a man could drown in them. 'Thank you,' she whispered, and left the tent.

As Mark fumbled in his shirt pocket for the rubber band to put around the rolled up paper, he watched the old black-robed woman go through mechanical motions in the corner. Tapping the rolled sheet against his open palm, Mark considered again the vision that had filled his mind all day, obsessing him, distracting him from his scientific pursuit. The woman in white . . .

'Old woman,' he said in Arabic.

She seemed not to hear, her hands fluttering over an unseen task.

'*Shaykha,* I want to talk to you.'

She did not turn around.

'You speak Coptic, *shaykha.* Possibly a dialect I am unfamiliar with. I would like to learn it.'

No response.

'If you wish payment, you can have it. All the tea you want.'

Her back remained annoyingly turned to him. Mark thought for a moment, then said, '*Nima tra tu entek?*'

Samira spun around, her eyes wide, startled.

'So, you *can* hear me,' he said in Arabic.

She pressed her thin lips into a line, then said in a wary voice. 'Where have you heard those words, master?'

'Are they Coptic?'

'No, it is the old tongue.'

'Is Coptic not the old tongue?'

'Older, master, it is the tongue of the *qadim.*'

Mark raised his eyebrows. *Qadim,* the ancients. The little eyes of the *fellaha* seemed to burn into his brain. 'What do the words mean?'

Samira folded her hands into the voluminous sleeves of her robe and regarded him skeptically. 'The words mean: *Who art thou.*'

'Who art thou . . . Of course, now I remember . . .'

187

Her eyes, like black diamonds, shifted back and forth across his face. 'Where did you hear those words, master?'

He frowned at her. 'I . . . in a dream.'

The fire behind her eyes flared. 'You have seen! It has begun! It has begun!'

'What are you talking about?'

A withered brown hand shot out and attached itself to his wrist with alarming strength. 'You must find the tomb, master, and you must find it soon, before we are all destroyed!'

Mark shook off her hand and laughed nervously. 'What are you babbling about?'

'The demons, master, they will destroy you and your friends, each in the manner ascribed to him. But once you have found the tomb and you have done what you have to do, the demons will go away . . .'

She lowered her voice to a coarse whisper and inclined herself toward Mark; the foul odor from her body made him flinch. 'The Seven must destroy you, master, for so it was ordained. Each of you will meet a terrible end. Unless you find the tomb and do what you must, for within it lies your salvation. But you must hurry!' Her eyes blazed like black flames. 'In the end it will be up to you, master. There will be the struggle, the final battle. Good and evil will fight for possession of you, and you must recognise that which is good and wage the final war against that which is evil '

'You're talking nonsense–'

'*Na-khempur!*'

'What?'

'The arrogant one,' she said contemptuously. 'He asked you the meaning of the word.'

'Do you know it?'

'It is indeed ancient, master. It belongs to the language of the gods who once walked the Nile Valley. It is older than the written word, older even than time.'

'What does *na-khempur* mean?'

'It means, master, to bleed . . .'

Mark stared at her for a long moment, suddenly aware of the beat of his heart against his ribs. 'He . . . he misunderstood. Mr Halstead only heard something that sounded like that . . '

Samira's lips ruminated over toothless gums. Her eyes were full of disdain. 'Find the tomb, master, before it is too late.'

As the Land-Rover slowed and the dust began to settle, Mark saw Abdul Rageb hurrying over the sand toward him. In all the years he had known the ascetic Arab, Mark had never seen him move so quickly.

'*Effendi,*' said Abdul hurriedly, his copper complexion a queer shade of ocher. 'Something has happened. You must keep the others away.'

Mark jumped down from the vehicle and peered over his foreman's shoulder at the stela site. A few *fellaheen* milled around the trench. 'Where are the teams?'

'I have sent them away, *effendi*. I have told them it is an American holiday.'

'Why?'

'You will see. Come with me, but do not let the others follow.'

Mark turned to Ron, who was climbing down from the second Land-Rover, and said when he came close, 'Keep everyone here. Abdul says there's trouble. Make up an excuse.'

Mark trudged over the sand behind Abdul, annoyed that the trenches were unattended, and was about to criticise the Arab when they reached the far end of the trench. It took a moment for the sight to register, then Mark had to reach out to his foreman for support.

The *ghaffir* assigned to guard the stela during the night was lying in the trench in two halves; he had been sliced through at the waist.

'Oh my god, Abdul . . .'

'I was the first to find him, *effendi*, therefore I was able to return the workers to the camp. Only these men know and their silence can be trusted.'

Mark barely saw the ashen, frightened faces of his foreman's assistants; he could not take his eyes away from the *ghaffir*. 'Why, Abdul?' he heard himself ask from far away. 'Why was it done?'

'I do not know, *effendi*. Nothing has been touched. The stela is as we left it yesterday.'

Mark was finally able to look up. He had never seen Abdul so shaken. 'Abdul, there's a feud going on here.'

'It would seem so, *effendi*.'

When Mark heard the approach of footsteps, he turned around too late. Halstead was already clutching his stomach and Alexis was gaping wide-eyed into the trench. 'I couldn't stop them, Mark,' said Ron. 'They insisted on seeing what the trouble was . . .' His blue eyes focused on the corpse and froze there.

Mark caught sight of dark movements on the sand, and when he looked up, saw vultures circling overhead. 'Abdul, you and your men get this body out of here! Dammit! The trench is smeared with blood!'

'I can take care of that, *effendi*.'

'Oh Jesus!' he shouted suddenly, feeling anger surge through him. 'I want this stopped! Who did it, Abdul?'

'My men say it is none of our workers. They say no one left the Workmen's Village last night.'

'They could have sneaked out.'

'My men are certain, *effendi*. They know their teams. They say there is no feud among them.'

'There has to be! That other one, the first *ghaffir*, you said he was unpopular. He had insulted another man's wife.'

'Yes, *effendi*, but I did not refer to any of the workers. These are *ghaffirs*, they do not mingle with the laborers.'

'Was this done by someone in the villages?'

'Possibly, *effendi*.'

Mark tried not to look into the trench again, but he could not help himself. More shocking than the spilled intestines and pools of blood was the expression on the dead man's face. His mouth and eyes were stretched open in a silent scream; the look was one of pure terror. 'All right, no work today. Clean this up as fast as you can, I'm going to El Till.'

He left the Halsteads in Yasmina's care and took Ron and Hazim with him. Mark handled the Land-Rover recklessly, slamming over boulders and mounds in a fury he had rarely felt. Before leaving the camp he had seen the *shaykha* huddled in a shadow, her raven's eyes glaring at him almost accusingly. And now, caroming in and out of the ruins of the ancient city, one sentence from Ramsgate's Journal echoed in his mind like the tolling of a great bell: *Mohammed's trusted assistant, God take him, was found sliced in two halves . . .*

When they reached the edge of the village and could go no farther by car, the three men got out and marched through the narrow streets in single file. Most of the houses were empty and the small children usually seen playing in the dirt were absent. Up ahead, they heard singing.

'What's going on?' asked Ron.

Coming to an alley, they found a crowd of people running behind a donkey-drawn cart laden with furniture. They were clapping their hands and shouting praises.

'It is a wedding,' said Hazim.

The three followed the crowd behind the donkey cart and presently came to a halt before a mudbrick house. Young men in skull caps and *galabeyahs* choked its doorway; they were clicking their tongues and chanting ribald love songs. Mark pushed his way forward and could see preparations for a peasant feast in the dim interior. A young *fellah*, holding a handkerchief up to his face and pretending to be bashful, was being clapped on the back by his friends. His hands were dyed with henna and he wore a new *galabeyah*.

191

Mark forced his way through the group, looking for the *'umda*. When he came out a moment later, he said, 'Let's find the bride's house.'

They wound through the village's dirty little streets, following the shrill cries of women. Finding the house, they found also all the women and children of the village preparing the young girl for her wedding night. She had already received the one bath she would have in her life; now her friends were reddening her hands and feet with henna and pinching her thighs for good luck. When gunshots were heard in the distance, red and white veils were draped over the girl's head and her friends sprinkled her with salt.

Mark and Ron and Hazim stepped away from the crowd and saw, threading its way down the narrow street, the groom's procession, headed by the donkey cart. Among the men was the *'umda*.

'There he is,' murmured Ron.

'Wait. Not yet.'

They dissolved into the shadows so not to be seen; the groom and his friends passed into the tiny house, leaving a path for the *'umda*. While the rest of the villagers clustered about the outside, the close friends and relatives were on hand for the virginity test. It was done quickly and primitively; the bride cried out in pain and blood flowed. Everyone cheered, honor was safe. Now the feasting would begin.

'It's not going to be easy,' said Ron as they stepped away from the wall.

'I don't care. I'm going to talk to the old man now whether he likes it or not.'

To Mark's surprise, as he was about to force his way through the throng, the peasants fell back and the *'umda* emerged from the house. As the mob closed behind him, he came up to the three men and gave them his best smile.

'You honor us today. Come join in the celebration.'

'We have to talk, *hagg*.'

The smile faded. 'We have nothing to talk about, Dr

Davison. The man came from El Hawata. Go speak to the *'umda* of El Hawata.'

Mark's brows shot up. 'You know about it?'

'There is nothing in this valley I do not know.'

'Then you know who killed the man.'

The old face darkened. 'That is one thing I do not know.'

'Listen, *hagg*–'

'Dr Davison, there is no feud. Our villages have been at peace for years and intend to remain so. I am not such a fool that I would allow a *tha'r* to interfere with the archaeological work. You are employing many of my men and you give us good quality tea. And I am not such a fool not to know what a *tha'r* would do to so profitable a situation. Whoever killed the man, Dr Davison, he was not of El Till. I will allow no vendettas.'

'*Hagg,* you are the most powerful man in this valley. You can dictate to the other *'umdas*–'

The old man held up a hand. 'Now you offend me, Dr Davison. Your *ghaffir* met with an accident, nothing more.'

'Now you listen to me!' cried Mark suddenly, startling everyone. 'And you listen well! Two deaths in my camp are enough! That is it! It stops now! If I have to call in the *ma'mur's* police I will, and then I will hire workers from El Minya and your people will see no more tea!'

Mark's outburst stunned the *'umda,* who gaped at him in astonishment.

'Keep your petty quarrels on your own ground, *hagg!* If there is one more incident, so much as a black eye, I mean it, *hagg,* the police will come and *my work will continue!* I promise you that!'

When Mark turned on his heel and marched away, Ron and Hazim had to run to keep up with him. They hurried away from the old man whom they left leaning on his staff in bafflement.

Ron called out, 'This isn't the way to the Land-Rover!'

'One more stop!'

They came to the western edge of the village where the fields began; a few men worked the *saqiya,* and an old woman stood knee-deep in the slime-covered pond delousing herself. Everywhere was silent.

The house they went to was set apart from the village, slightly larger and nicer. Children played with goats and chickens before the open doorway, and as the three visitors came near, they smelled the succulence of lamb roasting on a spit.

Mark stopped a few feet from the doorway and shouted in English, 'Domenikos! Come out, I want to talk to you!'

The children ceased their romping and stared up in wonder. Flies settled on their faces and covered their eyes. Presently a shape appeared in the doorway; the Greek was smiling and buttoning his shirt.

'I am honored! Please come inside and have tea!'

'I didn't come here for a friendly chat, Domenikos, I came here to threaten you.'

The porcine eyes bulged. 'I beg your–'

'Two of my men have been killed in the last four days. Now, I don't care if it's a tribal feud or if it was the work of one man. I'm here to tell you I want it stopped.'

'Dr Davison, I don't unders–'

'Maybe you'll understand this.' Mark stepped up to him and jabbed the man's chest with his finger. 'One more incident and the government police take over this village. I don't care if it jeopardises my dig, I don't care if everything comes to a grinding halt! The killing stops, Domenikos!'

Constantine blinked in bewilderment. 'Truly I do not know what you are speaking of. What have I to do with–'

'Just in case you thought I'd buy some of your protection.'

'But I didn't kill–'

'I don't care if you did or not. Just see that it doesn't happen again! Understand?'

'But Dr Davison–'

'Remember this, Domenikos,' Mark's voice dropped to

a threatening note. 'One more incident and I report you to the authorities. I'll tell them about the little deal you offered me, and I don't think your friends in Athens would like that.'

Mark whipped around and left the dumbfounded man staring after him as he and his companions stalked away.

Once inside the Land-Rover, Ron said, 'Now what?'

'Now, repeat performances at Hag Qandil and El Hawata.'

Lines of fresh laundry fluttered in the sunset breeze, and aromas from Samira's cooking settled over the camp. The group sat outdoors in the shade of the work tent, perched on folding chairs and drinking cool tea.

'You did the right thing,' said Sanford Halstead after hearing Mark's story. He was pale in the orange glow; after this morning's shock, Halstead had spent the day throwing up. There had been blood in the vomit, but he had told no one.

'That remains to be seen. I don't know who did the killing or why, but I think it'll stop now.'

'What if you do have to call in the *ma'mur's* police?' asked Hazim.

'You're the one with the answer to that. Have they the authority to stop our work?'

The young Arab sadly shook his head. 'I do not know. It depends . . .' He was becoming less enchanted with this expedition. He had found another scorpion in his bed. They seemed to appear only at night and when Abdul was not in the tent. Also, there had been that peculiar nightmare again: the enticingly long-limbed woman, naked, beckoning to him, taking him in her arms, only to have, at the last minute, her beautiful head transform itself into the ugly pincers of a scorpion. No, Hazim was no longer happy here. He was wondering if, after all, he should resign his position, go back to Cairo, and let someone with more stomach take his place.

'About the work,' said Halstead. 'What now?'

'We'll keep digging the trenches, and in the meantime I want all of us to inspect the tops of the cliffs for anything that might look like a dog.'

Mark could not sleep. Even after three cups of Ron's chianti and a glass of bourbon, he was sharply awake. He knew that it was anger and frustration that kept him alert. He also felt the beginnings of a headache.

Mark's eyes traced the ghostly path of the moon as it slowly rose over the tent; its halo glow could be seen through the Dacron roof.

He could not believe he had been in Los Angeles only two weeks before, dialing Nancy's number and getting a 'disconnected' recording. He also could not believe it had been just four months since that fateful rainy night in Malibu when Halstead had first knocked at his door.

Mark heard a sound on the other side of the tent wall.

Raising himself up on his elbow, he peered through the mosquito netting and could barely see, softly incandescent against the Dacron, a pillar of whiteness. It was like a fall of moonglow, a column of unearthly light that Mark perceived as an optical illusion; some *fellaheen* sitting around a fire or a *ghaffir* patroling the camp with flashlight. Still, it held his attention. Mark was captivated by it, compelled to leave his bed and steal across the tent. Lifting the flap, he looked out.

She was there again, standing at a distance, watching the camp. Through her gossamer body Mark could see the lights of El Hawata two miles away.

He came out of the tent, letting the flap fall back behind him. Mark stared at her for a long time trying to ignore the physiological responses of his body: the sudden thumping pulse in his head, the damp palms, the arid mouth, the sweat on his forehead that prickled like ice. Mark was curious about the illusion; he was drawn to it in scientific objectivity.

Then came the gentle tapping against his brain, like a moth against a window. *'Per-a em ruti. Bu pu ua metet enrma-a. Erta na hekau apen.'*

The throb in his brain increased; the headache intensified. Mark felt himself pulled to her. He moved over the sand as if in a trance – yet he was not. His mind was voltaic, he was charged with an awareness that seemed to expand to the stars.

'Speru ti erek tu em bak. Petra? Petra? An au ker-nek er-s. Petra?'

Mark came to a halt a few feet from her. As he listened to the alien sounds in his head, he filled his eyes with her astonishing beauty.

'Speru ti erek tu em bak.'

He tried to swallow but could not. Each breath was painful. Mark pressed his lips together, tried to take command of his body. She was a dream, an hallucination, nothing more . . .

'Petra?' she whispered. *'Petra?'*

And then Mark thought: I know! I understand!

The sudden realisation of it slapped him and made him fall back a step. Whatever she was – dream, illusion – he was both elated and afraid; he wanted to stay and yet run.

The woman seemed to sense his sudden understanding, for she fell silent, beholding him with mournful eyes.

Mark opened his mouth and tried to speak. His voice came out as a croak.

She waited, staring.

He ran his tongue over his lips and gulped the icy night air. Then he forced his mouth to move, concentrating so hard that his whole body quivered. *'Nima . . .'* he whispered. *'Nima tra tu entek?'*

And in his mind, he heard: *'I wait . . .'*

Mark staggered backward as if struck. It was as though the universe had exploded; his mind was blown to the far reaches of space. His pulse now pounded so violently his neck throbbed with pain. He repeated: *'Nima tra tu entek? Who art thou?'*

And the vision/illusion/dream said: 'I was asleep . . . waiting . . .'

But it was not English he heard. It was no language Mark knew. Suddenly the foreign sounds fell away and concepts filled his brain. He was hearing her voice, her words, and yet he understood, as if she spoke a language he had always known.

The woman now seemed to be having difficulty. 'I am she who has awakened . . I am . . '

The waiting was agony for Mark. He felt his body stretch to the limits of the galaxy; he wanted to shout and scream. He stood rigidly, trembling, sweat running torrentially down his back and chest. He watched as the dream-woman struggled with her thought, as though trying to remember.

Then, finally, he heard it.

More than a whisper now. A solid voice.

She said: 'I am . . . I am . . . I am Nofr'tay-tay . . .'

SIXTEEN

MARK WATCHED the cream coagulate on the surface of his coffee and vaguely heard Ron ask Samira for more *mehalabeyah*. Preoccupied, he didn't pay attention to any of the other conversation in the tent.

He couldn't get her out of his mind: Nofr'tay-tay, she had said. Nefertiti, Queen Nefertiti. A dream, an illusion, the product of an overworked mind. Nothing more. Yet he could not stop thinking about her.

'Hey!'

A hand was shaking his arm. Mark looked at Ron and tried to focus on his face.

'Let it go, Mark. We'll find the Dog. Don't worry, relax . . .' Ron faded away.

They had spent eight grueling hours, the seven of them, going over every crag and tor of the plateau and had returned to the camp with nothing more than sunburns and short tempers. But Mark wasn't thinking about the day: what preoccupied him now no one else could guess, for he had not spoken of it to anyone. Only the *ghaffir* had seen him, standing half-naked in the desert, dripping with sweat and babbling to himself. The *ghaffir*, thinking the American was drunk. The *ghaffir* who, patroling the camp, had blinded Mark with his flashlight and had made the incredible woman-in-white disappear. Her name, that was all she had had a chance to say.

Mark was jangled out of his reflection by the sounds and movements of everyone leaving the dining tent. Alexis Halstead, he knew, would head for her tent and pass through the heat of the day in a pill-induced sleep. Hazim would retire to write more letters to his numerous relatives. Ron would be in the darkroom, and Sanford Halstead would probably be doing his usual calisthenics.

Only Yasmina remained.

'You have been very quiet today,' she said to him.

Mark pushed his untouched dinner away and got up from the table. 'I have a lot of things to think about.'

'You should eat. You are losing weight.'

'Am I?' Mark rested a hand on his stomach; the beginnings of his paunch were gone, and the inch of flab that had sat over his belt two weeks before had also disappeared. His body felt hard, young.

He walked out of the tent with Yasmina, again slipping into singular thought. She walked quietly at his side until she reached her own tent, then she stopped and turned to him. 'Mark, I am worried.'

'About what?'

She looked around and lowered her voice. 'Mr Halstead. He has a bleeding problem and yet he will not come to me for treatment. Why?'

'Sanford Halstead is too macho to admit to any kind of weakness, especially to a woman.'

'Macho?'

'It means tough, manly. He needs to prove his masculinity, I guess. He has to be hard as nails and can't admit to anyone that he is less than perfect.'

'It is foolish. He needs a doctor.'

'Can you help him?'

She shook her head.

'Is it serious?'

'I cannot say without examining him. Has he spoken to you again of his problem?'

'No. I'd forgotten all about it.'

'Well . . .' She looked down and watched her toe dig into the sand.

'How's your tent? Any more insects?'

'Only a few . . .'

'Well.' Mark gazed at her bowed head, taking in the

200

thick black waves that tumbled luxuriously down her back and shoulders. She was so small, so quiet, so gentle; and yet, paradoxically, exciting, sexual. He wondered what she thought of him, although he could guess: no greater gap existed than that between Moslem and Western culture. He doubted whether she felt the same response toward him as he felt toward her: the desire to gather her into his arms, to drink in her kisses, to take her to bed with him right now . . .

Yasmina raised her swimming eyes and Mark was instantly embarrassed by his thoughts. She stared up at him, her lips slightly parted, as if waiting for him to say something. So Mark did, 'Well, good night then,' and watched her turn away.

After she had gone inside and he heard the netting zip closed, Mark walked away from the tents and decided to linger over a pipe before going to bed.

It was near the fragment of ancient wall that he found Alexis Halstead, frozen like a statue, poised as if listening.

'Mrs Halstead?' As he neared her, he smelled the familiar gardenias, but this time he smelled something else as well. Something queer, something underlying, barely perceptible . . .

He walked around to face her. Alexis's eyes were shiny and glazed, unblinking. Beneath the pungent spice of gardenias was a flat, vaguely replusive odor that Mark could not define. 'Mrs Halstead?'

Her eyes flickered and then focused on him; she looked as if she had just been awakened from a dream. 'I thought I heard wind rustling in the trees'.

Mark looked around at the still, desert night. 'There are no trees here, Mrs Halstead.' Then it came to him. It was the smell of stale alcohol.

'But I heard . . .'

'It's impossible, Mrs Halstead. You were imagining it.'

'Yes.' Alexis released a long, tremulous sigh. 'Yes . . . '

'Aren't you cold?'

She rubbed her arms a little, then took hold of herself

and gave her head a vigorous shake. 'No, I'm fine. This desert air is giving me the most peculiar dreams . . .'

'Why don't you go to bed?'

'I'm not tired. Sit and talk with me a while, please?'

After they were seated on the mudbrick wall, Mark reached into his shirt pocket and took out his pipe and tobacco pouch. He heard Alexis say: 'Desolate, isn't it?'

Mark nodded, filled his pipe and lit it.

'How do archaeologists stand it?'

Mark sucked on his pipe, his eyes staring straight ahead. He felt Alexis shift next to him. 'Dr Davison . . .'

'Yes?'

She laid a hand on his arm. 'Don't you sometimes wonder?'

'About what?'

'What it was like here three thousand years ago?'

He forced a laugh. 'Of course I do. It's my job to wonder, Mrs Halstead. I'm an Egyptologist.'

'Please call me Alexis.'

Mark was uncomfortable beneath her gaze. Alexis Halstead's steamy green eyes seemed to caress him, lick at him, undress him and rape him. It was Alexis Halstead and yet it wasn't; as though something had possessed her. And again, that familiar face, so hauntingly beautiful. Like an ancient profile carved in limestone . . .

Mark's thoughts shocked him. 'It's cold out here, Mrs Halstead. Why don't you go back to your–'

'I mean the *man*, Dr Davison, what does the man in you wonder about this city, the people who lived here so long ago?'

'Mrs Halstead–'

'Alexis. Please don't be a stranger. Let's be friends.' She leaned on him, her voice creamy.

Mark thought for a moment, then, knocking his pipe against the wall and starting to rise, said, 'Mrs Halstead, I make it a practise never to get involved with my employer's wife.'

She laughed softly as she stayed him with her hand. 'Do you have any policies against getting involved with your *employer?*'

'I beg your pardon?'

'Dr Davison, my husband did not hire you, *I* did.'

'What?'

'I read your books, you impressed me. When Sanford came home with the Journal I knew you were the one for the job. I did some research into you, and I discovered that you would not, or rather, *could* not say no to us.'

As she spoke, Alexis Halstead's voice hardened; her eyes became gemstones again. She leaned back, away from Mark. 'My husband hasn't a penny of his own, Dr Davison, he is a nobody. A capital 'N' nobody. When I met him I was an heiress and he was selling ties in a department store. I made a deal with him. That was nine years ago and it has worked out very well.'

'Deal?'

'I needed a husband, Dr Davison, but I didn't want a keeper. So I hired Sanford to play the part; he presents a good image and puts on an excellent act when called upon.' She clasped her hands around one knee and rocked slightly. 'I have never desired men, Dr Davison. I find sex with a man distasteful and a waste of time. I deplore any invasion of my body. But you see, paradoxically, I needed a man. When I was single, I was very rich and therefore a target for the fortune hunters. And for the jocks, too, who looked on me as a conquest. I could go nowhere, do nothing without the come-ons, the passes, the phoney lines. Some persisted too strongly, so I hired a husband. An actor who could play the part of the spouse I needed, but who in fact would have no designs on me himself. I found the perfect man selling ties at Bloomingdales.'

Alexis turned her calculating eyes on Mark. 'You see, Sanford is impotent—'

'Mrs Halstead—'

'He has no interest at all in my body. And he will do

anything for money. I set him up in a business, made him chairman of the board, gave him cars and suits and spending money. All I want in return is his last name and his presence at my side when I call for it.'

Mark thought: Oh Christ, and looked around the moonless desert for an exit.

'I always get what I want, Dr Davison. It wasn't difficult swaying that professorship vote; I have powerful friends at UCLA–'

He regarded her in blank surprise. 'What? What did you say?'

'Come now, Dr Davison, don't tell me you never connected the two. One minute you lose the professorship and the next, Sanford is standing on your doorstep. You can't possibly believe it was a coincidence.'

'You? You did that?'

Her lips curled in amusement and mockery. 'You really had no idea, did you! You disappoint me, Dr Davison! Of course you had the professorship. You knew that. Did you really not wonder why they voted you out all of a sudden when it had been so sure?'

Mark felt himself tighten. His teeth clamped until his neck cords bulged.

'It was a very close call, Dr Davison. I have a feeling that if you had gotten that post you would not have been as easily swayed to come to Egypt with us. Not with the professorship to lose. As it was, you had nothing to lose at all, I saw to that.'

'There are other Egyptologists,' he managed to say. 'For God's sake, *why me*?'

'Because I made up my mind to have you, that's why. You have a singleness of purpose that appealed to me. Your unswerving devotion to your science, even in the face of possibly losing the woman you love–'

'What!'

'I know all about Nancy. You had difficulty choosing between her and your profession, didn't you? That was the kind of man I wanted. Someone who would stop at nothing, let nothing stand in his way to get what he wanted, not even a woman. We're alike, you and I.'

Mark got to his feet and searched the black horizon for the Nile. He needed to fix on something; he could not look down at the woman who spoke with a voice that cut like a knife. 'We're not alike, Mrs Halstead,' he said rigidly. 'You are mistaken about me.'

'Am I?' She rose smoothly. 'You had your choice, Dr Davison, and you knew the risk. You chose Egypt. Do you really think Nancy will be waiting for you after this?'

Her words sliced through the air and cut him to the core. Mark saw the river in the distance, black on black, and felt his stomach turn to stone.

'That's something else I like about you,' he heard her say. 'You don't admit defeat. You fight back, you'll find that tomb for me, Dr Davison, *now* more than ever.'

He sank down on to the ancient wall and buried his face in his hands. The killing part was the truth in her words.

She remained towering over him, smiling in victory, her hard green eyes relishing the defeated sight of him.

And then, in the next moment, she swayed, as if about to faint, and brought her fingertips up to her temples. The green irises glazed over, the light in her eyes faded, her expression solidified, and, for a fleeting instant, Alexis Halstead was a marble statue.

Then she blinked, took in a deep breath and once again smiled down at Mark. Only now her eyes were warm and moist, her features soft, her body pliant. Alexis said in a melting voice, 'Yes, you'll find that tomb for me, Mark, I know you will. And . . . you're . . . not far from finding it either. You're . . . almost . . . there . . .'

Startled, Mark looked up. Alexis appeared again the way she had a few minutes before, sensual, enticing, breathing heavily. He regarded her in puzzlement. The voice was no longer hers, the green of her eyes had turned a queer shade. She looked at him but didn't see him, as if she were dreaming, sleepwalking again.

'What do you mean?' he said warily.

'I mean, the tomb is there, in the canyon, and you will find it soon. But you . . . face the wrong way . . . you must turn around . . .'

Her face clouded, her body swayed again.

Thinking she was going to fall, Mark sprang up and took hold of her arms. 'Go to bed, Mrs Halstead.'

'No, no,' she said breathlessly, her eyelids half-closed. 'I must talk . . . I must talk with thee. You must . . . listen. I am not she I am *she* and I need to say things to thee things that will tell thee where he lies–'

He gave her a gentle shake. 'Mrs Halstead, please go back to your tent. It's late. We're all tired.'

Her face contorted. 'I have to talk with thee! Why wilt thou not listen!'

Mark frantically searched the camp for help. Maybe Yasmina–

Suddenly Alexis broke free, stepping back and glaring at him with hard, angry eyes. 'What are you doing with your hands on me!'

'Mrs Halstead–'

'Don't underestimate me, Dr Davison! I cannot be bought at *any* price!' She spun around and sprinted over the sand, her bright red hair dancing like a halo of fire around her head. Mark stared after her in stupefaction, and in the next moment felt a cold breath sweep across his neck.

Turning, he found himself gazing at the woman in white.

At once his mind cleared and his emotions fled. All was forgotten in an instant; she shimmered before him like a carnival hologram.

Then he heard: *'Nima tra tu entek?'*

And he whispered: 'I am Davison.'

Later, he would remember other things: that the wind had died suddenly, that the moon had clouded over in a cloudless sky, that the woman was naked beneath her diaphanous robe. But for now he was filled only with the simple curiosity and awe of a scientist faced with a baffling new mystery.

They spoke haltingly at first, each adjusting to the other's thought patterns. The woman's ancient words translated themselves in Mark's brain, and his whispered English seemed to alter as he uttered it until the two conversed in a universal tongue.

'What are you?' he asked.

'I am Nofr'tay-tay.'

'Not *who* are you, *what* are you?'

'I am Nofr'tay-tay.'

'Am I dreaming? Do I imagine you?'

She floated on the air, her delicate face molded in sadness. 'I was asleep and now I am wakened.'

'Are you real, alive?'

'Yes . . .'

Mark sat back down on the wall, his hands dangling over his knees. She was closer to him than she had been before; he saw the details, the sharp stunning perfection of her features. 'Why are you here?' he asked.

'I have slept! I have slept, lo, these millenia–' She raised her slender arms and held her palms up to the sky. 'I am in pain! I hunger! I am lonely! So alone . . .'

'What are you? Are you a dream? A ghost? How is it we can communicate?'

Nofr'tay-tay lowered her arms and gazed forlornly at Mark. 'I do not know.'

'You speak strange words and yet I understand them.'

'Thou . . . thou has studied them, Davison. Thou has studied my language and it is there, buried deep within thee. I have called it forth.'

He stared up at her in astonishment. 'Studied it . . .' he whispered. Then his mind was suddenly alive with characters and pictures; he saw the columns of hieroglyphics, heard his own voice years ago speaking into a tape recorder, testing the strength of his theory. The words she uttered now – *petra* (what), *tennu* (where), *tes-a* (myself) –

had all been part of that three year study.

'You say you are Nofr'tay-tay. Do you have a husband?'

'Yes.'

Mark slid to the edge of the wall. 'Where is he?'

'He sleeps . . .'

'Where?'

'In the canyon . . .'

Mark felt a lump gather in his throat. 'What is his name?'

'He is Aton-Is-Pleased. He is 'Khnaton.'

Mark dragged a sleeve across his mouth; he fought to contain himself, to keep from shattering the fragile moment. She seemed so breakable, so tenuous; the thread between them seemed no more than a spider's filament. 'Can others see you?'

'No.'

'Can they hear you?'

'No.'

'Why not?'

'I do not know, Davison. If I am a puzzle to thee, thou art no less of a puzzle to me.'

'When do you exist?'

'In the now time.'

'Is it your future or my past?'

'I do not know.'

Mark struggled with his sanity. *I'm dreaming! I'm talking to an hallucination!* 'Do you know anything about me?'

'No.'

'I am searching for a tomb. Do you know where it is?'

'Listen!' Nofr'tay-tay raised a milky arm and held her hand by her cheek. 'Someone approaches.'

Mark looked around. The camp was dark and silent. 'We're alone.'

'No, my one, someone comes. I must go. But I will return, Davison. Listen to the Old One . . .'

As he beheld her, she vanished, her radiance dimming

slowly like a dying star. Then Mark heard a rustling sound behind him and, getting to his feet, saw Samira moving through the shadows toward him.

When she was a few feet from him she paused and fixed a glittering black eye on him.

'What is happening?' he asked in Arabic. 'Explain it to me.'

'It begins, master. And now you must move quickly.'

'Have I been dreaming? Is she just an invention of my imagination or am I going crazy?'

'The time has come, master. The battle will soon begin. We must hurry!' Her black robes fluttered in the night breeze. 'You must come with me now, master.'

'Where?'

'I have something to show you.'

Before he could question her further, the old woman turned away from him and hobbled over the sand. Bewildered, Mark followed.

She led him up the Royal Wadi, always ahead of him, never looking back, following the limestone walls with her hands. Their way was lighted by the full moon and stars, but still it was awesomely dark and Mark had to hurry to keep her in sight. Three times he called out to her to stop – once in Coptic – but Samira did not acknowledge him. Like an injured crow, she flapped her way up the gradually narrowing wadi, twice falling on the rubble.

The air grew increasingly chill. They turned up a narrow ravine that branched off the wadi just before the Royal Tomb; the bare rock walls loomed close. Mark followed the old woman's example and steadied himself with his arms outstretched, hands flat on either wall.

This deep cleft rose up from the main wadi and became at times so steep and perilous that Mark and Samira had to scramble up on their hands and knees. His shirt, soaked with sweat, clung to him like a shroud of ice; his breath came out in short, steaming jets. Still the old woman pushed on, staying always in front, silently scaling the cliff without once looking back.

The climb was a long and treacherous one; once at the top, on the desert plateau, Mark sank to his knees and heaved in the biting air. A raw wind swept over him; his lungs protested the painful arctic air. When Mark ran his hands over his face, he found his palms were cut and bleeding.

Samira, also gasping for breath and lurching so badly Mark thought she was going to collapse, kept walking. He tried calling after her but had neither the strength nor the breath. Then he doubled over and fell face down on the sand.

When, after he had recovered a short while later and was tasting sand, Mark hoisted himself up, he saw Samira a few yards from him, crouched in the dirt with her knees drawn up to her chest. She was swaying and softly chanting, the way she had done when he and Yasmina had found her behind the mess tent, and as Mark dragged himself to his feet and staggered over to her, he saw in the silvery moonlight that the *fellaha* was again chewing leaves.

'What's this all about?' he demanded. His voice severed the desert silence and shot up to the stars.

All about him was a stark lunar scape: the surface terrain of the plateau at night was vastly different from its daylight aspects. Here the eery jutting peaks of spar and crystalline carbonate appeared as alien ruins; they might have been broken pillars and castles of an extraterrestrial civilisation. The gorges and ravines streaked the tableland like mammoth, slithering snakes; it was a ruthless, menacing world.

He squatted before the old woman. 'Why did you bring me here!'

Although her eyes were open, she seemed not to see him. Unblinking and swaying, she continued her maddening song.

'Goddammit!' he shouted. 'You crazy old witch!'

Mark straightened and looked around in the darkness for a path down. He knew he could never find the way they had come up. And too many of these ravines descended into deep pits or box canyons that would trap him. Come tomorrow, Abdul might not find him soon enough and then the desert predators would claim him.

'Listen!' he shouted. 'Lead me back to the camp!'

Samira maintained her zombie-like humming, her eyes fixed to the east.

Exasperated, Mark bent down and seized her bony shoulders. 'I don't know where we are! Get me back!'

When he started to give her a shake, the old woman's hands shot up and grabbed his forearms in a shockingly strong grip. 'Wait, wait, master. Almost, almost.'

'Wait! Wait for what? Jesus!' He shook off her hold and backed away. He made a quick three-hundred-and-sixty degree scan of their position and tried to calm himself. We can't have come far, though it seemed like we climbed for hours. Why did I follow her? Abdul . . . Abdul will start looking in the morning. How long would it take? Days–

'Master!'

When he looked down at her, Samira's right arm was held out straight before her, and extended from it was a twisted brown finger. She was pointing at the horizon. '*Now*, master!' she cried.

Mark spun around. He saw the pale beginning of dawn, the first wash of a pastel sunrise. And just above the horizon, sitting on the line which could now be seen as the edge of desert and the beginning of sky, was a brilliant pinpoint of light.

While the morning breeze picked up and played through his hair, Mark watched with bated breath as the white beacon hovered over the edge of the world. It held him hypnotised as the sky grew lighter; then Mark saw the golden crown of the sun, a bare sliver on the horizon, and kept his eyes on it until the light was too bright and he had to turn away.

He stood for a long time on the plateau, the blackness

giving way to a tawny dawn, listening to the *fellaha's* chanting. When the sun was fully risen and the star no longer visible, Mark heard himself whisper, 'I'll be damned . . .'

He had found the Dog.

SEVENTEEN

'Sɪʀɪᴜs . . .' sᴀɪᴅ Ron, absently tapping his empty paper cup on the table.

'Like Ramsgate said, childishly simple.' Mark felt a little better. After he had stumbled into camp he had taken a vigorous shower and eaten a hearty lunch; now he relaxed in the mess tent with his feet up, dressed in freshly laundered bush jeans and a dark green army fatigue shirt. He had not slept in thirty-two hours. 'It all fell into place as I stood there, watching the sunrise. When I realised what the light in the sky was, I also remembered that today is 19 July. The star is Sirius and the ancient Egyptians used its annual heliacal rising to mark the start of their flood.'

'What is heliacal rising?' asked Yasmina.

'It means rising with the sun. You can only see the star just before sunrise, after that the sun is too bright.'

'But why just today?' asked Alexis, her voice distant, detached.

'Let me show you. Hazim, may I borrow your notebook for a second?' They all leaned close as Mark made a rough sketch. 'This line is the horizon. This circle is the sun. Now, we all know the sun rises in the east and sets in the west. However, what we haven't been keeping in mind is that the sun also moves along the horizon in a north-south fashion. While its *daily* path is east-west, its *yearly* path is south-north. For half the year the sun rises somewhere down here. But as the earth's axis tilts us away, we observe the sun to move slowly northward.'

'Downstream,' said Ron.

'Exactly. Now, here is Sirius.' He dotted the tip of the pen next to the circle that was the sun. 'For part of the year, Sirius cannot be seen because it is behind the sun. But as the sun "moves" northward, Sirius appears to the south of it and can be seen on the horizon. Like this morning.'

'Always on July nineteenth?' asked Yasmina.

'Always. The Egyptians knew this; they were great astronomers. They observed that this star always made its first appearance in this spot *every three hundred and sixty-five days*. That's how they established their year. To the Egyptians, Sirius was sacred.'

'Then what's this Dog business?'

'Partly my fault for mistranslating the riddle, partly the fault of three thousand years separating us from the men who carved the stela.' Mark drew the hieroglyphs that appeared in the last line of the stela. "When Amon-Ra, downstream traveleth, lieth, the Criminal, underneath, the Eye of Isis, to be provided with". Very simple, except I fell into the same error Ramsgate did, and I have no excuse other than I already had his translation so firmly rooted in my mind that I didn't leave myself open for other possibilities. This symbol here,' he tapped the tall triangle, 'has, as do most hieroglyphs, two meanings. It is the verb "to be provided with". It also stands for the star Sirius. Because I had a preconceived notion of what this line said before I even read it, I failed to pick up the second meaning of this symbol.'

'How can you be sure it is the second meaning we want?'

'I know, because once I realised it referred to the star, I then recalled that the star Sirius was sometimes referred to as the Eye of Isis. So, reading the new translation, we have: "When the sun moves northward on the horizon, the Criminal lies beneath Sirius, the Eye of Isis." '

Halstead sniffed and brought a handkerchief to his nose. 'That still doesn't explain the Dog.'

Mark returned the notebook and pen to Hazim. 'Mr Halstead, Sirius is the brightest star in the heavens, it is *the only fixed* star, and it is located in the constellation Canis Major. We know it as the Dog Star.'

The handkerchief came slowly away. 'Dog Star . . .'

'The ancients didn't have that name for it, but we moderns do. The *sebbakha* told Ramsgate to look beneath the Dog. His mistake, and mine, was in forgetting that terminology has changed over three thousand years. What was an Eye to them is a Dog to us.'

'But how,' said Hazim, 'can you be absolutely certain?'

'Shortly after sunrise, Samira led me to the edge of the plateau. I looked down and saw, far below, our little box canyon with the sun just starting to illuminate the trenches. Then I saw my shadow, two hundred feet down, fall directly over the base of the stela.'

The young Arab widened his eyes in amazement.

'What we will do, Mr Sheikhly, is tomorrow, before dawn, take the surveying equipment up to the plateau, and when the star appears, use the transit to calculate its path toward the stela. From there we triangulate, and using the coordinates the stone and the star give us, we should locate the tomb somewhere in the wall of the canyon.'

They all pondered this a moment, then Yasmina murmured, 'We are near the end . . .'

Mark smiled at her, recalling the gentle way she had washed his hands and daubed ointment on them.

'A pity we have to wait until morning . . .' said Alexis, staring at her fingers.

'I'm afraid if we tried starting this afternoon by only guessing where the star is, we could be off by many feet, in which case we would miss the tomb entirely and end up digging down to China.'

'Isn't the star visible at night?' asked Hazim.

'Yes, it is, now that it has made its first rising, but there is no way we can work in the dark.' Mark got to his feet and stretched. 'Morning is not that far off and I believe we could all do with the rest. Mr Halstead? Halstead, are you all right!'

'Sanford?' said Alexis, also rising.

Halstead lifted his head and exposed a handkerchief soaked in blood.

Mark was sitting on his cot with his shirt and shoes off, unable to sleep in the intense afternoon heat. Spread before him was a topographical gridmap of the plateau; he was looking for their canyon.

Ron, sitting cross-legged on his own cot, sipping wine, watched Mark work over the map for a long moment, then said, 'I'm sorry, Mark, but I don't like it.'

Mark, pinpointing the canyon and circling it, said without looking up, 'What don't you like?'

'This whole thing. I've got a feeling, Mark, a *scary* feeling.'

Mark looked up and frowned. 'About what?'

'You know what. This whole project.'

Mark turned away, unable to meet his friend's eye. 'I don't know what you're talking about.'

'Sure you do. We all know what's happening here, only no one's had the guts to talk about it.'

'What are you talking about?'

'The nightmares for one. Everyone's having them. And acting weird. Mrs Halstead, she walks around like a zombie. And whenever she looks at you, Mark, there's an insane look in her eyes, like hunger, like she's starving or depraved. And Halstead, bleeding. And Hazim, killing scorpions in his tent, and–'

'Cut it out, Ron.'

'It's the seven gods, Mark, they don't want us here.'

Mark scowled at his friend. 'I can't believe what I'm hearing. You, a man of science–'

'And what about you? What's troubling you? Look at the dark circles under your eyes. You've aged ten years in this place.'

Mark looked down at the grid map and again considered telling Ron about the vision (or whatever it was) of Nefertiti. But now was not the time, not with Ron romanticising the ancient curses, making something fantastical out of normal, explainable happenings. When you're in the desert you should expect to encounter scorpions and swarms of insects. And Sanford Halstead obviously had a blood dyscrasia. And his wife was popping too many pills–

'I want to leave, Mark.'

He snapped his head up. 'What?'

Ron remained calm, in control. 'We're headed for bad things. The closer we get to finding the tomb, the worse the nightmares get. And this . . . this *feeling* I have. Sure I'm a man of science, Mark, an Egyptologist. And as an Egyptologist I can appreciate better than anyone the power of the ancient Egyptians.'

Mark regarded his friend in bafflement. 'You can't mean it!'

'I do. And I think the others feel the same way. Mark–' Ron uncrossed his long legs and slid to the edge of the cot, speaking more earnestly. 'Those two *ghaffirs,* they died the same way Ramsgate's *ghaffirs* died. And his wife Amanda started sleepwalking. His interpreter came down with a bleeding problem. *Mark, it's happening all over again!'*

Mark tossed aside the grid map and reached for his flask.

The maddening part of it was: he agreed with Ron. He felt it, too, and yes, there was something weird going on. But that tomb was out there and the Heretic was in it and the man who found the tomb would be more famous than Howard Carter.

'Look at you,' said Ron. 'You're drinking more now than you ever have.'

But even more than that – more than the hunger for recognition . . . was the lure of the ghostly woman who called herself Nofr'tay-tay. He couldn't leave her, not until he had figured her out . . .

'What's that?'

Mark looked up. 'Someone's shouting. It's Yasmina!'

The two were immediately on their feet and running out of the tent. They dashed barefoot across the compound, following Abdul; the three arrived at the Halsteads' tent at the same time. Mark pushed his way in first.

He stopped short.

Sitting on the bed with Sanford Halstead propped up in her lap was old Samira. She was bringing a cup to his mouth. Then Mark saw Yasmina and Alexis, locked in a physical struggle, the younger woman shouting until her face was apple-red.

'Hey!' shouted Mark.

The three women looked up at him in surprise. Samira stopped the cup a few inches from Halstead's lips.

'What the hell is going on here!'

'The old witch is trying to poison him!' said Yasmina, wrenching free from Alexis.

'It's not poison,' said Alexis breathlessly. 'It's medicine. It will stop the bleeding.'

Mark narrowed his eyes at the two people on the bed: black-clad dirty old Samira and pristine, Sanford Halstead, who appeared dazed. 'What is she giving him?'

'It is from the pouch which hangs from her belt,' said Yasmina. 'I happened to come in to see how he was and I caught her mixing it into a cup of tea. I have tried to stop her but–'

'He is not well!' came a wizened voice from the bed. 'This will help him. It is good medicine, master.'

'What is it?'

The beady eyes watched him warily. 'Good magic, master.'

'Open the pouch please, *shaykha.*'

Her eyes flew open. 'No! You cannot see!'

He spoke patiently. 'I only want to know what you're giving him.' Mark took a few tentative steps toward her and Samira instantly recoiled, putting the cup down and clutching the soporific man to her bosom like a cat cradling a mouse. 'No, master! It is good magic, but no one must touch it! It is for the sick one! He bleeds!'

No one saw Ron move; he darted from the doorway and was on top of the old crone before anyone realised what was happening. She shrieked like a monkey and clawed at him, but when Ron backed away, he had her leather pouch in his hands.

'I only want to see what's in it, *shaykha,*' said Mark gently.

Ron emptied the contents into his palm: a brittle sprig from a tree and some black powder.

'What's this?' asked Mark, picking the twig out of the powder.

'It is a sacred relic, master. It is a piece of the sycamore tree Our Lady rested under when she fled into Egypt with the Baby Jesus.'

'And this black powder?'

She pressed her lips together and thrust out her chin.

'I know what it is . . .' murmured Ron, rubbing some of the powder between his thumb and forefinger. 'It's ground-up mummy.'

'What!'

'It is good magic, master! This one bleeds not from sickness but from the devils!'

'You can't give him this, *shaykha.*'

Samira's hand shot out like a snake and moved so quickly that Mark barely realised what had happened. The cup was already at Halstead's lips when he flew forward, dashed her hand away and sent the cup and contents flying across the tent.

'*Ya Allah!*' she shrieked.

'*Shaykha,*' Mark tried to control his anger; he knew the old woman's intentions were noble. 'He cannot drink this.'

She glared up at him with volcanic rage. 'You make a grave mistake, master. I can help you fight the demons–'

Mark frowned down at her in frustration. He didn't

want to upset her; she had led him to the Dog. 'Please, *shaykha,* let me handle this.'

When Abdul stepped forward, the *fellaha* raised a hand, staying him. Then she very carefully maneuvered herself out from under Halstead, gently laid him down, and straightened up with queenly dignity. 'I cannot help you after this, master. I have done all I can. Now you are on your own.'

Mark opened his mouth to speak, but Abdul moved smoothly to stand behind her. As she departed, Samira picked up the pouch and twig out of Ron's hand and snorted disdainfully.

Mark watched Yasmina bend over Halstead and feel his pulse. Then he looked at Alexis who was sitting on her cot, staring at her hands in confusion.

Yasmina tried to get the shirt off Halstead, who was nearly asleep. 'I should send him back to Cairo.'

'No!' Alexis snapped her head up, her pupils flaring. 'He would not stand for it. Sanford remains here at the dig.'

'He needs hospital treament—'

She glared at Mark with frosty green eyes. 'Sanford stays here, Dr Davison. It is what he wishes.'

As Yasmina picked up her medical bag and headed for the door, Mark opened his mouth to say something further, but saw by the look in Alexis's eyes that his words would be futile. So he turned on his heel and followed Yasmina into the sultry afternoon.

'I am sorry, Mark,' she said as they walked back to her tent. 'I handled that poorly.'

'You did the right thing. I doubt that mummy alone would hurt him, but who knows what she had mixed in with it.'

They stopped before her tent. 'I have some tea which I have made myself,' she said awkwardly. 'Will you share it with me?'

'Let me go put a shirt on.'

Abdul had had to cook supper because Samira could not be found; it was a palatable stew of rice and lamb and beans, but definitely missing the old *fellaha's* tasty flair.

It was a silent group that ate.

Halstead, pale but steady, had insisted upon joining them when he awoke. Alexis, sitting next to him, was remote and detached; eating as if in a dream, not tasting her food. Across from Mark, Ron chewed the bits of lamb with little relish and washed it down with chianti. At the other table were Hazim, who scribbled constantly in his notebook during the meal, and Yasmina who picked at her food.

Mark thought about her as he ate, about the relaxing and enjoyable hour he had spent drinking tea in her tent. She had been a little more open towards him, speaking of her difficulties in social quarters, how she so desperately wanted to be accepted as a peer among men, yet how unobtainable this was in a Koranic culture. She had spoken passionately of it then, her fight for liberation, and yet now, during supper, she isolated herself, as her Moslem sisters in Cairo would do, eating apart from the foreigners, demurely, not taking part in their conversation. Mark recalled now how she had recoiled when he had accidentally brushed her arm.

And then there was Abdul, who had been looking for Mark and, having found him in Yasmina's tent, had immediately stiffened. Mark had caught it this time and had recognised it: Abdul was old-world, he very much disapproved of Moslem mingling with Gentile, even if the latter were an old and respected friend.

Other things were on Mark's mind as he ate. The hallucination of the previous night, just before Samira had taken him up to the plateau. Conversing in the ancient tongue with an unexplainable vision. And Alexis Halstead's aberrant behavior, almost as if she had a split personality. But what concerned him most now was old Samira's absence. Since going up on the plateau with her he had gained a new-found respect for the old woman, and was even more anxious to engage her help in studying the ancient tongue. But she had disappeared and no one knew where.

A vague rumble in the distance brough Mark out of his thoughts. He looked at his companions, then saw Abdul working over the stove.

Mark went back to eating.

A second rumble was heard, and this time Yasmina raised her head. She and Mark stared at one another.

A third, louder noise – like a crack – made the others stop chewing and look around.

'What is that?' asked Alexis.

Mark shook his head uncertainly. 'I don't know . . .'

Then a sudden clap, like a bang, jarred the night, and in the next instant everyone was on their feet.

'It sounds like thunder,' said Ron.

'That's imposs–'

Another crash tore through the tent, shaking it. Everyone ran outside.

The sky was clear and bright with stars; the moon was just starting its ascent. When another rumble sounded, everyone turned in the direction of the cliff. 'It sounds like a storm on the plateau,' said Hazim.

'Rain?' said someone else.

Mark kept his eyes on the ridge. The thunder sounded like cannon fire. Next to him he heard Ron murmur, 'I don't like this.'

The group continued to stand and stare up at the crags overhead, listening to the thunder roll nearer, like massive wagons pounding over the plateau, until Hazim slapped his hand to his forehead and cried, 'It is raining!'

The others turned to him. His hand came away; his face was wet. Then they too, felt the tiny prickles of the first raindrops.

'What a relief!' said Halstead, smiling for the first time in days. 'It'll cool the air!'

The rain started to come down harder, pelting the tent

in a crackle that sounded like machine gun fire. When it suddenly fell in a torrent, everyone screamed and ran inside, laughing. Only Mark and Abdul remained outside in the downpour, looking up.

'It is because of the High Dam, *effendi*. It has unbalanced our weather.'

Mark continued to look up at the night sky. He knew what Abdul was talking about. Lake Nasser had such a vast surface area that its tremendous evaporation had created a new climate in the Nile Valley: vegetation now grew in the desert where none had been able to survive before; an increase in the annual rainfall; an insidious dampness that was creeping into the ancient monuments and starting to rot them, like the tomb paintings in the Valley of the Queens which had been preserved by Egypt's natural dryness for three thousand years.

But could Lake Nasser be blamed for this? A fierce rain and thunder storm in a sky that was sparkling, cloudlessly clear?

When Mark finally ran back into the tent he heard Ron say 'I always suspected you didn't know enough to come in out of the rain!'

The clamor inside the tent was almost deafening; such a heavy downpour played a thunderous symphony on the Dacron roof. The walls flapped wildly, and as the tempest increased, with the thunder crashing directly overhead and a frightful wind howling through the compound, the laughter in the tent died down.

The seven stood in awed silence, listening to the upheaval around them; the ground shuddered with each crack of thunder and the rain came down harder still. Seven pairs of frightened eyes looked to one another for reassurance. Mark glanced at Abdul and didn't like the look on the Arab's face: naked fear.

Then Mark remembered the Royal Wadi and thought: *Oh Jesus!*

'Hey,' said Ron between thunderclaps. 'What about the generators? In this kind of wet–'

223

At that exact moment, the lights went out and the ventilating fans slowed to a stop. For one frozen instant, everyone blinked into the darkness. Then someone cried out – another screamed, and they all started pushing one another.

'Stay calm!' shouted Mark. 'We have flashlights and lanterns! Stay calm and don't panic! Sit down if you can!'

The darkness was incredible. Mark had never seen such total blackness, such pure and absolute night. Only in tombs had he ever seen such utter blackness. He fought down his own rising panic as he fell to his knees over the crates which stood against one wall and fumbled inside them. There were four flashlights and two battery-operated lanterns, which he distributed among his companions. Seven ghostly faces, their features distorted in the false light, listened in dread to the storm.

Yasmina had to shout to be heard. 'The *fellaheen* in the Workmen's Village! They have no protection!'

'There's nothing we can do!' Mark clapped his hands to his ears. The roar was like being inside an inverted plastic bowl with water rushing over it.

'And the villages!' she cried. 'Their houses will dissolve!'

'They've dealt with rain before, Yasmina!'

'Oh God,' said Ron, 'my equipment! What if the tent leaks? All my paper, my film!'

A crash of thunder toppled one of the lanterns. As Mark reached out to right it, a slender copper hand curled around his wrist. The grip was so tight it was painful. He looked at Abdul's face; the Arab was like something out of a horror movie. The light played queer tricks with his features, hollowing out his cheeks, sinking his eyes into dark recesses, making his nose and cheekbones jut. Abdul looked skeletal.

'*Effendi,*' he said as quietly as he could. 'Have you forgotten the wadi?'

'No, dammit, I haven't.'

'We must evacuate.'

'How? Run through this downpour, through the mud? There's no shelter for miles! We wouldn't get more than a quarter of a mile without getting lost and separated. Not even the Land-Rovers could make it through this!'

'If we stay, *effendi*–'

Mark glared at his foreman and pulled his wrist free: Deep welts were etched in his skin. 'There's nothing we can do, so we might as well not panic the others.'

Mark lifted his face to the tent roof. He pictured the wadi – the watercourse – which opened out just yards from their camp. A gorge in the plateau sculptured by centuries of freak desert storms and flash-floods. That's why none of the villages was built in the line of its path: its waters would appear suddenly and in great volume, spilling into the valley like a burst dam, churning everything in its way. Nothing would survive.

End quickly, thought Mark, panic starting to rise in him again. End soon! Don't be up on the plateau. Be raining just down here so the wadi won't be any threat–

Another hand found its way to his; Yasmina, sitting next to him, leaned close, her small cold fingers creeping under his for shelter. He held her hand tightly as they all sat in mortified terror.

And then, as suddenly as it had started, the storm ended. The cessation of rain and thunder dropped a sudden blanket of silence that was almost as loud as the storm had been. For an instant, no one moved. Then Hazim whispered, 'Is it over?'

'Stay here, all of you,' said Mark. 'Abdul, let's look.'

They unzipped the flap warily and looked out. Then Mark took a step forward. Abdul followed. They stood in the calm desert night, unspeaking and unmoving.

'How bad's the damage?' Ron called from behind.

Before Mark could reply, the lights flared up and the generators could be heard humming again. 'Hey!' called Ron. 'That's not possible!'

Mark moved to one side as he felt his friend come through the flap. He heard Ron sharply suck in his breath, hold it, then let it out slowly. 'Holy Jesus Almighty!'

The others came out now, timidly, one by one, until the entire group stood before the tent, gaping dumbstruck at the scene.

From where they stood, across the plain to the Nile and the lights of El Hawata, the ground was as dry and dusty as it had ever been.

Mark drove the Land-Rover himself, impatient with another man's caution; he plowed through the rubble and caromed off boulders as if driving himself and the machine to destruction. He was consumed with a passion that could find release only in reckless, maniacal driving. Far behind, the other Land-Rovers picked their way up the narrow gorge, blinded by the cloud of sand Mark left behind. Once, Abdul grabbed the dashboard and cried, *'Ya Allah!'* The *ghaffir*, grey-faced, clung to the seat with his eyes screwed shut. But Mark kept his foot down on the accelerator, crashing over rock and shale, blasting his way up the ravine as if to tear all thoughts from his mind.

It wasn't enough that, without old Samira's help, they had been able to locate the spot where he had first seen the star; it wasn't enough that they had seen Sirius rise and had had sufficient time before the sun dimmed its brilliance to calculate its coordinates with the stela base; and it wasn't enough that Mark had been able, using the surveyor's transit and topo map, to pinpoint the position of the tomb. Nothing in the world could put the maddening frustration of last night's storm out of his mind.

It was a wind, he had told the others, just a fierce wind that had *sounded* like thunder and rain.

But he had seen in their blank faces the emptiness of his words; they had all *felt* the rain, had heard its roar, and had seen the tent walls flap insanely. That had been no ordinary wind.

It had driven Mark into a rage. The mood of the expedition was deteriorating; little enthusiasm had been generated upon watching Sirius rise in the biting dawn. Mark had now gone fifty-one hours without sleep; anger kept him moving.

The ravine narrowed to the point where he was forced to slow down. As he did so, the dust settled a bit and before them yawned the canyon. '*Effendi,*' said Abdul, pointing.

Mark stopped the vehicle. 'What is it?'

'I will take a look.'

Mark gripped the steering wheel until his knuckles were white as he watched Abdul swing down and pick something out of the gravel. He took a quick look at it, then offered it to Mark.

'Oh, my God . . .' It was Samira's leather pouch and it was spotted with fresh blood. 'Abdul, I'm going ahead on foot. You keep the others back here. Don't let them move this Land-Rover.'

Mark was almost glad of the emergency, it was one more thing to keep the storm out of his mind. He scrambled over the barren rocks as if running for his life; he pushed himself as he had pushed the car.

Coming to the entrance of the canyon, Mark stopped and scanned it with his field glasses. He didn't know what he was looking for . . . a crumpled black heap, perhaps – but the floor was sunny and sandy and clear. He looked up at the sky; no vultures.

Back at the Land-Rover, he found everyone waiting quietly. Abdul, he noticed, had hidden the *fellaha's* pouch.

'What were you doing?' asked Sanford Halstead.

'Just making sure of my coordinates,' said Mark, avoiding the man's eyes. 'This is a good vantage point. Okay everybody, let's go!'

They had been working for three hours. The sun was climbing to its zenith and the canyon was turning into an oven. Abdul's *fellaheen* had been deployed in an arc near

227

the base of the eastern wall; the sounds of their axes and shovels echoed up to the sky.

Mark felt his stamina wane. The others, succumbing to sleeplessness and the heat, sat lethargically in the Land-Rovers. Eight four-by-four test holes were being sunk by the *fellaheen*. Mark labored in the one he thought the most likely; it was at the very center of his coordinates. The others were being dug to allow for a slight shift in the earth and the heavens in three thousand years.

Mark knelt over a rocking screen, his back screaming for relief, sweat dribbling into his eyes. He pushed himself because he needed a find. He also knew the others needed it as well, something to jar them out of their stupefaction and bring them back to reality. Finding the tomb now would dispel all preoccupation with the 'storm'.

'*Effendi*,' said a tall shadow standing over him. 'You exhaust yourself. There is enough time, *effendi,* please rest now.'

'Abdul, mind your own business.'

A hurt pause. 'Yes . . . *effendi.*'

Mark tossed away the trowel, ripped off his gloves and started digging with his bare hands. When a scorpion scurried away from his advance, he ignored it. Dimly, he heard a *fellah* cry out when startled by a snake, but Mark pressed on.

The sun stood directly overhead, pounding waves of killing heat on to the curved backs of the workers. The temperature was over one hundred degrees and the air did not circulate at all. A few *fellaheen* collapsed; Yasmina and Ron ministered to them. But Mark kept going blindly on.

His head started to throb. Tiny pinpricks sprouted all over his body. He itched terribly. But his hands kept digging.

'*Effendi*–'

'Keep them working!'

'Mark–' came Yasmina's voice.

'Get back to your patients!'

He paused long enough to rip off his shirt, then continued digging. Mark moved recklessly now, forgetting the rocking screen, diving into the sand and plowing it up like a dog going after a bone. It wasn't anger any more, or frustration, or dreams of glory. He drove himself in manic desperation. His mind was blank; his eyes saw bright colors flash around him. A dull roar filled his ears. He didn't hear Ron shout from the Land-Rover, or see Yasmina run to him, or feel Abdul's strong hands seize his bare shoulders. Mark's hands flew with a will of their own, blistered and bloodied.

He screamed, 'NO!' as several arms pulled him back.

Pinwheels burst in the sky; indigo and vermilion and all the most dazzling colors of the spectrum skyrocketed from the exploding sun.

Then Mark heard a clang, like a bell tolling, and he felt himself drift slowly backwards on to the sand.

'What happened?'

'Classic words,' said Ron.

Mark blinked up at his friend. 'I . . . I passed out?'

'You pushed yourself too hard,' came another voice.

Mark raised his head with a wince and saw Yasmina sitting at the foot of his bed. He also saw that his hands were bandaged like white lobster claws.

'What's this?'

'The step did it. You should be grateful you have any fingers left at all.'

'Step? What step?'

'You mean you don't remember? Jesus, we were lucky to pull you away when we did, the way you were digging. Sand, okay, but solid rock you cannot dig through with bare hands.'

'Ron! What are you talking about!'

'The step, Mark. You uncovered the first step leading down to the tomb.'

EIGHTEEN

AT A time that should have been filled with excitement and celebration, only depression and gloom was shared by the group. No one could put aside the memory of old Samira's brutally abused body.

Mark looked up from under the canopy Abdul had had erected near the site and saw that the seventh step was being cleared away. Delicately holding a pencil, he was sketching the project from all angles with an unerring accuracy that made up for Ron's inability to produce any photographs. In the two days since his uncovering the first step, the workers had excavated what Mark calculated was fully one half of the stairway. He watched as they worked, their white *galabeyahs* bright in the sun, their copper hands sifting and digging and wielding the tools of archaeology. Two of Abdul's most competent men assisted Ron on each step, for Mark's bandaged hands prevented him from digging. The rest formed an assembly line sieving the cleared sand; like ants, gradually exposing the ancient steps leading down into the mountain.

There was an uncharacteristic nervousness among the workers. They labored without the usual chatter, and unprovoked arguments erupted without warning. It was because of the *shaykha's* body.

'Some of them wish to return to their village, *effendi,*' the foreman had said earlier. 'They say they have bad feelings about this place.'

'Let them go. We have more men than we need now, anyway.'

Mark couldn't blame the *fellaheen* – the sight of Samira's body had stunned everyone.

The old *fellaha* had been found the night before, lying not far from the camp, stripped naked, her mouth crammed with the same brown matter that had clogged the throat of the first *ghaffir*. Her face was swollen and plum-purple, her wrists and ankles bruised, testifying to her struggle against terrible strength, her withered body lying twisted in the sand as if she had writhed and wriggled.

The engorgement of blood on her face – its dark blue color – indicated that she had been alive when the brown stuff had been forced down her throat.

'There was great anger against her,' Abdul, grey-faced, had said close to Mark's ear. 'When she did not answer the *'umda's* call to help Iksander's mother, the villagers took this to mean that she had turned her back on them. Iksander's mother died, therefore they needed justice.'

Mark had felt a hammering in his skull and had heard his voice, flat and stony, say, 'Yes of course, that's what happened. Will you . . . bury her, Abdul? Say the proper prayers for her?'

'Yes, *effendi*. Will you be talking to the *'umda* about this?'

Mark had shaken his head. 'This is their land, Abdul. It was their justice . . .'

He had been unable to look away, despite the overpowering stench from her putrefying body; it was the look on her face that held him: the bulging, glassy eyes – the stark horror in them. What could so terrify the *shaykha*? She who seemed afraid of nothing?

'*Effendi.*'

Mark squinted up at Abdul's silhouette. 'Yes?'

'We have reached the top of the door.'

Everyone knelt in the sand around Mark as he squatted before the stone wall. They were crouched at the base of the eastern canyon cliff, staring down at the spot that had been cleared by the *fellaheen*. Sharply and distinctly, the natural limestone strata of the wall came to an end, and directly beneath it, disappearing below the sand, was a smooth, handcarved block of white stone lying horizontally in the limestone. At its center were carved two hawk eyes that traditionally topped funerary stelae.

'What are they?' whispered Halstead.

Mark reached out and gingerly ran his fingertips over the carving. 'The Eyes of Horus. The deceased was supposed to be able to look through them and see the light of day.'

'But they look . . .'

'Mutilated. They are. And deliberately. This was no accident. Here, you can see the chisel marks.'

'But why?'

'Offhand, I'd say it was to blind them.'

Everyone stood up and brushed the dust from their hands. Halstead said, 'How long will it take to clear away the entire door?'

Mark looked at the stone stairway descending into the earth. 'The threshold is about ten feet directly below us. I'd say another day, maybe two.'

The cries of the mourners of Hag Qandil filled the valley. As the seven ate dinner in silence, they each fixed on the wailing and pictured again the *shaykha's* body.

Sanford Halstead pushed away his barely touched plate of greens and said woodenly, 'Have you any way of telling at this point if the tomb is intact?'

Mark swung his head. He, too, was still shaken by the old woman's death. He felt her loss sharply; there had been so much he had wanted to ask her.

'Those mutilated eyes on the tomb door,' said Halstead, 'could that be the work of tomb robbers?'

Mark tried to keep his mind on the tomb, on his reason for being there. The stricken looks on his companions' faces reminded him that he was their leader; they needed his strength, his stability. If he were to show weakness now, the whole project could collapse. 'Tomb robbers would have had neither reason nor the time to do it. No, that is the work of the priests.'

'Why would they go to the trouble of carving the eyes on the lintel and then turn around and disfigure them?'

'Because you have to have eyes in the first place to be blind.'

'What do you mean?'

'Whoever's buried in that tomb, the priests didn't want him to be able to look out. Just to be sure, they gave him eyes and then blinded them.'

Everyone stopped eating and stared at Mark.

He examined his fingers. The bandages had come off but the fingertips were still sore. Then he saw an insect crawl out from under his plate. He slammed his hand down on it.

'Can't something be done about this, Davison?' said Halstead, batting a fly away.

'Hazards of desert living.'

Hazim al-Sheikhly, who had been scratching in his pocket notebook, cleared his throat and said, 'Dr Davison, I will not be accompanying you to the site tomorrow. I will take a felucca to El Minya, for I must telephone my superiors.'

Mark turned his head sharply.

'It is time to make a report. By the time they will have sent their representatives down to us, the door will be cleared. My superiors must be on hand for the opening of the tomb.

Mark scowled. 'I was hoping we would be allowed a few more days of freedom before . . .'

No one noticed that Hazim's linen napkin, crumpled by his plate, quivered slightly, nor did anyone hear the tiny scratching sounds of eight sharply hooked feet on the tablecloth.

'You see, Dr Davison, we have been here now for two

weeks, the ministry will be looking for a progress report . . .'

The corner of the napkin lifted a fraction as a small yellow head poked out. A pair of red lidless eyes surveyed the situation; two bony pincers opened and closed experimentally.

'And we have made without a doubt a wondrous discovery. I agree with you, Dr Davison, that a few more days of freedom would be preferred, but I cannot withhold the news any longer . . .'

A slender yellow tail, glossy and segmented, rose into an arc beneath the napkin.

'. . . I would be reprimanded.'

Mark shrugged in resignation. 'I hope at least we can keep the press at bay.'

'I shall recommend that in my report.' Hazim slipped the notebook into his shirt pocket then dropped his hand on to the napkin.

'Allah!' He jerked his arm back with such force that he tumbled off the bench and sprawled on to the floor.

When the scorpion emerged, its tail still poised, and scurried across the table, everyone screamed and jumped back. Mark seized his plate and crashed it down on the creature before it could drop over the edge. While everyone else stared in shock, Yasmina immediately ran to Hazim's side, opening her medical bag.

'I need to see it!' she said as she rapidly bound his arm with a rubber tourniquet. 'I need to see the scorpion!'

Mark shuddered as he cautiously lifted the plate. The tablecloth was clean.

'Hey!' cried Ron. 'It got away!'

'It can't have,' said Mark, stepping back and hastily looking around the floor. 'I know I got it.'

'Oh fuck, man, it got away!'

Sanford Halstead whipped about and dashed out the door.

'Jesus, come on!' Ron had a flashlight in his hand and was wildly sweeping the beam under the table.

Hazim lay groaning on the floor, muttering in Arabic, while Yasmina examined his hand. 'I need some ice.'

Mark glanced at Alexis, who was staring in a daze at the clean tablecloth, then he went to the refrigerator. When he had the cubes bundled in a napkin, he knelt next to Yasmina and held the ice pack on Hazim's hand. 'I must know the species, Mark,' she said. 'I did not see it.'

'I don't know scorpions.'

'Was it fat or slender?'

'Slender, I guess.'

'Hairy?'

'I don't know.' Mark looked over at Ron who was down on one knee with a flashlight.

'Was it yellow?'

'Yes.'

Yasmina reached into her bag and withdrew a needle and a five cc syringe. As she filled the barrel from a small glass vial, she said softly, 'The deadly species.'

Hazim, Mark saw, had broken out in a sweat. He lay with his eyes closed, muttering.

'Will he be all right?'

'The antevenin will take care of him, but he will be sick for a few hours.' She rolled up Hazim's sleeve and injected his deltoid muscle. 'Now we must get him to his tent.'

Mark massaged the back of his neck as he and Yasmina stepped into the cool evening. They had had problems with Hazim. After being put to bed, the young man had grown restless and delirious. His pulse had nearly doubled and his temperature had shot to a hundred and three. Mark had had to secure Hazim to the cot while Yasmina had administered a barbiturate. Then they had sat with him until the convulsions were controlled and his temperature was down.

'His symptoms are unusually severe,' said Yasmina as they slowly walked across the compound. 'He will be ill for about twelve hours, and then he will be all right. But he will not be able to use his hand for a while.'

'Abdul will keep an eye on him.'

As they neared her tent, they were joined by Ron, who was loping over the sand, shaking his head. 'I don't know where the sucker got to. I had four men search every molecule of that tent.'

'There must be a hole somewhere.'

'Not that we could find.' Ron wrapped his long arms about himself and shivered. 'Never could stand spiders! What I need is a drink!' He trudged past them into his darkroom.

Mark looked down at Yasmina. 'Are you all right?'

She regarded him in mild surprise. 'Yes, why should I not be?'

'You look . . .' he took hold of her shoulders, 'tired.'

'I could not sleep. The *shaykha–*'

'I know.'

Tears welled in her eyes, and when a drop tumbled down her cheek, Mark gently wiped it away. 'Hazim told me only yesterday,' she said in a timorous voice, 'that he wanted to leave. He said he wanted to return to Cairo and turn the job over to someone else.'

'Why?'

'He cannot sleep here. He has bad dreams. And there have been other scorpions.'

'How do *you* feel about staying?'

'I will stay where I am needed, but . . .' her face darkened. 'I am frightened here. Perhaps, when he is past the crisis and can travel, he and I should go back to Cairo.'

Unwittingly, Mark pressed his fingers into her shoulders. 'Are you that afraid?'

She bowed her head. 'I, too, have had dreams . . .'

'But I need you here!'

Yasmina looked up, startled.

'Please don't leave,' said Mark awkwardly.

'Do not worry, Mark. I will wait until a replacement is here before I go. Perhaps Dr Rahman–'

'That's not what I'm talking about. It's not a doctor I need, it's you–'

She stepped back, pulling out of his grasp. 'No,' said Yasmina softly. 'If you need me, I will stay, but as the doctor, not for any other reason.' Then she turned blindly and disappeared into her tent.

A minute later Mark stepped into the warm glow of his own tent, sat down on the edge of his cot and pulled off his boots. He could hear the faint opening notes of Vivaldi on Ron's cassette.

As Mark started to remove his socks, he heard a sound on the other side of the tent wall. Pausing, he listened. It could be barely heard, sounding curiously near and far off at the same time: a swishing, like a giant pendulum slicing the night air. Mark put his foot down and sat frozen on the edge of the cot; a draft penetrated the Dacron, a frigid gust like the sudden opening and closing of a freezer door. Mark shivered reflexively.

Then he winced. A dull pain shot through his head.

His eyes wide and staring, his hands dangling uselessly over his knees, Mark strained to hear the sound draw near through the formidable darkness beyond the camp.

Swish. Swish. Swish . . .

And then a feeling of dread, filling his soul as an ache now filled his head, made him swallow painfully and shudder violently.

It was coming again–

The tent flap drew back.

He whipped around, a strangled cry in his throat.

'Dr Davison?'

He squinted up at Alexis Halstead, at the flaming corona around her face: her hair was disheveled, her clothes untidy. 'May I come in?'

He eyed her cautiously. 'Yes . . .'

Alexis looked around the tent and pulled the wooden chair out from the small desk. As she sat down, she said, 'Such a strange chill out!'

Mark regarded her quizzically. She had that look to her

again: remote, distracted, 'Mrs Halstead . . . did you see or hear anything out there just now?'

She looked at him with unfocused eyes. 'No . . .'

Mark thought a moment, listening to the night silence beyond the tent wall, then resumed taking off his socks.

Alexis's steamy green eyes followed his every move. 'I heard you mention to your friend earlier that you have some bourbon.'

'Yes I do.'

'May I have some?'

He reached under the bed and withdrew an unopened quart of Wild Turkey. 'I brought this along to celebrate the discovery of the tomb.' He filled two glasses on his night stand and handed one to Alexis.

She took a tentative sip, then winced slightly.

'Something wrong with the bourbon?'

'No . . .' Alexis brought a hand up to her temple and massaged it.

Mark studied her face in concern. Yasmina had told him that Alexis had asked for more sleeping pills. 'Aren't you sleeping well, Mrs Halstead?'

Her eyes roamed around the tent. 'I've been having dreams . . .'

Mark waited upon her next word, and when it didn't come, he said, 'Dreams?'

'Strange dreams . . .' Alexis took another sip, a long one, her eyes glazing over as she spoke. 'I never used to dream at all. If I did, it was in black and white. But since we've been here at Tell el-Amarna I've had the most vivid and colorful dreams every night. They wake me up and then I can't get back to sleep.'

Mark took a swallow of bourbon. The headache intensified. 'What are the dreams about?'

Alexis inhaled deeply and let her breath out slowly. Her eyes became more remote, her voice more distant. 'I see things. And I feel things. Strange emotions. Sometimes I wake up and find I've been crying in my sleep.'

Mark leaned forward, his elbows resting on his knees.

The light in the tent seemed to dim; the walls felt closer. 'What sort of things do you see?'

'Towers . . . tall, white towers. And walls. And gardens. And I see people. I walk with them. I'm one of them. I dream that I am another woman, and I'm one of these brown people. There's a man, an ugly man–' Alexis frowned down at her glass. Her voice grew thin. 'And in my dreams I feel this need to . . . look for something.'

Mark gazed at her limestone profile, her hair like a fire-fall.

'In my sleep . . . I feel myself change. I become this other woman and she . . . she makes me think strange thoughts, makes me feel emotions I've never before . . .'

Alexis suddenly jerked her head back and frowned at Mark. 'Silly things! Dreams!'

She leaned back in the chair and drank down the rest of her bourbon. Mark took another sip, watching her over the rim of his glass. When she looked at him again, the wildness in her eyes startled him. 'May I have a refill?'

'Yes, of course . . .'

When her glass was full, Alexis relaxed instantly. She fluffed her hair off her shoulders. 'You're still mad at me aren't you?'

'For what?'

'The deception. The way I hired you.' She emitted a queer, high-pitched laugh. 'Men are funny creatures! They're happiest when feeling superior to a woman. I'll wager if it had been Sanford who had lost you that professorship you wouldn't be nearly so angry.' Alexis tilted her head back, arching her long white neck. 'Men have always bored me. They're like children. So unreliable and insecure. Constantly demanding that their egos be fed. So tiresome!' She took another draw on the bourbon. 'Now women, on the other hand, can be counted on. They aren't silly or vain. And they know more about the art of making love than men will ever know!'

Mark picked up the bottle and refilled his glass. When

his eyes met hers again, he saw that they were warm and tropical; there was a peculiar light behind them.

'I've never met a man who knew how to really make love,' she said archly. 'All they think of is thrusting and jabbing and satisfying themselves. A woman's touch is gentle and full of magic. When you think about it, only a woman can really know how to satisfy another woman. It doesn't surprise you, does it, that I have female lovers?'

He did not reply.

'No role-playing, no dominance, no ego to flatter. Just equal loving and equal gratification.' Alexis tossed down the rest of the bourbon and held out her glass.

'Mrs Halstead, do you really think you should–'

'It helps me to sleep, Mark. Please . . .'

He filled her glass and placed the bottle by his feet. 'Mrs Halstead, why don't you go to bed?'

Her lips curled into a smile. 'Is that an offer?'

Mark's eyes widened.

She laughed huskily. Alexis now almost seemed to steam. She was a jungle, all vines and ferns and mysterious undergrowths. 'Come on, Mark, don't tell me you haven't thought about it. I've seen the way you look at me. Wouldn't you like it?'

'Mrs Halstead. . .'

She put her glass down and came to sit next to him on the cot. Alexis laid her hand on his thigh and said, 'My husband is asleep and your roommate is in his darkroom. Mark, you're the first man who's ever excited me.'

He tried to fight the overpowering scent of gardenias, the humidity in her eyes, the feel of her firm breast against his arm.

'Let's experiment,' she whispered. 'I'll do anything you want.'

Her breath was warm and moist on his face; her hand was creeping up his inner thigh. 'Listen, Alexis–'

With her free hand she started to unbutton her blouse.

'Let me take you back to your tent'.

'We can't do it there,' her lips were on his ear. 'Mark,

tell me, do you want it?'

By now her blouse was open, exposing her bare breasts. Mark reached up and drove his fingers into her luxuriant hair. 'Yes,' he murmured. Then his mouth was on hers.

Alexis responded as if she were on fire; her arms circled his neck as she devoured his kiss, sucking on his tongue, stealing the breath out of him. Mark groaned as his hand sought her breasts; he explored them, caressed them, pinched the firm nipples until she also groaned.

As they squirmed on the bed, Mark's bare foot knocked against the bourbon bottle and it fell on its side, spilling the liquor.

'Damn!' he hissed, pulling himself away and reaching down for it. As he did so, his eyes focused on the metal box beneath his cot, the box containing Ramsgate's Journal, and for one hypnotic moment he stared at it.

'July 18, 1881: My poor Amanda, bewitched, possessed! Making unthinkable overtures to Sir Robert! My Amanda who has always been the soul of propriety and chastity, offering herself to Sir Robert! What madness has possessed her!'

Mark snapped back up and gaped at Alexis with a mixture of horror and revulsion.

'What's wrong?' breathed Alexis, her eyes half-closed, her arms reaching out to him.

'Mrs Halstead,' he said, rising unsteadily. 'This isn't right. You have to go back to your tent.'

'Oh Mark, Mark.' Her arms snaked up to him. 'What do you want? Just say it and I'll do it.

'I shouldn't have let this happen. I'll take you back.'

'Do you want me to take it in my mouth, is that it?'

Mark seized her wrists and jerked her to her feet. 'Mrs Halstead!'

She smiled dreamily as he took hold of her by the shoulders and gave her a shake. 'Alexis! Snap out of it! Look, I don't know what pills you took before you came here, but it's my fault for letting this get out of hand.'

'Thou doest not understand . . .' Alexis cried in a tight voice. 'She resists me, she will not allow me to speak with thee! The end is nearing, Davison, I must tell thee the secrets of everlasting life!'

Mark hastily buttoned her blouse and tried to steer her to the doorway, but she resisted him. 'Fool, Davison! Listen to me! I know the secrets! Thou must hurry, for time is running out! But she is . . . but I . . .' Alexis blinked and shook her head drunkenly. 'She will not do my bidding. I must speak with thee, but all she can think of is gratifying her lust. She will not let me through, Davison.'

Mark fixed an arm firmly around her waist and pro- pelled her out of the tent.

All was dark and deserted. He guided Alexis across the compound, and said when they arrived at her tent, 'Go to sleep, Mrs Halstead.'

Her eyes fluttered open; she frowned.

'Mrs Halstead?'

'Yes. . . I'm sleepy . . .'

'Are you all right?'

'Yes . . . I don't need her now . . .' Alexis turned away from him and fumbled her way through the flap. Mark waited until he heard the cot creak beneath her weight, then silence was all around him once again.

A wind rose up suddenly, whistling through the camp, lifting fine sand into swirls and eddies. Mark shivered and closed his eyes against the flying grit. When the breeze died, the night seemed colder, sharper.

His head thumped painfully.

Mark turned away from the Halsteads' tent and looked out at the dark expanse of desert. He heard someone singing.

It was faint at first, as if coming from far away, then the voice, a woman's, grew louder, and he was able to distinguish the words.

'*Ta em sertu en maa satet-k. Uben-f em xut abtet ent pet.*'

242

Mark was drawn over the sand toward the sweetly sad song. The haunting melody seemed to reach out and embrace him, as if gently urging him along.

He found her sitting on the broken bit of ancient wall; her hands lay idly in her lap, her head was bowed. Nofr'tay-tay seemed unaware of him. *'Bodies pass away since the time of the gods, and young men come in their place. Ra shows himself at dawn; Atum goes to rest in the Western Mountains.'*

Her willowy body swayed with the melody; her voice was high, enchanting. *'Men beget and women conceive. Every nostril breathes the air. Dawn comes, all children are gone to their tombs.'*

She lifted her hand and took a long look at Mark. 'Hello, Davison.'

He frowned at her, feeling the pulse in his temple.

'Do I make thee nervous?'

'You make me doubt my sanity.'

'Doest thou not believe in me yet?'

'You're a figment of my imagination.'

Her face was clearer this time, more solid. No longer could Mark see the distant village lights through her. Yet still she glowed, as if cloaked in phosphorus. And tonight, carried on the breeze, was the fragrance of crushed gardenias: her perfume.

'That is why I try to speak through *her*. In this incarnation, thou doest not believe in me! What am I to do, Davison?'

Mark studied the vision with a clinical eye. This time he could trace the pattern in her lotiform collar, pick out the vulture and uraeus on her headband, distinguish scarabs of lapis-lazuli in her bracelet. Beneath her robe of gauze: pink nipples and smooth, unblemished skin.

Impulsively he said, 'Have I found the tomb I'm looking for?'

'Thou has found a tomb, Davison.'

'Have I found 'Khnaton's tomb?'

'Yes.'

His eyes were locked on her face. She was expressionless, a mask of calcite, challenging him with deep oriental eyes. Mark wiped his hands down his pants. 'And . . .' he felt a trickle of sweat tumble between his shoulderblades, 'when I open the tomb, will I find him there?'

'Yes.'

Mark felt his legs give way. He sank on to the sand and stared up at the beautiful incandescent woman. 'I must be going mad. My mind is telling me what I want to hear.'

The woman's aura flared for an instant. 'How darest thou doubt me! Do I not tell thee what thou asks? Davison, I am vexed.'

'I'm sorry, but how do I know this isn't my mind playing tricks on me? How do I know I'm not hallucinating?'

'Thou art of mule-headed blood, my one, but I will be patient. I will tell thee something thy mind does not know. I can tell thee how the witch died, will that satisfy thee? It was done by the hands of the Upreared One.'

'What–'

'She challenged the will of the gods and she lost. The witch died in a long and terrible agony, for such is the power of the Upreared One.'

'That substance in her mouth . . .'

'One will make thee to eat thy own excrement.'

He shook his head violently. 'No!'

'Canst thou not see, my one, that thou art in danger?'

'From what?'

'The Seven that were put there. Thou must know them, Davison, and thou must fight them. There are seven and each will punish according to his ordination. Thou must beware of the Seven, Davison, for each will kill in its own way. And for thee, as thou art the leader of thy companions, for thee Davison is the most terrible punishment of all . . .' her voice echoed on the desert night, '. . . slow dismemberment.'

Mark rubbed his hands over his face. 'I must be going mad!'

'Doest thou doubt me still? I have great knowledge, my one. I am the sum of the mysteries of the ancient ones.' Nofr'tay-tay rose gracefully, her robe shimmering as she moved. 'Come with me, my one, and I will show thee wondrous things!'

Mark awoke with a shaft of light stabbing his eyes. He found himself lying in bed fully clothed; the morning sun was streaming through the netting of the open window. Dazed, Mark struggled out of bed, moaning with the throb in his head, and when his bare feet touched the floor, he cried out. Looking down, he saw that the soles were cut and covered with dried blood.

Mark stayed where he was on the edge of the cot and cradled his head in his hands.

It came back to him in patches at first; then more and more returned until he remembered his entire experience on the plain.

He had followed her to the ruins, walking in the freezing night air but untouched by the cold; treading barefooted over sharp rubble and rocks, but unaware of them. His eyes and mind had been filled with her radiance, always walking before him, her slender arm outstretched, pointing. Nofr'tay-tay had led him down fantastic avenues where plumed horses pulled electrum-plated chariots and palm trees stood in neat rows and house fronts were ornamented with brightly painted columns and papyrus grew in lotus pools and brown children ran naked and beautiful men and women in flowing gowns walked in contentment beneath the rays of Aton.

She had led him past mighty palaces where colorful banners flew atop massive pylons. Past temples teeming with holy men in white robes, their heads shaven. They paused beneath the Window of Appearances; they entered lush courtyards populated with exotic flora and gazelles. Mark saw Minoans in the streets, slender feminine people who hawked wares from their island across the Great Sea. And there were woolly Babylonians, fringed and bearded, haggling with animated gestures. Taverns gave out sounds of musical instruments and drunken singing. Everywhere they went, every road they walked, there was pavement and freshly painted buildings and trees and noise and life.

They walked through desolate ruins where walls were no more than two feet high, and Mark saw only the magnificence of the great Temple to the Sun. He followed the vision of Nofr'tay-tay over sand and rock, but he felt beneath his feet grass and smooth marble. The sky was black and sprayed with stars, but Mark saw a stunning blue and felt a hot sun on his neck.

They had walked for miles, crossing the plain and doubling back; they had walked all night, and all the while Nofr'tay-tay had spoken to him of the splendors of Akhet-Aton.

Now, holding his head in his hands, Mark felt utterly defeated.

More light suddenly poured into the tent and he heard Ron say, 'Good thing you're awake!'

Mark lifted his head with great effort. 'What is it . . .?'

'You look awful! Really tied one on last night, didn't you? Well, I hate to do this to you, but you're needed outside pronto.'

'Why?'

'Something's going on and you're not going to like it.'

NINETEEN

MARK BLINKED in bewilderment at the approaching delegation, but his surprise quickly turned to anger.

'I don't like the look of this,' he heard Ron murmur close to him.

Mark did not respond. He stood before his tent with arms folded, keeping a displeased eye on the visitors. This was not what he needed right now. He wanted to be alone, to sit by himself and think about last night's dream. He wanted to linger over the memory of Nofr'tay-tay, savor his 'walk' with her, recall to mind the incredible sights he had 'seen'. But he did not want this.

The *'umda* was accompanied by three young men in striped *galabeyahs*, two veiled women carrying wrapped bundles, and Constantine Domenikos, the Greek. The frail old man was astride a donkey; the others walked.

No one spoke as they approached. The padding of hooves and feet over the sand was the only sound to disturb the morning's crisp stillness. Mark stood with Ron, Yasmina, Abdul and the Halsteads.

When the donkey came to a halt, the *'umda* was helped down and escorted forward by one of the youths. *'Ah laan,'* he said, raising his hand, but Mark saw unfriendliness in the old face.

'Welcome, *hagg,* what brings you here?'

'An unpleasant duty, Dr Davison. I come as a representative of all four villages. We have need to talk.'

'My ears are open.'

The old man ruminated his thin lips. 'Is there no place

we can sit? No tea for guests?'

'We have work to do, *hagg*. State your business.'

The tiny eyes flared brightly. 'You disappoint me, Dr Davison, I had thought you civilised.'

'Civilised!' spat Mark contemptuously. 'And what do you call yourself, *hagg*? What do you call what you and your people did to the *shaykha!*'

The old man trembled. 'She did not die by our hands! We respected the *shaykha*, we needed her! And now the people of Hag Qandil blame *us* for her death when it is *you* who have killed her!'

'Say what you came to say, *hagg*.'

'For years!' cried the wavering voice of the *'umda*. 'For years we have venerated that which is *gadim*. And for years we have welcomed and respected the work of the foreign scientists in our valley. But now it has all gone wrong and we wish you to leave.'

Mark's arms dropped down. 'You're joking!'

'You have broken ancient taboos, Dr Davison. You have let bad magic into the valley. Now we wish you to go.'

'What the devil are you talking about?'

The *'umda* gestured with his staff and the two black-clad women came shyly forward. The first spread her arms and let the bundle fall open. A dead animal spilled out and thudded to the ground before Mark and his companions.

Mark gave the beast a quick glance, then said, 'You have had two-headed calves before, *hagg*. You cannot blame this on our presence.'

Then the second woman knelt and gently unwrapped her burden. Mark fell back a step, and Alexis released a muffled cry.

'This was to be my grandson,' said the *'umda* sadly. 'But he was born four months too soon. The evil magic has caused my daughter to miscarry.'

Mark collected himself and said, 'The fetus is deformed, nature aborted it not I. Your daughter is nearly fifty years old, she is too old for any more pregnancies.'

'Our water has gone bad! An infestation has attacked our bean crop! Our women cry out in the night with bad dreams! You must go away from here!'

'We're not leaving, *hagg*.'

'I demand to speak to the government man.'

Mark turned to Yasmina. 'Where's Hazim?'

'He is still not well, Mark.'

'I'm sorry, *hagg*, Mr Sheikhly is indisposed at the moment. But it doesn't matter. We have official permission to work here.'

'I will go to the *mudir*.'

'You can go to President Sadat for all I care. We stay.'

A crimson tide flooded the old man's cheeks and his eyes blazed with fury. For a moment, Mark was afraid the *'umda* was going to have a stroke, then the seizure passed and the old man said in more humble tones, 'I beg of you, Dr Davison. *Please go away from us.*'

Mark looked over at the pudgy face of Constantine Domenikos and found it curiously noncommittal. To the *'umda* he said, 'You are letting superstition frighten you, *hagg*. There is no evil here. We are only scientists doing our job. Surely we can all live in peace.'

'No peace, Dr Davison.' The old man seemed to deflate. He said unhappily, 'I know that you will persist and that catastrophes will occur. So I must do what I can to prevent it. My men will be called back to the village.'

'Is it more payment you want? More tea? Coca-Cola?'

The old man swung his head side to side. 'How you misunderstand me!'

'Then it's the artefacts you're after! Threats won't work, *hagg*. I'm going to see to it that whatever is brought out of the tomb – and don't pretend you don't know about it – is taken to the Cairo Museum.'

'What an unhappy hour this is! Dr Davison, my people want only peace, and since you will not grant it to us, then I will call the workers back to the village. They will listen to me.'

'I can send to Luxor for workers.'

'We shall see, Dr Davison, we shall see.'

Mark watched the old man hobble back to his donkey and mount the beast with great effort. Before turning away, the *'umda* raised a bony finger and said, 'I have warned you.'

The group standing before the tent watched in silence as the pathetic little delegation ambled away, then Mark turned to Abdul and said, 'Get these corpses out of here.'

'*Effendi,* what will we do about the workers?'

'I don't know. Surely he can't have the power to call them all back.

'No, *effendi,* I think I can persuade the men from Hag Qandil to stay for a high price. But remember, *effendi,* that we depend upon the *'umda* for our water and fresh food.'

'As soon as Hazim is better, he'll be reporting to Cairo. When the officials come here, they can bring a fresh team with them. In the meantime, we need only a handful of men to finish clearing away the tomb entrance. For supplies, we can go across to Mellawi. Now please, Abdul, get these things out of here.'

The gaunt Arab nodded and solemnly gathered up the two bundles. As he walked away, Ron said quietly, 'Think there will be trouble?'

'I don't know. For one thing, we do have the government on our side. Especially with the tomb found. There's no way the old man can move us from this valley. Things might get uncomfortable, but he wouldn't be so foolish as to get the officials mad at him. Don't forget what his people did to the *shaykha.* That's murder, Ron.'

As the others headed for the mess tent, which was giving off odors of burnt coffee and sizzling grease, Yasmina came up to Mark. 'You are limping. What is wrong with your feet?'

'I forgot to wear my shoes.'

'Let me look at them.'

They went into her tent where Mark sat down on a

folding chair and Yasmina knelt before him. 'This must be very painful.'

'I guess.'

Yasmina reached behind Mark to her utility bench and said, 'Roll up your sleeve, please.'

'Why?'

'I am giving you a tetanus booster.'

When she returned to his feet with a pan of soapy water, she said, 'How did this happen?'

'I . . . I went for a walk and forgot my shoes. How is Hazim?'

She gently washed off the blood and sand as she spoke. 'I do not understand it. Abdul awakened me this morning to tell me that Mr Sheikhly was having convulsions. His hand was swollen and purple, which is unusual in the sting of the yellow scorpion. I gave him morphine and now he sleeps, but I am perplexed.'

'And how is Halstead?'

'He is the same. He came to me this morning and asked me what he can do to stop his bleeding problem. When I asked where he was bleeding, he would not tell me. There is nothing I can do for him.'

Mark shook his head. He looked around the tent, at the cluster of dried flowers decorating the photograph of an elderly man, at the Koran on her night table, at the small bar of lavender soap in a delicate bisque dish. Then he watched her slender brown hands work over his wounds.

'Are you unhappy here?' he asked quietly.

She dried his feet with a soft towel and then smeared them with an orange balm. Yasmina did not look up as she spoke. 'Not unhappy, Mark, but afraid. The *'umda* is right. There are bad forces here, and we are tampering with them.'

He continued to gaze down at her, recalling his night spent with Nofr'tay-tay, and considered telling Yasmina about the visions. She would understand.

'I think we should all go away from this place, Mark,' she went on, applying the bandages. 'I do not wish to leave you, nor will I leave Hazim. So we must all go together, as we came, in one group.'

Mark sucked in his lower lip, feeling a pang of disappointment. No, perhaps she wouldn't understand after all. None of them would . . .

In the mess tent, an irate Sanford Halstead was waiting for him. 'It's gotten out of hand, Davison,' said the man in supreme agitation, pacing and slamming a fist into his palm. Ron and Abdul were also in the tent; Yasmina stood behind Mark.

'What are you talking about?'

'I want to leave, Davison. I want to pack up and go.'

'You can't be serious!'

'Do not presume to tell me what I can and cannot be, Davison!' Halstead held a thick wadded cloth to his nostrils. 'I have no intention of ending up like Neville Ramsgate!'

Mark looked at the faces of Ron and Abdul, both grave and unreadable. 'Surely, Mr Halstead, you don't believe in these demons–'

'I do not care, Davison, if it's demons or *fellaheen*. I have no intention of getting slaughtered. That old '*umda* meant business. First he'll pull away every man we've got, then, when we're defenseless, he'll send someone to murder us in our beds!'

Stunned, Mark looked from Halstead to Abdul – whose heavily lidded eyes were noncommittal – to Ron, who said, quietly, 'I agree with him, Mark.'

Mark sank down on to the bench. 'But why?'

'I don't know about any demons or curses, all I know is we're not wanted here and there have already been three grisly murders. It happened a hundred years ago to Ramsgate. Just when he was about to open the door of the tomb, he died, and I don't think it was from smallpox. Mark, these people want us out of here and they'll stop at nothing to get rid of us.'

252

Mark drove his fingers through his hair. 'This is madness! Here we are on the threshold of a fantastic discovery and you let a few locals scare you off!'

'Mark . . .' Ron reached over and laid a hand on his friend's arm. 'Face reality. We're in danger here–'

'No!' Mark slammed a fist on the table.

'Then let's simply back off until the government teams get here. That's all we ask. Let's go up to Minya and send a wire and sit it out until the officials arrive.'

'No!' Mark snatched his arm away from Ron's grasp. 'We continue working.'

'You're not being reasonable! Jesus, Mark, you're getting more and more irrational every day. What happened to the cool, pragmatic scientist? Look at you, man!'

Mark swiveled away from his friend's accusing eyes. They didn't understand! How could he make them see? He *had* to stay here, he couldn't leave, no matter what. The tomb was too important, and then there was *her,* how could he leave her before finding out what she was, where she came from, Nofr'tay-tay . . .

'Mark!'

He blinked at Ron.

'Be reasonable, man. That's all I ask. Let's go to El Minya right away, this afternoon–'

'I said no. Listen, Ron.' Mark spoke rapidly. 'How long do you think that tomb would last in our absence? Once we set foot on the other side of the river, those villagers will swarm down on it and break it up, pillage it, destroy the delicate artefacts, sell the gold to Domenikos, and all the while we're sitting in Minya waiting for the government to step in!'

Ron stared at Mark for a long moment, then said with a frown. 'I don't know . . . I hadn't thought of that.'

'No!' cried Halstead, the handkerchief now bloodstained. 'I say we go! This is *my* expedition and *I* say what goes–'

'Sanford!'

Everyone spun round.

Alexis Halstead, tall and majestic, stood in the doorway like a conquering queen. 'We do not leave.'

'But Alexis–'

'Sanford, one more word and I will send you back to where you came from.'

He beheld her with horror, shrinking beneath her virulent green eyes.

'Now then,' she strode into the tent and stood with feet apart, hands on hips. 'You're all getting hysterical. We are not going to let a few simple-minded farmers keep us from what is ours. I will not stand for it. This is *my* expedition and I say we stay.'

They all gazed up at her, at the imperial defiance in her eyes, the challenging stance of her magnificient body.

'If you wish to call in government help, Dr Davison, then do so. Whatever you need, get it. But we stay. And that's all there is to it.'

Mark was down on his knees, cleaning the top of the tomb door with puffers and soft paintbrushes. Two feet had been cleared down from the lintel, and inscriptions were clearly read in the stone. With his pipe clamped between his teeth and a sweat-soaked bandana around his head, Mark worked long and painstakingly in the hot sun to expose the hieroglyphs.

The handful of *fellaheen* Abdul had been able to bribe to stay continued to clear the stairway; nine steps were now uncovered, closer to the entrance and deeper into the earth. Halstead sat with Alexis beneath the flapping tarp, swatting flies, while Ron worked with his tripod and cameras. Yasmina had chosen to stay back at the camp with Hazim.

When the last character of the bottom-most column was exposed, Mark sat back and massaged his shoulders. Now he could concentrate on reading what he had brought to light.

He looked it over first, roughly translating it in his

mind, then he picked up his clipboard and did a more precise job. As the words went down on paper Mark felt himself become detached from the pen and hand that wrote them.

'Here lieth the Heretic, the Criminal, He-Who-Has-No-Name, and a curse upon the traveler who uttereth the name of this man and giveth him life, for he will see the incarnation of Set, he will see the personification of the Powers of Evil and of Darkness and of the forces of the waters which resist light and order, and he will see the seven-times-seven Companions as beasts and creatures which dwell in the dark waters and as beasts and creatures of sand and rock, and he will sorrow before them.

'Behold the Guardians of the Heretic, for they watch in eternal vigilance!'

The seven figures which appeared on the topstone of the stela were carved here again; below them the inscription continued.

'Beware to the traveler who goeth upstream that he not disturb the contents of this house, nor enter in, nor remove anything out. And beware to the traveler who goeth downstream, that he uttereth not the name of the Criminal, for such is the vengeance of the Terrible Ones:'

Mark dropped his pen and fell back from the door. Droplets of sweat found their way down from his bandana and trickled into his eyes. As the hieroglyphs blurred before him, Mark felt the heat of the day turn to a snapping cold, and for a moment he shivered. 'Ron, come here . . .'

Ron squatted next to him and inspected the carvings. 'So,' he murmured out of the hearing of the others. 'Ramsgate didn't mistranslate after all. Here they are, exactly as he wrote them in his Journal. The seven curses . . .'

Yasmina closed the book and regarded Mark with black, liquid eyes. She did not speak.

Unable to meet her gaze, Mark toyed with his pipe, cleaning it, refilling it, but not lighting it. As the night breeze howled mournfully through the compound, he tried to think of something to say.

'And you had thought that Neville Ramsgate might have been wrong?' she said at last.

They were sitting in her tent, drinking mint tea. 'Egyptology was in its infancy in 1881. It wasn't even called Egyptology then. And Champollion's decoding of the Rosetta Stone had not yet received wide publication. You see, Yasmina,' he finally looked at her. 'This is no ordinary tomb door. When I first read about it in the Journal, I was sure Ramsgate had not translated accurately.'

He looked down at his pipe. 'Egyptian tombs were always guarded by gods and goddesses of light and resurrection, never by demons. Any curses that were on the tomb were mild and intended only to keep tomb robbers out. The inscriptions always invoked the passing traveler to speak the name of the deceased in order to revive his soul. But . . .' he waved a hand at the Journal, 'this . . .'

Yasmina considered the bizarre inscriptions, then said softly, 'It is almost as if . . . the priests of Amon, instead of trying to keep tomb robbers out, were trying to keep whatever is in the tomb *in.*'

Mark raised his eyes to her.

She went on: 'The priests of Amon must have been terrified of Akhnaton's spirit, for they have not written his name on the tomb door. Without his name written somewhere, his soul will not know its identity and therefore it will exist only in a twilight. Without its name, the spirit is powerless. Mark . . .' her eyes were wide, timid, like those of a deer. 'Why did the priests fear Akhnaton's soul so?'

'I don't know.' He absently rubbed his forehead. 'Other

than that he was a heretic and had tried to do away with worshipping many gods, we only know Akhnaton as a peaceful man, a dreamer, a poet. If there was an evil side to his nature, it isn't known to us today.' Mark winced.

'Are you all right?'

'I must need glasses, I get these headaches–'

She started to rise but he reached out and took hold of her hand. 'Don't bother. Aspirins won't help. Nothing will. They come and go suddenly.' He forced a smile. 'It'll pass.'

Yasmina looked down at her hand cradled in his. Mark's calloused fingers curled around hers; she tried to pull away but he would not let go.

'Yasmina–'

'No, Mark. It cannot be so for us. Please do not make it difficult for me.'

'Then you feel it, too?'

'Mark, please–'

His hand suddenly jerked away and slapped the side of his head. His face twisted in agony.

Yasmina shot to her feet. 'What is it!'

'The pain! Oh God, it's coming again . . .'

Ron was so warmed with wine he did not feel the queer chill in the night air as he crossed the compound. Nor did he hear, beyond the edge of light, in the drowning darkness beyond the tents, a peculiar hissing sound, like steam under pressure, and then a rhythmic clicking sound, like the sticky tongue of a giant snake flicking in and out.

Once inside the tent, he hung out his DO NOT DIS-TURB sign, zipped up the flap and unrolled the black opaque cloth, snapping it in place at the bottom. After punching the ON switch of his cassette player, Ron pushed through the curtain of film strips hanging from the wire which bisected the tent, reached under the work-bench and retrieved a fresh bottle of wine. He whistled along with the 'Concierto de Aranjuez' as he filled a paper cup and took a quick swallow.

It was only when he stashed the bottle back under the bench that he noticed the sudden cold in the air. Ron leaned forward and squinted at the thermometer over the workbench; it said sixty-eight degrees. He shrugged and set about his work.

In mixing the developer, Ron was now using sterilised water on the off-chance that some quirky Nile impurities had caused the previous fogging, and as he carefully measured out the water and slowly stirred in a packet of Kodak Microdol-X, he thought he heard a scraping sound behind him. Pausing in the mixing, he listened. Between him and the arctic night there was only the strumming of classical guitar.

After he had poured the developer into the tank, Ron reached up for his OM-2, which sat on the shelf above the work area. He felt something scratch the back of his hand.

Yanking it back, he got up on his toes and inspected the shelf. Then he looked at his hand. Nothing.

Ron removed the leather camera case and dropped it on the table. Then he flicked off the light bulb overhead and the tent was plunged into total darkness.

He worked quickly to open the back of the camera and lift out the cartridge, noticing as he did so that his fingers were stiff, as if unusually cold. Ron felt around for the bottle opener, found it on the table, and pried open the film magazine. Handling the film by its edges, he slowly unrolled it, detaching the paper backing as he went.

Something tapped his leg.

Ron felt his hands tremble as he tried to work quickly but deftly. The film seemed to resist him. He stretched his eyes wide in the darkness but could see nothing; his hands worked on their own in the utter blackness of night.

Something fell lightly against his back. Ron flinched.

He hurried now, fumbling with the film and nearly dropping it. He felt around the tabletop for the tank apron, seized it and hastily rolled the film on to it.

Then he felt a cold breath against his neck.

With his fingers flying haphazardly, Ron groped for the developing tank, nearly spilling it, jammed the roll of film into it and reached for the lid. As he was about to slam it down on to the tank, a cold and scaly lump slapped the side of his face.

Ron screamed.

In blind terror he scrambled for the door, ripping the opaque cloth out of its snaps and clawing at the zipper.

'Help! Jesus, help me!'

Something pummeled his arms; icy slime gripped his hands, paralysing them. Something flicked at his face; a cold sting exploded in his cheek.

'Help! Get me outa here!'

Something took hold of his hair and jerked him back from the door with such force that Ron was toppled off his feet. He thrashed about, fighting unseen bombardments all over his body. He rolled around on the floor screaming, knocking over boxes and smashing bottles of chemicals. In the blackness, something hissed at him and coiled around his ankles. He struck out frantically, tasting blood in his mouth and feeling warm moisture spread over his chest. A clammy tendril encircled his neck, tightening with each outcry. Ron tried to pry it loose, but his arms were pinioned.

And as he lay crucified to the floor, he felt the hair on his head gather up into a knot and start to draw away from his scalp.

Ron stretched his mouth and shrieked long and agonisingly.

Then he saw stars where the tent flap had been and he felt someone step over him and was dazzled in the next instant by a sudden flash of light. Throwing an arm over his eyes, Ron heard Mark shout, 'Jesus, what happened?'

'Get it off me!' shrieked Ron. 'It's got my hair!'

'Hey!' Mark fell down to one knee and put his hands on Ron's shoulders. 'What happened?'

He slowly drew his arm away and gaped up at his friend. 'Where is it? Did you see it?'

'See what? What are you talking about?'

Shakily, Ron pushed himself up on his elbows and looked around the tent. A mess surrounded him: scattered photographic papers, spilled fluids, broken glass. Then he looked down at himself. His shirt was slashed across the chest and a thin red welt was rising on the skin. His wrists and ankles were entwined in curls of film strips.

'What the hell . . .'

'I knew you'd do it someday.' Mark reached under Ron's hair and carefully extricated a length of wire. 'Your clothesline, my friend.'

Ron ogled dumbly at it. Clothespins and weight-clips were stuck to his sleeves and pant legs, film strips lay scattered all around, the wire was coiled around his neck and twisted up in his long hair. 'No . . .' he whispered.

Yasmina appeared in the doorway, her medical bag in hand. 'What happened?' Behind her came Sanford and Alexis, looking stuporous and bewildered. Abdul pushed between them and gazed questioningly at Mark.

'He got tangled in his drying wire in the dark.'

'No . . .'

'Can you stand up?'

'Let me look at him first,' said Yasmina.

'No . . . I'm all right . . .'

With Mark's hands supporting him under the arms, Ron managed to get to his feet. In a daze he untwined the wire from his neck and arms, staring at the film strips in dumbfoundment.

'Come on,' said Mark gently.

But Ron pushed angrily away. 'Hey! There was something in here with me! I'm telling you! It was slimy and scaly and it attacked me, man. It fucking *attacked* me. It tried to pull my hair out!'

Mark took a firm hold of Ron's arm. 'You're mistaken. There was nothing in here. I opened the flap myself and, believe me, *nothing* came out. You were working in the dark and you accidentally got tangled in that wire–'

Ron wrenched his arm free. 'I'm telling you there was

something in here! I heard it breathing!'

Yasmina withdrew a hypodermic syringe from her bag and started to fill it, but when Ron saw it he backed away. 'No you don't. No tranquiliser for me. Goddamit, why won't you believe me!'

Mark held out his hands. 'Ron, there was nothing–'

Ron spun around on his heel and stormed away.

Mark drove himself to the brink of exhaustion. Despite warnings from Abdul and pleas from Yasmina, he worked at the tomb door in a heat of such intensity that even the *fellaheen* had to quit. Abdul stood with him now, holding a sunshade over him as he squatted before the door with his puffers and brushes; more than half was already cleared and nearly all the steps exposed. Three more horizontal rows of hieroglyphs gradually materialised before Mark, and finally the seals of the royal necropolis at Thebes: each one depicting a jackal with nine captives. The seals were unbroken.

Then Mark saw something that made him look closely with a magnifying glass: etched into the stone were several fine vertical lines that extended below the sand down to the threshold beneath.

'What are they?'

'I don't know. They start at around the six-foot level and disappear below the sand. They look like scratches.' Mark stared at Ron's hands as his friend turned a lens over and over; the backs of them were black and blue.

'You figure tomorrow will be the day?'

'It looks like it.' Mark started to lift the cup of Wild Turkey to his mouth, then stopped. He watched his friend's involvement with the broken lens as Ron sat cross-legged on his cot, turning it in his fingers.

'Ron?'

'Yeah?'

'You all right?'

A pair of winter-blue eyes met his gaze; they were

charged with pain and indignation. 'What do you think?'

'Look, I'm sorry. I just didn't see anything, that's all.'

'Right.'

'Come on, for God's sake, you'd been drinking wine all day–'

Ron suddenly sprang off his cot.

'Where are you going?'

'I'm going to be prepared. Next time that thing comes after me I'm going to get a picture of it!'

As Mark listened to Ron's crunching footsteps fade away, he felt a cold fist suddenly seize his stomach. He took a long draw on the bourbon and felt it burn going down, but it didn't warm him.

Mark suddenly felt very alone. He looked over at the photograph of Nancy on his night stand and wondered, for an instant, who she was. Then he impulsively grabbed his jacket, picked up his pipe and tobacco and headed out of the tent.

A hundred feet from the compound, standing on a rise of ground that had once served as a look-out point for Akhnaton's police was Alexis Halstead, dressed only in a nightgown. Mark zipped the jacket up to his neck and approached her cautiously; when he was a few feet from her he could see that her eyes were open and that she was faintly smiling. He could also see that she was asleep.

'Hello, Davison.'

It was her voice and yet it wasn't. The night wind swept her long hair off her shoulders and pressed the diaphanous gown against her naked body. Mark stared at her in wonder, unaware of the cold wind that cut through his jacket and the start of an ache inside his head.

'Mrs Halstead?'

'Yes . . . and no.'

His vision blurred. For an instant he saw double, as though he had crossed his eyes – a pain shot through the back of his skull . . . and then Alexis Halstead looked different.

It was the same body, the same gown, the same long white limbs, but on her head, transparent – like a double exposure photograph – was a black braided wig. And around her neck, a heavy lotiform collar.

The hallucination fascinated him, held him rooted as he watched her fluctuate, the solid vision of Alexis Halstead superimposed on a fragile, wavering image.

'It is the only way I can speak with thee, Davison, for alone thou doest not believe in me.'

'Nofr'tay-tay . . .'

'Thou thinkest I am nothing more than a dream. When I showed thee the wonders of my city, thy thoughts were baffled and disbelieving. I must make thee know that I am real.'

Alexis's red lips curved upward. She held out a milky arm. 'Thou wilt listen to *her,* for she governs thee, Davison. I know not how, I know not what power this red-haired one wields over thee, yet I can read it in her sleeping thoughts. This one has power over thee. She will be my instrument.'

He took a cautious step closer, narrowing his eyes. He plainly saw the stunning features of Alexis Halstead, and yet blurring them: black oriental eyes, lips that did not move, lids that blinked and through which he could still see green irises.

'It grows late, my one, we have little time left. So hard have I tried to communicate to thee what must be done. Walk with me, Davison.'

Spellbound, he fell into step beside her, marveling at the double vision, at the change in Alexis's voice, recalling her previous episodes of sleepwalking.

'Thou thinkest this woman insane, that she suffers from two personalities. Perhaps thou wilt never believe in me, Davison, but at least thou wilt listen now. If I speak through these lips, thou wilt do my bidding as surely as thou must do *hers.*'

He thrust his hands into his pockets, fascinated.

'Thy thoughts are troubled, Davison. It is the inscription on the door of the tomb. Thou art puzzled.'

He looked at her in surprise. 'Yes, I am. How did you–'

'Thou thinkest the inscription is like no other in all of Egypt. I will tell thee, Davison, it is because the man inside is like no other.'

'He has no name, no Eyes of Horus through which to see the light of day.'

'Thou art right, Davison. My beloved 'Khnaton is a prisoner in that house. He was not put there for his own safety but for the safety of the world. Or so believe the priests of the Hidden One.

'Why?'

'They believe he was a criminal. They believe he has committed great wrongs and would continue to do so from his grave.'

'Is that why they've taken his name from him?'

The braids of her heavy black wig rose a little in the breeze. 'It is heresy to speak his name for they do not want him wakened. He lies in a deep, dreamless sleep. He knows not who he is. He has no awareness. They have sealed him in a limbo for eternity.'

'Why wasn't he buried in his original tomb in the wadi?'

'The priests of the Hidden One were afraid those who loved 'Khnaton and were loyal to him would come to the tomb and give him life, so the priests carved a new house to hold him, a secret one that no one would find.'

'And the seven gods?'

'They were placed there to prevent anyone from uttering 'Khnaton's name.'

'Is it that simple to waken him? Merely to utter his name?'

'No, it requires more than that, my one, for 'Khnaton was entombed without a name on his body. His corpse lies without identity. There was no one to write his name on an amulet and place it over his heart.'

'Was he murdered?'

'Not even the priests of the Hidden One would dare

touch the divine person of the Living God. When 'Khnaton saw that his dream had collapsed and that chaos ruled the land, he sickened at heart and died. Now his brother Tutankhaton rules in his place and he is a mere boy.'

'If they wanted Akhnaton out of the way for good, why didn't the priests destroy his body?'

'They feared a cataclysm, my one, for it is the most foul deed to desecrate the body of Pharaoh. Although corrupt men, they knew the consequences of such a sacrilege. And yet, they feared to preserve him for then his spirit would walk the land. The priests were in a perplexity.'

'They found a solution.'

'Until someone opens the tomb and gives my husband his identity. Then the priests will understand wrath.'

'I'm afraid the priests are gone. Akhnaton has been asleep for three thousand years.

'Can it be so? It seems the blink of an eye.'

She came to an abrupt halt and brought a slender hand to her cheek. Mark fumbled in his pocket for his lighter, and when he struck a flame, he saw Alexis's face in the illumination.

Killing the flame Mark said softly, 'You're crying . . .'

With a graceful sweep, she dashed the tears from her cheeks. 'I have been so alone these thousands of years, waiting for my beloved! I cannot exist without him! He is my soul and my breath! The loneliness, Davison, you cannot conceive of the loneliness, wandering this empty valley . . .'

'But I thought–' he said haltingly. 'I had heard that you had left 'Khnaton to live in seclusion. Isn't that true?'

Alexis regarded Mark with doe-eyes. 'It is true, but for reasons unknown to anyone. In the later years, a sickness came over 'Khnaton, a condition for which the doctors could find no cure. He became . . . not himself; they said he had the holy sickness. I believe he was only tired and disillusioned. 'Khnaton was not himself when he fought with me. In his extreme moments, when great pain filled his head, he would clutch his scalp and pull at his hair and utter damnations against Aton. He said that his god had failed him, that Aton had abandoned him. But it was not so. Aton has always been benevolent and watchful over His children. It was a time of trial, a time of testing, but 'Khnaton had not the strength to see it through. He spoke of returning to Thebes, of restoring Amon. We argued. And when I saw that my presence only vexed him further and increased his pain, that my intense love for him and for his god drove him to insanity, I removed myself from him, knowing that the day would come when he would call for me. Those were lonely years, living apart in another palace.'

'Were you ever . . . re-united?'

'My beloved died before I could see him again. I rushed to his bedside, but life had already ebbed from his poor, tormented body. Did you know him, Davison? Did you know his goodness and compassion? He was a tormented man, for he so loved the world that he would embrace it with his own arms if he could. 'Khnaton's heart was too frail for the vices of men. He was an . . . Innocent, he was naïve; he called all men brothers and was blind to their crimes. Then it was too late. They used him, they toppled him. Disillusionment and disappointment were the weapons that killed him.'

'Can't *you* bring him back? Can't *you* speak his name?'

'I cannot. It must be done by one who lives. Davison, thou wilt do it for me.'

'Do what?'

'Inscribe his name on an amulet. Even on a scrap of papyrus. And place it upon his body. Then seal the tomb again so that he will never come to harm. Then 'Khnaton will live again and his soul can fly to the Western Land and live in eternal bliss.'

'But . . .I can't do that!'

'Why not?'

'Because–' Mark cast wildly about for the words. 'You don't know why I'm here, why I came to this valley–'

'Thou art a traveler.'

'I'm a scientist. A man of learning. I came to study your ways.'

'Thou art out of Babylon, Davison? I guessed this by your beard.'

'No, I . . .'

The frigid air penetrated his jacket. He trembled uncontrollably and thought: I came here to open the tomb and take your husband's body away! He's going to be put in a glass case in a museum hundreds of miles from here for millions of people to come and ogle . . .

'Thy thoughts are turbulent, my one, I cannot read them. Thou art in conflict. Have I done this?'

'I'm sorry . . . it's the cold.'

'It is summer.'

'Well, I'm freezing!'

'Davison . . .' Alexis stretched out a long, tapered hand and rested it gently on his arm. Through the nylon sleeve, Mark felt a patch of warmth. 'Do what I ask of thee. I beg . . . Give my beloved life once again.'

There remained two steps and the last row of hieroglyphs to be cleared. Mark and Ron worked together in the pit, carefully scooping the sand, sifting it, pouring it into baskets and passing it up to one of the workers outside the trench. The stairway was steep, its descent at a sharp angle, so that the two men worked in the shade of the walls created by the excavation. Before them, the tomb door loomed tall and forbidding.

Sanford Halstead sat at the side, fanning himself, while Hazim, who felt a little better this morning and had insisted on coming, sat in one of the Land-Rovers with Yasmina. Alexis sat apart, cross-legged in the sand, her face blank. Mark looked up once or twice from his work but saw no flicker of memory in her vacant eyes. She did not remember their night walk. Afterward, Mark had not slept. Her astounding knowledge, the incredible words Alexis had uttered, the bizarre optical illusion of looking at two women . . . whoever or whatever Nofr'tay-tay was, she was right: speaking through Alexis Halstead had made him listen. And because of this he knew what lay on the other side of the tomb door.

'Mark.' Ron's hand touched his forearm. 'There's something here, beneath the sand.'

Mark took off his gloves and gently palpated the surface of the spot where Ron had been working; he felt the soft dirt move beneath his fingers. Except in one place. 'There's something under here all right. Give me that whisk broom.'

As if dusting fragile china, Mark delicately swept the brush over the surface, back and forth in slow swings, while he and Ron kept a sharp watch for the object to emerge.

Presently, something white, like a piece of chalk, jutted from the sand. Mark continued his sweeping while Ron reached down every so often and gingerly cleared away the sand.

The object grew with the removal of the dirt. It jutted up from the final step, which was still buried, and stood just inches from the base of the door.

Ron hissed and jerked his hands back as if he had been bitten.

'Jesus,' said Mark, dropping the whisk broom and staring at what they had uncovered.

Poking up through the packed sand, as if reaching up to seize the two men, was a skeletal human hand.

TWENTY

RON CLICKED his last shot and said, 'That'll do it.' He had been photographing for an hour, recording every stage of the excavation of the skeleton. Mark had just finished brushing away the last of the dirt, now it lay exposed on the final clean step at the stony base of the door. Everyone else – Abdul, the Halsteads, Yasmina, Hazim, and the *fellaheen* – stood along the rim of the pit, gazing down in silence. They had not said a word for the past hour.

Mark ran his eyes over the startling find, from the bony feet which lay inside leather boots, along the legs and pelvis, covered with tatters of cloth, over the ribcage and arms, all of which were still joined by yellow bands of cartilage, to the skull which was matted with tufts of brown hair. The skeleton lay on its side with its knees drawn up and one arm curled beneath it. The other arm was partially outstretched; held rigid by hardened tendons and cartilage, the bony fingers pointed to the columns of vertical scratches etched in the door. It lay twisted and grotesque, frozen in its death agony, slumped at the door of the tomb.

Finally someone's voice broke the stillness. 'He must have been a member of the Ramsgate party.'

'The boots,' said Mark without looking up. 'They wouldn't have belonged to any of the *fellaheen*. And the shreds of clothing. Not native cloth.'

'Neville Ramsgate himself, perhaps,' said Halstead.

Their voices were carried away on the wind. All eyes

were fixed on the skull-face which was still covered in part by taut, leathery skin. The mouth was stretched wide in a silent scream.

'The scratches on the door,' said Ron. 'It looks like he was trying to . . . get into the tomb.'

Mark didn't respond. A new thought was forming in his mind, an idea that jelled as he continued to stare at the death grimace; something about the skeleton that had not at first occurred to him, but which now started to tug at the back of his mind. Something was not right. Something that should be here but was not . . .

'*Effendi,*' said Abdul from his vantage point at the edge of the trench. 'See there, *effendi,* at the back of the skull.'

Mark shifted slightly and tilted his head for a look. Then he bent forward and put out a fingertip. It explored the contour of bone, then fell through a small round hole at the base of the skull. Standing, Mark narrowed his gaze on the door at eye level, going over the hieroglyphs, inspecting the claw marks, and eventually finding what he had overlooked. Pulling a knife out of his shirt pocket, Mark leaned over the skeleton, braced himself with one hand and dug the tip of the knife into a tiny hole in the stone.

'What is it?' asked Halstead.

Mark pried a small object from the hole, examined it in his palm, then handed it up to Halstead.

'A bullet!'

'And I'll wager,' said Mark, again kneeling next to the skeleton, 'it matches the hole in the skull *and* that pistol we found.'

'I don't get it,' said Ron. 'Who shot him?'

Mark studied the skeleton for another moment, trying to seize upon the elusive thought that gnawed at the edges of his mind, then stood up once more and brushed off his hands. Turning so that he faced the steep flight of stairs leading up to the surface, he said, 'We can reconstruct the action. Whoever he is, he ran down these stairs, maybe because he was being chased, fell against the door, clawed at it, then was shot through the back of the head. He sank down and was left there.'

'But why?' said Halstead. 'Who was chasing him? And why did he try to get into the tomb?'

'I only said we could reconstruct the action. I didn't say we could explain it.'

'Why would anyone try to get into the tomb like that? I mean,' Halstead's voice was tight, 'he *clawed* at it!'

'Your guess is as good as mine.'

'And why,' said Ron, 'didn't he get cremated with the others?'

'I assume the Pasha's men found him like this and, being afraid to touch him, buried him where he was.'

'But they touched the other bodies.'

'Yes . . .' Mark rubbed his beard as the elusive thought started to come into focus.

Halstead said: 'I can't imagine why the officials buried him here but never reported the tomb.'

Then Mark had it. He looked down at the skeleton, at the stringy ligaments and parchment skin, at the posture of the body, lying exactly as it had fallen a hundred years ago, and thought: The desert scavengers didn't touch the body. The jackals and the vultures. Not even the white ants . . .

Halstead was saying, 'The Pasha's soldiers come into this canyon, find a camp full of corpses, cremate them and burn everything else, and then come over here and just fill in this stairway? Without throwing this body on the fire as well? Without letting the authorities know about the newly discovered tomb? It doesn't follow! Something's wrong here!'

'Maybe,' said Ron quietly, 'they never came this far. Maybe they were afraid to come to this end of the canyon.'

'What are you talking about?'

Ron looked up at Halstead, his eyes glassy. 'Maybe they were frightened by something.'

Mark spoke suddenly: 'Let's get this thing out of here.

271

Abdul, you and your men move it as carefully as you can, we might need to study it later.' He looked at his watch. 'It's almost noon. We'll quit for the day. In the morning we'll open the tomb.'

They were sitting in the mess tent after lunch. Mark, sipping a glass of cold tea, said, 'What do you think, Hazim?'

The young man looked up from his own glass and seemed to have trouble focusing on Mark. 'What do I think about what?'

'This skeleton. Are you going to report it?'

'The authorities will not be interested . . .'

Mark watched a fine sweat glisten the grey face and saw that the whites of Hazim's eyes had yellowed. 'Are you all right?'

'Yes . . . I am feeling better.'

He looked at Yasmina, who gave a barely perceptible shake of the head, then said, 'The discovery of this skeleton changes things.'

'How so?' said Halstead.

'Those death certificates in the ministry's file. Either one of them is in error, or that skeleton is someone we don't know about.'

'They were all in error and you know it,' said Ron. He was staring moodily into his untouched tea.

'What do you mean?'

'I mean, there was no smallpox here and you know it, Mark. The Ramsgate party was *killed*, every one of them. Remember the bodies we found in the pit? Dismembered *before* cremation.'

'Then you're saying the Pasha's officials falsified death certificates. Why would they do that? And if there was no disease here, why burn everything? Why quarantine the area?'

'Maybe they were trying to hide something.'

'Davison,' said Halstead. 'I still want to know who

buried Ramsgate or Sir Robert at the bottom of the steps without reporting the tomb.'

'It's obvious, Mr Halstead, that nature did the burying. If he had been covered with sand immediately after his death, we would have found a more preserved corpse. A mummy, actually. After he was killed, he must have lain in the pit exposed to the elements, decomposing until the wind and sand did the job of filling in the grave.'

'Then that means the Pasha's men never got to that end of the canyon. Why?'

'Maybe something kept them away.'

Everyone looked at Ron. 'Like what?' said Halstead.

'Like whatever chased Ramsgate to the bottom of those steps.'

A chill silence fell over them in the stagnant heat of the tent; seven faces became masked in private thought. Halstead dispelled the quiet by saying, 'Davison, read the inscription on the door.'

'Why?'

'Just read it.'

Mark picked up his clipboard and flipped to the translation. 'Behold the Guardians of the Heretic, for they watch in eternal vigilance. They are the Hidden One, the Upreared One, the One Belonging to the Cobra, Set the Slayer of Osiris, the Devourer, Akhekh, and She-Who-Binds-The-Dead-In-Chains. Such is the vengeance of the Terrible Ones:

One will make of thee a pillar of fire and consume thee.

One will make thee to eat thy own excrement.

One will wrench the hair off thy head, pulling the scalp off thy skull.

One will come and dismember thee.

One will come as a hundred scorpions.

One will command the insects of the air to devour thee.

One will cause an awesome bleeding to drain thy body unto death.'

Mark's last words continued to hang in the air long after he had finished and laid the clipboard down.

Finally, Ron said, 'Seven gods, seven punishments.'

'I don't like it, Davison, not one bit. I want to know what we're dealing with. What are you hiding from us?'

Mark's brows arched. 'Hiding? Nothing.' He glanced at Alexis.

'You can't tell me there isn't something odd about that inscription! In the four months it took you to prepare for this trip, Davison, I did some reading. This is no ordinary inscription. Those curses are meant more than just to scare off tomb robbers, they're there to see the tomb is never opened! Why?' Halstead's voice rose to a shout. *'What's inside it that the priests were afraid of?'*

In a weary voice, Mark said, 'Only a dead man, Halstead, nothing more. They thought Akhnaton was evil so they sealed him up. It's that simple.'

'That's what the *sebbakha* meant when she told Ramsgate he was setting the devils free . . .' murmured Yasmina.

'Three thousand years of ingrained superstition, Halstead, passed down from generation to generation.' Mark sadly shook his head. 'The only evil that exists in this valley is within ourselves.' He turned to Abdul. 'Get your men prepared for the opening of the tomb tomorrow. That door will have to be handled with extreme care.'

The taciturn Arab turned away from his stove and regarded Mark with a shadowy expression. 'We have lost the rest of the men, *effendi.*'

'Oh for Chrissake–'

'The skeleton frightened them. They say they had dreams last night. Monsters coming after them, ordering them back to their villages.'

'How many are left?'

'The three government *ghaffirs* and four men from El Hawata. I have offered them very large payments, *effendi.*'

'Have them move their camp into the canyon and keep the *ghaffirs* posted at the door of the tomb. When Mr Sheikhly telephones Cairo tomorrow, he'll have another team sent to help with the emptying of the tomb's contents.'

Mark turned to the antiquities agent. 'Or would you rather make the call this afternoon.'

'No, no,' whispered Hazim. 'I am still a little weak. Tomorrow is good. Now I must rest . . .'

As everyone was about to rise, Ron stood at the tent flap and cried, 'Holy Christ Almighty, you're not going to believe this!'

Mark shot to his feet. 'What is it?'

'There's a swarm of them coming!'

Mark ran to the door. 'A swarm of what?'

'*Tourists!*'

Seizing his binoculars from the table, Mark dashed out of the tent. About one hundred yards from the camp, heading toward the ruins of the Workmen's Village, was a string of donkeys, each bearing a rider.

'There's about thirty of them,' said Ron, joining him.

As the rest of the group emerged into the bright sunlight, squinting and shading their eyes, Mark inspected the scene through his Nikons.

'Christ, it's one of the boats. The *Isis* or the *Osiris*.'

'What are they doing here? Tours never stop here.'

'I think I can see why . . .' He handed the glasses to Ron.

Scanning the parade of donkeys straddled by brightly colored, sun-hatted tourists, Ron said, 'Isn't that Sir John Selfridge?'

'The same. Out of Oxford. It's one of those lecture tours. That could mean more than just a stopover. Days, maybe.'

Mark and Ron stood in sullen silence as they watched the string of riders wend its way over the ancient mounds and into the maze of mudbrick walls. As the people started to dismount, one animal continued trotting; it headed for the camp, bearing a man in white slacks, white shirt, and white Panama hat.

As he neared, he waved and shouted. 'Hullo!'

275

'What does this mean?' asked Halstead.

'Leave it to me. Don't say anything.'

The visitor reined in his little beast and slid to the ground. Lifting off his hat and running a handkerchief over his bald head, the short, bandy-legged man approached the quiet group. 'Hullo! John Selfridge here! How do you do!'

Mark accepted the sweaty handshake. 'Hello, Mark Davison.'

'I know, I know! When they told us at the landing that work was going on here and who was conducting it, I was simply flabbergasted! I've read your work, Dr Davison, most impressive.'

'Thank you. Dr Selfridge, my assistant Ron Farmer.'

'Of course, of course!' They shook hands. 'Read your stuff on mummies. Top drawer. I say, they didn't tell us in Cairo there was work going on here. Sorry if we've disturbed you.'

'Not at all, Dr Selfridge.'

The little pink man fanned himself with his handkerchief and eyed the dining tent. 'Been here long, have you?'

'Two and a half weeks.'

'I see . . .' The stout Oxford scholar looked at the blank faces of Mark's companions and again glanced overtly toward the mess tent. 'Uh . . . what sort of project, if I might ask?'

'We're reconstructing one of the funerary temples.'

'Indeed! I believe Peet and Woolley attempted that and it didn't work.'

'That was over forty years ago, Dr Selfridge. We have technology now.'

'Fascinating! I should love to see it.'

'I'm sorry, but we're still in the blueprint stage. You understand.'

'Yes, yes, of course.' he waved an arm toward the Workmen's Village. 'Will my people be in your way?'

'Not if it's just for a little while.'

'An hour at the most, I assure you. My local guide is showing them the choicest bits. After this we'll be going up to visit the Royal Tomb.'

Mark felt Halstead stiffen behind him. 'I'm afraid you can't go up the wadi.'

'Why not, Dr Davison?'

'There was a rockslide. It's completely blocked.'

'Such luck!'

'Will you be visiting the tombs in the cliffs?' asked Ron.

John Selfridge licked his lips and cast one last impatient glance at the dining tent. 'We were going to, but I'm afraid the heat's got to most of our members. We have to push on. A lot to see in two weeks, you know.'

'Won't you be mooring here for the night?'

''Fraid not, have to be in Assyut in the morning. I say, have you something cold perhaps—'

'Dr Selfridge, I'm sure you'll excuse us if we don't invite you in, but we're working against a deadline and have to utilise every bit of daylight. We were just getting back to work.'

The amiable smile fell. 'I see. Well.' Selfridge lifted his hat, ran the handkerchief over his shiny pate once more, then said, 'It was nice to have met you, Dr Davison. All of you . . .'

Ron called out after him, 'Have a nice trip up river!'

They continued to stand in silence as they watched the little man remount, then, as he trotted away, Mark turned to Abdul. 'Watch them. Let me know when the boat has left.'

He was sitting at his little writing table, working out a schedule for the tomb's exploration and eventual systematic emptying; suddenly Ron drew the tent flap aside and stood for a long time in the doorway, unspeaking. Mark swiveled around and looked up at him. 'What's wrong?'

'It's happening all over again.'

'What?'

Ron's lips were pale, his face grave. 'We're going the same way the Ramsgate expedition went. A curse for each of us.'

Mark threw down his pen. 'Ron–'

'I want to show you something.'

'What is it?'

But Ron didn't answer. He turned on his heel and went back out into the night. Curious, Mark followed. They entered the work tent where Ron fumbled with the light before they walked all the way in. Spread before them on the work table was the skeleton.

'I want to hear you explain this one away,' said Ron solemnly. 'I want to hear your scientific explanation for this.'

Ron stepped up to the bench and stared down at the skeleton. When Mark came to stand next to him, he said softly, 'While you were working on the excavation schedule, I examined this body.'

The light bulb overhead swung on its wire, tossing eery shadows this way and that; as the light fell on to and then off the skull, its expression changed.

'First,' said Ron, 'look at the hands. The index finger is longer than the ring finger.'

'So?'

'Look at your own hand.'

Mark stretched out his right hand; the index finger was shorter than the ring finger. 'So what does that–'

'Now look at the brow ridge and the mastoid processes.'

Mark had to lean close. As the smell of decay rose to his nostrils, the corpse grinned up at him.

'And finally,' said Ron, 'the pelvis. A dead give-away.'

'What are you getting at?'

'This body, Mark. It isn't a man, it's a woman.'

Mark's eyebrows went up. 'A woman . . . are you sure?'

'No doubt about it. And I took a magnifying glass to the symphisis pubis. She's around forty-years-old.'

Mark could not take his eyes off the leering skull.

'Okay, so this is Amanda Ramsgate. So?'

'I got to thinking. It's not unusual for partners to have a falling out, one man shooting the other. But Amanda? Why should anybody shoot her?'

A picture flashed in Mark's head: the tomb door and the long vertical scratches made by the corpse's fingernails.

'There must be a reason, Ron.'

'Sure! Amanda Ramsgate ran down the steps and tried to claw her way into the tomb so either her husband or Sir Robert shot her. What could be simpler?'

'Then what's *your* explanation?'

'I don't know . . .' Ron turned away and walked over to the door. 'Maybe she wasn't shot on purpose, maybe it was an accident. Maybe whoever did the shooting was trying to kill something else . . .'

The two friends gazed at one another for a long time, then Ron shook his head and walked out of the tent.

Mark looked back down at the skeleton, taking in the tatters of clothing, the tufts of hair still matted to a leathery scalp, the prehensile hands petrified into claws. Then he, too, spun around and left the tent.

But Mark didn't return to his own quarters. He trudged over the rubble and away from the camp. And when he was alone and in darkness, he murmured, 'Where are you? I need to talk to you?'

A cold wind came up, fluttering his shirt, a sick ache welled inside his skull, and then she was before him, shimmering, translucent. 'Hello, Davison. Thou believest in me now.'

'We have found a woman's body. Who is she?'

'Is she not with thee, Davison? But no . . .' Nofr'tay-tay's smooth forehead wrinkled in a frown. 'It was before thy time. There were others . . . I remember now. I tried to speak to her. But it was to no avail. I told her in dreams about 'Khnaton. When she was in danger, she ran to him.'

'What was the danger she was running from? Was it a man with a gun?'

'What is a gun, my one?'

'A weapon.'

'She ran from the Upreared One who chased her. Another, her husband, hurled a weapon at the demon and it sounded like thunder, but he killed his wife instead. The Upreared One cannot be killed by physical means.'

'Thunder . . .' Mark saw it all unroll before him like a slow motion film. The demon chasing Amanda, she running screaming to the tomb, Ramsgate shooting at the monster, the bullet passing through it and killing Amanda.

What madness had overtaken them that they had all hallucinated so horribly!

'I read thy thoughts, my one, and thou art in error. The gods are not visions, they are real.'

Mark started to shake. 'I don't believe that!'

'The scavengers of the desert did not touch the woman's body, Davison, is that not proof of the power of the Seven?'

'There has to be an explanation—'

'Fool, Davison!' Her aura flared and blinded him. 'Thou vexeth me beyond endurance. Open the seven holes of thy head, O man of learning. If thou believest only what thou seest with thine eyes and hearest with thine ears, then be assured, *thou wilt see the demons.*'

His stomach felt as if he'd swallowed a live coal; it burned with an intensity that caused Mark, every so often, to grimace. It was the tension of the moment . . .

'Have you decided?' asked Ron.

Mark reached out a shaky hand. 'Here. We'll pierce a small hole here and shine a light in to get a look.'

'What if the door's too thick to remove as a whole?'

'We'll section it with a bandsaw.' Mark reached for the hammer and chisel and, before driving them into the stone, took one last look at his companions. They were all in the pit with him, even ashen-faced Hazim, supported by Yasmina.

Mark said, 'Okay, here goes.' He seated the tip of the chisel in the center of the door between two rows of hieroglyphics, took in a deep breath, held it, raised the hammer high, and brought it down with a clang.

TWENTY-ONE

THE INSTANT the last fragment gave way, a tremendous wind rushed out through the hole, whistling by with such force that everyone fell back, fearing the door would explode.

'Jesus!' cried Ron, jumping away from the rush of putrid air.

They stared at the hole in bewilderment, listening to the whine and feeling a hot, foul breath on their faces. Then the wind gradually died and all was quiet again.

Mark scrambled for the flashlight. Focusing the beam through the five-inch diameter opening he had cut, he cautiously bent forward and peered in.

'What do you see?' asked Halstead, pressing close.

'I see . . .' Mark drew back, incredulous, 'Absolutely nothing!'

'What?' Ron took the flashlight from him and pressed his own eye to the hole. He tilted the beam from every angle, twisting his position for a better view, then he also came away and said, 'You're right. Can't see a thing.'

'Okay. Everyone out of the pit. We're going to cut this thing open.'

The grinding of the bandsaw filled the canyon with a fierce buzzing that sounded like dive bombers swooping in and out. Mark and Ron did the work, wearing sunglasses and surgical masks, while the rest of the group sat tensely outside the trench, watching the door come away in heavy blocks.

Mark and Ron moved cautiously, pausing every now and then to shine a light into the gradually widening opening and making sure they weren't damaging anything on the other side. But, as daylight filled the space beyond the door, they saw before them a long, empty shaft; a dark corridor that was forbidding and abysmal and seemed to have no end. When they finished removing all of the door, creating an aperture wide enough for a man to stand in, they all gaped wordlessly into the interminable void stretching before them.

'Are we going in?' asked Halstead.

'I'd better go in alone. You can't just barge into a tomb. Some of these were rigged with traps and pitfalls.'

'I'm going in with you,' said Ron.

'Okay. Grab a flashlight. Abdul, stay close, we might end up calling for help.'

Yasmina reached out and touched his arm. 'Please be careful.'

Mark gave her hand a squeeze. 'Don't worry. Ready, Ron?'

His friend nodded gravely.

'Okay everyone, here goes . . .'

Mark went first, sweeping his broad flashlight beam in a circle; the walls were close together and roughly hewn, the ceiling was low – he and Ron would have to proceed in single file and slightly stooped over. Mark bent his head and stepped over the threshold. As he moved warily forward, he heard Ron step in behind him.

Mark kept up a slow sweep with his beam as he took steady and cautious steps. The floor was not as rough as the walls, but it was gravelly, and each footfall sounded like a splintering crash. Every so often he paused to aim the beam directly ahead, but it dissipated into the darkness; he and Ron were creeping down a long, narrow and eternal tunnel.

Once, Mark looked back over his shoulder and saw, beyond Ron, the doorway. It was a small rectangle of daylight with a scalloped border of silhouetted peering faces.

'Whew!' whispered Ron when they had gone nearly a hundred feet. 'Air smells bad! It's making me gag!'

'It's three thousand year old air. The last men to breathe it were the priests of Amon.'

Ron dashed his light over the ragged walls. 'This is weird, Mark. No paintings, no inscriptions, nothing. How far into the mountain do you suppose this goes?'

Mark didn't reply. He felt a tightness creeping up his legs and invading his bowels. Ahead, the darkness waited.

'Hey,' whispered Ron nervously, 'can't you just see it? We go on and on until we come to a door at the other end and when we open it there's a bunch of Chinese staring at us . . .'

Mark stopped suddenly and put out a hand to steady himself.

'What is it?'

'I think we've reached the end.'

Aiming his flashlight at his feet, Mark saw that the toes of his boots overhung a ledge; before them yawned an indefinable pit. 'Shine your light over me,' he said softly, crouching down in front of Ron. 'Let's see what's down there.'

Two circles of light traveled over a clean stone floor, up walls that were white and smooth, along a ceiling that was roughly hewn. The hundred-foot shaft had ended and opened on to a small, bare room that was sunk eight feet below the floor of the shaft.

'Looks like we've come up empty,' whispered Ron, trying to hold the beam steady in his trembling hands.

'Maybe not. Look over there.'

Directly across the chamber, set into a smoothly plastered wall, was another stone door. It appeared to have been hastily sealed into place.

'We'll need a ladder of some kind. Lights and equipment.' Mark turned to his friend. 'I lay odds, Ron, that on the other side of that door lies the man we've been looking for.'

The food went untouched. Nobody felt like eating, and Abdul's hastily cooked *ful* was unappetising.

'So,' said Mark, 'The ultimate decision is up to you.'

The antiquities agent, sitting grey-faced and staring unhappily into his tea, did not immediately reply.

Mark looked at Yasmina who shook her head, then said, 'We're all set, Hazim. The equipment's ready. All we need is your authorisation to open that door.'

Hazim had, at the last minute, been unable to travel to El Till and make the phone call as planned. Upon their return from the canyon, he had collapsed on to his cot and Yasmina had had to give him a shot to ease his pain. Now, one hour later, sitting shakily in the dining tent with all eyes on him, the sickly young man wished he could curl up and die.

'It is . . .' he said in a weak voice, 'Not an easy decision to make. My superiors should be here now. They should have been on hand for the opening of the first door.'

Mark understood the poor man's dilemma: in his current condition, Hazim would be replaced and thus lose his connection with the dig. Expecting to feel better each day, Hazim had put off reporting to Cairo; now he was forced into the decision. Mark said, 'Let's go to El Till right now and make the call.'

Hazim wagged his head. 'These village telephones are unreliable. It will take hours for the call to go through. I cannot . . . Dr Davison, I am tired, please let me sleep.'

'Hazim, we need authorisation to go ahead with the tomb opening. You're hesitant to give it, and you can't travel to a telephone. Let me go to El Till and I'll make the call.'

'You could be at El Till for hours. By then the ministry will be closed. Let us wait until morning, please, and I will fell better then.'

As Mark considered this, Alexis said in a startlingly staccato voice, 'There is enough daylight left to open the inner door. It doesn't make sense to sit around waiting for the go-ahead to do something we're going to do sooner or later anyway. I thought Mr Sheikhly *was* the authority here. I thought that was why he came along, to represent the government. Surely he can speak for the ministry.'

Mark turned to the poor man and said quietly, 'Hazim, would you rather we took you to the hospital at El Minya?'

'No!' A look of panic rippled across his handsome features. 'We are too close. The credit for this tomb goes to me. I cannot give it up now.'

'But you're not well–'

'I am well enough to exercise authority here.' Hazim's breathing became labored; his face glistened with sweat. 'Mrs Halstead is right. I was sent here to represent the ministry. As their agent I take full responsibility . . . Dr Davison, you may open the inner chamber . . .'

Everything was ready. The rope ladder was secure, the chamber brightly lit, the hammers and chisels and saws placed by the door.

The seven descended the shaft one by one until they all stood in the twelve foot by twelve foot ante-chamber, staring up at the most astonishing sight they had ever seen.

'This is incredible!' breathed Halstead. 'That is absolutely . . .' His voice died away.

On the wall before him, looming high up to the ceiling in outsized proportions, towered seven awesome figures. They were monsters, fantastical half-human, half-beast mutations, each one frozen in a pose that made it appear the demons had once moved and were caught in the middle of an action: one had a hand raised as if in salute; one had both arms held out as if ready to clasp someone; another held a scythe above his head, ready to swing it down. In colors as bright as the day they were painted, the Seven stood at attention, all of them in profile, each glaring down with one menacing eye. They were the seven monster guardians of the tomb.

In the center stood a naked muscular man, his angular body painted in gleaming gold, his powerful arms hanging at his sides – this was Amon the Hidden One. To his right, raising a hand in obeisance, stood She-Who-Binds-The-Dead-In-Chains, a long-limbed, shapely woman who had the head of a scorpion. Behind her, standing on its hind legs, was the Upreared One, a wild boar with human arms. At the end, facing Amon, stood an unidentifiable beast, its four legs poised as if ready to spring, its mane and eyes a flaming red – this was Set the Slayer of Osiris. On the other side of Amon, also in profile and facing the Hidden One, was Am-mut the Devourer, a beast with the hind legs of a hippopotamus, the front legs of a lion, and the head of a crocodile; its leering grin revealed a row of sharp pointed teeth. Behind Am-mut stood Akhekh the Winged One, an antelope with wings and a bird's head. And lastly came Apep, Belonging to the Cobra – a man who wielded a scythe and upon whose shoulders, where his head should have been, writhed a glistening snake.

The seven visitors gazed in dumbstruck wonder at the mural, each one mesmerised by the hypnotic eye of one of the gods. No one moved or blinked; all seven held their breath.

Halstead stared in horror at Amon, the golden god in the center, the demon that had visited him in his nightmares.

Hazim, leaning on Yasmina, could not tear his gaze away from the scorpion-headed goddess.

Ron was mesmerised by Am-mut the Devourer, feeling the beast's crocodile eye burn into his brain.

Alexis, imprisoned by the red, flaming eye of Set, heard herself whisper, 'They're so . . . *lifelike* . . .'

Mark found that his voice was tight, he had difficulty speaking. 'The hermetic seal of the tomb has kept the colors vibrant. In time, they'll fade . . .'

No one moved.

The seven gods stood majestically and horrifyingly

before them, twelve feet tall, the detail minute and precise, down to the pleats in the loincloths and the nipples on the bare chests. One thing, however, was glaringly absent. Not one word, not one hieroglyph, had been written anywhere.

Halstead's voice was tremulous. 'What the hell kind of tomb painting *is* this!'

'I don't know,' whispered Mark. 'I have never in all my experience seen such a mural. It is totally contrary to ancient Egyptian religion.'

'I don't understand! The other walls are blank and this one has these ghastly things painted on it! The priests of Amon can't have been *that* afraid of Akhnaton, can they?'

'I don't know.'

'And we still don't know for certain this is his tomb. I mean, what the hell is on the other side of that door that they wanted to frighten us away with these . . . these monsters!'

Mark forced himself to turn his back on the mural. 'This *is* Akhnaton's tomb, Mr Halstead.'

'How can you be so sure? Maybe it isn't even a tomb! Maybe it's a repository for some horror the ancient Egyptians wanted to keep from being found!'

'Halstead–'

'They went to some extremes to keep us out of there, maybe we should leave it alone and get the hell out of here!'

'*Sanford!*'

Everyone looked at Alexis. Her voice had been high and edged with hysteria. She seized her husband's arms and said angrily, 'Stop it right now! Do you hear me? No one's leaving! We're going to open that door and see what's on the other side!'

Halstead regarded her in pale-faced terror. 'I don't like it!' he cried, dragging the back of his hand across his bloody upper lip. 'I don't want to die–'

'They're looking at us,' came a quiet voice. It was

Yasmina. 'The antelope with the bird's head. It's looking right at me.'

Mark stared at her in one frozen moment of horror, then suddenly slapped his hands together in a loud crack. 'We've got work to do!' he said in a forced voice. 'The sun will be setting soon, so we have to move quickly. I want that door opened.'

It was a plain limestone block with no markings other than the necropolis seals of Thebes. Mark and Ron studied the door, tapping it in various places with the hammer, then settled on the direct center as the place to start.

Seating the tip of the chisel and raising the hammer, Mark braced himself. He didn't know what he expected – a rush of foul wind, a howling of the violated dead – but when he drove the chisel into the stone, his body was wound tight, ready to spring and run.

The others watched in rigid anticipation, concentrating on the point of the chisel, trying to ignore the seven giants that stared down at them from the wall.

Each strike of the hammer was a jarring, reverberating clang. The noise ricocheted around the chamber then funneled up the shaft and could be heard echoing out into the canyon. Each impact created a spray of splinters and dust; everyone was tense and braced.

Mark struck one last time and the chisel fell through.

The group froze for one expectant second, then released shaky sighs and relaxed an inch. Mark pushed away from the door and ran a trembling hand over his face; his beard was soaked with sweat. Raising the tools again, Mark steeled himself against his fears and began hammering once more.

When the hole was large enough to look through, he pointed the flashlight into the space on the other side. There was nothing to see.

By the time the bandsaw had cut through most of the

door, the air in the chamber was thick and difficult to breathe. But no one would leave. Slowly, square by square, the burial chamber opened up before them.

Mark dropped the saw and, picking up his flashlight, leaned in through the sawn-off door. 'What do you see?' asked a strained voice.

'Well,' Mark's mouth was uncommonly dry. 'It's a burial chamber all right . . .'

'Is there a sarcophagus?' asked Halstead.

Mark took in a deep breath. 'Yes . . .'

Everyone fell back, exchanging nervous looks. Mark and Ron went into the burial chamber with their flashlights.

After a quick sweep of the bare walls, smooth floor and rough ceiling, the two Egyptologists gazed at one another in the gloom.

'This is it,' murmured Mark. 'No other rooms. Just this. We've reached the end.'

'And there's nothing here.'

'Nothing,' said Mark, 'except for these.' And he rested the beam of his flashlight on the two massive granite sarcophagi that stood in the center of the room.

There had been no inscriptions in the tomb to identify the bodies, nor any markings on the two stone coffins to indicate who – or what – lay inside. And Mark and Ron had been unable to move the lids. So the seven had returned to the camp in a saturnine mood, each unable to shake off the icy horror they had felt upon looking up at the gods. Now, four hours later, the camp was dark and silent. Hazim slept fitfully in a barbiturate twilight; Halstead groaned on his bed, a pack of ice held to his nose; Alexis lay in a deep, dreamless slumber, barely breathing, her face in death-like repose; Abdul, kneeling on his prayer mat by his cot, chanted solemnly toward Mecca; and Yasmina lay curled on her side, blinking into the gloom. Only the two Egyptologists were up and about:

Ron in his darkroom, Mark wandering the dunes beyond the boundary of camp light.

He shivered and thrust his hands into the pockets of his windbreaker. In all his accumulated months in Egypt, Mark had never known a night as chill as this. The nights seemed to be getting gradually colder and colder, as though a mammoth glacier had descended upon them. He looked over at the dark, deserted ruins of the Workmen's Village. They were all gone now, the *fellaheen*, no one remained.

Mark shifted his thoughts to the sarcophagi, the granite lids that hadn't budged beneath his and Ron's pushing. The logistics of their removal would have to be worked out. When Hazim called Cairo in the morning, Mark would request some hoisting machinery–

'Davison . . .'

He stopped short. Nofr'tay-tay was suddenly before him.

'Thou hast found him,' she said. 'Now thou must give him life.'

'I found two coffins.'

'Yes, my one.'

'Who lies in the other?'

Her eyes were sad; she held out her hands. 'Doest thou not know? It is I, Davison. I lie in the other coffin.'

Mark brought a fist up to his throbbing forehead. 'This is insanity!'

'Davison, thou must listen! Thou must be made to understand. Hear me out, I beg of thee . . .'

He brought his hand away and looked at her in confusion. 'There are no cartouches in the tomb, no inscriptions, no canopic jars. There are no amulet bricks at the four cardinal points. I don't understand.'

'Pity us, Davison! Search your heart for the wellspring of mercy and compassion that surely must be there! Thou must set us free!'

'*Free from what!*'

She spoke hurriedly, beseechingly. 'The coffins are our

prisons. The priests interred us without identity, they sentenced us to an eternity of unawareness; a death that is not death. We two sleep namelessly, but I remember. My beloved does not. He slumbers in a twilight where I cannot reach him and where he cannot hear me. I have tried, lo, these thousands of years to waken him, but it cannot be done by me.'

'How is it you're a free spirit?'

'I do not know, Davison. I wakened, that is all . . .'

'Then you can go. You can leave this place, fly to the sun–'

'I cannot!' she cried. 'I will not leave my beloved. Yes, for reasons unknown to me I have wakened and my spirit lives. But I will not leave my dearest 'Khnaton, my husband, he who is my very essence! How can I enjoy the bliss of the Western Land knowing that he continues to lie in that cold tomb, unaware, dreamless? Davison, thou mule, *how can I leave my beloved!*'

Mark screwed his eyes tight. 'I'm going mad . . .'

'Thou must perform the act soon, my one, to set us free, for the Seven are enraged. Thou must set us free before the gods can stop thee.'

Her voice rose to a wail. 'I long to be with my beloved again! Give us our names, Davison, recite the resurrection spells, then we can leave this place, my beloved and I, and enjoy the bliss of the Western Land.'

Mark's stomach churned in anger and frustration. *'Why me?'*

'Because thou alone can speak my tongue.'

'It isn't fair! I have another obligation! I have to take those mummies to–'

'How I have tried!' she wailed to the sky. 'All these long and empty years. How I have tried to communicate with another, and yet I had not the power. That other one, long ago, whose head was split by thunder, I tried to possess her, but I failed for the woman was so filled with unrequited passion that she became a wanton. I could not make her do what I wanted.'

'Amanda Ramsgate . . .'

'And the other, with the flaming hair. She fights me; her own strong will clashes with me. When my love for 'Khnaton infuses her body I cannot control her as thou has seen. Thou must be my instrument, Davison. Thou knowest our ways, our beliefs. How long I have waited for one such as thee to come to this valley, a man who knows the ancient ways. The knowledge is already there, Davison, in thy brain. Thou knowest that the souls of the dead cannot fly to the Western Land without an identity. If no one utters the proper spells and incantations, the soul is trapped forever in the body. And if that body is destroyed, then the soul is destroyed. Write out our names, Davison, upon our corpses and recite the ancient prayers. Then will our souls be released and we can dwell in eternal bliss. And then, Davison, thou must protect our mummies and see that no harm comes to them, for thou knowest, my one, that the soul must come back to the body periodically to rest . . .'

Mark wanted to cry out, to throw back his head and howl. Yes, he knew! How well he knew! The ancient Egyptian beliefs of afterlife. That the soul rode with the sun by day and slept in the body at night. But the soul had to know where the body lay. All those mummies, scattered the world over, encased in glass in foreign museums; where were *their* souls? What calamity had Egyptologists wrought in the name of science? The soul returning to the tomb to rest, only to find the tomb empty, the mummy gone. What anguish and torment had been caused in the name of science! And he, Mark Davison, was going to commit that same crime – carry the corpses far down the Nile so that the souls of the king and queen would stumble in darkness and gloom, bewildered and lost . . .

He gazed at her across the sand, charging the night with the collision of his passion against hers.

'Believe in the gods of Egypt, my one, for they are but manifestations of Aton! They exist . . .'

'They don't!'

'Hurry, Davison, before it is too late. Thou wilt have freedom from the demons when thou hast set us free, but while we sleep thou art in grave danger.'

'Why don't you leave me alone?'

'It begins, Davison. Behold!' Nofr'tay-tay held out a ghostly arm, pointing. 'It begins . . .'

Mark turned and saw the flap of the darkroom move to one side. Ron stepped out uncertainly and looked around, as if sniffing the air. Mark hurried across the compound. 'What's wrong, Ron?'

The blue eyes made a slow sweep of the sleeping camp, squinting at the fringe of darkness beyond the light. 'Something's coming,' he said softly. 'Something's coming this way.'

Mark's body rocked in an uncontrollable shiver. 'I don't hear anything.'

'It's not something you hear. It's a feeling. I was at the developer when all of a sudden I was overcome by a feeling of utter . . . *hopelessness*.' He fixed his gaze on Mark's face. 'You feel it, too, I can tell by your eyes.'

Mark tried to keep from grimacing as a sharp pain volleyed between his temples. Yes, he felt it, just as he had felt it twice before: an awesome dread, a draining of the soul, the impulse to fall to his knees and weep.

'Listen!' Ron held up a hand. 'You can hear it now.'

Mark's eyes stretched wide against the black wall that stood at the edge of camp glow. There it was, in the distance but coming closer, through the inky night, at first only a whisper, then louder: *plock-plock, plock-plock . . .* The irregular sound of a drunken footfall, like the lub-dup of a heartbeat, *plock-plock, plock-plock,* someone staggering in a stupor, plodding blindly, mindlessly, heavily over the cold sand.

It drew near.

Ron stretched his mouth in a wide, silent scream.

Mark fell back against the tent pole, pinioned, transfixed.

It had walked all the way from the tomb: up the long

passageway, up the thirteen steps, across the dark canyon, down the wadi, along the base of the cliff toward the cluster of little white tents; slowly, inexorably, the bare feet thudding over the sand in a zombie's walk.

Then they saw her. She stumbled out of the darkness and into the light: a tall, slender-limbed woman of creamy skin and shapely body; long-armed and long-legged, her transparent dress revealing small firm breasts and pink nipples, wide hips and a triangular shadow between her thighs.

On her shoulders, where her head should have been, were two red lidless eyes and the bony pincers of a scorpion.

A high, strangled sound, like the wail of a cat, escaped Ron's throat.

She hesitated at the rim of darkness, the yellow glistening pincers clicking open and closed, then she started forward again, arms dangling, the stagger of a corpse.

She stopped at the doorway of one of the tents. Mark tried to cry out, to scream a warning, but he had no voice, no breath, like in a dream, paralysed. He could only stare in horror as the milky, slender arms rose up and out, as if to embrace a lover, and then the creature stepped into the tent.

A howl rose up to touch the silent stars; released, Mark slid to his knees. A light went on, and then another. Yasmina appeared in the doorway of her tent, hastily donning her robe. Sanford Halstead stumbled half-naked out of his tent, looking bewildered.

A second howl shot up to the black sky, then Ron could move. Pushing away from the tent he reeled across the sand and flung aside the flap the creature had walked through.

On the floor, kneeling and glassy-eyed, was Abdul. He threw back his head and howled a third time.

Now the others were there: Yasmina clutching her medical bag, Halstead staring mindlessly, Ron, his chest heaving in sobs, and finally Mark falling against the tent pole, gaping at the body of Hazim al-Sheikhly.

He lay on his back, naked, eyes wide and lifeless, his skin swarming with yellow, hairless scorpions, stinging over and over again . . .

TWENTY-TWO

MARK TRIED to take command of his hands, but with no success; when he poured the bourbon, he shook so badly the liquor slopped out of the glass and on to the floor.

When the tent flap drew aside, he uttered a cry and dropped the glass. It was Yasmina.

Looking drawn and weary, with her hair disheveled, she came to sit opposite Mark on Ron's cot. 'They are sleeping now.'

Mark retrieved the glass, pressed the flask against the rim and managed to pour a shot. He drank it down in one burning gulp.

'Let me give you something,' said Yasmina.

'No, I'm all right now. Don't worry, I have no intention of getting drunk.' He deposited the flask and glass on the night table then ran his fingers through his hair. 'So they're quiet now?'

'I gave Mr Halstead and Abdul shots to let them sleep. Strangely, Mrs Halstead never woke up when Abdul screamed and she continues to sleep deeply now.'

'Ron?'

'He is setting up cameras and wires around the camp. He said that when the next one comes, he will get a photograph of it.'

Mark emitted a bitter laugh. 'That's Ron!' Then he buried his face in his hands and groaned. 'My God, she warned me . . .'

'Mark,' said Yasmina softly.

He brought his hands away.

'We must leave here.'

'No.'

'We must leave here, all of us, and at once.'

'That's what they want,' he said in a tight voice. 'Domenikos and the *umda*. Don't you see! They're trying to scare us off. We've found the tomb for them, they want it for themselves. They can sell those mummies for a lot of money.'

'Mark,' she said quietly, firmly. 'You do not believe what you are saying. You saw the creature that killed Hazim. Ron said she was a demon, the goddess from the tomb. She-Who-Binds-The-Dead-In-Chains.'

'You don't believe that nonsense!'

Yasmina studied Mark closely. His irrational behavior was manifested by erratic hand gestures, an uncharacteristic wildness in the eyes, a note of hysteria in the voice. He clearly did not want to face the truth. For some reason, he desperately wanted to remain here . . .

She got up from Ron's cot, tightened the sash of her robe, and came to sit next to Mark. Laying a hand on his arm, she said quietly, 'Let me give you something to help calm your nerves. You have been under a strain.'

'No.' Mark struggled to get a grip on himself. He drew in a few deep breaths and let them out slowly. 'It was the shock of seeing Hazim . . . I'm getting over it now.' He draped a hand over hers and fabricated a reassuring smile. 'Don't worry about me, Yasmina.'

'But I am, Mark, I cannot help it.'

He gazed into the comforting depths of her dark eyes and felt himself grow calm. Then he became aware of the warmth of her body as she leaned against him. 'You're very brave, aren't you?' he murmured. 'You're the only one of us who's managed to keep cool, running around giving shots, comforting the sick, taking command of the hysterical. It's supposed to be the other way around. You're supposed to be uncontrollably hysterical and I'm supposed to be the man with nerves of steel who comforts you.'

He fell silent, staring at her as she stared back, barely aware of the sound of Ron erecting his tripods beyond the tent wall.

'What I will do, Yasmina, is telephone Cairo in the morning. I'll guard the tomb myself. Abdul and I can do it. You and Ron will take the Halsteads and Hazim's body to El Minya.'

She shook her head firmly. 'No, Mark. I will not leave you. And I do not think government agents and police will help. It is an unearthly power we are dealing with. We have no weapons against them.'

He gave her hand a squeeze. 'I'm sorry, Yasmina, but I won't leave.'

Her eyes misted over. 'Then I shall stay, too.'

Against the vast silence of the midnight hour could be heard the clinking and swearing of Ron Farmer, as he set up three cameras upon tripods at angles to one another around the camp. To the shutter cables he attached thin wires and stretched them between tents, accidentally tripping off a flash now and then and muttering, 'Shit!'

'If you are so afraid,' said Mark quietly, 'why would you stay?'

She opened her mouth and then abruptly turned away.

Mark caressed the small hand beneath his, marveling at the emotions charging him. It had not been like this with Nancy, not even in the very beginning. Nancy had come into his life at a time when he had no one, no friends, no family. He had just emerged from all those years of study and sacrifice and self-denial, holding down a job and going to school full-time, with no social life, no girl friends, not even casual acquaintances. The day he had received his PhD and an offer to go to Aswan, Mark had been ready for a woman to enter his life. He wondered now, marveling at the effect this remarkable woman had on him, if it could have been anybody then: if not Nancy, then someone else – and he would have called it love just the same.

'Do you know, Mark,' she murmured, still looking

away, 'when I first met you I hated you. I expected you to be like all the others who come to my country and exploit the *fellaheen* and treat them like animals. But you–' She brought her face around, tears in her eyes. 'You were different. You were kind to the workers, you treated them humanely. And then I saw what love you have for our past, how you cherish our heritage, that you would not sell to Domenikos what belongs to Egypt. My hatred started to change, to turn into admiration, and then . . .'

'And then what?'

'I cannot say it, Mark. Even if I feel it, I cannot say it.'

He lifted his arm and laid it around her shoulders, drawing her against him. 'Then I'll say it for you–'

'No, you must not. Mark, I am *fellaha!* Our worlds are separated by more than miles; there is religion, and tradition, and our different heritages. You asked me once why, if I fight so hard for the liberation of Egyptian women, I continue to segregate myself from the men in the dining tent. It is because I cannot help it! Although my mind longs for equality, my spirit was too long with the *fellaheen.* I am imbued with the old ways, Mark, I am a prisoner of the old traditions!'

A tear tumbled down her cheek. 'Possibly I shall never change, Mark, not in my heart, not enough to be able to *freely* love a man so foreign as you. I shall have difficulty enough with one of my own kind. The old ways have a strong hold on me!'

He gazed down at her in painful comprehension. He knew too well what she spoke of: in Cairo he had many Egyptian friends, all young and educated and progressive. And yet, on social occasions, while the men sat in the parlor with their strong coffee, the women retired to the kitchen. Once, Mark had tried to get the women to join them – women who were business and economics students at the University of Cairo – and they had been appalled at his suggestion.

Gently placing a hand on her cheek, Mark brought her face close to his. 'We can change the old ways, Yasmina.'

'No!' she sobbed. 'It is not possible! You have seen how

Abdul looks at us when we are together. As much as he respects and admires you, Mark, he disapproves of anything between us.'

'Do you love me?'

'I cannot–'

'*Do you love me?*' He took hold of her shoulders. 'Tell me, Yasmina. Say it!'

The tears fell and streaked her cheeks. She was crying freely now. 'Mark, I am not a virgin! Not after the year I spent in the *mudir's* house! No Moslem man will want me, how can *you* want me?'

He gathered her into his arms and pressed her face into his neck. 'Because I love you and I want you. And I want to hear you say the same thing.'

Her thin shoulders rose and fell with anguished weeping. Her voice came out muffled, halting. 'And if I did love you, Mark, what good would it do? You will soon return to America and we shall never see one another again.'

He took her by the shoulders again and held her at arm's length. 'You'll go with me, Yasmina.'

She raised her eyes, red and swollen. 'I cannot go with you, Mark. I have dedicated myself to helping the *fellaheen*. They need me, Mark, they need someone who cares for them! I can never go away from here, they are my life.'

'And what about me! What am *I* then!'

She bowed her head and did not reply.

'All right. I can stay in Egypt. I can work for the government.'

'No, Mark,' she said, her voice suddenly calm, her weeping subsided. 'You would not be happy here. For a little while, perhaps. But Cairo is so very different from your home in California. How long would it be before you hungered to be among your own kind, to go to parties where the men and women mingle, where they drink alcohol, to live in a freedom we do not have in Egypt? How long before you crave an American movie, a hamburger, your Pacific Ocean?'

Her words stabbed, made his heart rise up and stop the

301

breath in his throat. No, he could never live in Cairo, not indefinitely, for the rest of his life. It was too different: the crowding, the filth, the poverty, the strict Moslem laws . . . tolerable for a while, so long as one knew the visit was going to end.

'And how would we live?' she asked quietly, wiping the tears off her cheeks. 'I must work in the villages up the Nile, traveling and teaching and researching. What would our children be? Who would be our friends? There would be such prejudice, Mark. It might last for a little while, yes, but how long would our love sustain us?'

Defeated, his hands fell from her shoulders.

'Mark,' she was in control again. 'In Moslem law only a woman's husband may touch her. And if she is unwed, no man may touch her, not even in friendship.'

He nodded mechanically. Again, his friends in Cairo: one girl engaged to an architect for seven years, and in all that time not even so much as a kiss . . .

'But the end is near, Mark, it is almost over and we will part forever, perhaps never to meet again. And so . . .' her voice faltered. 'If it is your wish, for this one night–'

He placed a finger on her lips. 'No, not like that.'

'Then let me sleep with you, Mark. Hold me until sunrise. I am so afraid . . .'

Exhausted, they lay down on the cot, he with his arms around her, Yasmina with her head on his chest. They listened to the ancient wind cry mournfully through the valley.

Mark's eyes snapped open. He blinked up at the dark roof. How long had they slept? Yasmina, curled like a kitten against him, was still asleep.

Mark listened. It was a sound that had wakened him. It came again: a crying, echoing, haunting, *Davison* . . . A woman's voice, dreamy, unearthly, *Davison* . . . A sorrowful, beckoning call.

And then the pain.

He rolled his head to one side and moaned.

Yasmina sat up. 'What is it?' she whispered.

'It's . . . it's coming back.'

Davison . . .

She looked over her shoulder. 'Someone is calling you, Mark.'

'No,' he seized her arm. 'Don't go out there.'

Yasmina rose to her feet. 'Who is it, Mark? Who's calling you?'

'It's only the wind.'

Davison . . .

Yasmina tilted her head. 'No . . . it sounds like a woman. We must see.'

He jumped up and reached the tent flap before Yasmina. Drawing it aside, he saw Alexis Halstead, draped in a glowing white robe, standing out on the sand. "*Davison* . . .'

'Allah,' whispered Yasmina. 'That is not her voice!'

Mark seized his head and groaned.

'What is it, Mark?'

'It's coming back, can't you hear it?'

She listened. She heard it. From the black night beyond: *swish, swish, swish* . . . Something rising high in the air and then slicing down with force. An axe, a sword . . .

'Stay inside, Yasmina!'

'Mark–'

He pushed her back into the tent and staggered outside. 'Which one is it?' he cried, stumbling toward Alexis.

'It is the one for thee, Davison. *It comes for thee*.'

'No!' He reeled in the sand, pounding his temples. 'I don't believe in this! It's not happening!'

Ron appeared in the doorway of his darkroom. 'Mark, what's–' He looked at Alexis, his mouth fell open.

'Beware, Davison. Save thyself. Run to the tomb, for there is thy salvation.'

Ron blinked at Alexis, 'What the hell–'

'When we are resurrected, Davison, the demons will return to their dark world. But thou must hurry.'

Closer now: *swish, swish,* at the edge of the compound.

In the next instant it emerged into the light.

Mark froze in horror. The thing had the shape of a man, broad-shouldered and narrow-hipped, but where its neck and head should have been was a thick, writhing snake rising up out of the shoulders, a cobra poised to strike. The thing hesitated, swaying uncertainly, an outside lantern illuminated its features: the naked, muscular chest, the pleated loincloth, the sinewy arms, the glistening scaly body of the snake weaving back and forth as two brilliant green eyes flashed. Then Mark saw that in one hand the monster carried a long curving scythe that glinted in the lantern light.

'Oh Jesus!' cried Ron. 'Run, Mark! Run!'

Then the green eyes of the snake fixed on Mark and the thing started toward him.

The long determined strides of the monster brought it closer and closer as the snake eyes held Mark in hypnotic fascination. He was unaware of Ron and Yasmina screaming behind him. Their cries went unheard as the monster moved steadily nearer.

When it was a few yards away, one tightly thewed arm slowly rose, and the great scythe swung high in the air.

From Alexis: 'Save thyself, Davison . . .'

Mark stared up at the flashing reptillian eyes; they were emeralds of fire. A strip of tongue, split at the end, flicked in and out of the monster's snake head.

With the massive scythe held high, the monster came close. Mark continued to gape up at it, bending his head back as the twelve-foot demon now towered directly over him. The scythe caught the light of the lanterns, gleaming as the hand that held it made sure of its grip; then the scythe started to come down.

Mark heard, '*Effendi!*' and felt a great weight fall against his body. The impact sent him flying, sprawling in the sand. Mark shook his head and pushed himself up on his hands; he stared up at the monster as, with its free hand, it knocked Abdul's turban off his head.

Abdul did not react in time, for an enormous fist took hold of his hair, and as the Arab screamed, struggling and wriggling beneath the hold, an unseen wire was triggered; a flash went off as the scythe came down with a loud whine and neatly sliced through Abdul's neck as if he were a sheaf of wheat.

Mark had to clutch himself to fight down the trembling fits that came over him. He was alone in the dining tent.

A sound was heard at the entrance, he started; but when he saw Yasmina appear, Mark sagged. His voice was gravelly as he said, 'How are they?'

She slumped down on the bench opposite him. 'Mr Halstead put his wife to bed. He saw the whole thing from his tent and when Mrs Halstead dropped in a faint, he would not let me touch her. And he would not let me give him a tranquiliser.' Yasmina looked at her hands as if they were alien things. 'The blood from his nose and mouth–'

Mark screwed his eyes tight and tried once again to reconstruct the events of the past hour: Alexis calling him out of his sleep; the materialisation of the 'thing'; it coming toward him; his utter helplessness to move or cry out; Abdul interceding, saving Mark's life, then lying there on the sand, blood gushing from the stump of his neck.

Mark buried his face in his hands and tried to press out that final, horrifying vision – of the demon towering over him, one hand bringing up the scythe again, the other holding Abdul's dripping head aloft – but it was imprinted upon his brain, like a brand, and Mark knew there would be no forgetting it.

And then, just as quickly as it had started, the horror had ended. As they had all looked on in stupefaction, the demon had dissolved before their eyes and Abdul's head had dropped to the sand with a sickening thud.

After that, it was all dreamlike. Halstead sobbing over his wife's slumped body. Ron viciously seizing the camera and running back to the darkroom. Yasmina kneeling over poor Abdul . . . And then a few minutes later, with her help, Mark gently carrying Abdul's remains to the work tent where Hazim lay.

'I'm cold,' whispered Mark. 'I've never known the night to be . . . this cold . . .'

Yasmina came around to sit next to him, to lean on him; she took one of his icy hands and cradled it between hers. 'It is almost dawn.'

'I don't know what to do with . . . his body,' Mark murmured, laying his cheek against her hair. 'I'll go to the *'umda's* house and call the police.'

'How will you tell them he died?'

'I don't know . . .'

'What will happen after that?'

'Once the authorities from the Ministry of Antiquities are here, I guess . . . we'll continue the work. Those sarcophagus lids have to be removed and the mummies examined–'

Yasmina released his hand and drew back from him. She regarded him sadly, pityingly.

'What's wrong?'

'Do you not yet know, Mark, that we are not meant to disturb those coffins? That is the reason for all this. From the start, the *fellah* in the ruins, having a heart attack while brewing tea. He *saw* something, Mark, that scared him to death.'

Mark's face took on a bleak, hunted look.

She stood up and tugged gently at his arm. 'Come.'

They trudged wearily across the dark compound; overhead, the sky was a canopy of ice. In the east a wash of pale blue was extinguishing the stars. Entering her tent, Yasmina switched on a single bulb and went over to the workbench. Reaching for a bottle of yellow tablets, she said quietly, 'Take these, Mark.'

'I don't want to sleep. Why don't you take the pills?'

'Because that luxury is not mine. I have a duty to the sick ones, I cannot abandon them. Mark, go lie down, please.'

He regarded her helplessly, then heaved a rattling sigh and left the tent.

He was awakened an hour later by the sound of a motor, and was more surprised by the fact that he had slept than that someone was starting up one of the Land-Rovers.

Excited shouts brought him to his feet and he stumbled to the tent flap. Squinting into the bright morning, he saw Ron and Yasmina running after the vehicle that was grinding away from the camp.

'What's going on?' he demanded.

'The fuckers stole our Land-Rover, that's what!' shouted Ron.

'Who?'

'The last *ghaffir* and Abdul's assistants! They've deserted us! We're alone out here, man, sitting ducks!'

Sanford Halstead appeared from his tent, his face pasty and stubbled with beard. 'What's going on . . .?'

Mark whipped around. 'I'm going to El Till.'

Ron followed him into their tent. 'I'm going with you.'

'No.' Mark hurriedly tore off his shirt, splashed cold water over his bare chest and arms, then roughly toweled himself dry. 'You stay here and keep the others calm. I'll have the police here in an hour.'

'No way, man! I'm not staying here!' Ron also peeled off his shirt, which was stained with photographic chemicals, and pulled his Greenpeace T-shirt over his head. 'We stick together.'

'Now listen, Ron. We can't both leave. That'll open the way for Domenikos to steal the mummies.'

'Jesus Christ!' screamed Ron. 'You still believe all this is the work of one fat Greek?' He snatched a film strip off his bed and thrust it in Mark's face. 'Look at this, take a good look!'

Mark saw Abdul standing tall and erect, his head several feet above his shoulders, a startled look on his face.

Mark turned away.

'The fucking demon didn't photograph, Mark! And you still say Domenikos is doing this? We're in a death-trap, man!'

Mark's voice sounded like cardboard. 'I'm going to use the 'umda's phone and then I'll be right back. By noon everything will be under control.' He fell to his knees by his bed and reached under as far as he could. With a grunt, he pulled out a small crate that was still sealed.

'What's that?'

'Something I take along on every expedition but which I've never had to use. It's a last resort.' He splintered up the boards and exposed, nestled in straw packing, four Smith and Wesson .38 police specials.

'Oh no, man . . .'

Mark pulled one out along with a box of cartridges. Working swiftly and quietly, he slid the button on the left side of the gun, flipped out the cylinder, and carefully loaded a .38 caliber shell into each of the chambers. After he had checked to make sure the shells were flush with the back of cylinder, he snapped it into place and gave it a spin.

'It won't work against the demons!'

'Listen, Ron.' Mark got to his feet and held the gun out. 'You'll need it if Domenikos or anyone else comes into the camp.'

'You poor sucker . . .'

The tent flap lifted and Sanford Halstead, with a bloody handkerchief to his nose, peered in. 'What's going on in here?'

'We'll be right out, Halstead,' said Mark.

'Wait a minute . . .' Seeing the pistol, Halstead came all the way into the tent. 'What's that for?'

'We have to protect ourselves and the tomb.'

'We won't be needing guns, Davison,' said Halstead grimly. 'We're leaving the camp.'

'What!'

'And you can't stop us.'

Mark looked at his friend. 'Ron?'

'We've gotta get out of here, Mark. We've gotta save ourselves.'

'You can't mean that! Look, I'm going to El Till right now and I promise you the police will be here within the hour.'

'Now you listen, Davison!' shouted Halstead through his blood-soaked handkerchief. 'I don't know what that thing was that got the Arab, but I'm not going to stick around to see if it feels like coming back! I don't give a damn who or what it was, I know when my life is in danger!'

'So where do you think you'll run to?'

'We're going to Mellawi. Let the government come and finish the tomb work. I've just resigned.'

As Halstead turned to go, Mark grabbed his arm. 'You can't abandon the camp! Don't you see? That's just what they want!'

'Fine! Let them have the blasted camp! No mummies are worth that much to me!' Halstead gave Mark a shove and strode out of the tent.

'I can't believe this is happening!'

'And I'm joining him,' said Ron, hurrying out after Halstead.

Mark stood for a moment, weighing the weapon in his hand, then, tossing it on to the cot, grabbed his shirt and also ran out of the tent.

They were already in a Land-Rover when he reached them. Sanford was seated, his head resting against the window, Ron behind the wheel. Yasmina was wringing her hands. Seeing Mark, she ran to him. 'I could not stop them! He must not travel! He is too ill, stop them, Mark!'

He looked at Halstead's shirt, now spotted with blood that seeped up from his skin. 'Look, just give me an hour. I'll have the police here and a doctor—'

As the four-wheel-drive started to pull away, Mark shouted at them one more time. Then he spun around, said to Yasmina, 'You stay here with Mrs Halstead,' and ran for the remaining Land-Rover.

Five minutes later, in a cloud of sand and gravel, the two Land-Rovers swerved to a halt. No one waited for the air to clear; they jumped down and started to run to the river.

'Wait!' cried Mark, going after them. 'Come with me to the *'umda's* house! You'll be safe there!'

Ron shouted over his shoulder, 'Come with us and make your phone call from Mellawi!'

Mark glared after them, clenching and unclenching his fists. Then he ran roward the *'umda's* house.

The village was strangely quiet. The narrow streets were deserted; not even a solitary child played in the dust. Doorways were barred with bales of sticks or lengths of cloth, no sounds came from the dark windows. The fields were equally empty, the plows stood unattended, the wind whispered through the mudbrick hovels.

When Mark reached the *'umda's* house he saw that the windows were covered with straw and the wooden door was closed. Mark gave it first a loud knock, then tried to push it in. The house was locked tight.

He turned away and followed the path to the isolated residence of Constantine Domenikos. No children played in the front yard this morning; the windows and doors were covered.

Mark put his hands on his hips and looked out at the deserted fields. A solitary buffalo gnawed idly on some grass.

Mark marched back to the *'umda's* whitewashed house. Pounding on the door, he shouted, 'Come on out, I know you're in there! I won't leave until you talk to me!'

He paused to listen; the howling wind rushed through the tiny deserted plaza.

'Goddamit!' he shouted. 'I need to use your phone! We have government business, *hagg*, we demand to use your telephone to call the authorities!'

Still nothing, only emptiness and the nagging feeling of being watched by a hundred unseen eyes.

Then he heard running feet. Someone was approaching from one of the narrow alleys leading to the *'umda's* house. Mark turned around and braced himself. Ron Farmer emerged into the plaza, supporting a staggering Halstead.

'What happened?'

'They won't take us across,' said Ron. 'We offered them a thousand dollars, but they won't take us across! They say we'll cause them to drown!'

'How many men are down at the river?'

'Just the felucca owners. Where's the *'umda?'* Ron looked around. 'Where are all the people?'

'I don't know.'

'Uh oh,' said Ron, peering past Mark's shoulder.

Mark turned around and found four very large *fellaheen* slowly approaching; in their hands were heavy clubs.

'Where is the *'umda?'* he demanded in Arabic.

The four men stopped before the *'umda's* door.

'We demand to use the *hagg's* telephone!'

Then one of them spoke. It was in a frantic, rapid tongue. Mark responded angrily. When they were finished, Mark groaned and his shoulders slumped a little.

Halstead, whose mouth was bleeding at the corners, said, 'What was that all about?'

'They say that when the *ghaffir* pulled into the village earlier, the *'umda* tried to call the *ma'mur.'*

'And?'

'The call never went through. The phone is dead.'

'Well, get the old man out here! We want a boat!'

'It's no use, Halstead, he's dead, too. They say he died at the telephone. He died standing up, with his eyes open. Now they want us to leave.'

'But we need to cross the river!'

311

'Halstead, the boatmen don't want us in their boats!'

'Then we'll *take* their damned boats!' He turned to Ron. 'Farmer you're a sailor, can you handle a felucca?'

'I don't know. I'm an ocean sailor, not a river man. The Nile's like the Mississippi, full of hidden sandbars. You have to know it. I don't think I can do it.'

'Then we'll just take our chances. Anything's better than staying here!'

Halstead pushed away and stumbled off. Ron ran after him.

When they reached the landing stage, they were met by a group of *fellaheen* guarding the boats with pitchforks.

Halstead stopped short. 'Bargain with them, Davison. Tell them they can have whatever they want. The camp, the tomb, whatever.'

'Are you crazy?'

'Tell them!'

Mark tried to talk to the grim-faced men who stood at the Nile's edge like soldiers, but the look in their eyes took the courage out of his words. 'It's no use, Halstead, they won't listen to us.'

'We've got to get across, Davison!'

'Okay, okay. Don't panic. Listen, there are other landing stages at El Hawata and Hag Qandil. We'll return with our tea and Coke–'

'Mark,' said Ron.

The *fellaheen* were starting to walk toward them.

'Mark, I think they mean business.'

'Oh shit!'

Before the *fellaheen* could get any nearer, the three turned on their heels and started running away from the river. Behind them, they could hear the dull padding of bare feet on the dirt.

Halstead staggered and fell twice, and Ron and Mark had to drag him by the armpits. His nose haemorrhaged so badly they had to strip off his shirt and bunch it up against his face.

They got to the Land-Rovers and started the engines

just as the *fellaheen* let fly their pitchforks; they rained on the roof and sides of the cars and were followed by angry shouts and curses.

The four-wheel-drives literally flew over the mounds and ruins, and when the three arrived back at the camp, dropping to their knees and gasping, Halstead said, 'The guns! We can shoot our way to the boats!'

Mark reached out for him as he reeled away. 'Halstead, don't be a fool! If we go back now there'll be a hundred of them waiting for us! *It'll be a bloodbath*!'

As Mark bolted forward to stop the man, Sanford Halstead swooned in a heap in front of Mark's tent.

Mark looked up as Yasmina entered the tent. 'Well?'

'He is very ill and cannot be moved. He needs a doctor, Mark.'

He studied his hands. 'I'm going to have to find a way across the river. But it can't be done in daylight.' He looked at his watch. 'The sun will be setting in a few hours.'

'How will you get across?'

'I don't know. Steal a boat, maybe. I don't think I could swim it, although I sure as hell might try. Whatever,' he looked up at Yasmina. 'I have to do it alone. That means the four of you here by yourselves. Can you handle it?'

She hesitated. 'Yes . . .'

'Would you rather I didn't go?'

'You must go, Mark. You will find no help in the other villages and there is nothing to the east of us but desert. You must go to Mellawi and contact the *ma'mur's* police.'

The sound of a car door slamming and a motor starting up made both of them turn towards the flap. 'Now what?'

Mark and Yasmina ran out and found Ron about to drive away. Mark shouted after him and the Land-Rover stopped.

'What are you doing?' said Mark, running up to his friend.

'I'm going to the tomb.'

'Why?'

Ron's hands twisted on the steering wheel until they were bloodless white. 'I want to see what's in the sarcophagi.'

'Ron, not now–'

'I want to know that we're risking our lives for.'

'Ron, listen–'

Ron looked at Mark with killing eyes. 'It won't wait, Mark. I have to know. I have to see what is in those coffins. You can do what you want, I'm going to the tomb.'

The deadly calm in Ron's voice alarmed Mark. 'Wait a second, I'll go with you.'

To Yasmina, Mark said, 'Will you be all right here with the others?'

'They sleep now.'

'Come with me a minute. Ron, I'll be right back.'

Mark led Yasmina to his tent where, once inside, he turned to her and said, 'There's no way I can stop him. I have to go with him. But I promise I'll be back before dark. Here,' he picked the gun off the cot. 'I want you to have this with you at all times.'

Yasmina stared at the pistol as he placed it in her hand.

'Will you use it if you have to?'

'Yes.'

'If the Halsteads waken before I return, tell them I've gone for help. It's a lie, but it'll keep them calm. You'll be all right?'

'Yes . . .'

He took her by the shoulders and gave her a hard, brief kiss on the mouth, then hurried out of the tent.

'It's a mistake, Ron.'

'I don't give a shit.'

'Right now, the mummies are safe. No one can get at them. If we move those lids, there'll be no way we can protect them from robbers.'

'Somehow, Mark, I think robbers are the least of our worries.'

Mark was silent for the rest of drive, and as they entered the canyon, he noticed two disquieting things: the afternoon was growing late and the gas gauge in the Land-Rover was reading almost empty.

When they pulled up to the tomb entrance, Ron jumped out, ran to the rear of the vehicle and hauled out a massive coil of nylon rope. 'I hope it's long enough,' he said as he headed down the steps. 'If not, I'll use gunpowder to blast the lids off.'

Ron plunged through the doorway with Mark at his heels. The two nearly ran down the hundred-foot shaft, their flashlight beams paving a feeble path before them. Mark and Ron hastily climbed down the rope ladder, kicked the excavating tools out of their way and stepped through the door of the burial chamber. As they did so, Mark noticed that the camping lanterns were smashed and strewn over the floor; there would be no light in the tomb except what came from their flashlights.

They worked rapidly and without speaking, wrapping one end of the rope around a sarcophagus lid and making it secure. As Ron started to leave, uncoiling the rope as he went, Mark restrained him and said one last time, 'This is a mistake, Ron.'

Ron's face was that of a stranger in the dim battery light. 'Yeah, but it won't be our last. When you hear me honk the horn, start pushing on that sucker.'

Mark rested his flashlight on the lid of the other sarcophagus and got himself into position. He saw that, with Ron's departure and the removal of the second flashlight, the tomb was terrifyingly dark. Except for the small halo created by his own beam, everywhere was cloaked in the most awesome darkness Mark had ever seen. As he heard Ron's footsteps shuffle up the shaft and as he placed his hand on the cool granite, Mark felt his throat constrict in fear.

An eternity went by before he heard the start of the motor. Then, finally, the horn. Mark heard the distant grinding of wheels, heard the rope snap up off the floor, and felt, a moment later, the sarcophagus lid start to move beneath his weight.

Then the Land-Rover fell silent and Mark heard Ron's footsteps in the shaft. A few seconds after that, a flashlight beam came into the burial chamber and Ron said, 'How'd we do?'

Mark had difficulty finding his voice. 'About six inches . . .'

Ron shone his light on the edge of the lid and saw that a tiny space had appeared between the lip of the lid and the inner surface of the thick sarcophagus wall. 'Okay, let's give it another shot. About three feet should do it, that's all we need to see what's inside.'

Hearing Ron leave again and take his light with him was agony for Mark, who was by now sweating so badly his shirt was cold and wet and uncomfortable. His bowels crawled with unnamed fears and apprehensions; he pushed away imagined horrors that tried to invade his mind. Mark forced himself to concentrate on the task at hand; moving a mass of stone as if it were nothing more than an exercise in physics.

But, as the lid once again started to move beneath his hands, as the dark space started to widen and yawn, Mark felt a scream gather in the pit of his stomach and begin to rise up in his throat.

The scraping of the lid drowned out the comforting, familiar sound of a car motor; it was the grating noise of a rusty gate opening the way to Hell.

As he pushed and grunted and as the lid inched slowly away from him, Mark felt great drops of sweat run down his face and gather at the tip of his nose. By now he was leaning far over the open coffin; directly below him was a black universe. He screwed his eyes tight and wrestled with the vision of a monstrous hand suddenly flying up and seizing him–

'How was that?'

Mark screamed.

'Hey!' Ron ran around the sarcophagus and took hold of Mark's arm. 'It's me! Hey, come on!'

Mark fell back from the sarcophagus and leaned on Ron, breathing heavily, 'You . . . startled me . . .'

'Hey,' Ron put an arm around Mark's shoulders. 'You worked too hard on that, you only had to guide it, the Land-Rover did the work. Come on, pull yourself together.'

Mark took in great gulps of air; when he swallowd there was a biting, metallic taste at the back of his mouth. 'I'm okay . . .'

'You sure?'

'Yes . . .' Mark coughed a little, then found a stronger voice. 'I'm okay now. Let's take a look at what we've uncovered.'

Standing close together, the two Egyptologists warily aimed their flashlight beams into the black pit beneath the sarcophagus lid.

They stared for a very long time.

TWENTY-THREE

HALF AN hour later they were peering into the second coffin.

Ron had gone back to the Land-Rover and had pulled the first lid all the way off, so that it had crashed to the floor and broken into two pieces. Then he and Mark had removed the lid of the second sarcophagus, also splitting it. Now they were able to study the coffins' contents in their entirety.

Mark's voice was low and conspiratorial as he said, 'I've never before seen such excellent preservation.'

'They're perfect in every way,' whispered Ron. 'It's like . . . like they were just brought here from the house of embalming. There's no sign of decay or deterioration or anything!'

As the two Egyptologists bent over the first coffin, their flashlight beams roamed up and down the mummy, revealing every perfect detail: the precise way in which the body had been wrapped, the geometrical balance of the bandage strips, the whiteness of the linen.

The sarcophagi contained two small people, both wrapped with equal care and in identical fashion. But no funerary masks sat on their faces, no amulets or spells were woven in with the gauze. They were plain, featureless bundles, neatly, tightly wrapped, lying in boxes of cold granite.

'This one is female,' said Ron quietly, 'See the placement of the arms.'

Mark had already noticed it. The other mummy had its

arms crossed over its chest, signifying it to be the body of a king. This one, small and doll-like, had one arm across the chest and one straight down at the side, in the manner of a queen.

'Who do you suppose it is?' said Ron, his voice hushed.

Mark's beam caught something. A tiny scrap of papyrus tucked pathetically between the folds of bandage across the chest. Already knowing what it was, he gingerly reached down and gave it a gentle tug. Yellow and brittle but sufficiently preserved to be read, the papyrus strip came out easily. He focused his beam on the writing.

Ron bent over so that his long blond hair caressed the queen's arm. 'Hieratic script,' he murmured. 'Written in a hurry. Looks like just one word. I think I can read it . . .' Ron twisted around. He gazed at the papyrus for a moment, then slowly drew back. He stared at Mark across the coffin and said in a whisper, *'Nefertiti!'*

Mark kept his eyes on the peaceful, almost serene lady before him and murmured. 'This is why she's free. This is why she remembers . . .'

'What?'

He raised his head. 'I guess we'll never know who put it there. One of her daughters, perhaps, or maybe little Tutankhamon. A loved one who managed to bribe a priest, or who stole into the house of embalming and, under threat of death, secreted the papyrus into the bandages. Maybe,' he looked over his shoulder, 'they intended to do the same for Akhnaton but got caught . . .'

'What are you talking about?'

A distant thunderclap disturbed their silence. Reflexively, Ron and Mark turned to the black doorway leading to the anti-chamber. 'Rain?' said Ron, shivering with the memory of the last time.

But when the second crack sounded, Mark, said, 'That's not thunder, that's gunfire!'

They scrambled out of the tomb and fell into a brilliant fiery sunset. Ron hastily snatched the rope off the trailer hitch then clambered into the Land-Rover as Mark pulled away. More gunshots sounded as they bounced and careered through the narrow gorge and into the main wadi. 'Jesus, man, step on it!' cried Ron, flying off the seat with each jolt.

Mark glanced down at the gas gauge and grasped the steering wheel so hard his hands hurt.

As the gunshots grew louder, Mark and Ron neared the mouth of the wadi; ahead of them, the giant complex of the ruins of the Workmen's Village stood in the final blaze of a spectacular sunset. But before they could reach the ruins the Land-Rover slowed and came to a halt.

'What did you stop for?'

Mark swung down to the ground. 'Out of gas! Come on!'

They ran the rest of the way, sprinting over the sand, dodging rubble mounds, hurdling over waist-high walls. The camp, its tents tangerine in the dying sun, seemed farther away than ever before. Mark and Ron gasped lungfuls of air, stumbled and staggered over rocks, and cursed with each report of gunfire.

When they reached the camp, holding on to one another, the sun had set and they saw Yasmina, kneeling in the sand at the center of the compound, holding a gun in both hands. Her arms were outstretched, she aimed the pistol at Ron and Mark.

'Hey!' they cried. 'It's us!'

Mark ran to her, looking quickly around, then yanked the gun from her hands. Yasmina's eyes were wild, her face distorted. 'Beasts!' she screamed. *'Allah! Beasts!'*

Mark took hold of her around the shoulders and tried to bring her to her feet. Then Ron shouted, 'Oh fuck!' and grabbed the gun.

As he fired blindly, a black shape, squealing and weaving, dashed through the compound.

'What the hell–'

Before Mark could react, another one appeared, running straight for him, an enormous ugly black mass shrieking as it lunged.

Ron fired directly into the beast but it kept running.

'They're big as Saint Bernards!' cried Ron as he hastily picked up the cartridges which had spilled from the box and nervously tried to cram them into the cylinder.

Another monster appeared, then another. Yasmina put her hands to her ears and screamed.

They ran on the hind legs of a hippopotamus and the forelegs of a lion; their heads were crocodiles', leering, grinning, snapping.

'Into the tent!' shouted Mark. 'Come on!' He yanked her up by the arm and, as he started to run, a tremendous blow exploded against his legs; he flew up in the air and landed flat on his back.

More beasts materialised, grunting and squealing through the compound; Mark tried to move, but the breath had been knocked out of him.

'They bite!' cried Yasmina. 'They will tear your flesh off!'

Ron, having reloaded, released a thunderous barrage of fire into the monsters. They zig-zagged around him, nipping at his legs, shrieking as if in pain. He tried to fire a last time, but the gun only clicked. Ron looked frantically around him, for more bullets; they had all been scattered in the sand. Throwing down the revolver, he grabbed hold of one of Mark's feet. 'Get the other foot!' he shouted at Yasmina.

A swarm of beasts was bearing down on them. Their ugly mouths were stretched back to reveal rows of sharp pointed teeth.

'Pull!' screamed Ron.

Yasmina seized Mark's other foot and, with Ron's help dragged Mark on his back toward the dining tent.

A vice clamped around Ron's ankle; he cried out. Yasmina kicked the beast in the side of the head and it let go. Others came running, snapping and growling like dogs. They caught the edges of clothing and tore them off. One got Mark's upper arm and sank its teeth into it. When Ron kicked the animal away, a bloody gash was left in

Mark's deltoid muscle.

Ron and Yasmina ran as they dragged Mark to the door of the tent, kicking at the monsters and yelling. Fumbling with the tent flap, Ron reached down and, with one great effort, managed to get Mark around the waist and heave him into the tent. Yasmina scrambled in after him, throwing herself on to the floor, while Ron quickly zipped up both the flap and inner netting.

Then he stood back, heaving, and stared in horror as dark masses squealed and hurled themselves at the tent.

Hearing a moan, Ron turned around and saw Mark rolling around on the floor, clutching his upper arm.

Then he saw something that made his blood turn to ice.

In the convoluted light of several flashlights placed around the tent sat Sanford and Alexis Halstead. 'You sons of bitches!' he screamed. *'Why didn't you help?'*

'Ron . . .'

He looked down at Mark. Yasmina was wrapping a cloth around his arm. 'Ron, don't . . .'

Ron turned away and, glaring at the two at the table, heard a sudden stillness fall over the camp.

'They're gone,' groaned Mark.

'It is all right,' soothed Yasmina, stroking his forehead. 'You have a muscle wound but no artery damage. The bleeding will stop soon.'

Mark tried to get up but she pushed him back down. 'Lie still. I will give you something for pain. Here,' she took his free hand and laid it over the bandage. 'Press hard and do not let go.'

Yasmina rose shakily to her feet and looked around the tent for her medical bag. Seeing it, she started for it. Then Ron took a step forward and cried out.

'What is it?'

'My ankle . . . I think it's broken . . .'

She fell to her knees and lifted his pant leg. In the leather of the boot which had protected the ankle were several deep punctures. She gently unlaced the boot and peeled down the sides to reveal discolored patches of blue on the white skin.

'Move your foot up and down.'

As he did so she palpated the bones with her fingertips. 'I do not think it is broken. Sit down and I will bind it for you.'

She took another look at Mark, then went for her bag.

Half an hour later they were still sitting in silence, no one speaking, listening to the howl of the cold night. Finally, Mark, whose arm was tightly bandaged and who had been given Demerol, said, 'We're going to have to find a way out of this. And soon. The generators are broken. We have little food. We could try getting into the Land-Rover that's left–'

'And go where?' said Ron. 'At any one of the other three villages they'll kill us if we come near. I'm sure all the boats are being guarded. We can't go up over the plateau and head for Beni Hassan because we don't have enough gas. And if we stay here . . .'

He let his voice fade. Ron's initial fury with the other two in the tent had quickly dissipated when he had seen their state. Sanford Halstead, frequently pressing an already blood-soaked sheet to his face, had awakened earlier with a spreading bloodstain on the seat of his pants. And Alexis sat in a trance.

Ron felt sorry for them. His ankle was all right now that it was bound, Mark had recovered and was holding up, and Yasmina's hysteria had passed. It was up to the three of them now to save the group.

'What . . . were those things . . .?' came Halstead's thin voice.

Mark didn't like to look at the man's face; where it wasn't smeared with blood it was flour-white, and the eyes seemed to have receded.

'I don't know,' he said softly, closing his eyes against the memory. But he did know: they were Am-mut the Devourer, the fantastical beast that sat by the Scales of

323

Truth in the Underworld, ready to devour the deceased's heart if Osiris judged him a liar.

Mark covered his face with his hands, again seeing Abdul's head swinging by its hair. Abdul, who had run *to* him when everyone else had run away. Abdul, who now lay in the work tent covered by a sheet, his body starting to give off a stench.

'. . . exorcism.'

Mark brought his hands away. 'What did you say?'

Ron spoke urgently. 'Do you remember that piece I did for the *National Enquirer* a while back? The one on ancient Egyptian exorcism?'

Mark nodded warily.

'If I can still remember all the right words–'

'You're not serious!'

'Why not! If we can't get away from those demons, then we have to try to get rid of them!'

'Ron, we have to think of a way to get out of here! These people are sick! One of us has to go for help!'

'Davison . . .' came Halstead's feeble voice. 'Let's do what Farmer says. It's our only hope . . .'

'It's a waste of time!'

'Mark, the demons aren't going to let us get away.'

He shot to his feet. 'Well, I sure as hell am going to give it a try!'

'What are you going to do?' asked Yasmina.

'I'm going to take the Land-Rover and go down to the river south of El Hawata. From there I'll find a way across, if I have to pay my way or shoot my way across. I'll even swim across if I have to.'

But no one was listening to him. Halstead said, 'What do we have to do, Farmer?'

'First we need an altar of sand, then we'll need a sistrum. Let me see,' he looked around the tent. 'What can we use for a sistrum?'

Mark opened his mouth to say something, then clamped it shut and stormed to the door. As he unzipped the netting, he heard Ron say, 'What we have to do is call upon the gods of light to help us. We have to get a fix on the constellation of Orion . . .'

Mark flung the tent flap open and burst out into the night. Yasmina ran after him.

Inside his tent, Mark drew one of the revolvers out of the crate and started loading it. 'Please do not go,' pleaded Yasmina. 'You cannot leave us now!'

'Come with me,' he said flatly, without looking up.

'I cannot abandon them, Mark!'

As he slid the gun into his belt, he looked directly at her and said, 'What about me?'

She faltered. 'I–'

Mark's hands shot out and he seized Yasmina so hard she winced. 'Now listen to me! The only thing we have to be afraid of is our own insanity! The only way to stop it is by bringing law and order to this place! First I had the ignorance of the *fellaheen* to bang my head against, now my own people have turned crazy! One last time, are you coming with me?'

'No,' she whispered.

He let go of her, giving her a little push, then grabbed a box of shells and his windbreaker and ran out of the tent.

He stopped outside, causing Yasmina to bump into him.

In the center of the compound, kneeling, Ron and Halstead were piling up sand and packing it down like children building a sand castle at the beach. Behind them Alexis stood in the doorway of the dining tent, her eyes wide and blank. Halstead held a fork with a little bag of hard beans impaled on it in one hand. As he shook it, it gave off a sound like a baby rattle.

Mark and Yasmina stared in disbelief as, when the 'altar' was completed, Ron raised his arms to the sky and cried out: 'Horus purifieth and Set strengtheneth; Set purifieth and Horus strengtheneth!'

'Jesus God Almighty,' whispered Mark.

Ron's voice tolled like a prophet's, reaching to the plateau and sailing up to the heavens. 'We call upon thee

O Children of Horus! We call upon the Four that dwell in Meskheti!' With his long blond hair and Greenpeace T-shirt and blue jeans, Ron Farmer cried out: 'Hear us Mestha! Hear us Hapi! Hear us Tuamutef! Hear us Qebhsen-nuf! The servants of Light make offerings to thee!'

Mark watched in horror as Ron solemnly picked up a bundle by his knees and opened it up, gently laying the frozen lamb shanks on the mound of sand.

He raised his arms again. 'Ye shall be cut in pieces and your members shall be hacked asunder, and each of you shall consume the other!'

A wind started to blow, rushing down from the plateau and whistling through the camp. Ron's platinum hair started to fly as he cried: 'Thus doth Ra triumph over all his enemies, and thus doth Heru-Behutet, the great god, the lord of the heaven, triumph over his enemies!'

The wind grew fiercer, creating a curious noise in the wadis: it sounded like a hundred voices moaning and wailing. The sand started to swirl; the tent walls snapped in and out. Halstead's shirt now clung to him in bloody patches. His skin rose in purple welts and ruptured and ran with blood. It trickled from his nose and mouth and ears, pooling on the sand at his knees.

'Hear us O gods of Light!'

The moans grew to a roar; the ground shook. Yasmina tried to take hold of Mark's hand and he drew her against him.

The pathetic twosome in the center of the camp, ludicrous in their posture and pitiful in their solemnity, chanted together: 'We call upon Horus, vanquisher of Set! We call upon–'

'Mark!' cried Yasmina, pointing.

He saw it. In the thrashing wind, a long black vein started to cleave the sand; a twisting, writhing line that began at the edge of the camp and wound its way towards the kneeling men, like a ground-fault opening up.

Then Mark realised that it was a fat, glistening snake

that had materialised out of the night, its hellish eyes gleaming as it slithered toward the altar.

Ron's eyes were fixed on the three stars of Orion, his voice could barely be heard above the violent wind. 'We beseech thee Horus and Isis and Osiris! Ye are the light and the resurrection!'

'Ron!' shouted Mark, but his voice was flung back in his face.

The wind was now so strong that it felt like a solid wall. The massive serpent crept toward the unaware twosome, flicking at the sand with its split tongue.

A ripping sound joined the wind and Mark watched in terror as the south wall of the work tent started to tear.

He tried to take a step forward but could not. Mark brought up an arm to his eyes and tried to open his mouth to shout, but the wind rushed down his throat and filled his lungs as if to burst them.

The giant snake moved over the sand, its great head fixed on the couple at the altar; its mouth drawn back in a leer.

Through the cover of his fingers Mark noticed the dining tent start to lift in the gale. He saw Ron's lips moving, but couldn't hear his voice.

Then he felt Yasmina's hand fall against his chest. It slid down his abdomen until she had hold of the gun. They clung to one another, pressed against the tent wall, unable to move, the furious wind pinning them back like an invisible hand.

But Yasmina was able to inch the gun out of Mark's belt.

The wind seemed to take a grip on her arm and try to wrench it; Yasmina screwed her eyes tight and called upon all her strength. Wrestling with the hold the wind had on her, she managed to raise the gun a few inches. It whipped from side to side.

The two at the altar were oblivious of the fury about them. Their eyes were riveted to the stars; their mouths pronouncing the names of ancient gods. Alexis stood rigidly, as the tent behind her rose high and toppled on to its side.

The serpent reached the altar and raised its grotesque head. The tip of its snapping tongue was inches from Ron's chest.

Then Yasmina wrapped her finger around the trigger and squeezed.

She pulled it again. And again.

And the wind ceased abruptly and the night was crashingly silent.

Mark cautiously opened his eyes and, wiping sand out of them, saw Ron and Halstead kneeling and staring in horror at the squirming, contorting monster on the altar.

Mark and Yasmina were transfixed for a shocked moment as they watched the snake contract and writhe and shrivel and curl up in the sand until it disappeared. Then they were able to move.

Yasmina ran to Halstead, who had collapsed as soon as the wind had died. His body was wrenching in convulsions; a ribbon of blood spurted out of his mouth in a high arc.

'Mark!' she wailed.

But Mark was gaping at Alexis, who was staring at him across the compound. She raised an arm and pointed a long, tapered finger at him. 'Save thyself . . .'

'Mark!' screamed Yasmina. 'He's dying! Help me!'

Alexis's green eyes held him immobile, her face was death-white against her flaming red hair, and her voice, dreamy, sing-songy: 'Thou art my salvation, Davison. Thou alone. Go now, my one, and give us our identities.'

Then he heard Ron saying, 'Oh Jesus, oh fuck–'

Mark turned around and saw Sanford Halstead moaning in a pool of blood, writhing as the monster snake had done. His shirt and pants were soaked with blood; the red stuff oozed like sweat from every pore in his body.

Mark stared in mindless terror at the blood welling up in Halstead's bewildered eyes, trickling down to mingle with the blood in the sand. It gushed from his mouth and nostrils; it spread over the fabric of his pants; it seeped from his skin. Halstead's eyes darted from side to side like those of a frightened animal. He tried to lift his hands but could not. Great purple ridges rose up on his skin and burst open like over-ripe plums. He rolled his head from side to side and gazed accusingly at Mark through a veil of blood.

Then a final gurgle filled the night – a brief, tormented plea – and Halstead succumbed to the mercy of death.

For a moment, none of the remaining four moved. Then Ron shot to his feet and glared at Mark. 'You stupid shit!' he cried. 'This is all *your* fault! You're the cause of this !'

Mark gaped at his friend. 'Ron . . .'

Ron's eyes were charged with rage and insanity. '*I* know what to do!' he screamed, spittle flying from his mouth. '*I'll* stop it! *I'll stop it!*'

He spun about in the sand and sprinted away, leaping over the altar and disappearing into the shadows.

'Stop him, Davison . . .' wailed Alexis in a faint voice. Her rigid body teetered slightly, the queer light in her eyes flickered. 'He goes to destroy us. Save us, Davison, I beg of thee . . .'

Behind the battered work tent Ron got down on his hands and knees and scrambled about in the dark. He rifled through the scattered parts of generators, got caught in the electrical wires, and smelled the stench of putrefaction coming from the bodies that had been battered to the floor by the wind.

Then his hands fell upon what he was looking for. A can of gasoline. It was undamaged and full.

Hoisting it up with both hands, he staggered to his feet and half-stumbled, half-reeled back to the center of the camp.

He stopped when he saw Alexis Halstead, both arms outstretched; she advanced upon him.

'No!' he shrieked, whipped about and darted away.

'Hey!' shouted Mark, shaking himself out of his stupor.

His friend kept running; Mark dashed after him and caught him at the Land-Rover, 'Ron, don't–'

'Let go of me, man! It's the only way!'

'Don't, *please!*'

They struggled, the gas can sloshing between them. 'I have to do it, man! I'm going to burn those mummies! They're the cause of it all! Without the mummies to guard, the demons will go away! It's our only chance for survival, Mark!'

'You can't do it! You can't destroy them!'

And then Ron suddenly jerked back from Mark and flew high in the air, dropping the gas can and screeching.

Mark stared in paralysed horror as he watched Ron scramble backwards into the night, screaming, arms flailing about his head, his boots creating two tracks in the sand. He was being dragged by the hair; behind him a monstrous shape, black on black, pulled him over the sand like a rag doll.

Mark's mind went blank, his body held in place by an unseen power. Before him, disappearing into the darkness, struggling like a fish flopping on a hook, Ron Farmer trailed helplessly behind Am-mut the Devourer.

A bright light stabbed his eyes and shot a pain through his head. Mark recoiled, flinging his arm across his face. He heard Yasmina's voice: 'Where is Ron?'

'What . . .?'

She lowered the flashlight and stepped closer to him. 'Mark, where did Ron go?'

'He . . . he . . .'

'Mark!' She dug her fingers into his shoulder, pressing the moist bandage of his upper arm so that he cried out in pain. 'He is right, Mark! Ron is right! We must destroy the mummies!'

He beheld her in stunned horror. 'No . . . not you, too . . .'

'Yes, Mark! Look at me! Listen to me! I am not possessed, I am sane! Listen, damn you!' She gave him a shake. 'Your friend is right. It has all happened because of the mummies! We must destroy them before the gods destroy us!'

Behind her, Alexis Halstead stood like an ancient statue, arms still outstretched. In his brain, Mark heard the familiar whisper: 'Save us, my one, save us, save us . . .'

'We can't, Yasmina!' he wailed. 'I promised her!'

'Damn you, Mark! Damn you to Hell for your ignorance! How do you know *she* is not the evil one! *How do you know!*'

He gaped at her, dazed.

'Mark, how do you know she is what she says she is? How do you know she is not one of them? She is *using* you, Mark. Whoever she is that has a hold of Mrs Halstead, she is a sorceress! She is an evil goddess! Oh Mark, you fool!'

He blinked at Alexis. 'No . . . I'm right . . .'

'Maybe the ancient priests had a good reason for sealing that tomb! Maybe they were sealing in evil, Mark! You cannot save them! You will unleash an ancient horror upon the world! I know what she is asking of you!'

In his brain: 'Do not listen to her, my one. She lies. *I* speak the truth. Write our names upon our corpses, recite the resurrection spells, but hurry, hurry, hurry . . .'

'Mark, you will give that monster his name and then he will again walk the earth as he did three thousand years ago! Don't you see, Mark? She has *used* you! You are her instrument for setting chaos free upon the earth again!'

Mark stretched his mouth wide to cry out, but instead an unearthly scream tore the night. 'Ron!' he whispered. 'Oh my God!'

'Don't go–'

'Ron!' Mark pulled away from her.

'Please–'

He turned and ran over the sand, following the sound of the screams, leaving Yasmina and Alexis behind.

Mark found him lying in the sand at the edge of the Workmen's Village. He stopped for a minute to steel himself, gulped down his fear, then gently and lovingly knelt next to him. Gathering Ron into his arms, Mark felt hot tears sting his cheeks.

The scalp had been ripped off Ron's head.

As Mark cried over him, clasping Ron's body to his chest, a stirring of life was sparked, and his dying friend moaned.

Mark drew back a little so that he could see Ron's face. Just above the eyebrows was a long jagged tear where the skin had been torn apart; above it was red, glistening muscle. Ron's head was smooth and shiny, like a billiard ball, purple veins mapped the muscle and silvery fascia – the long blond hair had gone.

Ron's eyes fluttered open, his lips parted slightly. He tried to speak but streams of blood ran down from his skull, down his face, into his mouth and over his chest.

'Don't talk,' said Mark, choking back a sob and gently wiping the blood out of Ron's eyes.

'No,' came a hoarse whisper. 'You were right, man. I'm sorry. I wasn't myself there at the end, you know? This isn't your fault. It had to happen . . .'

Ron coughed, and blood spattered Mark's face. Lovingly laying a hand along his friend's cheek, Mark murmured, 'You don't have to say anything.'

'You see . . . it *had* to happen, we were just the patsies.' His throat bubbled as the words came out with increasing effort. 'Listen . . . you've made a fantastic find, Mark. You'll be famous. You can't let the demons get you, you have a date with Johnny Carson. Oh fuck–'

'Ron?'

'Listen, man, will you take care of *King Tut* for me?'

'Yes,' whispered Mark. Then he saw Ron release a long, rattling sigh and his staring eyes lost their life. As he gently laid his friend down on to the sand, the big sad eyes of a baby seal looked up at Mark through spreading stains of blood.

He got blindly to his feet and staggered back to the camp. Mark fell against the Land-Rover, sobbing. And leaning against the vehicle with Ron's mutilated head before his eyes, tasting the bitter salt of his tears, Mark felt a new emotion start to build within him. It began at the pit of his bowels, welled up through his stomach and burst through his lips in a madman's scream. Raising a fist to Alexis he shouted, 'You fucking bitch! You want me to set you free? I'll do better than that! I'm going to do what should have been done three thousand years ago!'

He scooped up the gasoline can and flung it into the Land-Rover.

'No, Davison,' wailed Alexis. 'I beseech thee!'

'Yasmina's right!' he screamed, neck veins bulging. '*You're* the evil one! Ron was right, you have to be destroyed!'

'Davison, Davison, Davison–'

Mark seized Yasmina's hand and roughly pushed her into the Land-Rover.

'Davison! Davison, wait, wait, wait I beg, save us, save us–'

As he started the ignition, a look of surprise swept over Alexis Halstead's face; she swayed and fell back a step, as if slapped, and said, 'What–'

In the next instant an explosion of white light filled the night. With her arms fluttering helplessly and her hair dancing off her sholders, Alexis Halstead was suddenly turned into a pillar of fire.

Mark and Yasmina stared as Alexis, in a final moment of lucidity and understanding, cried out in mortal pain. Her clothes blackened and curled and dropped off as flames licked her entire being; the skin reddened and blistered, at first giving off a succulent aroma, then the skin darkened and blackened and fell away in chunks and the smell turned to a gagging stink. Her face and hair were the last to be consumed. As she continued to stand, bewildered, on two blackened legs, the face started to melt and char, her mouth opened and a high pitched sound came out, like a song. Her hair was spectacular, a brilliant torch to illuminate the world; a tongue of flame rose up to the stars, blinding the two who looked on in astonishment.

The burning was long and agonising; she did not run, as if bound to a stake, and she screamed until the very end. Then the flames died and a charred corpse crumpled to the ground.

Yasmina doubled over and buried her face into her knees. Mark thrust the Land-Rover into reverse and ground away from the camp.

TWENTY-FOUR

As the Land-Rover bounced and caromed up the gorge, Mark and Yasmina could hear a jungle of unearthly sounds far behind them. They were the grunts and squeals of demons overrunning the camp. Mark knew there was no turning back.

The canyon was filled with an eery light as if a lightning flash had been caught and held. It illuminated every detail: the stratification in the limestone, the black pit where the charred bones of Ramsgate had been found, the five long trenches, and at the far end, the roped-off steps leading down to the tomb.

Mark drove like a crazed man, barely missing the trenches, pressing the accelerator to the floor as if to crush the seven gods beneath his foot.

He didn't wait for the Land-Rover to stop. He flew out, swung the gas can down, and ran to the stairs.

Below him yawned the black doorway of the tomb. The words of old Samira echoed in his head: 'The worst punishment for you, master, for you are the leader. Slow dismemberment . . .'

Yasmina, unable to move from the vehicle, watched in terror as Mark slowly descended the stairs. Then an uncanny buzzing brought her back to herself.

On her bare arm, crawling up toward her shoulder, was a giant wasp.

Spellbound, she looked down at the seat: it was now alive, a squirming black mass of enormous beetles, covering the seat and floor and windows like a moving blanket.

She felt hundreds of little prickles sweep up her legs, into her boots; then they crawled up her neck and infested her hair.

She could no longer see Mark through the beetle-covered windshield; could not cry out, for her mouth was suddenly full of crawling things.

Hideous, hard-shelled bodies and jointed legs swarmed under her clothing, between her thighs, into her nose and ears.

Yasmina shimmied in silent, peristaltic fear.

Black things sat on her cheeks. Yellow bodies scurried over her breasts and under her armpits. She felt the thousands of stings, the bites, was deafened by the droning, thundering in her head as if they crawled over her brain.

In her death throes, Yasmina managed to move her lips against the locusts which swarmed into her mouth. It came out garbled, muffled, but she was able, using her last breath, as the insects crawled down her throat, to whisper: 'Praise be to Allah, Lord of the Worlds, the Beneficent, the Merciful . . .'

As Mark took the second step down, a wind howled through the canyon and an invisible force lifted him off his feet, tossed him high in the air and let him fall with a crash.

The gas can got away from him, rolling into the nearest trench.

Mark sputtered and gasped for breath and tried to get up. Then he felt a blow against his ribs, like an unseen foot kicking him. He howled and doubled up.

As he tried to rise up again, an invisible hoof slammed the side of his face; he saw stars flash in his head and felt a burning pain shoot down his spinal cord.

Mark shook his head and once again tried to get to his feet, but instead of hoisting himself up, he rolled over and over along the sand until he was at the edge of the stairway, then he curled up into a ball and flung himself down the steps.

He crashed down on each one, banging his knees and elbows and tailbone, but he protected his head with his arms so that when he landed at the bottom he was still conscious and able to move.

Bizarre lights swarmed over the canyon; brightly colored streaks shot from wall to wall, like lasers; demonic shrieks and outcries filled the night in a horrifying chorus.

Then Mark looked up and saw a giant leering down at him at the head of the stairs.

It was Apep, the broad-shouldered man with a snake for a head. And it started to descend.

Mark scrambled to his feet, felt the ground sashay beneath him and dropped down again. He panicked, reaching out for the walls to pull himself up; his hands scraped rough limestone, sheering off the skin.

Only one thing drove him on now: to destroy the mummies. Once done, he knew, the demons would leave, having nothing more to guard.

The snake-headed monster took each step slowly and torturously, and Mark heard in his brain: *It will be a slow one for thee: an arm at a time, then each leg, until thou desirest death.*

Mark found his balance, got to his feet and lunged for the door.

A mammoth hand shot out and seized his arm. He felt a hot, seering pain go through his shoulder, then he was released and plunged headlong into the shaft.

Crawling, dragging himself the one hundred feet and catching his dangling severed arm on the rough-hewn walls, he thought: So this is what it's like to die . . .

Then the floor suddenly ended and he tumbled to the bottom of the ante-chamber, and as he lay there moaning, he thought: I'll just stay like this, it would be so easy . . .

But then he thought of the mummies and tried to draw strength from his vengeance; he imagined what it was going to feel like to tear the mummies apart with his bare hands . . .

Mark felt the flashlight beneath him and snapped it on,

illuminating the seven monsters towering over him on the opposite wall.

'You bastards!' he whispered hoarsely. 'You haven't won yet. Not while I have a breath in me, I'm not beaten yet . . .'

But the chamber started to swim and Mark fell back, banging his head on the floor. At first, pinwheels filled his vision, then his eyes cleared and focused on the four demons standing over him. They had stepped down from the wall: Amon the Hidden One, the Upreared One, Am-mut the Devourer, and red-haired Set peered down at him. On a voiceless command they each took hold of one of Mark's extremities, and each held in its other hand, Mark saw, a blunt ax.

First thy feet, he heard in his brain, *then thy hands, then thy knees and elbows, like hewing a tree for lumber . . .*

Mark closed his eyes. The terror was more than he could physically endure; he felt his sphincter relax, a warm wetness spread over his pants. As he saw the first ax rise high in the air and come down toward his foot, he heard another voice, remembered from a cold night spent with the dazzling vision of Nofr'tay-tay: 'Believe in the gods of Egypt, Davison, for they are but manifestations of Aton . . .'

Then his mind did strange things. As the first ax hacked through his ankle and mortal pain exploded in the universe, Mark remembered something from long ago.

In his post-graduate days, a seminar on the Egyptian gods, so much detail and unnecessary data, stored away, forgotten. Until now.

With his eyes closed, but sensing the swinging down of the second ax, Mark saw before him the ancient papyrus he had studied and the hieratic script. Then he took in a gulp of air and croaked: 'O great Sisters of the resurrection, I am thy son, thy heir. Gentle mothers, I call upon thee. Sweet Isis, who knew sorrow and mourning and who restored Osiris, I humbly . . .' A pain shot up Mark's leg; he cried out. 'I beseech thee, Isis, Great Mother. And sweet Nephthys, mother of Anubis and protectress of those who . . .' Colors flashed in Mark's head; he felt a kaleidoscope of pain and agony. 'Protectress of those who flee from Set . . . divine Sister, I implore thee, come to thy lowly servant. I believe in thee . . .'

When his right hand came away beneath the ax, the pain turned into something sublime. As he repeated the spell, Mark's cracked lips fell easily into the ancient syllables: *'Ii kua xer-ten ter-ten tu ne ari-a ma ennu ari en ten en xu apu amiu ses en enb-sen . . . Isis, Nephthys . . .*

Then night enveloped Mark and he opened his heart to welcome death.

When Mark came to he was lying on his back and he saw that the ante-chamber was filled with a soft light.

He lay as he was, staring up at the ceiling, trying to remember what had happened.

He had had a dream. But it eluded him now; only vague snatches of it could be recalled: two beautiful, fragile women with feathery wings encircling him, laying their perfumed bodies over him and murmuring, 'Thou hast called me Nephthys. I embrace thee. Thou art not weary any more. I give thee breath.' Gentle, tinkling voices, softly brushing his ear. 'I am Isis. Thou hast called me by my name. Thou hast found me and I restore thee. I salute thee, arise . . .'

There was more, much more, but it all blended together into one dreamy scenario. Together, in harmony, caressing him with their great, fluttering wings, they had chanted: 'This is our brother! Come let us raise up his head; let us gather his bones for the protection of his limbs. Come, let us protect him. In our presence let him be weary no more. O, Osiris-Davison, stand up thou unfortunate one that liest there! I am Isis! I am Nephthys!'

In the dream, he had felt a wonderful peace wash over him and a glow had surrounded him and he had felt his soul rise out of his body to the serene chanting of the sweet, winged goddesses.

But Mark could remember nothing more, only a sense of having traveled a great distance and of having slept for centuries.

He awoke completely rested and no longer tired. Sitting up, he found his body whole; there was not a scratch, not a bruise anywhere.

Staring in bewilderment at his healed hands and flexing his fingers, Mark did not hear the footsteps coming toward him down the shaft.

Then he heard a sound and, turning, found Yasmina standing in the ante-chamber.

They gazed at one another for a long moment, then, slowly getting to his feet, Mark whispered, 'Yasmina, I thought they had gotten you . . .'

'They had, Mark, as they had gotten you.'

'What happened?'

'I do not know. I prayed. But listen, Mark, whatever it was that happened, we have not much time. The Seven will be back. Mark . . .' She took a step toward him, 'I understand now. I was on the threshold of death and I called out to Allah. I was brought back. And in my passage, I suddenly saw it all open before me. We must write their names and recite the spells. We must give them life, Mark, not destroy them.'

He took a step backward. 'How can I be sure?' he asked in a strangled voice. 'How do I know? What if the priests of Amon were right?'

Yasmina held out her hands in supplication. 'Set them free, Mark.'

He continued to fall back. 'I don't know what to do!'

'Mark . . .'

He whipped around and stumbled into the burial chamber which was suffused with the same ghostly light. He fell against one of the sarcophagi and peered in. A man lay beneath the bandages, a man who slept in forgetfulness, who had no power without his name. Who was he? What was he? The Devil incarnate, or the Son of God? It would be so easy to reach in, so easy to take hold of the brittle body and wrench it apart, scattering the pieces, destroying forever any chance of reviving this dormant spirit . . .

'No!' howled Yasmina, running to him 'Do not wreak vengeance upon them! They are innocent! Set them free!'

Mark stared into the deep swimming eyes of Yasmina, filled his head with her voice and nearness, then said in a lifeless tone, 'I'll do whatever you want.'

'We must hurry. There isn't much time. Even now, the demons are returning.'

Mark looked around the chamber for something to write on, and finding nothing, tore off a piece of his shirt sleeve. Then he picked a sharp stone out of the dust and debris, pierced the tip of his index finger with it, and squeezed until a drop of blood rose up. Very carefully he drew on the cloth the hieroglyphics that spelled Akhnaton's name.

When this was done, he leaned over the sarcophagus and hesitated, gazing down at the bandaged head of the king, wondering what face lay beneath. Then he felt Yasmina gently urge him on and, as he heard in the far distance a wind start to build up in the canyon, Mark reached down into the coffin and laid the piece of cloth on the mummy's chest.

Remembering long-forgotten phrases, Mark whispered, 'I give unto thee, Beloved of Ra, He-Who-Pleaseth-Aton, whatsoever has come forth from thy body that thy heart may not cease to beat through want thereof. Thy voice shall never depart from thee; thy voice shall never depart from thee. Hail Akhnaton, thy two jaws are unlocked, thy *ka* is unfettered. The way to the Sun openeth to thee . . .'

Mark closed his eyes and chanted: '*Rer-k xent-k tu Ra maa-nek rexit neb* . . .'

And as he murmured the ancient spell, Mark felt another voice join his. It was deep and resonant, quiet at first then growing in strength with each spoken word. They chanted in unison, Mark and the other, filling the burial chamber with the ancient resurrection spells that were written before the memory of man, at the dawn of time.

And Mark felt a strange sensation come over him, a lifting, elating sense, as if he were rising off the floor and expanding up to the sky.

Ta-k-tu er ra-k em Ra uben-k em xut Osiris an 'Khnaton!'

Mark became overwhelmed with a feeling of such joy and happiness that his body trembled violently. His voice rang out; not his own voice alone, but mingled with another.

" *'Khnaton an Osiris maaxeru t'et-f a neb-a sebebi heh unt-f er t'etta ne nebu suten suteniu aphi neter neteru Osiris!'*

Mark saw the earth grow small beneath him; he saw moons and planets and constellations swirl around him. *'A ta ret per em axex an ten-a a am snef per em nemmat an ari ahnnuit a neb Maat 'Khnaton!'*

The cosmos opened before him; galaxies flew by, he saw before him the limits of space, the gateway to the universe. *'A tennemui per em Osiris! 'Khnaton! 'Khnaton!'*

Then there were eternal fields of wheat and an azure sky and a green river and, finally, the dazzling brilliance of a thousand suns.

He brought his arm up to his face and shielded his eyes. Giving one last cry, Mark slumped down over the sarcophagus.

When he lifted his head, feeling dizzy and drained, Mark found Yasmina gazing down at him, her hand resting on his shoulder. She said, 'It has worked. They are rising.'

Straightening up, Mark rubbed his eyes against the optical illusion: two shimmering columns of incandescent light, sparkling, swirling, one over each sarcophagus. The spirits of the king and queen, ascending.

But against the night, like an obscenity, came the cacophony of a thousand hellish voices.

And inside Mark's brain, a fluttering whisper: 'They

return, Davison, to stop what thou hast done. They can yet undo all thy doing; they can destroy us still. Fight them, my one, while my beloved and I make our flight. For if you do not, all will be lost . . .'

He staggered back against the wall, hands pressed against the cold stone, and cried, 'I can't stop them! They're too much for me! I have no power, no weapons!'

The pillars of diamond-fire continued to rise up from the coffins – phosphorescent columns, slowly lifting up to the ceiling. And again the fragile whisper: 'Thou hast the ultimate weapon, my one, for thou art on the side of Good. Thou hast Aton, the One God, invoke His name . . . I beg of thee, for there is no more time . . .'

A great rushing wind flooded the chamber, howling and shrieking around Yasmina and Mark, whipping their hair about their faces, deafening them with an inhuman roar. Mark sank to his knees, screwing his eyes tight. Yasmina, immobilised, stared at the effulgent shafts, quivering in the center of the tempest.

And then shuddering black shapes, towering, looming, stepped down from the wall on the other side of the door; the demons stretched their hideous limbs and drew breaths of life, called once again to their eternal duty.

The lambent spirits of the king and queen slowly rose, but they were too frail, too brittle to withstand the onslaught of the demons of the ancient Underworld.

Yasmina saw their light start to flicker.

'Mark!'

He snapped his eyes open, jerked back his head, banging it on the wall. The monsters were marching toward the sarcophagi: snake's head writhing, scorpion's pincers opening and closing, Amon's golden body gleaming. They staggered and stumbled in death-walks, wielding their weapons, advancing upon the egg-shell columns, dimming their brilliance, choking the wondrous light of the burial chamber with their evil and horror.

Mark managed to push himself to his feet. He worked his jaw, forced his lips to obey. A strangled voice came out. 'In the name of the One God!' he cried. 'In the name of Aton, He-Who-Is-Upon-The-Horizon, I command thee to depart!'

Apep, emerald snake's eyes flashing, swung out with his scythe; Yasmina jumped back, feeling the wind of the blade rush past her face.

Mark fixed his eyes upon the steadily rising spirits, filled his sight with their brilliance. 'I invoke the name of Aton, the Good God, the One God, who is also Vishnu the Preserver and Brahma the Creator and Allah the Merciful and Jehovah the Vengeful!'

The demons loomed over him, swaying, teetering, their arms held aloft. Behind, the ghostly columns continued their ascent.

Tears burned Mark's eyes, his jaw chatered in abject fear. With the devils standing before him, he felt the breath die in his throat. Sobbing, he reached down for a shard of limestone, grasped it in his left hand and, using the sharp edge, sliced open the palm of his right. He cried out.

Yasmina, pressed against the opposite wall, her eyes fixed on the fluctuating columns, watching them flicker and wane and threaten to extinguish, like candle flames, felt Mark dash past her and out into the ante-chamber.

Screaming, he slapped his hand on to the cold wall where the gods had once stood. Mark dragged his bloody palm this way and that, streaking the white plaster with crimson lines. And as he did so, he shrieked: 'I invoke the power of Aton, who is also Jehovah, who is also Allah, who is Brahma; the Unknowable, the All Powerful, the Merciful . . .'

He brought his bleeding hand up and down, around and over, again and again, covering the wall with the same symbol, slashing, swiping, hurried, frantic.

'And the Holy Ghost, and Jesus, and Vishnu, and Shiva, and–'

A howling chorus filled the burial chamber; a foul, gagging wind rushed out, knocking Mark to his knees.

'I call upon Aton!

'I call upon Allah!

'I call upon Jehovah!

'The God of Gods, King of Heaven, He-Who-Is-On-The-Horizon!'

He slapped his palm against the wall over and over again: down, across, and in a loop. It was the *ankh*, the ancient symbol for eternal life, the Cross of Aton.

Shrieks and cries and yowls were carried on the hot, putrid air. Yasmina watched spellbound as the demons started to freeze and grow rigid in their poses. While Mark chanted and painted the cross on their wall, the gods ceased their advance, they solidified into grotesque effigies of the manifestations of Evil.

Mark, exhausted, fell against the wall, his cheek pressed against its smooth surface, his hand moving jerkily, his voice a coarse whisper: 'Let the powers of the One God vanquish thee . . .'

Then, one by one, the gods fell: Amon and Set and their five hellish companions crumbled to the floor, disintegrating before Yasmina's eyes as the two shimmering columns surged with light.

Mark lay against the wall for a long time, breathing heavily, oblivious of the throbbing pain in his right hand. Yasmina came out of the burial chamber and slumped next to him, laying her face against his back. 'It is over, Mark. You have won.'

He stared blankly for a moment, then slowly, achingly got to his feet, bringing Yasmina with him. He gazed in astonishment at the blood-smeared wall, the red *ankhs* slashed over the places where the gods had once stood.

'They are gone, Mark. The demons are gone.'

'The king and queen?'

Her eyes were misty with sadness. 'They are gone, too. You have set them free at last.'

He pushed away from the wall and staggered into the burial chamber. On the floor between the sarcophagi were seven little piles of paint dust. Inside the coffins, the mummies lay in repose.

'She was a great lady,' Mark heard himself say as he gazed down at the little doll-like body before him. 'She could have gone to the Western Land three thousand years ago and enjoyed the bliss of eternal life. But she chose to remain here, in this god-awful place, roaming this valley for thirty centuries, looking for someone to resurrect her husband. How she must have loved him . . .'

Yasmina frowned and looked down at the delicate body, the small bandaged head and wondered, fleetingly, what Mark was talking about. Then she whispered, 'What will you do with them?'

'The authorities will have to be brought in. There are five deaths to explain. And I'll have to show them the tomb. They'll take the mummies to Cairo and put them on display.'

He groped for her hand. 'She waited for three thousand years to be reunited with him. When they return here to rest, the mummies will be gone and so their souls will perish.'

Mark raised his eyes to Yasmina. 'One last duty to perform.'

She looked at him questioningly.

'I'll take them in the Land-Rover. This canyon is riddled with deep crevices. I'll find one within Akhnaton's sacred boundaries. It won't be difficult to bury them deep into the mountain and conceal the entrance so that no one will ever find them. And then I'll carve their names into the rock so that they will know where their bodies rest. Yasmina, will you help me?'

'Yes.'

As he reached in to gather the frail body in his arms, Yasmina said, 'What did you mean, Mark, when you said she searched this valley for three thousand years for someone to resurrect her husband? How do you know?'

He paused, leaning over the sarcophagus. 'It's a long story, Yasmina, and we haven't much time. But later, after we've taken care of them, after we've buried them and recited the prayers to guide their souls back, after we've called the authorities and talked to the police and the newspapers, after everything is finished . . .' Mark gazed across the darkness at her.

'There will be time,' Yasmina whispered. 'We will have all of eternity.'

THE SHINING
by Stephen King

Danny was only five years old but in the words of old Mr Halloran he was a 'shiner', aglow with psychic voltage. When his father became caretaker of the Overlook Hotel his visions grew frighteningly out of control.

For as winter closed in and a blizzard cut them off completely, the hotel seemed to develop a life of its own. It was meant to be empty, but who was the lady in Room 217, and who were the masked guests going up and down in the elevator? And why did the hedges shaped like animals seem so alive?

Somwhere, somehow, there was an evil force in the hotel — and that too had begun to shine.

NEW ENGLISH LIBRARY

'SALEM'S LOT
by Stephen King

Almost overnight, the population of 'Salem's Lot has
gone from 1319 to nothing. *At least to nothing human!*

Thousands of miles from the small New England town
of 'Salem's Lot, two terrified people still share the
secrets of those clapboard houses and tree-lined streets.

One is an eleven-year-old boy who never speaks. Only
his eyes betray the grotesque events he has witnessed.

The other is a man with recurring nightmares of a placid
little township transformed into a tableau of unrelenting
horror, a man who knows that soon he and the boy
must return to 'Salem's Lot for a final confrontation
with the unspeakable evil that lives on there . . .

NEW ENGLISH LIBRARY

NEL BESTSELLERS

T 51277	'THE NUMBER OF THE BEAST'	*Robert Heinlein*	£2.25
T 51382	FAIR WARNING	*Simpson & Burger*	£1.75
T 50246	TOP OF THE HILL	*Irwin Shaw*	£1.95
T 46443	FALSE FLAGS	*Noel Hynd*	£1.25
T 49272	THE CELLAR	*Richard Laymen*	£1.25
T 45692	THE BLACK HOLE	*Alan Dean Foster*	95p
T 49817	MEMORIES OF ANOTHER DAY	*Harold Robbins*	£1.95
T 53231	THE DARK	*James Herbert*	£1.50
T 45528	THE STAND	*Stephen King*	£1.75
T 50203	IN THE TEETH OF THE EVIDENCE	*Dorothy L. Sayers*	£1.25
T 50777	STRANGER IN A STRANGE LAND	*Robert Heinlein*	£1.75
T 50807	79 PARK AVENUE	*Harold Robbins*	£1.75
T 51722	DUNE	*Frank Herbert*	£1.75
T 50149	THE INHERITORS	*Harold Robbins*	£1.75
T 49620	RICH MAN, POOR MAN	*Irwin Shaw*	£1.60
T 46710	EDGE 36: TOWN ON TRIAL	*George G. Gilman*	£1.00
T 51552	DEVIL'S GUARD	*Robert Elford*	£1.50
T 53296	THE RATS	*James Herbert*	£1.50
T 50874	CARRIE	*Stephen King*	£1.50
T 43245	THE FOG	*James Herbert*	£1.50
T 52575	THE MIXED BLESSING	*Helen Van Slyke*	£1.75
T 38629	THIN AIR	*Simpson & Burger*	95p
T 38602	THE APOCALYPSE	*Jeffrey Konvitz*	95p
T 46796	NOVEMBER MAN	*Bill Granger*	£1.25

NEL P.O. BOX 11, FALMOUTH TR10 9EN, CORNWALL

Postage charge:

U.K. Customers. Please allow 40p for the first book, 18p for the second book, 13p for each additional book ordered, to a maximum charge of £1.49, in addition to cover price.

B.F.P.O. & Eire. Please allow 40p for the first book, 18p for the second book, 13p per copy for the next 7 books, thereafter 7p per book, in addition to cover price.

Overseas Customers. Please allow 60p for the first book plus 18p per copy for each additional book, in addition to cover price.

Please send cheque or postal order (no currency).

Name ....

Address ....

....

Title ....

While every effort is made to keep prices steady, it is sometimes necessary to increase prices at short notice. New English Library reserve the right to show on covers and charge new retail prices which may differ from those advertised in the text or elsewhere.(6)